"Gritty, imaginative, sexy!
You MUST read Laura Griffin."

—Cindy Gerard, *New York Times* bestselling author
of the Black Ops series

TWISTED

"With a taut storyline, believable characters, and a strong grasp of current forensic practice, Griffin sucks readers into this drama and doesn't let go. Don't plan on turning the lights out until you've turned the last page."

—*RT Book Reviews* (Top Pick)

"Griffin excels at detailing the mystery and the chase, and forensic science junkies will love the in-depth look at intricate technology."

—*Publishers Weekly*

"Mesmerizing . . . Another fantastic roller-coaster ride."

—*Night Owl Reviews*

"*Twisted* is a masterpiece of romantic suspense."

—*Joyfully Reviewed*

SNAPPED

"*Snapped* rocks!"

—*RT Book Reviews* (Top Pick)

"Electric chemistry between two believable and interesting characters coupled with the investigative details make this page-turner especially compelling."

—*BookPage* (Top Pick for Romance)

"Laura Griffin mesmerizes. . . . A captivatingly passionate romance where danger is around every turn."

—*Single Titles*

"If you want a knock-your-socks-off romance, here it is."

—*The Reading Frenzy*

Also by Laura Griffin

TWISTED

SNAPPED

UNFORGIVABLE

UNSPEAKABLE

UNTRACEABLE

WHISPER OF WARNING

THREAD OF FEAR

ONE WRONG STEP

ONE LAST BREATH

LAURA GRIFFIN

SCORCHED

A TRACERS NOVEL

*To Cheryl Ann —
Enjoy!
— Laura
Griffin*

POCKET BOOKS

NEW YORK   LONDON   TORONTO   SYDNEY   NEW DELHI

Pocket Books
A Division of Simon & Schuster, Inc.
1230 Avenue of the Americas
New York, NY 10020

This book is a work of fiction. Names, characters, places, and incidents either are products of the author's imagination or are used fictitiously. Any resemblance to actual events or locales or persons, living or dead, is entirely coincidental.

Copyright © 2012 by Laura Griffin

First Pocket Books paperback edition November 2012

POCKET and colophon are registered trademarks of Simon & Schuster, Inc.

For information about special discounts for bulk purchases, please contact Simon & Schuster Special Sales at 1-866-506-1949 or business@simonandschuster.com.

The Simon & Schuster Speakers Bureau can bring authors to your live event. For more information or to book an event contact the Simon & Schuster Speakers Bureau at 1-866-248-3049 or visit our website at www.simonspeakers.com.

Manufactured in the United States of America

10   9   8   7   6   5   4   3

ISBN 978-1-4516-1739-9
ISBN 978-1-4516-1744-3 (ebook)

To Kevan

ACKNOWLEDGMENTS

Each book is an adventure that would not be possible without the help of so many people. I owe a special thank-you to the forensic science and law enforcement professionals who answered my research questions as I wrote this story, including Kyra Stull, Jennifer Rice, D. P. Lyle, and Erik Vasys. Any mistakes here are mine.

Thanks also to the hardworking team at Pocket Books, including Jae Song, Renee Huff, Jean Anne Rose, Parisa Zolfaghari, and my talented editor, Abby Zidle.

Finally, I would like to offer my heartfelt thanks to the readers who have made it possible for me to get up each day and do what I love. Thank you for reading.

SCORCHED

CHAPTER 1

§

The Black Hawk flew well below the radar and Lieutenant Gage Brewer sensed more than saw the water below. Light cloud cover, no moon. Perfect conditions for an op like this, which was exactly what made him itchy. Gage and his teammates had trained long and hard to expect the unexpected, and there wasn't a SEAL among them who trusted an operation that got off to a perfect start.

"Going black," came the voice in Gage's headset. At his CO's order, the helicopter went dark except for the faint red glow of the control panel.

A ripple of movement as the eight men of Alpha Squad triple-checked gear and prepped for battle. Gage reviewed the mission. Tonight's landing zone was the size of a driveway—just small enough to make things interesting. He visualized the layout of the vessel they planned to fast-rope onto in a matter of minutes. The *Eclipse* was a handcrafted yacht, custom built in Maine specifically for this voyage—which had gone horribly wrong when Somali pirates seized the boat. Less than three hours after capturing the yacht, the pirates had used a satellite phone to call in an eight-figure ransom demand.

Gage pictured the captain, the man he was tasked with rescuing: fifty-two-year-old Brad Mason of Sunnyvale, California, who fancied himself an adventurer. According to the intel Gage's team had received, Mason was some kind of computer genius who had made billions with his software company before taking a year off to sail around the globe with his family.

Gage didn't doubt that a man who'd made a freaking billion dollars off something he'd invented was smart. But his genius didn't extend to tactical matters, apparently, because the guy had posted updates about his journey and details of his route on Facebook, making him a prime target for the brazen and surprisingly high-tech pirates who roamed the seas just north of here. But dumb-ass moves aside, the guy was an American citizen under attack on the high seas, and the SEALs had been ordered to get him out of harm's way.

Along with his daughter.

Avery Mason, seventeen, had taken a year off of high school to go on the expedition. A copy of her varsity soccer photo had been passed around the briefing room a few hours ago. She was a blue-eyed, freckle-faced brunette, and one look at her had set the entire SEAL team's mood to extra-grim.

Conspicuously absent from the rescue list was forty-eight-year-old Catherine Mason, who had been shot and thrown overboard yesterday, after the pirates' first deadline passed without a ransom drop. Mason's extended family had been allotted twenty-four more hours—of which three remained—to come up with the ransom, or else Avery would die.

No one doubted the pirates would make good on their threat. That was the bad news. The good news was the seven Somalis on the yacht were lightly armed—only a half dozen AKs and some handguns among them.

The helicopter swooped lower. Sweat trickled beneath Gage's flak jacket as he contemplated the battle plan. The sweat was from heat, not fear. After eight years in the teams, there wasn't much that rattled him anymore. Dodging bullets and IEDs and operating behind enemy lines had taught Gage to be cool under pressure, to take what life threw at him. And whatever shit came down, he and his team would get the mission done and get out, because failure was not an option.

Not usually.

A vision of Kelsey flashed through his mind, and Gage wondered where she was tonight. He shouldn't think about her now. But even as he commanded himself to focus, he wished for one more moment to tell her . . . what? There was nothing left to say. And yet before every op, he felt a burning need to talk to her.

"Two minutes."

His CO's voice snapped him back to the task at hand. Joe Quinn sounded calm, resolute—the way he always did before an operation. There was a determination about him that steeled his team, no matter what the risks in front of them. Just the tone of his voice reminded them of the SEAL creed, which went with them everywhere.

If knocked down, I will get back up, every time. I will draw on every remaining ounce of strength to protect my teammates and accomplish our mission. I am never out of the fight.

On the horizon, the faint flicker of the target vessel. The helo dipped lower. As they neared it, the boat was just a lone white speck in the darkness. The pirates had switched off almost all the lights and kept belowdecks so as not to make themselves easy targets. Even the pirates on the mother vessel—a dilapidated shrimping boat being used as a communications headquarters—had kept a low profile. The Somalis had learned their lesson when some of their comrades had been taken out by SEAL snipers a few years back.

"It's go time."

Quinn's words sent a jolt of adrenaline through him. Gage ditched his headset and stood up. Beside him, Derek Vaughn did the same. As the two largest men of Alpha Squad, Gage and the Texan would be working in tandem to get the hostages off the yacht and onto an inflatable boat that would take them to the frigate that had been lurking nearby since the early hours of the crisis.

"Aces, man," Derek said over the din, his usual way of wishing Gage luck. Behind him, Mike Dietz slapped him on the back while Gage traded insults with Luke Jones—another routine. SEALs were a superstitious bunch.

And that was it. They'd trained. They'd practiced. They were ready.

The door opened and the noise increased, making it difficult to communicate except by hand signal. The first man kicked the rope out. One by one, the commandos disappeared into the night. The pilot struggled not to suddenly gain altitude each time a three-hundred-pound load of man plus gear came off the rope. Gage waited for his cue, gripping the thick nylon in his hands. Quinn signaled *go*. Gage jumped out and slid down so fast that his gloves smoked.

The boat came alive with lights. A flash of muzzle fire as one of the pirates hosed down the squad. Derek took out the shooter just as a bullet zinged past Gage's ear.

"Go, go, go!"

Gage's boots hit the deck. He sprinted for the hatch and slid down the ladder, planting a brutal kick in the face of a man at the base. The man went down like a stone, but he looked unarmed. Gage swiftly zip-cuffed him as Derek leaped over them and kicked open the forward cabin.

"Cabin one clear," Derek shouted.

Weapon raised, Gage kicked open one of the aft cabins. Pitch dark. He switched on the light attached to his helmet. On the bottom bunk was a bloodied man whose face was a nearly unrecognizable pulp. Looked like Brad Mason had been beaten with the butt of a machine gun.

"Hostage one secured," Gage said into his radio, as Mike—the team corpsman—quickly moved to check Mason's pulse. Despite the thunder of boots and the *rat-tat-tat* of gunfire up on deck, the hostage hadn't moved.

"Alive," Mike announced, but Gage was already kicking open the second aft cabin. He aimed his M-4 into the dimly lit space.

Empty bunk.

A low moan, and Gage turned his attention to a lump in the corner. Someone curled in a fetal position. Gage crouched beside her and used his free hand to lift her face. Avery Mason's blue eyes drifted shut and her head lolled back.

"Hostage two secured," Gage reported. Her hair was matted with blood. He noted the blood on her shorts and thighs.

"Sitrep on the hostages," Quinn demanded over the radio.

"Alive but injured. Girl's got a gash on her head and I think she's been drugged. Scratch the boat evac. We need the helo back here."

"Yo, Brewer, up and out."

He glanced up to see Derek in the doorway with Mason slung over his shoulder in a fireman's carry.

Gage scooped up the girl and positioned her limp body over his left shoulder. He moved for the ladder just as a man burst out from one of the cabinets.

Pop!

Pain tore through Gage's shoulder as he squeezed the trigger. The man dropped. Luke lunged around the corner and put a bullet in his chest, just to be sure.

Gage managed to hang on to his gun as he grabbed the rail with his free hand and hoisted himself up the ladder. On deck he did a quick head count. Three pirates dead, four cuffed—plus one casualty below.

Cursing their crappy intel, Gage eased Avery Mason onto the deck beside Mike, who was briskly bandaging her father's leg injury.

"Knife?" Gage asked, looking at the nasty wound.

"We need that helo." Mike glanced up at him. "Shit, you're hit."

Gage looked at the patch of blood that was rapidly expanding on his right shoulder. Derek said something to him, but it was drowned out by the *whump-whump* of the approaching chopper, the rescue basket dangling from the hole.

Suddenly the helo lurched right, then left, doing evasive maneuvers. Gage swung around to face the shrimp boat, which was a dim shadow on the now-gray horizon.

"A fucking stinger!" Derek shouted.

Gage's pulse spiked as a trail of fire arced up from the distant boat. All eyes turned skyward as the pilot shot off tracers to fool the heat-seeking missile, but it was too late. The tail rotor exploded. The helo tipped sideways and cartwheeled into the water with a giant splash.

"Joel!" Gage dropped his gun and ripped off his flak jacket. His teammates frantically did the same. Water rained down as Gage sprinted across the deck and dove off the boat.

The ocean hit him with an icy slap.

> *Basilan Island, the Philippines*
> *24 hours later*

Kelsey Quinn kneeled on the ground, tapping the sifting screen until the dirt disappeared and the tiny plastic object came into view.

"What is it?" Aaron asked over her shoulder.

Kelsey glanced up at her field assistant, who towered over the four Filipinos clustered around him.

"Tagapayapa," a woman muttered in Tagalog.

"What?" Aaron looked at the Filipino anthropologist with puzzlement.

"Pacifier." Kelsey pulled an evidence bag from one of the pockets of her cargo pants and labeled it with a permanent marker. She dropped the pacifier inside and darted a concerned glance at the woman whose face held a mix of sorrow and resignation.

The anthropologist held out a slender brown hand. "May I?"

Kelsey gave her the bag and watched as she squared her petite shoulders and trekked across the campsite to the intake tent, where this latest bit of evidence would be labeled properly and entered into the computer. Kelsey sighed. As a forensic anthropologist, she had traveled the world unearthing tragedy, and it amazed her how people who had seen the most suffering always seemed to have the capacity to deal with more.

Kelsey got to her feet and dusted off her kneepads. Her legs and shoulders ached from being on screen duty all morning.

"Ready for a break?" Aaron asked.

"Think I'll wait till noon." She checked her watch and realized her mental clock was about two hours behind.

"You're doing it again, Doc." Aaron passed her his water bottle and watched reproachfully as she took a gulp.

"Can't be helped." She handed the bottle back and repositioned her San Diego Padres cap on her head. "We've only got ten days left. There's no way we'll finish the second grave site in that amount of time. What'd you hear about those klieg lights?"

"Nothing yet."

"Dr. Quinn? Need your eyes over here."

Kelsey glanced across the campground at the doctor standing beside the radiography tent. It was a welcome interruption. She could tell Aaron was about to launch into one of his lectures, and she was too tired to argue with him.

"Get me an update on those lights," she told Aaron, then remembered to smile. "Please." She jogged across the camp and ducked into the largest tent, which was blessedly cool because of the giant fan they used to keep the expensive equipment from overheating. Dr. Manny Villarreal, a short man who happened to be a giant in his field, was seated at a computer with his usual bandanna tied over his bald head. Today's selection was army green to match his scrubs.

Kelsey zipped the tent door shut. She tilted her head back and stood for a few moments, letting the decadent eighty-degree air swirl around her.

"When you're done slacking off . . . ?"

"Sorry. What's up?" Kelsey joined him at a computer, where the X-ray of a skull appeared on the screen.

"Victim thirty-two," Manny said. "She came out of intake this morning."

"She?"

He gave her a dark look. "Irene recovered a pink headband."

Kelsey glanced across the tent at Irene, whose un-enviable job it was to painstakingly disentangle every set of bones from the accompanying clothing and personal items. After being separated from the bones, each item had to be photographed and cataloged before being examined by investigators.

"You're the expert," Manny continued, "but I'm guessing the profile comes back as a four- to five-year-old female, about thirty-eight inches tall, based on the femur. In addition to the headband, Irene cataloged a pair of white sandals. What we didn't find were any bullets or signs of bone trauma."

"What about lead wipe?" Kelsey asked. The opaque specks typically showed up on X-ray after a bullet crashed through a human skull.

"None," Manny replied. "And as I said, no broken bones. So no obvious cause of death." He leaned back in his chair and gazed up at Kelsey, and a bleak understanding passed between them.

If this child hadn't been marched to the edge of a pit and shot to death, like the rest of the people in the grave with her, then she'd died by other means. Most likely, she'd been buried alive and suffocated.

Kelsey's chest tightened and she looked away.

"I— Excuse me. I have to get some water."

With that completely transparent excuse she ducked out of the tent and stood in the blazing tropical sun. She felt light-headed. Her stomach churned, and she knew Aaron was right. She needed a break—a Coke at least, or a PowerBar to get her energy up before she did something embarrassing like faint in the middle of camp.

Lead from the front, her uncle always said, and he was right. Uncle Joe commanded Navy SEALs for a living, and he knew a thing or two about leadership. Kelsey needed to work hard, yes, but she also needed to set a good example for the six members of her team who had been toiling in the heat for weeks in the name of human rights. Kelsey was spearheading this mission on behalf of an international human-rights group with backing from her home research lab—the prestigious Delphi Center in central Texas. She needed to be sharp and in charge, not passed out from exhaustion. She was young to be managing such a big job, and she knew more than a few people were expecting her to fail—maybe even hoping for it. She needed to prove them wrong.

Kelsey wiped the sweat from her brow with the back of her grimy arm. She traipsed across the camp and rummaged through a plastic food bin until she found a granola bar.

"Ma'am Kelsey?"

She turned to see one of her team members, Juan Ocampo, emerging from the jungle with his metal detector and his shaggy brown dog. Milo aspired to be a cadaver dog, but in reality was simply a well trained mutt who went everywhere with Juan. Kelsey didn't mind the pup. She liked him, in fact; he was good for morale.

Juan stopped beside her. His blue International Forensic Anthropology Foundation T-shirt was soaked through with sweat and his face was dripping.

"You need to come with me," he said, and the low tone of his voice told her he didn't want the others to know about whatever he'd found.

Kelsey shoved the rest of her granola bar into her back pocket and followed him into the jungle. A route had been cut through the dense tangle of trees and vines, but the terrain was steep and uneven. Kelsey was glad for her sturdy hiking boots as she made her way down the path she and so many workers had traversed for weeks now. That's how long it had taken her team to recover the remains of dozens of civilians whose bus had been hijacked by a death squad working for a local politician. Aboard the bus had been a rival politician's family on their way to file nominating papers for the upcoming election. Each member of the family had been bound, tortured, and shot. The other passengers had been mowed down with machine guns and left in a shallow grave.

Kelsey swatted at mosquitoes as she neared the first burial site, where a pair of local police officers stood guard over the workers. Like most policemen in the Philippines, they carried assault rifles rather than handguns—yet another cultural difference she'd found unnerving when she'd first arrived in this country.

To Kelsey's surprise, Juan walked right past the grave site. He veered onto a barely visible path through the thicket of trees. Milo trotted out in front of him.

Kelsey's nerves fluttered as she tromped down the hill. He couldn't have found another pit. They'd counted fifty-three victims already, the exact number of passengers that local townspeople believed had been on the bus when it went missing during last year's election season. If there was another group of victims, surely her team would have heard something during their interviews with local families.

"You find gold in them thar hills?" Kelsey used her best John Wayne voice in a lame attempt to lighten the mood. Juan glanced back at her. He'd once told her he'd been named after the American actor and loved all his movies.

"I was out here this morning, ma'am, walking Milo." Juan's formal tone said this was no time for jokes.

Please not another death pit.

"I had the metal detector on, and it started beeping."

Kelsey glanced at the device in Juan's hand—one of their most useful pieces of equipment. It detected not only bullets and shell casings—which were valuable evidence—but also belt buckles, jewelry, and other personal objects.

"Look what I found." He stopped beside a ravine, and Milo stood beside him, wagging his tail. Juan shifted a branch and nodded at the ground.

Human remains, fully skeletonized. Kelsey crouched beside them, feeling a familiar mix of dread and curiosity.

"Male," she conjectured aloud. "Five-eleven, maybe six feet."

The height was unusual for a native Filipino. She studied the rotting clothing. Denim and synthetic fabrics withstood the elements better than soft tissue, and it looked as though this man had died wearing only a pair of jeans. She glanced around for shoes but didn't see any.

"What'd you hit on?" She nodded at the metal detector.

"Something under his head. I think there is a bullet, but I did not want to move anything."

"Good call." She frowned down at the remains.

"Do you think he tried to run?"

"Different postmortem interval from the others, I'm almost sure of it." She glanced up at him. "He's been here longer."

Kelsey dug a latex glove from one of her pockets and pulled it on. She took out her digital camera and snapped a photograph before carefully moving a leafy branch away from the cranium. She stared down at the skull, and it took her a moment to realize what she was seeing.

"I'll be damned," she muttered, leaning closer.

On the road above them, the hum of a motorcycle. The noise grew louder, then halted, and she and Juan traded looks. Kelsey surveyed the trees lining the highway—the same highway the bus had been on when it was hijacked. Branches rustled. Kelsey stood and Juan reached for the pistol at his hip.

"Ma'am Kelsey!"

A boy stepped into view. Roberto. Kelsey breathed a sigh of relief and shoved her KA-BAR knife back in its sheath.

"Phone call, ma'am." He scrambled down the steep hillside and emerged, grinning, from a wall of leaves. Roberto had appointed himself the camp errand boy and spent his days zipping back and forth to town, fetching supplies for the workers in exchange for tips. He reached into his backpack and produced the satellite phone that usually lived in Manny's tent. The boy looked proud to be entrusted with such an important piece of equipment, and Kelsey handed him some pesos.

"Sir Manny said it's important," Roberto told her. "The call is from San Diego."

Kelsey's stomach dropped. *Oh God, no*. She jerked the phone to her ear. "Hello?"

For an eternity, only static.

"Kelsey?"

Just the one word and Kelsey knew. *Gage*. She'd been expecting this call for years. Her heart felt like it was being squeezed by a fist, but she managed to make her voice work.

"Mom, what is it?"

"Baby, it's your uncle Joe."

CHAPTER 2

San Diego, California
Two months later

Gage pulled his pickup truck into the parking lot of O'Malley's Pub, way more than ready to put an end to his crap day.

It had started at 0430 with a training op on San Clemente Island and ended less than an hour ago with a brutal run through the obstacle course on base. Under normal circumstances, he liked training ops—especially ones that involved high-altitude jumps. And the O-course hadn't been a problem for him since BUD/S training.

But these weren't normal circumstances. Gage was coming off a shit week following a shit month at the end of a shit year. His shoulder hurt like hell despite endless rounds of physical therapy, and his head was in the wrong place. Gage couldn't find his zone—hadn't been able to in months.

O'Malley's was quiet for a Friday, which suited him fine. He took a seat at the bar and ordered a beer. After knocking back the first swig, he stared at the bottle and forced himself to confront the nagging possibility that maybe, just maybe, he was losing his edge.

A young blonde approached the counter. As if to confirm Gage's depressing hypothesis, she ignored the empty stools next to him and chose one three seats over. She tucked her purse at her feet and barely gave him a glance before flagging the bartender to order a drink.

Ouch. Not the response he usually got from women in bars—especially this one, which was popular with SEAL groupies.

On the other hand, Gage really couldn't blame her. He'd come here straight from the base, not even bothering to shower after his sixteen-hour ass-kicking.

Gage glanced across the room at Mike Dietz and Derek Vaughn, who had managed to clean up before coming out. They'd left the base not long before Gage, so they must have set the world record for speed showering. Clearly they were looking to get laid tonight, whereas Gage was simply looking to get hammered. It had been that kind of week.

Derek caught his eye and walked over. "Hey, Brewski," he drawled, "you want in on this game?"

"Nah, I'm good."

"Come on, bro." He glanced over his shoulder at the two brunettes who were hanging around the pool table. "Callie's sister's in town. You need to come meet her."

"Really, I'm fine."

"You're killing me."

"Let Dietz talk to her."

"He has to cut out after this. Some family thing." Derek clamped a hand on his shoulder, and Gage made an effort not to wince. "Seriously, do *not* leave me hanging here, man. You can have Tara. She's older, but probably no less talented than her baby sis." He grinned and slapped Gage on the back. "Come on. It'll snap you out of your shit mood."

Gage glanced at the women and he knew Derek was wrong. Nothing would snap him out of his mood tonight.

"You're not still hung up on Kelsey, are you?"

"Hell no."

"Then what's up?" His brow furrowed. "Having a bad day?"

It was common knowledge that Gage had taken Joe's death two months ago harder than anyone. And it wasn't just because he knew the man's family and had once dated his niece. Even before all that, Gage had had a special bond with him. Joe Quinn had been a demo expert, same as Gage, and he'd taken Gage under his wing during his very first year in the teams.

"I'm fine," Gage said, and his friend gave him a long, hard look.

"Not so sure about that. Those are two hot-looking women. But, hey, your loss. Lemme know if you change your mind."

Derek returned to his game of pool, and Gage nursed his beer while watching the mirror behind the bar. The blonde was still there and she had a drink in front of her now. She stirred it with a slender red straw as she glanced over her shoulder again and again. Gage checked his watch. Ten after nine. Her date was probably ten minutes late. Suddenly she smiled and jumped up from her stool as a man in service khakis entered the bar. He crossed the room in a few strides. The woman

SCORCHED   19

threw her arms around his neck and kissed the hell out
of him.

Gage felt a stab of envy and looked away. He remembered Kelsey kissing him like that—in this very
bar, too—right before he'd drag her home with him to
set his world on fire. That's how they'd been together—
weeks and months of no contact, then completely unable to keep their hands off each other when they finally
got together.

Which wouldn't be happening again anytime soon.
Or ever.

Last time Gage had seen Kelsey was at her uncle's
funeral. She'd been seated at the front of the church
with her boyfriend at her side—some FBI hotshot she'd
dated back before she met Gage. Seeing the two of them
together had been hard enough, but when they'd stood
to leave the church and Gage glimpsed the ring on her
finger, it was like a kick in the gut. He'd been blind-
sided by hurt and anger—which made the entire day of
Joe's funeral all the more torturous.

Good times. Gage tipped back his beer. He felt
someone behind him and knew who it was when he got
a nose full of cheap perfume.

"Hey, sailor."

Callie's sister had a friendly smile, and Gage did
his best to return it. It wasn't her fault he was in a foul
mood.

"Hey there," he said.

"I'm Tara." She rested her hand on his forearm and
eased close, giving him a perfect view down her low-cut
shirt. "My sister says you know your way around a pool
table. Wanna play with us?"

Gage looked down into her pretty blue eyes. She was young. Built. Eager to please. If he couldn't have Kelsey, he should have someone else. He couldn't wallow in celibate misery his whole life, could he?

Problem was, he'd been down this road and knew where it went, and waking up tomorrow with some girl in his bed wasn't going to solve his problems, just create a few more.

Gage glanced at the mirror behind the bar as a woman who looked remarkably like Kelsey stepped through the door. He blinked at the reflection.

No way.

But there was no mistaking her. Six feet tall. Long auburn hair. In a bar filled with hot and available women, she stood out in her jeans and no-nonsense T-shirt. She rested a hand on her hip and scanned the room.

Gage drank in the sight of her body, her lips, her skin. She'd gotten some sun recently. He remembered she'd been on a dig when they'd called her about Joe, but that was probably over by now and she was back to her job at the crime lab.

But what did he know? Maybe she'd been on her damn honeymoon.

"Uh, hello? Earth to Gage?"

He snapped his attention back to the woman beside him. Her friendly smile had dimmed.

Then he glanced over her shoulder at Kelsey, who was indeed still standing there, in the flesh, in the middle of O'Malley's Pub. What was she doing here?

Kelsey spotted him and froze. She glanced at the woman beside him, and for an instant the startled look on her face made him feel good. He could tell she wanted to bolt, but instead she walked straight up to the bar and ordered a drink.

"Excuse me, would you?" Gage picked up his beer and walked over to Kelsey. She'd chosen a stool on the corner, which didn't leave him a place to sit, so he rested his bottle on the counter and stood beside her.

"Hi."

"Hi." She avoided his gaze, but smiled at the bartender as he delivered her beer.

"What brings you to town?"

She glanced over her shoulder at the pool table, where Derek and Mike were finishing a game. Gage ignored their curious glances.

At last she looked up at him. "I came to visit my grandmother. We're cleaning out Joe's house."

He'd figured as much. Joe had never married, and Kelsey was the closest thing he had to a kid. He'd helped raise her after her father died in a car wreck when she was young.

So now she was here to help go through his stuff, probably put his house on the market. It made sense. Gage hadn't actually believed she'd flown all the way out from Texas just to see him.

She reached down and picked up her purse from the floor.

"I was hoping I'd run into you," she said casually, unzipping the bag. "We came across something, and my grandmother thought you might want it."

Her grandmother.

Kelsey handed him a white envelope. He hesitated a

moment before taking it. Joe's family had wanted him to have this, whatever it was. The very idea humbled him.

Gage opened the envelope and pulled out a photo that he recognized instantly. The picture was from Afghanistan. Half of his team stood on a mountaintop, lined up in full gear. They'd just flown out from Bagram for a six-month tour, most of which had been spent assaulting cave complexes. Just three years after the towers had fallen. They'd been full of energy and optimism, good and ready to kick some terrorist ass.

Gage studied the faces: Derek, Mike, Luke, a few others who'd left the teams. It was a snapshot in time, but he felt a surge of love for these guys who had had his back on so many different occasions. They'd taken bullets for one another. It was impossible to describe what that meant to anyone who hadn't been there.

Gage couldn't look at Joe's face. He ran his thumb over the edge and focused on the rugged Afghan landscape. At times it was hell on earth. Other times it was beautiful.

He glanced up, and Kelsey was watching him with those bottomless brown eyes. He cleared his throat. "Thank you."

"You're welcome."

Gage unbuttoned the front pocket of his BDUs and tucked the envelope inside. He looked at Kelsey and felt a sharp stab of regret. After their breakup, she'd done a damn good job of keeping her distance. He didn't really blame her. The breakup had been his choice, not hers. The last time she'd flown out to visit him, she'd told him she couldn't handle the long distance anymore, the constant stress of his deployments. She'd given him an ultimatum—her or the teams. Torn between Kelsey and the SEALs, he'd done the only thing he could do—he'd chosen the SEALs. But it wasn't the end of him wanting her. And it wasn't the end of his bitterness. Even now—*especially* now, with her sitting there beside him—he still harbored a deep resentment toward Kelsey for making him choose between her and his job. And toward the man who'd come along in his absence and put a ring on her finger.

But along with his bitterness was something else, something he tried not to think about but couldn't ignore with Kelsey sitting so close. Truth was, he missed her. He missed talking to her, hanging out with her. He missed that little line she got on her forehead whenever he ticked her off. Hell, he even missed her freckles.

And, yes, he missed the sex. He itched to touch her right now and had to rest his hand on the bar to keep from running it through her hair.

"Is that why you came looking for me?" He held her gaze for a long moment, not sure what he wanted her to say. He knew what he wanted to say to *her*.

How could you get engaged to someone so soon after we broke up? Was it that easy to move on?

But he didn't ask, because the answer was a resounding *yes*.

"Actually, there was something else, too." She cut a glance at the pool table, and her businesslike voice told him the other reason wasn't nearly as personal as he would have liked.

"Joe had some books and CDs in the office at his

house." She looked back at him, searching his face for
something. "Apparently he was learning Tagalog. Was
he headed to the Philippines?"

Gage didn't say anything. He couldn't talk about
the when and where of what they did, and the fact that
he couldn't had been an ongoing source of friction between them. Kelsey had always accused him of being
too closed off—not just about the job itself, but about
how it affected him personally. Maybe so. But Gage had
never been big on talking. Like most SEALs he knew,
he was a doer, not a talker.

She sighed, obviously frustrated by his silence. "I was
just on Basilan Island."

"Why?" He frowned.

"We were excavating a mass grave there."

Gage clenched his teeth at this news. Basilan Island
was home to some extremely dangerous people, and the
military ops going on there were totally covert. Gage
had been involved in a few, and he'd heard rumors.
There was some serious shit happening in the Philippines right now, and he didn't like the idea of Kelsey
anywhere near there. He didn't want her in the same
hemisphere.

"Has the island become a haven for Al-Qaeda?" she
asked, completely point-blank. Gage had often admired
her straightforwardness, but it could be annoying, too.

"Was your team on its way there?" she persisted. "Is
that why Joe wanted to learn the language?"

"That's classified."

Classified. She hated that word, and Gage couldn't
count the number of arguments they'd had over it.

She shook her head and looked away. "I should have

known I'd be wasting my time trying to talk to you."

He bristled. "Hey, you came to me, babe. Don't blame me for wasting your precious time. And what does it matter now, anyway?"

"It *matters* because I'm working on something that could be important." She picked up her beer and took a sip. She looked flustered now, and he didn't know whether it was because they were fighting again or because this was a touchy subject. She plunked the bottle down and looked up at him. "I was hoping you might give me a little information so I don't make a fool of myself raising a stink about something that could be nothing."

"I can't talk about operations. You know that. You need information so bad, why don't you ask Blake?"

Kelsey's *fiancé* worked counterterrorism. And Gage could tell by the look on her face that she'd already asked him.

"What, 007 wouldn't talk to you? So you decided to try me? Maybe you thought I'd bend the rules just to do you a favor?" He leaned closer to her. "Sorry, babe, no can do. You want someone to bend the rules for you, go ask your boyfriend."

She looked away and muttered something.

"What?"

"You know, I predicted you'd be this way."

"That's me. Mr. Predictable."

"You know what's really disappointing, Gage? I'd hoped we could be friends now." She stood up and collected her purse. "After Joe and everything and all the crap that happened, I'd hoped we could at least have that."

She pulled out her wallet and left some bills on the bar. Gage caught sight of her hand.

"Hey." He grabbed her wrist as she turned to leave. "Where's your ring?"

She jerked her hand back and glared up at him. "I left it at home."

Kelsey moved for the door, and Gage's shit luck continued as Callie picked that exact moment to slide onto the vacated stool. "Come on, Gage. We need you to come play."

She rested a hand on his waist and gave him a coy smile. It was a smile that had worked on him before, and he could tell Kelsey knew that as she glanced back and then stalked out the door.

Kelsey's flight was late getting into San Antonio, and it took nearly an hour for her to claim her luggage and retrieve her car from long-term parking. As she steered her Chevy Tahoe onto the interstate, she checked her watch. After nine already, which meant she was going to be up past midnight doing laundry.

It was either that or wear a bikini to work tomorrow instead of underwear. It wouldn't be the first time. Laundry was always the first chore to get scratched off her list when life got hectic, and these past few months her life had been hectic in the extreme.

She shifted into the far left lane and tried to make up some of the time she'd lost on the tarmac in San Diego. Her shoulders ached and she had a knot in her back from hauling boxes for the past five days. She couldn't wait to go home and stand under a scalding-hot shower, then throw on a fuzzy bathrobe and flop onto the couch for some mindless television between laundry loads. She couldn't remember the last time she'd felt so beat.

She'd underestimated how much work it would be to pack up Joe's two-bedroom bungalow. Yes, the place was as spartan as Kelsey remembered it. His home exhibited the meticulous order of a lifelong military man. But it had been just Kelsey doing the work. Grandma Quinn was nearly eighty, so Kelsey had set her up on Joe's sofa and brought her things to look at as they decided which papers and mementos and personal items would go where. Joe's entire closet had gone to Goodwill, and any furniture her grandmother didn't want—which was most of it—had gone to the resale shop run by the church. Kelsey had packed a shoe-box of stuff for herself. It contained photos and a few personal items, including a glossy clay "bowl" Kelsey had made in an art class her freshman year of high school. It was lopsided and hideous and decorated with purple peace signs, but Joe had kept it in a prominent place on his dresser and used it for loose change. Kelsey got misty-eyed the moment she saw it.

She still couldn't believe he was dead. She'd been numb at the funeral, both from jet lag and shock. But for the past few days with her grandmother, Kelsey had been living completely in the moment. And the moment sucked. Day after day, she'd watched her grandmother grieve for yet another son she hadn't expected to bury. And Kelsey had been forced to confront the stark truth that she had very little family anymore—with Joe's death, just her mother and Grandma Quinn. Kelsey was accustomed to having a small family, but it had never seemed so lonely before.

Just last weekend she'd been to a birthday party for a friend's little girl. Kelsey didn't know much about parenting, but even she could see that the horde of toddlers and the snow-cone station and the bouncy castle were completely over the top. Still, she'd experienced a pang of envy as she'd watched a crowd of aunts, uncles, and grandparents gaze on adoringly as the little princess blew out her candles. Kelsey would never have that. Even if she met someone who truly wanted to spend his life with her—and she was 0-for-2 now—she would never have one of those obnoxiously big families that so many of her friends were lucky enough to have.

Her thoughts went to Gage. Seeing him at the bar had stirred up her emotions. Maybe she shouldn't have gone. But she really *had* wanted to give him the photograph and she'd also wanted his take on Joe's work in the Philippines.

Which of course was a sore subject. Gage had always refused to talk about work with her, and his silence drove a wedge between them. Just their brief conversation the other night had brought her old resentments bubbling to the surface.

Along with other feelings.

She pictured him back at O'Malley's. He'd looked good, but that was no surprise. He'd always been a magnet for women with his powerful build and his piercing blue eyes. Since she'd first met him, he had a way of looking at her that made her tingle from the inside out. She'd once made the mistake of telling him what that look of his did to her, which was obviously why he'd been using it on her back at the bar.

But that was about sex, not a relationship. They'd

always been good at the sex part—it was everything else
that had given them trouble.

Kelsey swerved around an eighteen-wheeler doing a
plodding sixty in the left lane. Her phone chimed from
the cup holder. She eyed it suspiciously, almost certain
she knew who was calling.

She checked the screen. Yep, Blake.

She sighed.

Was it personal or business? Or personal disguised as
business? She wouldn't put it past him to call her with
some issue about a case they were working on and then
slip in a few questions about her trip. And Kelsey knew
that even if she dodged his inquiries, he'd manage to
glean some detail that would somehow answer his real
question—namely, *did you see your ex while you were in
California?*

Blake had a jealous streak when it came to Gage, and
Kelsey didn't blame him. But that didn't mean she owed
him answers. Not anymore. Their engagement was off
and she was determined to keep their relationship on a
purely professional level from here on out. They were
mature adults. Surely that was possible.

Her phone kept chiming. She muttered a curse and
answered it.

"Hi."

"When'd you get back?"

She took a deep breath. "Just now. What's up?"

"I got those test results back—the DNA you asked
me to send to Quantico."

"Wow." She was surprised by the news, as well as the
fact that this *was* evidently a business call. "I thought it
would take longer."

"I thought it would, too. The lab's usually pretty backed up, but they managed to get to it. And guess what—you were right."

Her stomach tensed. "About what?"

"This guy *was* in the system. Not only that, he happens to be on our terrorist watch list. *And* he happens to be American, which you also predicted. His name's James Hanan aka Ibrahim Antel. So, now you've got some explaining to do. How the hell did you know that?"

"I didn't. I just had a hunch."

Silence. "You care to elaborate? I could put that in my report, but it might raise a few eyebrows."

"The stature, for one," Kelsey said, getting comfortable now that she was talking about work. "He was significantly taller than the average Filipino male, so I doubted he was native. And his dental work told me he spent much of his life in a first-world country."

"That doesn't explain why you thought he'd be a criminal."

"That was mainly because of the implants."

"Implants?"

"Cheek implants. And I saw evidence of recent rhinoplasty. Not only that, it looked like he'd had his jaw sculpted."

"You can tell he had a nose job?"

"From the bone scarring at the top. I could tell he'd had a nose-narrowing procedure in which the surgeon removed the nasal bones on either side, reshaped them, and then repositioned them. There are tiny marks visible where the bones have been reset."

"Sounds like he spent a lot of money to alter his

appearance. Still, he could have been a tourist who wandered off on a hike."

"He could have," she agreed. "But I heard some rumors while I was down there about extremist groups training in the jungle, so it seemed to fit."

"Hmm," he said, and that one sound confirmed Kelsey's suspicions. "I'm impressed. And I know some other people who are going to be, too, soon as I pass this up the chain. I've been doing some investigating. You know, we thought this guy was in Jakarta. His turning up in the Philippines is going to cause some concern. We've been learning about increased activity there—training and recruitment. But it's been tough to get good intel. We're going to be interested to know exactly where you found him. I'm hoping you have some maps?"

She did. They were in the case file in her carry-on bag—along with the other files she'd been reviewing on the plane. But she was *not* going over to Blake's tonight.

"Kelsey?"

"I do."

"Any chance I could get a look at them? Also, I need to get a statement from you about cause of death. You mentioned a gunshot wound, but we're going to need specifics."

Damn it, he wanted a meeting. She should have expected this.

"When?"

"I'm working on a brief for the assistant director for CT, Rick Bolton. I was hoping to have it by tomorrow."

Silence stretched out as Kelsey raced down the highway. He wanted to notify the *head* of counterterrorism about what she'd found. That had been her goal ever since she'd first seen those bones and realized what they meant. To hold up that process because of personal issues seemed ridiculously petty.

"If it makes you feel any better, I've got company," he said, clearly interpreting her hesitation for what it was. "Trent's on his way over to work on another case."

In other words, Blake wasn't going to try to talk her into bed while his coworker was sitting there. Kelsey checked her watch and sighed. Blake knew her weakness. A case needed her, and she'd never been able to say no.

She was definitely going to work tomorrow with a purple polka-dot bikini under her clothes.

"I'll be there in ten minutes," she said.

"The gate's open."

She took the next exit and made a U-turn under the freeway, locking her doors as she did because she had to cut through a seedy part of the city to get to Blake's neighborhood. He lived downtown, near San Antonio's River Walk, which when they'd first started dating, Kelsey had thought was romantic. But it hadn't taken her long to realize his choice of neighborhood had nothing to do with a fondness for the tree-lined riverfront where tourists like to stroll and shop and drink margaritas. No, his choice had been purely practical—one of his coworkers had been getting divorced and had offered him a deal on the condo. And although Kelsey liked the condominium itself, parking her SUV anywhere near it was a challenge. She circled the block twice before spotting an empty space.

Kelsey did a quick appearance check. She wore her

typical weekend combo of jeans, T-shirt, and Nikes. She glanced in the mirror and saw that her hair was limp. Her eyes were bloodshot. Her makeup had worn off, and her freckles were on prominent display. She looked like a woman who'd spent the past ten hours in airports, and the cherry Chapstick in her purse would do little to rescue her—which was probably for the best. This was business. She got out of the car and went around to the back to retrieve the case file from her bag.

The brown accordion folder had been steadily expanding since her return from the Philippines. Those unidentified remains had become her pet research project. She tucked the folder under her arm now, slung her leather purse over her shoulder, and headed for Blake's.

Kelsey had made a career out of identifying anonymous bones. All too often, the remains that came through her lab belonged to people who had been murdered, and since the vast number of murder victims were killed by someone they knew, getting an ID was crucial. Kelsey's work at the Delphi Center helped investigators identify the victim, narrow the suspect pool, and ultimately make an arrest.

Forensic anthropology wasn't just a job to her—it was a calling. From the moment when she'd held that first human skull in her hands and stared down into those sightless eyes, she had known it was her mission in life to give a voice to people who couldn't speak for themselves.

Kelsey neared Blake's condo and glanced around for Trent Lohman's car. She didn't see it, but she hoped he was here. The gate to the courtyard Blake shared with his neighbor stood open. Kelsey mounted the Saltillo tile steps leading to his door. The condo had a split-level floor plan, with the master suite down and the living area and guest room up, overlooking the River Walk. The festive sounds of a mariachi band drifted up from a restaurant as she rang the bell and waited.

Blake opened the door with his BlackBerry pressed to his ear. Typical.

She stepped in without comment and noticed the rolling suitcase parked in the hallway. Was he coming or going? His travel schedule was no longer her business, so she didn't ask. She walked into the living room, where his laptop sat on the glass coffee table beside a half-finished Heineken.

"Yeah . . . yeah . . . No, that's good. We'll put that in." He shot her a look of apology as he stood in the foyer.

Kelsey sank onto the couch. He was watching basketball playoffs and she idly checked the score. At last, he ended the call.

"Sorry." He sat down beside her. "That was Trent. He's on his way."

"You two working on a big case?" Kelsey deposited her purse on the table alongside the accordion file.

"Aren't we always? Here, I want you to see this." He shifted his laptop to face her, and Kelsey watched video footage of a dark-haired young man sitting in a courtroom.

"This is James Hanan's arson trial, back in Tennessee, when he was only nineteen."

"They filmed it?"

"It was news in Memphis. He set fire to a church outbuilding, got sent up for three years, out in one."

"He looks really different."

"From what? A corpse?" He smiled at her.

"You can tell a lot from a skeleton." She opened the file and pulled out an eight-by-ten photograph. It had been taken in an autopsy suite in Manila at the country's main forensic center. The skeleton lay spread out on a steel table. All the bones had been cleaned. She handed the picture to Blake and then passed him a close-up of the skull.

"I only have photos, unfortunately," she said. "The bones themselves are with the Filipino authorities. I'd recommend going through the embassy if you want to send someone out to look at them."

"These are the implants?" Blake hunched over the picture, which showed small pockets of silicone arranged beside the skull.

"They were recovered with the skull. Notice the marks on the mandible and the nasal bones here? Those are from an osteotome, or bone chisel. After his surgery, he would have had a receding jaw and a very narrow nose, totally unlike how he looks in that video." She handed over another picture. "Here's a back view of the skull where you can see the entry wound in the parietal bone. Someone shot him in the back of the head."

The stony look on Blake's face prompted Kelsey to voice what had been on her mind for weeks now.

"The extensive plastic surgery has me concerned," she told him. "Why would he go through all that effort and expense, unless he planned to resurface someplace? Someplace where authorities were on the lookout for him, such as America." She didn't want to sound alarmist, but she could tell from Blake's guarded expression that he'd thought about this, too.

The computer screen changed abruptly, and she glanced at it. The new footage was taken in a wooded area. A line of men in green fatigues lay in the dirt, shooting at paper targets with machine guns.

"This is from a training camp in Indonesia." Blake put the photos aside. "He's the second one from the right."

"Hard to see with the beard."

"I asked Trent for confirmation on this ID. He knows our tech who specializes in facial recognition software. We've had it analyzed and managed to get IDs on everyone you see there. See this guy?" He pointed to one of the men who was crouched down, tinkering with something that looked like a homemade explosive. "We've been looking for him for years. He's thought to be involved in the Bali outdoor market bombing back in 2009. Thirty-three people were killed, including four American tourists. And this man here?" He pointed to another commando in the background. "We think he was involved in a foiled bomb plot against the American embassy in Manila back in 2010."

Kelsey couldn't take her eyes off the video. Now they were thrusting guns in the air and cheering as someone hoisted a mannequin from a tree limb. The mannequin was clad only in combat boots and an American flag, and the crowd cheered as someone set fire to it. Her stomach knotted as she thought of Gage.

"So much hate," she murmured.

Blake squeezed her knee. She looked up at him.

"What happened to your hands?"

She glanced down at the razor-thin cuts on her knuckles and fingers.

"Oh, you know. Corrugated boxes and packing tape." She stood up and glanced around. "Do you mind if I use your bathroom?"

He looked irritated by her formality. "You know where it is."

She took her purse with her and shut herself in the guest bathroom. She couldn't explain the sudden tightness in her chest. Maybe she was tired. Or still feeling the emotions of her trip to California. Or maybe it was watching that training video and seeing what a mob of young men were so eager to do to an American soldier. To soldiers like Gage.

She bent over the sink and splashed water on her face. She looked in the mirror.

Eight months. Eight *months* and still she couldn't stop worrying about him. She'd thought when she and Gage broke up that it would magically go away, that she'd be free again to watch the news and read the paper without this terrible dread in the pit of her stomach. But she still thought of him everywhere she went. She still dreamed about him. She had *conversations* with him in her head, and even though she knew it probably meant she was crazy, she actually enjoyed them. She enjoyed joking with him and laughing with him and flirting with him.

She needed to get past this. It was time to get over Gage Brewer and move on with her life. He had dumped her. Flat. She'd given him a choice: her or the teams. And—big surprise—he'd chosen his precious SEALs.

His rejection still stung, even though she should be over it by now. But the reality was, she missed him—so much sometimes that it put an ache in her chest. Some nights she lay awake, thinking of all the ways she could have settled for less and how they might still be together if she'd been willing to put up with being an accessory in his life instead of an equal partner.

Kelsey took a deep breath. She'd made her choice. He'd made his. And if her visit to San Diego had proven anything, it was that nothing had changed.

She dug a bottle of ibuprofen from her purse and downed two tablets. Then she ran a brush through her hair and used a tissue to dab away the makeup smudges under her eyes. What she needed most was a good night's sleep. She'd leave the file with Blake and get it back from him later. Nothing good was going to come from hanging around his place all night.

She stepped into the hallway and was surprised to see two men standing in the foyer—Trent and a short, stocky guy she didn't recognize. And Blake . . . was on the floor, motionless. *What on earth?*

Kelsey saw blood.

She gasped and both men looked up, startled. They exchanged glances. Trent jerked his head in her direction, and the short man lunged toward her.

For a split second she couldn't move. Then adrenaline kicked in and she dashed into the bedroom. She slammed the door and turned the thumb latch. Shrieking now, she watched as something rammed against the door, making it shake on its hinges. She glanced around frantically. She rushed to the glass door leading to the balcony.

A muffled *pop pop!* Bullet holes in the wood. She

clawed at the curtains, desperate for the door handle. Her mind reeled.

He's shooting! He's got a silencer!

She yanked open the slider and lurched onto the balcony as the bedroom door burst open.

She screamed—a shrill, piercing sound. She was on a second-story balcony overlooking a tile patio. She glanced at the neighboring balcony and then the tile patio below. The curtains moved behind her. She heard cursing. She scrambled onto the adobe wall and leaped onto the neighbor's balcony, where she landed hard and crumpled to her knees.

Omigod omigod omigod. He has a gun!

She cowered beside a propane grill and found herself face-to-face with a plastic garden gnome.

Noise on the other side. Voices. She crawled to the sliding door and pulled on the handle, but it wouldn't budge. The room was dark, silent. The neighbors weren't home. Kelsey's heart slammed against her rib cage. Her body quivered. She felt paralyzed with terror, but she couldn't stay here. She had to move.

A noise from within the apartment. She peered through the glass. A light went on in the hallway and a silhouette appeared.

Him!

Kelsey jumped to her feet. Blake's balcony was empty now. She hitched herself over the wall and looked down at the ground-level patio. More tile. A garden hose. A tricycle. The door behind her slid open and she leaped to the ground. Pain zinged up her legs, but she managed to roll sideways and under the overhang.

Noise at the side of the building. *Trent?* God, what was *happening?*

She scrambled to her feet and raced to a wrought iron gate. Terror shot through her as it squeaked open, giving away her location. She raced down the side yard between the condos. Carport. Empty. No one home, no one to help her. She spotted the main entrance to the shared courtyard and forced herself to *think.* She remembered a gate that led to the trash cans. But she'd have to double back.

Shouts behind her. Kelsey's pulse jumped. Instead of going back, she bolted for a concrete wall, about six feet high. She climbed it, ignoring the pain in her ankles as she scraped for a foothold. She pulled herself over and landed on her back on the asphalt. For a long moment, breathless shock. Then she rolled to her feet, sucking in air.

Voices nearby. *Trent's* voice.

She glanced around. She was in an alley behind a row of buildings. On one end, a brick wall. On the other end, traffic. She scooped her purse off the pavement and sprinted for the cars, keeping close to the concrete wall she'd just scaled, hoping the shadows might conceal her. *Blake is dead. Blake is dead. Blake is dead.* The words pounded through her brain, keeping time with her galloping heart. Her breath came in gasps. Her thighs burned. She ran as fast as her legs could carry her toward the noise and safety of the crowd.

A man stepped into view. *The short one.* Kelsey stumbled to a halt and glanced back over her shoulder.

Several buildings down, a door was propped open by a milk crate. She ducked low as she darted across the alley, praying he wouldn't shoot. She squeezed through the door and found herself in a dim lobby that smelled like ammonia. Hysteria bubbled up as she glanced around. Marble tile. Vintage staircase. There was an information board on the wall displaying the names of businesses. From upstairs came the high-pitched whine of a vacuum. A janitor. But she didn't want to risk getting trapped up there. She raced through the lobby and tried the front door. *Open.*

Kelsey rushed into the muggy night air and glanced up and down the street. A few parked cars. Some panhandlers on the corner near the River Walk. She hurried for the people as thoughts tumbled through her head.

They killed Blake. They're after me. What is happening?

She ran down a few stairs toward the noise. She stopped, chest heaving, and looked around. Mariachi music filled the air, along with the smell of fresh tortilla chips. She saw neon signs, riverboats, umbrella tables filled with people laughing and drinking.

She dashed into the nearest open door—a T-shirt shop. Kelsey ducked behind a clothing rack and peered through the glass. She gripped a hanger, suddenly aware that all her limbs were trembling. She surveyed the faces outside, looking for help.

Standing beside a lamppost was a man in a dark uniform. He turned.

Cop!

She hurried outdoors and ran toward him just as he moved aside.

The short guy. He stood beside the cop now and flashed a badge.

Kelsey's stomach plummeted. The uniformed officer listened and nodded. All the air seemed to rush out of her lungs as her brain put the pieces together.

She turned around and race-walked in the opposite direction, clutching her purse against her side, trying not to draw attention to herself as she wove through the crowds. She had to get out of here. She had to find her car—

Her car.

Just a few blocks away.

She realized with a sinking heart that her keys were back at Blake's, sitting on his coffee table.

Okay, *think*.

She glanced over her shoulder. Fear shot through her as she spotted the man with the now-familiar black crew cut weaving his way through the crowd.

Her gaze snapped to a riverboat gliding by. Too slow. She picked up her pace until she was nearly running, dodging around couples and families.

He wouldn't shoot her out here, would he? Would he shoot her in public?

She glanced over her shoulder. Their gazes met through a gap in the crowd.

Kelsey took off. She pushed through the pedestrians and sprinted over a footbridge. On the other side was a concrete water fountain. A crowd milling nearby. Another glimpse behind her. She couldn't see him, but he was back there, she knew it. Her limbic system had kicked in and her panicked brain *knew* she was being hunted. Kelsey ran past the fountain. She spotted the sign for a familiar hotel chain. She hurried past the revolving door and pushed through the handicapped entrance.

A wall of cold air hit her. She was in a lobby. A huge, air-conditioned, terrifyingly *empty* lobby. God, it was much too empty. All the people were either behind the counter or clustered near the elevator bank. A glass elevator soared up, up, up and stopped at one of the top floors.

She glanced around and felt horribly exposed. She saw another revolving door. A flash of yellow.

She raced across the lobby and shoved her way outside.

"Taxi!"

The cab rolled forward.

"Taxi!"

A squeak of brakes. She yanked open the door and dove into the backseat.

"Drive!"

The cab lurched forward. She was facedown on a seat that smelled like air freshener and vomit. She pushed herself up and glanced out the rear window.

The hotel receded. She watched it, searching the alleys and sidewalks and surrounding parking garages, waiting for the short, dark-haired cop to burst out and chase her down.

A *cop*.

And *Trent*.

And—dear God—*Blake*.

He was dead. Kelsey's chest convulsed as she pictured the blood pooling beneath him. Bile rose up in her throat and she remembered the red rivulets spreading out over the tile grout.

"Where to?"

She glanced at the driver, an enormous black man wearing an Astros cap. Kelsey stared at him blankly. *Where to?*

Her pulse pounded as she tried to think. She brushed her hair out of her eyes with a trembling hand and took a deep breath. San Marcos was north. Her home was north.

"South," she croaked. "Just drive . . . south. I'll tell you when to stop."

He smiled into the mirror and shook his head. "South it is."

CHAPTER 3

Elizabeth LeBlanc disliked airports, especially at rush hour. But today she wasn't complaining as she made a fifth lap around San Antonio International. Instead of sitting at a computer running background checks, like the other newbie FBI agents in her field office, she actually got to drive. Forget that she was under strict instructions to go straight from her office to the airport and back to her office again—which essentially made her a shuttle service. It was an opportunity to get out from behind her desk.

Elizabeth scanned the doors, looking for a man in a dark suit. Having never laid eyes on Supervisory Special Agent Gordon Moore, that was all she knew about his appearance, and it was based on a guess. But the passengers pouring through the automatic doors weren't wearing suits—in June in San Antonio, why would you?—and Elizabeth sighed as she checked the clock. He was officially late. The airport security guy waved her forward and looked completely nonplussed when she flashed her badge at him. She was about to roll down her window to explain when she spotted Moore in her rearview mirror.

Tall, suit, computer bag. This was definitely her VIP from Washington. It wasn't his attire that identified him, but the way he carried himself. Men throughout the Bureau had a certain look about them that made them easy to spot. Elizabeth threw the car into reverse and maneuvered into a gap near the curb, earning a honk from a pickup driver.

Moore noticed her, no doubt recognizing the "un-marked" gray sedan as a Bureau vehicle. He approached the car and she got out to offer him a handshake.

"Special Agent Elizabeth LeBlanc."

"Gordon Moore."

She was pleasantly surprised that he didn't rattle off his superior job title or try to sneak a peek down her blouse. He tossed his garment bag into the back of the car and hung on to his computer case as he slid into the passenger seat. Elizabeth hurried around to her side and got behind the wheel.

Okay, progress. She'd picked him up without incident and now all she had to do was get him back to the office in time for the briefing. If she sped the whole way, she just might make it.

"So." She checked her mirrors and pulled into traffic. "This your first trip to the San Antonio field office?"

It was a weak opening, but it was friendly without being personal, so she'd decided to use it anyway.

He glanced up at her from a stack of files on his lap. Not two minutes in the car and already he was working.

"No."

Okeydokey.

"It's not usually this hot in June," she said. "Actually—"

"Four twenty-nine Chavez Avenue. How far is that?"

"Uh . . . fifteen minutes maybe? Depending on traffic." Damn it, he wanted to go to the crime scene.

"Drop me off there. I'll get a cab when I'm finished if you need to get back to work."

Ha. Like she had more important things to do than chauffeur him around.

"I'd be happy to." She cleared her throat. "There's a briefing at six, though, and we'll probably have trouble making it."

"They'll wait." He glanced out the window as they entered the interstate.

"Sir?"

He turned to her, and she noticed the hard look in his dark brown eyes. *Damn.*

"Should I call and let them know or—"

"This won't take long." He stowed his bag on the floor and settled back in his seat, ending the conversation.

Elizabeth bit her lip, annoyed with herself. She should have just made the call instead of asking permission. She stepped on the gas and did her best to make good time to the home of Blake Reid, the FBI agent who'd been murdered yesterday. She knew exactly where he lived—not because she'd been assigned to the case, but because the story had been on the news all afternoon. "Murder on the River Walk" had already become the tagline.

Moore remained silent as she drove to the scene. By some miracle, she found a parking space at the

end of Blake's block. They got out. Moore seemed
unconcerned by the pair of news vans parked nearby
as they walked briskly toward the residence. The air
felt hot and muggy, and they were hardly out of the car
ten seconds before Elizabeth was sweating beneath her
navy blazer.

"What do you know about this case?" Moore asked.

"Not a lot," she admitted. "Mostly what I saw on the
news."

"You ever work with Reid?"

"No."

He gave her a sharp look, and she realized that might
have come out a little strong.

"I've only been with this office a few months."

He raised an eyebrow, and she could tell he'd picked
up on the edge in her voice.

A heavyset patrol officer got out of his car as they
approached.

"Evening." Moore flashed his badge. "Officer Resnik? I talked to Lieutenant Tooley a few minutes ago.
Mind taking us inside?"

The officer darted another glance at Moore's FBI
shield before ducking back into his car to retrieve a
key and a clipboard, which presumably contained the
crime-scene log.

"Sir. Ma'am." He nodded at Elizabeth. "Right this
way."

They followed him up the stairs. Elizabeth noticed
the fingerprint powder all over the door frame. Resnik
donned a pair of latex gloves from his pocket and used
the key to open the door.

"Crime-scene techs just left an hour ago." He passed

the clipboard to Moore. "Said someone might be back later to get a carpet sample."

Moore handed the clipboard to Elizabeth and she scrawled her information beneath his. Her first real murder scene. She felt a little numb. She glanced around and tried to seem calm as the officer left them alone in the condominium.

A square piece of butcher paper lay near the door. Moore stepped onto it and traded his black wingtips for a pair of paper booties from one of the cardboard boxes sitting there. He snapped on some latex gloves and handed her a pair. Elizabeth took his place on the paper and swapped out her navy flats.

"Ever been to a homicide scene before?"

"Just at Hogan's Alley," she said, referring to the area at Quantico where New Agents in Training—or "gnats," as they were affectionately known—practiced takedowns and worked mock crime scenes. "I'm brand-new, sir. Just graduated this year."

"Call me Gordon." He stepped into the kitchen and looked around, then opened the cabinet beneath the sink and checked the trash can. He used an index finger to tug open the refrigerator. "And new's all right. It's good to have a fresh perspective."

He stepped back into the hallway and crouched beside a pool of dried blood. Elizabeth saw little dots in the reddish-black where it looked as though a CSI had used a cotton swab to get a sample. Dark rivulets radiated out along the lines of the floor grout.

Elizabeth studied the walls but saw no sign of bullet penetration. Still, a slug could have lodged in the body.

"Cause of death?" she asked.

He stood up. "I talked to the ME. Someone snapped his neck, then stabbed him through the right kidney with a combat knife."

Elizabeth frowned down at the blood. "Not the most common way to murder someone." She glanced around the foyer. "Then again, it's quiet."

"It's also up close and personal."

He stepped over the puddle and walked into the living room, where numbered yellow markers on the coffee table took the place of evidence that had been removed.

"TV was on when the maid showed up at eight this morning," he informed her. "There was a beer on the table. Looked like he'd been home watching ESPN when someone came to the door."

"Someone he knew?"

"No sign of forced entry."

Elizabeth surveyed the room, taking in the spare furnishings, the empty bookshelves. The walls were bare, which wasn't that surprising given that Blake Reid was single. Most guys Elizabeth knew didn't spend a lot of time decorating their apartments. She glanced at the kitchen clock. It was 6:10. Any minute now her boss would be calling, wondering what she'd done with their VIP. Headquarters had sent one of their top investigators down to oversee the case.

"What's Reid's reputation?" he asked from across the room.

Elizabeth shifted on her feet. "I hear he's a good agent. His team took down that terrorist cell—what was it, two summers ago?"

He kept watching her and she decided, What the

hell? If he poked around long enough, he was going to hear this anyway.

"You mean personal reputation?"

"Whatever you heard around the office," he said. "Or what you know from your experience with him."

"Well, like I mentioned, I haven't been here long." She tucked her hands in the pockets of her blazer. "But he was pretty forward. He asked me out three times."

"What'd you say?"

"No."

"All three times?" He looked skeptical.

"I don't mix work and personal. And anyway, he was engaged to someone. At least that's what I heard. I thought it was pretty sleazy for him to be hitting on new agents when he had a fiancée up in San Marcos."

"Kelsey Quinn. What do you know about her?"

She shrugged. "Just her professional reputation, really. She's a forensic anthropologist at the Delphi Center. She's trained some of our people in bone recovery."

"I understand she and Reid were no longer together," he said.

"That's news to me."

"Did he hit on all the new agents or just you?"

"I know of at least two. And they said yes. You should talk to them if you want more about his private life. I really only saw him at work."

Gordon glanced around the living room. His gaze lingered on the coffee table.

"What's a combat knife, exactly?" Elizabeth asked.

He looked up at her. "Typically, a seven-inch, double-edge blade, partially serrated on the bottom for cutting rope, et cetera. KA-BAR makes them. They're somewhat expensive, but standard issue for active-duty Marines, Navy, spec ops guys."

"That doesn't really tell us anything," she pointed out. "I bet any ten-year-old can order one off the Internet."

"I'm sure you're right." He walked past her into the hallway. The light was on, and Elizabeth noticed the fingerprint dust on the switch. He paused beside a bathroom, then walked to the door at the end of the hall. The door got stuck on the carpet and he had to push it open with his shoulder. Elizabeth followed him into the room and looked around. The bed had been stripped. She guessed this was a guest room based on the lack of items on the dresser and nightstand. A band of sunlight seeped through a gap in the curtains and she peered outside at a balcony. No plants, no patio furniture. There was a nice view of the trees along the River Walk, but it didn't look as though Blake had spent much time outside enjoying it.

Gordon went back into the hallway. Elizabeth stood in the room a moment longer, looking around at the paint, the carpet, the draperies. Everything was very generic.

She followed the veteran agent down a carpeted flight of stairs to the ground floor. At the base was a hallway. Elizabeth poked her head left into a utility room and saw what looked like an exterior door to the carport. She turned right down the hall and joined Gordon in what was clearly the master bedroom. Tossed over the nearest chair was a suit jacket and tie. On the wall opposite the king-size bed was a huge flat-panel TV. The bed had been stripped here, too, but the nightstands on either side were blanketed with clutter: a TV remote, a *Sports Illustrated,* an alarm clock. Gordon pulled back the curtain to reveal a pair of French doors looking out on a private patio. He glanced up and seemed to be checking out the security system.

"No evidence of forced entry, you said?"

"None," he confirmed.

Elizabeth added that info to the up-close method of attack. Breaking a man's neck *and* stabbing him was not only violent but personal. And Blake was tall. It wasn't just any man who would be able to get the drop on a guy like him.

"So, are you assuming he knew his killer?" she asked.

"Don't assume." He glanced over at her as the phone buzzed in his pocket. He pulled it out.

"Moore."

Elizabeth sauntered over to the nightstand and pretended not to be eavesdropping. A *TV Guide* tucked under the *Sports Illustrated* was open to Sunday's date. She tapped the button on the alarm clock. It was set for 6:10 a.m.

"All right. And we have this confirmed?" Pause. "You mean the Delphi Center?"

Elizabeth glanced over at the dresser, trying to add to her catalog of clues. If this were *her* case, what would she make of all the items in this bedroom? What about his medicine cabinet? His refrigerator? His laptop computer? Any one of those things might hold the key to understanding Blake's murder. But she, of course, wouldn't be finding it because this wasn't her case. Gordon Moore had clearly brought her along to get the inside gossip on Blake's private life, but he didn't take her seriously as an investigator. And why should he? She was brand-new.

"Okay, repeat that." He dug a notepad from his jacket and glanced around. Elizabeth handed him a pen. "And this is from her supervisor?" He jotted something down. "Call the airline. Make sure she was on the flight. Then call me back."

He ended the call and shoved the phone in his pocket. "Kelsey Quinn didn't show up for work today."

Elizabeth caught the tension in his voice. "Anyone go to her place?"

"She's not there. And no one at her work has seen her since she flew to San Diego last week to visit family. She's got a grandmother there, apparently. And an ex-boyfriend who's spec ops with the Navy."

"Spec ops?"

"He's a SEAL."

Elizabeth stood there, digesting this, as he took out his phone again.

"Brenda? Gordon Moore here . . . No, I made it, but I need you to book me another one." He glanced at his watch. "First thing tomorrow I need a flight to San Diego."

Gage was back in the zone. He could feel it. As the C-130 climbed high into the night, he felt his worries slip toward earth and his mission crystallize in his head. His thoughts were clear, focused. His breathing was steady. He gripped the straps of the parachute in his hands and visualized exactly what he needed to do.

Gage loved night HALOs. The High Altitude Low Opening jumps gave him a rush like almost nothing else.

"Six minutes," yelled the loadmaster.

Gage checked his gear. Although temperatures in the Mojave soared well above one hundred during the day, it was butt-ass cold in the middle of the night at twelve thousand feet. So Gage and his teammates were in desert cammies, thick wool socks, tactical boots, and insulated aviator gloves to provide warmth. Gage had modified his gloves, cutting out the right thumb and index finger to make it easier to use his weapon and cut detonator cord. He inventoried his gear. His SIG Sauer nine-mil was tucked securely at his hip, on the opposite side of his body from his KA-BAR knife. He had his M-4 strapped to his back. His pockets were stuffed with extra ammo, along with a blowout kit that contained medical supplies. He was good to go.

"Three minutes."

The ramp at the back of the plane eased down, creating a roar throughout the aircraft. Gage and his three teammates lined up lightest to heaviest, which meant he was after Luke and Mike, but before Derek. Gage waited for the green light to appear and then stepped onto the vibrating platform. Mike disappeared, then Luke. Gage waited a beat and then plunged into the night sky.

A wall of cold air pushed against him as he hurtled toward land. On his first jump he'd clenched his teeth through this part and prayed that the guy who'd packed his chute had been paying attention. But now—nearly a thousand jumps later—Gage no longer worried about the chute opening and spent this time instead enjoying the thrill of being a human projectile rocketing toward earth at 125 miles per hour.

At three thousand feet Gage pulled the cord. His body jerked back as the chute unfurled and caught air. He switched on his night optical device and searched for the rest of his team against the backdrop of the empty desert. The NOD enabled him and his teammates to see the infrared lights on one another's helmets, and they maneuvered their bodies so that their canopies stacked like stair steps, which would help them land close together—but not too close.

Gage's heart thumped steadily. He sucked in air. As they neared the landing zone, he flared his chute to control the speed of descent. The ground flew up at him and then . . .

Freaking perfection.

They were clustered on the ground together in a space no bigger than a baseball diamond. But there was no time to gloat over the kick-ass landing. Mike and Luke already had their weapons ready, holding security as Gage and Derek took off their chutes. Then it was Gage and Derek's turn to stand guard as the other two bunched up the nylon. In a real-world op, they would break out shovels and bury their chutes out of sight of the enemy, but tonight was a training mission, and they weren't about to risk damaging nearly ten thousand dollars' worth of equipment. Mike and Luke stowed everything under a bush and covered it with camo netting while Gage and Derek stood guard.

In a quick huddle before takeoff, they'd debated skipping that step and letting everyone take care of their chutes simultaneously to whittle down their time. But Gage knew his CO might be lurking in the darkness somewhere, watching their every move through night-vision goggles. He'd be waiting for one small reason to give them a failing grade on this exercise, which would mean instead of taking the five days' leave Gage had coming to him, he'd be joining his teammates for some extra-hellacious PT work back at the base. Shortcuts didn't pay—not in the teams.

They finished up with the chutes and checked their compasses. No GPS, as part of tonight's purpose was to test navigation skills. Luke signaled the direction of the target and they moved out with Gage on point.

Slowly, silently, they crept through the desert. In contrast to the briny air of Coronado, the valley smelled of dust and sage. A thin layer of cloud cover and some stealth tactics would prevent them from being seen by the enemy—which tonight might be members of their own platoon ordered to try to ambush them on the way to the target. So the limited visibility was helpful, but could also lead to problems if Gage's team botched the calculations and walked right past the target in the dark.

Tonight's winning streak continued, though, and after an hour-long patrol in silent slow motion, they walked right up on their objective: a three-thousand-pound Tomahawk missile. According to their pre-op briefing, the weapon had missed its designated target and landed behind enemy lines without detonating. Now it was the SEALs' job to destroy it before enemy forces could get their hands on the valuable technology or convert it into an IED that would be used against American troops.

Mike and Luke held security while Gage and Derek took a knee and got to work unloading supplies from their rucksacks. Derek took out four pounds of C-4, which looked like modeling clay and smelled like hot asphalt. As the team's top demo man, Gage was in charge of the blasting caps, fuse igniters, and fuses. By itself, the C-4 couldn't explode, but mishandled blasting caps could blow off a finger—or some other valued appendage—so Gage never carried them in his pants pockets. He took a deep breath now and concentrated as he unloaded everything carefully.

Derek prepped two blocks of C-4—one for each end of the missile. Gage put blasting caps into each block. Then he readied the fuse igniters, all the while thinking hard about how much he did not want to botch this up. When everything was in place, he traded looks with Derek and then pulled the lanyards attached to the fuse igniters.

"Fire in the hole!" Gage shouted.

The smell of burning cordite filled the air as they sprinted for the cover of a nearby boulder. They ducked behind the rocks and Gage checked his watch. He waited. Three . . . two . . .

Boom.

The earth shook. Debris pelted down on their helmets. Gage waited a beat to make sure the explosion was over.

"Score!" Luke said, leaping to his feet. They no longer worried about noise discipline now that their cover was literally blown to bits.

"Time to haul ass," Gage said, and hustled out from behind the rocks. After a quick check to ensure that no overly large missile fragments remained, they bugged out, making the two-mile trek to the pickup point in less than fifteen minutes. They exfiltrated using a different route from before, just in case the enemy had somehow discovered their tracks and set up an ambush.

Ten minutes later, they were on a helicopter headed back to base, grinning at one another like a bunch of kids who'd just won a baseball game.

Mike slouched back against the side of the helo. "I'd give my right arm for a mile-high stack of Flo's pancakes."

Gage's stomach growled in response. Flo's Diner near base was a popular breakfast spot. He and Kelsey had gone there on more than one occasion to fuel up after a marathon night.

"Cowboy omelet," Luke said, and passed Gage a spare T-shirt to wipe off his greasepaint. "You in?"

"I'm in," Gage said, pushing away thoughts of Kelsey. He didn't want to believe that her broken engagement had anything to do with his good mood. And he damn sure didn't want to think it had anything to do with his recently rediscovered ability to do his job well. This wasn't about her. It was a good morning, simple as that. With any luck, it might end up being a good day, and maybe even a good week. Gage watched the first rays of sunlight hitting the San Bernardino Mountains and felt a lightness in his chest that had been missing for a long time.

The team was still talking about breakfast when they landed at Coronado. The base was alive with activity as new recruits grunted it out on the hard top doing morning PT. Lines of flush-faced men did sit-ups and push-ups. SEALs in training clawed their way up the sixty-foot cargo net on the obstacle course. Not a good place to lose arm strength.

Derek slapped Gage and Mike on the back as they jogged across the base. "Let's make this quick. I'm starved."

They hustled to the SEAL building, where they took off their helmets and weapons and stowed them in lockers. They still had to debrief and downstage the rest of their gear before they could have so much as a cup of coffee. On the way to the briefing room, Gage turned a corner and nearly crashed into Jeff Hallenback, his new CO.

"Vaughn. Dietz."

"Sir," they said in unison.

"Where's Jones?"

"He's in the head, sir."

"Find him and get to the briefing room, ASAP." The CO's gaze landed on Gage. "Brewer, come with me."

Gage straightened his shoulders as he followed his commanding officer back across the hard top. His mind raced. The op had been flawless, but the expression on Hallenback's face told him something was wrong.

Gage followed him inside the base's main head-quarters and down an air-conditioned corridor lined with black-and-white photographs of aircraft carriers. Gage had never been in here before, but the ball of dread forming in his gut far outweighed his curiosity.

Hallenback stopped outside a closed door and turned to face him.

"Some people here to see you."

"Sir?"

"They're with the FBI. Be direct. Be brief. And don't hesitate to stop the meeting if you want legal advice. I've got someone I can call." He pulled a handkerchief from his pocket and passed it to Gage. "Clean up your face before you go in there. I'll be down the hall." He nodded curtly and walked away.

Gage took a second to process the orders. His ears were still ringing from the helo ride and he was covered in grime. He wiped his face and stepped through the door.

Two civilians stood in the windowless conference room. In dark suits and white shirts they looked like his-and-hers ads for Brooks Brothers.

The man stepped forward and offered a handshake. "Lieutenant Brewer."

"Yes, sir."

"Take a seat."

The woman lowered herself into a chair at the end of the table and politely crossed her legs, leaving five empty seats. Gage took the one on the other end.

The man sat in the chair directly to Gage's right. "Do you know why you're here, Lieutenant?"

"No idea."

Gage dropped the "sir." Fuck this guy if he couldn't even be bothered to identify himself.

"We're with the FBI," the woman piped up. "I'm Special Agent Elizabeth LeBlanc and this is Supervisory Special Agent Gordon Moore."

Gage watched the blonde talk, but his real focus was Moore, who was clearly the one in charge. The agent was six feet, one-eighty. His demeanor came across as relaxed, but his gaze was sharp.

He leaned back in his chair now and looked Gage up and down. "You ever met an agent, Blake Reid?"

Shit.

"In Texas, two summers ago," Gage said. *Same time he'd met Kelsey.* "Why?"

"And do you remember the circumstances of that meeting?"

Gage gritted his teeth. He glanced at the woman—LeBlanc—who had her pencil poised above a yellow legal pad.

"I was in West Texas helping out on an archaeological dig." This was total bullshit. Gage had been guarding the dig, at Joe's request, after Kelsey's team had run into trouble with some of the nastier elements along the border. Joe had sent Gage down there on a quick PSD assignment, maybe thinking a little personal security detail would be a good break from combat.

Turned out to be not much of a break, though, as Kelsey's workers stumbled into evidence of a terrorist cell trying to infiltrate the United States. Blake's counterterrorism team was called in to head them off, which—despite numerous fuckups—the feds managed to do.

With Gage's help.

He stared at the two feds before him now. They were watching him closely.

"All due respect," Gage said sarcastically, "what exactly is this about?"

The woman looked at Moore, who was trying to stare a hole through Gage. Gage folded his arms over his chest and stared right back.

The woman cleared her throat. "Agent Reid—"

"Blake Reid is dead," Moore said flatly. "Where were you, Lieutenant Brewer, on Monday night?"

Gage's shoulders tensed, but he didn't blink.

"You're telling me someone killed him?"

He nodded.

Shit. Gage glanced at the BlackBerry sitting on the table near the woman. He wanted to call Kelsey.

"Why don't you walk us through your whereabouts since Sunday?" Moore said, very low-key.

Unbelievable. They thought he was a suspect.

"Lieutenant?"

"I was here Sunday." Gage's mind was still reeling and he looked at that phone again. It was Thursday. Why hadn't Kelsey called him? She had to be devastated. Unless—

"What time did you arrive—"

"Where's Kelsey Quinn?" Gage demanded.

Moore just looked at him.

"Blake Reid's fiancée—where is she?"

"*Ex*-fiancée, from what we understand."

Gage slapped the table. "*Where* is she?"

Moore stared at him, and Gage's blood ran cold.

"We were hoping you could tell us."

CHAPTER 4

"She's *missing*?"

The lieutenant's alert level went from code yellow to code red in the space of a heartbeat. It was remarkable to see. Elizabeth watched from the other end of the table as the SEAL leaned forward in his chair and got right in the face of a senior FBI agent.

But Gordon seemed unfazed.

"No one's seen Dr. Quinn since eight-fifty P.M. Monday when she paid the parking attendant at the San Antonio airport."

Brewer shot to his feet. "That was three days ago!"

"Sit down, Lieutenant. We need you to answer some questions."

The man stood there, face taut, hands flexing at his sides. He towered over Gordon, and Elizabeth could tell there was some sort of battle going on in his head: Should he walk out of here or cooperate?

He darted a look at the clock and then lowered himself into the chair. But even seated, he looked no less menacing, and Elizabeth had no trouble imagining this man snapping someone's neck with his bare hands.

But she didn't believe he'd snapped Blake's. It didn't add up.

"Walk me through your last few days," Gordon said. "Start with the weekend."

"I was here most of the weekend training."

"What time did you leave the base Saturday?"

"About 1930." The SEAL shot a look at Elizabeth as she scribbled that down. "Went to a bar. Met up with some friends. Had a few beers, went home."

"What time?"

"About 2300."

"Were you alone?"

"Yes."

"And then?"

"Went home, hit the rack, got up about 0500. Came to base for training all day. Went home about 1800, watched TV and went to bed."

"So Sunday, you basically worked and went home, is that correct?"

"That's correct."

"Is it uncommon for you to work weekends?"

"No."

"What about Monday?" Gordon asked.

The man darted yet another look at Elizabeth's phone. He cast a glance at the clock.

"Got up about 0500, went for a run."

"How long?"

"Twelve miles."

Twelve *miles*? Holy crap. Elizabeth jotted it down.

"Got here at 0800. Had a planning session with my team and left the base about 1300. Spent some time packing. Then watched some baseball and went to bed."

Gordon eased forward. "Packing for what?"

The man hesitated. "I've got leave coming. I was planning to go down to Cozumel, do some diving."

"And when did you plan to go?"

"This afternoon."

The room got very quiet. Just the sound of her pencil scraping against the paper. Pretty convenient timing for an international trip, but Elizabeth didn't look up from her notes.

"Back to Monday," Gordon said. "Did you see anyone Monday night or Tuesday morning?"

"No."

"Anyone at all who can corroborate your whereabouts?"

"No."

"Tell us more about Monday night. Did you call anyone? E-mail anyone? Leave your apartment for any reason?"

"I didn't get online, no. I was by myself, like I said, watching the game."

"And you didn't call anyone?"

"No."

"Anyone call you?"

"No." He glanced impatiently at the clock.

"What about Tuesday morning?"

"Reported to base at 1100."

"Eleven in the morning? Is that unusual?"

"We work unusual hours. Sir."

Elizabeth caught the contempt in his voice but didn't look up. This guy clearly didn't like FBI agents—a fact she felt sure wasn't lost on Gordon.

"I was here until late Tuesday, until late Wednesday, and then back before dawn today. Check the base records if you want."

"We have," Gordon said. "We spent most of yesterday, in fact, going over your background."

The SEAL's face hardened. He stood up. "That case, I won't waste any more time on this. I've got a meeting with my CO."

"One more thing, Lieutenant. I wouldn't be taking any trips out of the country if I were you."

"Is that a threat?"

"Just some friendly advice."

He scowled and walked out the door.

Elizabeth's shoulders slumped as the tension in the room disappeared. She glanced at Gordon.

"You don't really think he'll leave the country, do you?"

"Not the traditional way," he said. "We've got his passport flagged."

She glanced down at her notes. For some reason she still didn't comprehend, Gordon had handpicked her for his team on this. Out of all the available agents in the San Antonio field office, he'd chosen her. Why? She wasn't sure. She assumed he wanted her opinion, but she felt strange offering it to such a seasoned investigator. So since their arrival yesterday, she'd basically acted as his silent assistant while he checked in with the local field office and conducted preliminary research on Gage Brewer. Unfortunately, that research hadn't yielded much. Brewer didn't have a criminal record, and his military record—what they'd been allowed to see of it—was exemplary. They'd also learned that besides being Gage's ex-girlfriend, Kelsey Quinn was the niece of Gage's former commanding officer.

Elizabeth studied Gordon's pensive expression and debated whether to offer her opinion. Maybe she should keep her mouth shut. But then again, what was the point of her being here if she didn't at least attempt to provide insights?

"There are some holes in his timeline," she said. "But still this doesn't feel like a fit to me. You're thinking some kind of love triangle?"

"Kelsey Quinn's unexplained disappearance coincides with Blake Reid's murder. That tells me she's either involved in the crime or a victim herself." He checked his watch and stood up. "I've got to get back to the local office. I want you to keep tabs on Brewer. He'll be leaving here soon, and I don't want him out of your sight."

Elizabeth stood and collected her notes. "So . . . you don't want me to help search for Kelsey Quinn? I thought finding her was high priority."

"We don't need to find Kelsey Quinn. If she's alive, Lieutenant Brewer will find her for us."

Kelsey was missing.

Blake Reid was dead.

The two facts didn't get any less grim the longer they rattled around in Gage's head.

Gage pulled his pickup into an empty space at his apartment complex. There were plenty to choose from because most of the tenants had already left for work. He checked his watch and took the steps leading to his apartment two at a time. Kelsey had been MIA for almost sixty hours, and he didn't have a minute to waste.

It was possible he was too late already.

Gage went straight to the computer in his bedroom and logged on.

"Come on, Kels," he muttered as a torrent of messages flooded his in-box. He hadn't checked e-mail since Tuesday, and a desperate part of him was holding out hope that maybe she'd reached out.

Did you hear about Blake? Yeah, even though I wasn't planning to marry him anymore, I'm still racked with grief over it. Thought I'd head to the beach and drown my sorrow in a bottle of tequila, just FYI.

But no such message appeared in his in-box. As had been the case for months, he didn't have anything from her—just a crapload of junk mail and a note from his brother. It was what he'd expected, but still it sucked. Kelsey's radio silence was just one more shitty piece of news to add to the growing list of Really Shitty News he'd learned about today. Way, *way* down on that list was the fact that Gage, evidently, was suspected of involvement in Blake's death. The feds had made that clear. And although Gage had no doubt his story would hold, he wasn't happy to know that the lead detective in the case was wasting his time.

Sure, Gage was capable of killing Blake Reid. He'd even fantasized about it a time or two when he'd been shitfaced drunk and loaded with resentment. But Gage *hadn't* killed him. And Kelsey *couldn't* kill him. It wasn't in her nature. Even if the rumors were true and Blake had been cheating on her, Gage couldn't picture her putting a bullet in the man's gut.

Which meant someone else had killed him.

And now Kelsey was missing, which meant that either she was somehow complicit in the murder or she'd been abducted—or worse—by Blake's murderer.

Another possibility—that Kelsey had been spooked by something and gone into hiding—was what Gage was counting on. The odds were long, but he was betting on it, anyway.

Gage got a strangled feeling in his chest. Why hadn't she reached out? If she was alive, why hadn't she tried to contact him? Even with all the shit they'd been through, he'd always thought that deep down she knew she could depend on him. But maybe she didn't know. Maybe that run-in back at O'Malley's had sealed his fate. He'd been an asshole, and she'd finally written him off.

Gage hoped that was it. The other explanation—the *likely* explanation for her silence—was too hard to think about.

He shook off the dread. He needed to be positive. He needed to be proactive. To accomplish his objective he needed to believe, with every fiber of his being, that she was still alive.

He checked his watch again. Time to move. Every hour that ticked by put Kelsey in more danger. Not that she couldn't take care of herself. She was smart, and if she *was* on the run, then she'd managed to elude the FBI for several days, which meant she'd done a better-than-average job of covering her tracks. But Gage suspected the person who'd killed Blake was better-than-average, too. And Kelsey was a scientist, not an operator. If and when Blake's killer caught up to her, she didn't stand a chance.

Gage stripped off his filthy clothes and jumped in the shower, going over the plan he'd formulated on the drive home from the base. He scrubbed off the dirt and sweat and greasepaint clinging to him as he went over every detail. He got out of the shower and felt himself stepping into combat mode even as he pulled on civilian clothes.

Gage unlocked the file drawer of his desk and grabbed his passport. He took his escape-and-evasion kit from his closet and shoved it into the roomy pocket of his cargo shorts. The kit contained a bare minimum of supplies he would need for a little E&E. Gage jammed his feet into sneakers and nestled his blue-and-orange Chicago Bears cap on his head. He grabbed his personal firearm—a SIG nine-mil—and tucked it in the holster at the small of his back, where it would be concealed by the loose-fitting button-down he wore over his T-shirt. An extra magazine in his pocket and he was good to go.

Gage glanced around his bedroom one last time as his cell phone buzzed from its spot on the desk.

Damn, maybe it was the feds calling him in for another interview. He should have turned it off.

But maybe it was her. He grabbed the phone.

"Brewer."

"Yo, you ready?"

"Just leaving," he told Derek, who'd agreed to do him a favor. *Anything you need, man. Consider it done.* Gage would have said the same to him, but given all the factors in play here, he felt obligated to give his friend one last out.

"You sure you're up for this?" Gage asked. "It could get messy."

Silence stretched out, and Gage could tell he'd insulted him.

"Vaughn?"

"Fucking 1100," he answered. "And don't be late. This isn't how I planned to spend my day off."

Lieutenant Brewer was definitely leaving.

Elizabeth watched him toss the duffel bag in the front seat of his truck, then fire up the engine and go tearing out of the parking lot.

"Subject is on the move," she said into her phone. "Heading north on Palmetto Avenue."

"I got him."

Elizabeth waited a few seconds before pulling out of the lot across from Brewer's apartment building. She couldn't see the backup car, but that was probably a good sign. SEALs were highly trained in evasive maneuvers, and she had no doubt that if Brewer spotted the tail, he'd be able to ditch it in a matter of minutes.

The trick was to keep him from spotting it.

Elizabeth moved through traffic, allowing a good distance between her vehicle and the black pickup. Fortunately, Gordon had placed enough importance on this task to provide her with not only a backup agent, but also a decent vehicle from the local office's motor pool. The white SUV she was driving was old enough and crappy enough not to stand out as an unmarked police unit.

Much *less* fortunate was the fact that Gordon had entrusted her with this task in the first place. She didn't understand why he'd wanted a newbie agent—even with help—to keep tabs on their prime suspect.

But he hadn't asked for her opinion—he'd simply given her the keys, along with explicit instructions: Don't lose him.

Despite the uneasiness niggling away at her as she tailed Brewer's black pickup onto Interstate 5, Elizabeth was determined to follow orders. She planned to be on him like a tick until he led her to Blake Reid's ex, who held the key to his death.

If she wasn't already dead herself.

Brewer veered into the left lane and picked up speed. They were heading north, and she wondered if his destination was the airport. An afternoon flight maybe? Was he hopping a plane to rendezvous with Kelsey, wherever she was? But the airport exit came and went with Brewer doing seventy in the left lane.

Elizabeth checked her odometer. She checked her clock. Her stomach growled at her—a reminder that she hadn't eaten since the candy bar in her motel room last night. That was nearly twelve hours ago, and her energy was flagging as she pushed north on the interstate, leaving San Diego behind.

Where are you going? she wondered, envisioning a map of Southern California. He had a flight to Mexico this afternoon from San Diego—Elizabeth had confirmed that—but as they got farther and farther away from the city, she concluded he had no intention of taking it. Their interview this morning had caused him to change his plans. With any luck, he was on his way to Kelsey.

The miles rolled by. The journey dragged on. Elizabeth's energy level dropped. Sign after sign reminded her of all the hamburgers and sandwiches and cups of coffee she could have used to recharge her system. She glanced at her fuel indicator and wondered how much gas Brewer had in his truck. If this was a true road trip, he'd have to pull over at some point, and maybe she could dart into a convenience store and—

The truck cut across three lanes of traffic and exited.

"Damn!" She pounded the wheel. "Damn, damn, damn!"

If she attempted to follow, he'd spot her for sure. She waited for him to disappear from view before easing over to catch the next exit.

Elizabeth's phone chimed and she snatched it up.

"Don't worry, I got him." Agent Frost's calm baritone voice made her breathe a sigh of relief. The man was almost as new as she was, but at least he knew the area.

"I'm just getting off," Elizabeth said. "Where's he going?"

"Can't tell yet. He's staying on the feeder. You might even come out ahead of him. Careful he doesn't see you. I don't think he's made the tail."

"I'll be careful." She eased off the highway and checked all her mirrors. Up ahead she spotted a black pickup slowing down at a stoplight.

"I see him," Elizabeth said, scanning the area. The light turned green, and Brewer veered into the right-hand lane. Her gaze landed on a sign, and suddenly her heart sank.

"Oh, no."

Brewer put on his turn indicator.

"Oh, shit."

"What is it? Where's he going?" Frost asked.

Brewer hung a right at the light. Her heart sank even lower as she followed him.

"LeBlanc? What's the word?"

"I think he made the tail. He's taking us to Disneyland."

Silence followed this announcement.

"That's not good," Frost said.

"I'm aware of that."

"Think he's meeting someone?"

"No."

She followed the steady river of cars along the landscaped route leading into the park. Her respect for the man expanded as she contemplated the looming disaster. What better place to ditch her than a park packed with six zillion tourists? Elizabeth glanced down at her attire and actually started to laugh. It was either that or cry. In her charcoal gray pantsuit, she was going to stick out like a funeral director at a birthday party, and she had no doubt that was part of the plan.

"Okay, I see him," Frost said. "Far left lane, correct?"

"Affirmative."

Elizabeth took a deep breath. She could do this. She hadn't lost him yet. She pulled into the far right lane and inched up to the parking booth behind a series of minivans. She took out her wallet and paid the attendant, trying to envision how this was going to look on her expense report.

"He's pulling into a space," Frost informed her.

"Keep an eye on him."

"He's getting out now. You want me to sit on the vehicle or follow him inside?"

Elizabeth considered the question as she found a parking spot. He could be planning to leave in a friend's car, a taxi, a bus. He could hop on the monorail.

"Forget the vehicle," she said. "We need to follow him."

Elizabeth got out of the SUV and stood for a moment in the blazing sunlight. Heat rose up from the asphalt. In seconds she was sweating, but ditching her jacket wasn't an option because it hid her holster.

"He's headed for the entrance," Frost said. "Navy blue Chicago Bears hat with an orange logo."

Elizabeth stood on tiptoes to peer over the sea of cars and people. "I see him." Luckily he was tall, which would make him easy to track.

Wishful thinking.

Elizabeth joined a stream of parents and strollers and ignored their curious glances at her attire as they flowed toward the park. She kept her eye on Brewer as he sauntered up to a ticket window. Elizabeth silently cursed him as she hauled out her wallet again and handed over another stack of bills.

If she didn't know how worried he was about his ex-girlfriend right now, she'd think he was laughing at her. Maybe he was. Maybe he didn't give a damn about Kelsey Quinn or Blake Reid or any of this, and his idea of fun was to spend his day jerking around a couple of feds.

Elizabeth passed through the entrance and joined a sea of tourists clad in brightly colored shirts and hats. The scent of funnel cakes wafted toward her and her stomach growled. She didn't even *like* funnel cakes, but she was nearly faint from hunger. She took out a five-dollar bill and tucked it in her pocket, just in case a vendor brushed past her and she had a chance to snag some food.

Brewer ambled through the crowd, looking right at home in his shorts and Nikes. She wasn't fooled by his attire, though. She would bet a week's pay he had a weapon tucked under that shirt or stashed into one of those many pockets.

He led her down Main Street, USA. Elizabeth had never been here, but as she scanned the storefronts, she realized that—at least conceptually—the place was like Hogan's Alley. Both were mock-ups of an American town. However, the Disney version had more color and landscaping and gingerbread architecture than the Quantico version. More mouse ears, fewer guns.

Brewer veered into a gift shop. Elizabeth glanced around. She spotted Frost standing near a restaurant window, pretending to read a menu. The sun glinted off his shaved black head, and he could have used a hat, but at least his jeans and polo shirt were less conspicuous than her business garb. With the tilt of her head, Elizabeth motioned for him to go inside. Brewer didn't know Frost, whereas he'd been in a conference room with Elizabeth just this morning.

Frost strolled down the sidewalk and slipped into the store.

A second later, Brewer exited. Elizabeth turned her back and pretended to be looking at a shop window as she watched his reflection in the glass. He didn't glance in her direction, but that didn't mean he hadn't noticed her. After a few moments, she turned and followed him. A balloon vendor provided some cover for her as she trailed him down the street.

She tried to think ahead, tried to deduce his plan. Would he get on a roller-coaster? It would be a good place to shake her, but he'd have to wait in line. Maybe he'd queue up for something less crowded, like one of the kiddie rides.

He slipped into a men's room.

Elizabeth jerked her phone out and called Frost. "He's in the restroom just north of the ice-cream parlor."

"Roger that. I've got the side street covered."

Elizabeth's head pounded. This wasn't good. She thought of all the things she'd read about SEALs and imagined him shimmying into an air duct and elbow-crawling into another building. She scanned every door to every building on that side of the block.

And then there he was, stepping out of the restroom and crossing the street to a churro vendor. Elizabeth watched with annoyance as he bought a snack and proceeded to chomp into it as he meandered down the road. He finished it off and pitched the wrapper into the nearest trash can. A few seconds later he eased up to a crowd of teenage girls who were waiting to have their picture taken with Goofy. Elizabeth's heart skipped a beat as she lost sight of him in the crowd.

Her phone chimed.

"You see him?" she asked Frost. "I don't see him."

"I lost him—wait. Scratch that. He's buying a hot dog."

Elizabeth blew out a sigh. "I see the storefront. Don't get too close, though. I'm pretty sure he knows I'm here, but he may not have seen you."

The Bears cap appeared above the teenagers.

"I'm going to hang back a ways," Frost said.

"I've got a better idea. How about *I* hang back? Maybe he'll think he lost me, and you can follow him out."

"Good plan."

It *was* a good plan. If he thought he'd ditched her, he'd probably start moving toward his real destination.

Elizabeth ducked into a shop and took a brief instant to soak up the air-conditioning. She grabbed a pack of M&M's from a shelf beside the cash register and handed the clerk her five-dollar bill, then stuffed the candy in her pocket and hurried out of the store. She scanned the area. No sign of Brewer.

But then she saw Frost standing across the street, glancing around, looking perplexed.

Elizabeth's shoulders tensed. She looked up and down the street. She studied the mob of teenagers, the food kiosks, the storefronts. There was a sign directing people toward Adventureland. Had he gone that route?

A sharp whistle.

She glanced at Frost and he nodded in her direction. He'd walked right past her! He was moving aggressively now that he assumed he'd shaken her. He wove quickly through the crowd and back toward the main entrance. She hurried after him as her phone chimed.

"He's leaving," Frost told her.

"I'm on it!"

For a moment she lost him in a cluster of teenage boys wearing matching green track suits. But then she spotted him again on the far edge of the group. She picked up her pace until she was nearly running. She glanced at the signs. His speed increased. He was moving toward the bus depot, and he was way ahead of her. Elizabeth broke into a run. She wove through parents and kids, darted around strollers and sidestepped souvenir vendors. Sweat trickled down her back as she spotted the line of buses waiting at the curb. He stepped onto the one in front. Elizabeth cursed her luck as the door hissed shut and the bus began to move.

She sprinted forward and pounded her fist on the side of it. "Wait! *Wait!*"

Brakes squealed. The door hissed open. She climbed up the steps. The seats were full and he stood in the aisle, his back to her, holding on to one of the loops dangling from the ceiling. She studied the cap, the broad shoulders, the loose-fitting shirt. She noticed a handicapped door in back and tried to figure out how she was going to block that exit once he figured out she was here.

Suddenly he pivoted and they were face-to-face.

She blinked.

The man smiled.

"Who are you?" she sputtered.

"Name's Derek Vaughn." He grinned down at her from beneath the brim of his Bears hat.

"But—"

The bus lurched forward. She stumbled into him. He caught her arms and looked amused as he steadied her on her feet.

"I take it you were expecting someone else?"

Trent sank onto a park bench and mopped the sweat from his brow. Acid filled his stomach as he gazed down at his phone. A full minute ticked by. Finally he dialed.

"I lost him."

Silence on the other end. Trent squeezed his eyes shut and waited.

"Do you want me to—"

"Forget him for now. I've located the woman."

Trent's chest loosened. He'd dodged a bullet.

"Where is she?" he asked, hoping the relief didn't come through in his voice.

"Call me in three hours. I'll give you instructions."

CHAPTER 5

Kelsey couldn't shake the feeling that she was being followed. She checked her rearview mirror again, and again spotted no other cars or headlights on the two-lane road.

Since arriving yesterday at this California logging town, she'd tried to keep a low profile. She'd spoken to only a handful of people. She'd spent almost all of today cooped up in Joe's cabin, cleaning—as if sweeping floors and swiping at cobwebs would somehow get her mind off of everything. But it hadn't worked. The place was tiny, and once she'd scoured everything and dusted everything and organized everything down to her uncle's fishing tackle, there was nothing to distract her. She'd finished her last chore this afternoon and had spent the remainder of the day thinking about Blake's death and the fact that the world's top law-enforcement agency was currently searching for her.

Kelsey's throat tightened as a fresh wave of fear washed over her. It was becoming a familiar feeling. She flexed her hands on the steering wheel and took a deep breath.

No one knows you're here, she told herself.

Very few people even knew about this place. Kelsey herself hadn't been here since she was a kid and had forgotten it existed until she'd come across a stack of utility bills in Joe's desk. Her grandmother said Joe had kept the place all these years because he spent so much time living with other people and needed a little solitude between deployments.

Solitude. Just what Kelsey wanted. She checked her mirrors again as she swung onto the dirt road leading to the row of cabins. The caretaker's home was the second one down, and Kelsey noted the flicker of a television in the main room as she passed by. She reached Joe's cabin and pulled right up to the front. Her little car sputtered and coughed when she cut the engine, and she eyed the dashboard mistrustfully. It had done okay on the drive up, but she'd put fifteen hundred miles on it in three days, and it probably could at least use an oil change.

Kelsey gathered her groceries and got out. The porch light glowed and she noted the freshly swept grooves in the dirt around the wooden steps, which told her no one had been tromping around here during her trip to town. Kelsey unlocked the door and paused to listen.

All was quiet except for the gurgle of the nearby creek and the whisper of wind in the surrounding woods.

Something buzzed, and Kelsey jumped. She caught her breath and pulled the cell phone from her pocket. Ben Lawson.

"What's up?" she asked. She'd told him only to call her if it was something important.

"You don't sound happy to hear from me."

"Is everything okay?"

"Just thought you'd want to know, the FBI was out at the lab again today, looking for you."

Kelsey felt a stab of guilt for involving him.

"You don't have to lie for me," she said, locking the door behind her. She dropped her grocery bags onto the sagging couch.

"I didn't. They talked to Mia. And anyway, you haven't told me where you are, so why would I have to lie?"

Kelsey stacked cans of soup in the cupboard as she thought about that carefully worded statement. She hadn't told Ben where she was, but she had no doubt he'd figured it out. Ben worked in the Delphi Center's cyber-crimes unit. He was a genius on computers and had been known to bend a few rules to track down information. Kelsey would bet that within minutes of her phone call last night, Ben had not only traced her call to the nearest cell tower, but also pinpointed her most recent credit-card transaction. The FBI could do the very same thing, which was why Kelsey had cleaned out her bank account on the way out of San Antonio. All her purchases—from her dinged-up Dodge Neon to her prepaid disposable cell phone—had been with cash. She was doing everything she could think of to stay off the grid.

"So, I ran down those numbers you wanted," Ben told her, and she heard the pride in his voice.

"That was fast. I would think hacking the phone records of an FBI agent might be something of a challenge."

"I got everything, no problem. But you said you're

most interested in the calls he made in the three days before his death."

Tears burned her eyes. *Death.* She still couldn't believe it. But she couldn't get emotional right now—she had to be objective.

"Kelsey?"

She cleared her throat. "What did you learn?"

"Well, almost everything was a Bureau call—him phoning his office, his coworkers, that kind of thing. There were two numbers that weren't, excluding a call placed to you. You have a pen handy?"

She grabbed the steno pad off the kitchen table, where she'd been sitting earlier and making notes. Ben recited several numbers.

"First one is the cell-phone number of a C. Weber in Provo, Utah. I'm working on that name. Second one is the main number for UC Berkeley. No idea where they routed the call. They've got tons of extensions."

"Interesting." She didn't know why Blake would be calling a university.

"There's something else you might want to know. I took a look at the phone records of another agent in Blake's office."

Kelsey's nerves jangled. Was he referring to Trent? She'd purposely avoided any mention of Trent because she didn't want Ben knowing details that might put him at risk.

"I thought you were only going to look at Blake?"

"I was," he said. "But then I got curious because of the high volume of calls between these two over the weekend. There's some interesting overlap with the non-FBI numbers they were both calling. For example, Agent

Trent Lohman called the Weber number multiple times. And Berkeley, too."

"When did he call Berkeley?"

"Twice last Thursday and once Friday."

A dog barked outside. Kelsey's pulse picked up as she went to the front window. She switched off the overhead light and moved the shade aside so she could look out. The cabin was dark except for a band of light coming in from the porch.

"This Weber person," she said. "You don't have a full name?"

"Just an initial. I should have more by tomorrow."

"Thanks." She gazed out at the darkened road running past the cabins, but saw no one. "Be careful, though. I hope you aren't leaving your fingerprints on this."

"Don't worry about me. Just take care of yourself, all right? I'll be in touch."

"Thanks."

She hung up and looked outside again. No more barking. She was being paranoid. Ever since she'd arrived here, she'd been hearing footsteps and jumping at shadows.

Kelsey stared down at her throwaway cell phone. She was tempted to make one more call, but she probably shouldn't.

On the other hand, how was she going to get herself out of this mess if she didn't track down some critical information?

She took a deep breath and dialed a number she knew by heart.

"Travis County Medical Examiner's Office."

"Dr. Froehler, please."

She held her breath and waited, hoping he was there. He worked a lot of late hours.

"George Froehler."

"Hi, it's Kelsey."

"Well, well. Wasn't expecting to hear from you."

It was a loaded statement, and she tried to interpret it. Did he know she'd left town? Were people looking for her? Would he call the FBI the second he hung up?

But she and Froehler went way back. She'd interned in his office one summer during grad school, and she happened to know the deputy medical examiner was fond of her. His drawn-out silence told her two things: First, he knew she was in trouble. Second, he wasn't going to ask questions.

"I understand you performed the Reid autopsy," she said, although this was a guess. Froehler was the workhorse at TCMEO, while the ME was more of a figurehead. "I had a quick question."

"The official report hasn't been released yet." His voice was guarded. She needed to tread carefully.

"Manner of death?"

"Homicide."

She waited, hoping he'd elaborate. From what she'd witnessed, she thought the weapon was either a knife or that gun with the silencer. But even with a silencer, guns weren't really *silent,* and Kelsey was pretty sure she would have heard a noise. She was almost certain Blake had been killed with a knife.

"I assume nail clippings were collected from the victim autopsy," she said. "Any blood or skin cells present? Any signs of struggle?"

"None."

Kelsey's heart sank.

"What about trace evidence?" she asked. "Hair, fiber, that sort of thing?"

Another pause, probably as he debated the wisdom of sharing anything with her. "We found one hair, on the back of the victim's shirt. It's inconsistent with the victim, so there's a strong chance it came from his attacker."

A breath of relief whooshed out. *Physical* evidence.

"The FBI was here today, taking custody of everything," Froehler said. "I assume it's at Quantico by now."

"I see."

"Anything else you needed, Doctor?"

Another bark, and she peered through the window. Still, she saw nothing.

"Kelsey?"

She heard the concern in his voice. In his guarded way, he was offering to help. Kelsey felt a twinge of guilt. This man had always been kind to her. He'd always been a mentor. But the sort of trouble she was in now was way, way beyond his ability to fix.

"I'm fine."

Silence.

"Thanks for the info," she added. "I appreciate it."

She hung up before he could say anything else. She'd involved him enough, and she didn't want to get him in trouble.

Kelsey stood in the darkened kitchen, thinking about what she'd learned. The FBI had a hair, which was good. Trent had been in Blake's apartment countless times, so fingerprints alone would do nothing to connect him to the murder.

Then again, the hair might not, either.

Next to bone and teeth, hair was one of the most durable elements of the human body. Kelsey worked with it all the time. But unlike DNA or fingerprint evidence, it wasn't unique to an individual. It was considered class evidence, which was much less useful for investigators.

Still, it was something.

And then there was Ben's information about the phone calls. Berkeley. Provo. She had been working on a timeline of Blake's activities, but she had no idea how phone calls to either of those places might relate to his murder.

Kelsey reached for an apple and nibbled on it, waiting for some sort of epiphany. Nothing came to her. The most perplexing question of all was *why?* What on earth had made someone who'd acted like one of Blake's closest friends decide to kill him?

Maybe the motive was personal, some sort of rivalry. Maybe Blake was having an affair with Trent's wife. Given Blake's penchant for womanizing, Kelsey figured it was possible. But what about the plainclothes cop who'd tried to kill her? If this was a crime of passion, why was *he* involved? The image of that man flashing a badge was keeping Kelsey up at night. It had shaken her faith in something she'd always taken for granted.

Maybe the whole thing had to do with one of Blake and Trent's cases. Or the bones Kelsey had recovered in the Philippines. Blake had told her he'd consulted Trent about that case, and that Trent had contacted someone in the Bureau who specialized in facial recognition software. But why would Trent be interested in some dead terrorist halfway around the world? More likely the motive was something much closer to home.

Unfortunately, none of the pieces fit together. Kelsey couldn't even envision the puzzle.

She finished the apple and tossed the core in the trash. The cabin was silent. Now that the phone calls were over, she was acutely aware of how alone she was. She stared down at her dirty jeans, which she'd been wearing since Monday when she'd fled Blake's condo. She couldn't run forever. She knew that. She didn't have the skills or the funds. Or the capacity for lying. Luckily, Kelsey's mom, a high-school French teacher, was in Paris with a group of students, so she wasn't likely to be contacted by the FBI right now. But her trip ended next week, and Kelsey didn't relish the thought of her mother returning home to find a couple of somber-faced agents waiting to question her about her daughter's whereabouts.

Kelsey had to come up with some answers soon and she had to contact the police. But she wasn't ready to step forward with her account of what happened until she knew which people she could trust. At the moment, anyone with a badge was off that list.

The back of Kelsey's neck tingled. She glanced at the door. Was that—?

Creak.

A cold burst of adrenaline flooded her veins. Someone was on the porch. For a moment she stood motionless, not breathing. Then she crept to the other side of the kitchen and took her purse from the counter. She'd bought a tube of Mace several days ago and she slipped it into her hand as she stared at the door.

A shift in the light—barely perceptible, but Kelsey caught it. Her pulse quickened. She wasn't imagining it. Someone was definitely out there. She glanced around, grateful for the darkness of the cabin, which would enable her to see someone before they saw her. But the cabin was tiny. How could she sneak out the back without someone in front noticing? What had once felt like a refuge now felt like a trap.

She slid the car keys from her purse. She eyed the phone across the kitchen and debated whether she could get to it without making a sound.

Creak.

All her blood seemed to drain into her toes. She reached for the back door and fumbled with the latch.

Thud.

Kelsey wrenched open the door. She jumped down the steps and raced around the side of the house, toward her car.

Suddenly she was scooped off her feet and jerked back against something hard. A hand clamped over her mouth.

"Don't scream."

The arm tightened, and Kelsey's heart did a flip.

Gage.

There was no mistaking the arm, the voice, the firm wall of muscle now pressed against her back. He loosened his hold and she sagged against him with relief.

"Someone's there!" she hissed.

"It's a woman."

His voice sounded low, warm—the way she remembered from so many dark encounters.

Kelsey pulled out of his grip. She peered over the bushes and saw a short, plump figure tromping down the dirt road.

The caretaker's wife. Not a homicidal maniac.

Gage took her by the shoulders and slowly turned her around to face him. In the dimness she saw those blue eyes gazing down at her and the hard angles of the face she knew so well. The familiar scent of him flooded her and she wanted to bury her head against his chest.

"Are you all right?" His voice was serious—as serious as she'd ever heard it.

"What are you *doing* out here?"

His jaw tightened. Instead of answering, he took her hand and led her around the back of the cabin and up the steps. The door still stood open. He pulled her inside and crossed the cabin in a few strides.

Kelsey shoved the Mace in her pocket and switched on a lamp as Gage opened the front door and picked up something from the porch.

"Boysenberry preserves." He glanced at her as he shut the door. "'Welcome to Piney Creek, from Joyce.'"

Kelsey pressed her hand to her chest. "God, she scared me to death! Why didn't she just knock?"

He plunked the jar on the kitchen table. "You didn't have any lights on. Maybe she thought you were asleep."

He leaned against the wall now and folded his arms over his chest. Kelsey's heart lodged in her throat as she took her first good look at him. With his broad shoulders and powerful build, he'd always looked to her like he might be able to leap tall buildings in a single bound. But her favorite feature was his penetrating blue eyes— which were fixed on her right now. He wore a desert-brown T-shirt that stretched taut over his chest, faded jeans, and sneakers. This was the closest he ever came to looking like a civilian, but it didn't really work because everything about him screamed *warrior*. Disapproval emanated from him, and she felt the need to explain herself—which was ironic considering that he was the one who'd been skulking around her cabin late at night.

She took a deep breath. "You heard about Blake."

He gave a slight nod. "Lot of people looking for you."

"I know, I just—" She swallowed the lump in her throat. "I had to get away."

"You're running."

She opened her mouth, but she couldn't bring herself to explain. She didn't want to involve him in this. She wanted him to walk right out that door and stay out of it.

At the same time, she felt impossibly grateful that he was here. Just seeing him, hearing him, being in the same room with him made her feel as if she hadn't completely lost her grip on the normal life she'd had only a few days ago.

His expression hardened. She recognized the look. He didn't like to be stonewalled, which was funny given that he was one of the least communicative men she'd ever met.

"Forget it. You can tell me later." He pushed off from the wall. "Right now we need to get you out of here." He walked around the room and picked up her phone from the counter. "You got a bag or something?

Anything besides the purse?" He held the phone out to her.

She gaped at him. "I'm not going anywhere."

"Rule number one, Kelsey. Never, ever go where the enemy might expect you to be."

"But nobody knows I'm here."

"I know you're here. Joyce knows you're here."

"But—"

"Save the argument. We need to—"

Glass shattered. Gage launched himself across the room and tackled her. They crashed to the floor and she smacked the side of her head.

He pushed up on his hands. "You okay?"

She managed a nod. "What—"

"Rifle." He glanced over his shoulder. A pistol seemed to have materialized out of nowhere and he gripped it in his hand. He turned around and must have seen her look of horror.

"Don't worry, all the shades are down—he's shooting at shadows." Gage reached across her to yank the lamp cord from the wall and the cabin went black. "We need to get out of here."

Kelsey's heart hammered. Her lungs didn't seem to want to work. *Someone was shooting at them.*

Gage moved into a crouch beside her. "Stay down. Grab your purse and anything else you need. And here, give me your keys."

Dazed, she fumbled around in the darkness and followed his commands. Then he folded her hand around something metal—a key.

"I'm parked two lots down, at an empty cabin. You're going to make a run for my truck."

"*What?*"

"I'll create a diversion."

Before she could voice any of her objections, he reached up and opened the back door. He went perfectly still as he peered into the darkness. When he seemed satisfied it was safe, he slipped out the door, ducking low and towing her behind him. Together, they eased down the steps.

Kelsey gripped the keys in one hand and Gage's arm in the other.

"Come with me," she whispered. "Let's stay together."

He shook his head. Then he pointed her shoulders toward the woods.

"Just over there, all right?" His voice was warm against her ear, but barely audible over the frenzied beating of her heart. "Count to five, then run like hell. Get in on the driver's side, then move over for me."

He gave her arm a squeeze and disappeared into the shadows.

Kelsey stood motionless. She felt a swoosh of wind, heard the rustle of bushes. A loud squeak as he yanked open the door to her car.

She'd forgotten to count!

The car sputtered to life. Kelsey glanced around, then darted for the nearest spruce. She felt like a cartoon character running from tree to tree, trying to make herself invisible. Her breath came in shallow pants. She scanned the area, but it was nearly impossible to see anything in the dimness. She sprinted for the next tree and the next.

Crack.

The sound was unmistakable this time, and her heart skittered. *Gage!* She wanted to scream at him. What kind of crazy plan was this?

Through the gloom, she saw the outline of another cabin. A black pickup sat out front. Kelsey made a mad dash, trying so hard to stay low that she tripped to her knees right beside the truck. She wrenched open the door and scrambled across the seat and over the gear shift. She huddled on the floor.

God, where were the *keys?* She groped around. Her hand encountered a soft-drink can, a hat. Her fingers closed around the key chain. She shoved the key in the ignition as Gage leaped behind the wheel.

"Go!" she yelped.

He started the truck and thrust it into gear. "Get down!"

She crouched into a ball on the floor as he shot backward, jerking his door shut as he went. He hunched low over the wheel, but his bulk was an inviting target, and Kelsey held her breath as they roared down the dirt road. The tires hit asphalt and he stomped on the gas.

Kelsey gazed up at him, unable to speak or breathe or even formulate a thought.

"You all right?" He glanced down at her.

She nodded.

"Stay down," he said, but even as he said it, he was straightening up to check his mirrors and switch on the headlights.

The car vibrated under her and she squeezed her eyes shut. It was happening again. She couldn't get away from it. And now Gage was involved.

She opened her eyes and looked up at him. His jaw was set, his lips pressed together in a grim line. He looked fierce, determined.

"Are they following?"

He glanced over his shoulder. He checked the mirrors again. Kelsey waited, sure that at any moment the windshield would explode.

"Gage?"

"We're good for now." He patted the seat beside him. "Come on."

Her arms quivered as she pulled herself into the seat. She dragged the seat belt over her body and it took two tries to get it buckled because her hands were shaking. She looked at Gage. Then she looked out the window at the woods rushing by in a blur.

"Where are we going?" she asked.

"I'll put some distance between us." He shot her a look. "Then we'll stop and you can tell me what the hell's going on."

CHAPTER 6

Elizabeth glanced around the dark motel parking lot as she gathered files from the backseat. It wasn't the best neighborhood she'd ever been in, but it wasn't the worst, either. Still, she didn't think it wise to leave anything in the rental car overnight. She hitched her computer bag onto her shoulder, grabbed her purse, and balanced a few more files against her hip as she slammed the door. She strode across the pitted asphalt, darting her gaze around.

"Need a hand?"

She whirled around as a figure emerged from the shadow between two cars.

Derek Vaughn.

The man was, quite possibly, the last person she wanted to see tonight.

"Are you lost?" she asked.

"Nope." He reached over and took the stack of files.

"Hey!"

"Let me give you a little tourist tip." He spoke in that lazy Southern drawl as he smiled down at her. "This isn't a great part of town. Not a good idea to walk through dark parking lots with your hands full. Makes that Glock you're packing next to useless." He tugged the computer bag from her shoulder and transferred it to his own. "Damn, you got encyclopedias in here?"

Rather than engage in a wrestling match over her stuff, she crossed her arms.

"What can I do for you, Mr. Vaughn?"

"It's Derek." The side of his mouth curled up. "And you can let me walk you to your room. This way?"

He started off in the direction she'd been walking. Elizabeth watched his back. He'd changed clothes since before, when he'd been dressed as Gage Brewer's twin. Now he wore faded jeans and a black T-shirt that fit snugly over his muscular build. Now that he wasn't wearing the Bears cap, she got her first look at the thick brown hair that curled slightly at the back of his neck.

"What are you, 103?" He glanced back at her.

Elizabeth huffed out a breath and followed him. They reached the concrete walkway in front of the rooms, and she sidestepped him to take the lead. She halted in front of 103 and flicked him a glance.

"How did you know?"

He shrugged. "The other ones look occupied."

She shook her head as she took out her key card. At least she didn't have to go raise hell at the front desk because they'd given out her room number. But still, she didn't like him sneaking up on her in a parking lot late at night. What was he doing here? Either he was hitting on her or he had information related to the case. She suspected he was hitting on her.

Elizabeth rested her hand on her holster as she stepped inside and flipped on the light. The room hadn't improved since this morning. It smelled of mildew and cigarette smoke. She gazed at the faded orange bed-spread and sighed.

"Nice digs."

She turned around, and he handed over the file fold-ers. He'd put her computer bag on the floor just inside the door. Maybe he sensed her uneasiness or maybe he simply had manners, but he hadn't entered her room without permission. He stood on the threshold, his shoulder propped against the door frame.

Where did they get these guys, Beefcakes R Us? At six-four, he was almost a foot taller than she was. Practically every SEAL Elizabeth had seen today had been almost as huge. She'd watched them doing their morning workouts as she'd waited for Lieutenant Brewer. All of the men she'd seen were impressive, but particularly the SEALs. They seemed to relish pain. And they were distinguishable from the others by their longer-than-regulation-length hair and—in some cases—their beards, which helped them to blend in in countries where American servicemen might not be welcome.

Derek Vaughn was eyeing her now with a look she couldn't quite read. Elizabeth stacked her files on the table. She tucked her hands into her pockets and saw his gaze drift to the sidearm at her hip.

Some men had a thing for women with guns.

"What can I do for you?" she repeated.

"Let me take you to dinner."

She stared at him.

"You're ticked off about earlier. Let me make it up to you."

SCORCHED 101

She watched him, annoyed now. She *was* ticked off about earlier. She was embarrassed, too. But she was also starving and it was nearly midnight. As much as she hated to admit it, she knew she'd be safer going on a quest for food with a jacked-up Navy SEAL beside her than she would by herself. Yes, she was armed, but as a young blonde, she tended to attract attention.

"What did you have in mind?" she asked.

"Ah, you know. Thought I'd show you some of the culinary adventures San Diego has to offer. Maybe a little international cuisine."

"You're talking about the IHOP across the street."

"Good coffee." He nodded at her files. "Looks like you plan to be up late. And they're open, too, which is always a plus."

Ten minutes later, Elizabeth found herself sharing a vinyl booth with a ridiculously attractive man whose mission tonight was probably to separate her from her tailored gray pantsuit.

She distracted herself by checking out the menu. After a waitress took their orders and filled their coffee mugs, Elizabeth folded her hands on the table in front of her.

He was grinning at her.

"What?"

"Big appetite for a little woman."

"I'm hungry."

"Good for you." He rested his elbows on the table and leaned forward. "So, Liz—can I call you Liz?"

"It's Elizabeth."

"Yeah, but what do your friends call you? Liz? Beth? Betty?"

"Betty?"

"No one goes by Elizabeth. Too much of a mouthful." Derek smiled, and something in his look made her stomach flutter. He had light brown eyes with gold flecks in them. Besides his build, he didn't look a thing like Gage Brewer. How had she confused them?

She took a deep breath. "My mother is Beth. I go by Elizabeth. Less confusing."

"All right." He leaned back and watched her. *"Elizabeth,* how's the investigation going?"

"It'd be going a lot better if we knew where Lieutenant Brewer was."

He looked at her blankly.

"Do you care to tell me?"

His eyebrows arched. "Is there a warrant out for him?"

"No."

"Then I can't tell you where he is."

"Can't or won't?"

"Can't because I don't know. *Won't* because even if I did know, he's my best friend."

She tamped down her irritation.

"What do you want with him, anyway? You just talked to him this morning."

She felt almost sure he knew the answers to all the questions he was asking. "We need to ask him some more questions. And we need to talk to his girlfriend, Kelsey Quinn."

"Ex-girlfriend."

"Whatever. She's been missing since Monday evening, the night Blake Reid was murdered." Elizabeth watched closely, to see if any of this seemed to come as a surprise. As she'd suspected, he seemed well aware of the situation.

Just as he was probably well aware of Gage Brewer's current location. Elizabeth tried a new tactic.

"So, what do you know about her?" She took a sip of coffee.

"About Kelsey? I know she's a nice lady. It's not every woman who spends her summer vacation in some armpit jungle digging up bones."

Elizabeth listened, intrigued by the admiration she heard in his voice.

"She's got an impressive career," he continued. "Top of her field. She's smart, too—lot of degrees under her belt. But I hope to hell Gage catches up with her before whoever killed Reid does."

"And what if Gage killed Reid?"

He smiled.

"What? It's an avenue we're currently investigating."

"Why, because Reid was killed with a KA-BAR knife? Because someone broke his neck?"

She gaped at him. "How—"

"You're not the only one who knows a few folks at the Bureau." He winked at her. "Relax, it's not like it's common knowledge or anything. I just happen to have a friend who's been following the case."

From the way he said "friend," Elizabeth figured it was a woman. Probably some San Diego field agent he'd taken out for pancakes a time or two.

Elizabeth took another sip of coffee and tried to appear casual. "So. Do you know why Kelsey broke up with him?"

Derek just looked at her, and she hoped he wasn't going to clam up.

"Maybe he was a bit too controlling? Or maybe he had a violent streak?"

"You're working the jealous-ex angle," he stated. "Only problem is you got your facts mixed up. Gage dumped *her.*"

"Why?"

"I don't know the details," he said, but Elizabeth could read his face and the message there was plain: *Even if I did know, I wouldn't tell you.*

She was an outsider here. He was having coffee with her and answering her questions, sure. But she now knew for certain that his motive wasn't to help the investigation. He was fishing for information to help his friend.

"I know she gave him an ultimatum," he added, probably sensing her annoyance. "She told him it was her or the teams."

Elizabeth stared at him. Kelsey Quinn gave an ultimatum to a Navy SEAL? The move was either stupid or desperate. And nothing she'd learned about Kelsey pointed to stupid.

"An ultimatum seems a little extreme," Elizabeth said. "Why do you think she did that?"

Derek smiled and shook his head. "You got me. Why do women do anything?"

Two large plates arrived, overflowing with eggs and sausage, followed by two smaller plates stacked with pancakes. Elizabeth forgot the investigation for a moment as the scent of food wafted up from the table.

"So, Elizabeth, I know you suits think us military guys are dumber than a box of rocks." He shook hot sauce over his eggs, and she noticed his drawl had become more pronounced. "But see, Gage is a SEAL. Means he's smarter than the average bear."

"Your point is?"

"Your theory doesn't add up. It's too easy. Why would Gage implicate himself? And why would he need to kill the guy twice?" He carved a sausage in half and took a bite.

He had a good point. It was one she'd spent considerable time thinking about. Even with the evidence pointing to a perpetrator trained in hand-to-hand combat, and even with the combat knife and the hole in Brewer's timeline, Elizabeth didn't actually believe he'd murdered his ex-girlfriend's lover. And if it was true Brewer had been the one to end the relationship, then she *really* didn't believe it.

Plus there was this morning. Elizabeth had seen the look on the man's face when he found out Kelsey was missing. If he could manufacture that reaction, he was an amazing actor.

Somehow Kelsey was the key. Elizabeth believed that and so did Gordon, which was why he'd ordered an entire team of agents to spend the day trying to track her down.

She recalled Gordon's reaction when she'd phoned in the news that she'd lost their suspect. Silence. That was it. And an excruciating pause that ended with her pathetic offer to come into the office and help the rest of the team.

It had been one of the low points of her short career.

Derek was watching her now over the rim of his coffee mug. "So come on, ask me."

"Ask you what?"

"How we pulled the old switcheroo." His mouth twitched at the corner, and she could tell he was laughing at her.

She shrugged. "I couldn't care less."

"Sure you could. Learn from your mistakes. Don't they teach you that at Quantico?"

She looked at him, irritated because he was right. Fine—she could play along.

"You were at the bus depot."

"Nope." He took a big bite of pancakes. "Damn, these are good."

Elizabeth pursed her lips.

"You were on the bus?"

"Honey, you're way off. Think earlier."

She gritted her teeth. It simply wasn't possible that she'd lost him before the bus depot.

"You weren't in the gift shop," she said. "I *saw* Brewer exit the store and—"

"—and cozy up to that drill team?"

She looked at him.

"Cute girls. All the way out from Nashville. They're performing in the parade tomorrow, by the way."

He'd been in the crowd somewhere. Surrounded by young women. Waiting for Gage Brewer to take his place.

How could they have planned that ahead of time? Or had they made the plan on the fly after spying the opportunity?

"So, what'd you stop for?" he asked.

"What?"

"In the gift shop. You ducked in for something."

She took a deep breath. "M&M's. I was trying to let him shake me. I thought if he believed he'd lost me, he'd let his guard down and the other agent could follow him more easily."

Derek shook his head. "See now, that was a tactical mistake. Gage spotted your buddy way back at his apartment. You underestimated him. Another tactical mistake? Stopping for snacks in the middle of an op. Gotta keep your eye on the ball."

Elizabeth felt her stomach tense. She was getting defensive. But she needed to look past that and get this man's information. She no longer had any doubt that he knew where his friend was.

"Explain something to me," she said. "If Gage and Kelsey's relationship was over, if he dumped *her,* as you say, why would he feel obligated to go looking for her?"

Derek sighed. "You really have no idea who you're dealing with, do you?"

"I guess I don't." She tipped her head to the side. "Why don't you enlighten me?"

He looked at her for a long moment. "Gage and I were swim buddies during BUD/S training. You know what that is?"

"The SEAL training course. I've read about it."

"During BUD/S, you don't go anywhere without your swim buddy. The ocean, the pool, the chow hall. Even when you go to the head, your swim buddy goes with you. You *never leave* your swim buddy. Ever. It's a serious offense, and you can get thrown out right there on the spot. It may sound silly to you, but it goes back to the age-old SEAL ethos that you don't ever leave a man behind, dead or alive. That's ironclad. You take care of your teammates. Your team is everything."

He held her gaze, and Elizabeth couldn't help but ease closer.

"So, we were in Hell Week—the hardest part of BUD/S. Guys had been dropping like flies. We were down to forty-three men from our original hundred and twelve. The guys that were left—they were pretty much hard-core, and every last one of us was hating life." He shook his head. "It was relentless. For days we'd been doing obstacle courses, surf drills, rock portage—where you have to dock this inflatable boat without getting your brains bashed out on these rocks. We'd been doing beach runs, night swims, log PT, and every damn thing we did, we were in boots and long pants and T-shirts, and we had to be wet and sandy. All the time. We froze our asses off."

"Sounds brutal," she said. Brutal? It made the FBI Academy sound like a health spa.

"Yeah, but there was a purpose to it. It's designed to make you reassess your commitment. Do you really have what it takes? And it's not always the biggest guys who end up being the toughest. A lot of it boils down to mental stamina—which is where Gage really has something on the rest of us." Another sip of coffee. "Anyway, all of it was straight up hell, but the worst was the sleep deprivation. You're going on fifty hours with no sleep—your mind starts to play tricks on you. So, it was the middle of the night, 'bout four days in, and we were doing log PT."

"What's that?"

"You get with your team—which by that point was only five guys, because so many had rung out—that's when you ring this bell announcing you quit. Your log is like a telephone pole, and first thing they tell you to do is get it wet and sandy, because God knows it's not heavy enough on its own. Next, you have to hold it up—arms straight—while you do sprints, squats, whatever they tell you. They tried to divide the teams up by height, but Gage and me being six-four—you can picture where the lion's share of the weight came down. And we'd been doing this for hours." He shook his head. "Our arms were on fire. Our legs. Our joints. I was delirious—didn't know my own name. At one point—and I don't even recall it, really—but I dropped to the ground. I remember lying there, facedown in the sand, and thinking, 'They finally did it. They finally killed me.' And I was so relieved, I wanted to cry."

Elizabeth tried to picture this huge man weeping in the sand, and she couldn't.

"Next thing I know, someone's hauling me to my feet. It's Gage. I could barely talk, but I remember telling him I was done. He's just as tired as I am, but he's in my face screaming at me, 'Don't you quit on me! Damn you, Vaughn! We didn't get this far so you could ring out!' I don't remember if he dragged me or carried me, but next thing I know, I'm back with the team, heaving that log over my head, stumbling forward, one foot at a time, with Gage yelling at me the whole way. One step at a time." He paused and looked at her. "That's the key, you know. If you think about the pain to come, you'll just give up. So you take it hour by hour, minute by minute, and the only thing you have through all of it is your team."

Elizabeth watched him talk, certain she'd never felt a bond like that with anyone.

"So, that's Gage," Derek said. "He's about loyalty. Kelsey's no longer his girlfriend, but she's someone in his life and she's Joe Quinn's niece besides. If Gage believes she's in danger, then his mission is to protect her. He will pursue that mission until she is safe or he is dead, because that's who Gage is."

She watched him, starting to see where the arrogance came from. She still didn't like it, but she was beginning to understand it.

He nodded at her plate. "Hey, I thought you were hungry."

She glanced down at her untouched food just as her phone vibrated in her pocket. She pulled it out and checked the e-mail message that had just come in from Gordon.

"Shit," she muttered.

"What is it?"

"I have to go."

He smiled. "You haven't even tried your pancakes."

"Sorry." She rummaged through her purse, then left a twenty on the table and scooted out of the booth. "Something's come up."

Gage sped down the two-lane highway, checking his mirrors at every curve. Finally satisfied that they hadn't been followed, he swung onto a dirt road.

"Where are we going?" Kelsey asked.

He glanced at her. For the past half hour she'd been silent except for the barely audible sound of her teeth chattering. The woman was petrified.

Gage passed a sign for a picnic ground and turned into a gravel lot. He pulled up to a split-rail fence and cut the engine.

"We need to talk."

She didn't answer. Gage watched her profile in the dimness as she stared silently through the windshield.

"Kelsey, look at me."

Instead, she pushed open the door and climbed out of the pickup.

He followed. She trudged past a pair of picnic tables into a clearing where a circle of stones was visible in the moonlight. It had probably once been a campfire pit, but this part of the state had had a burn ban for years.

She tipped her head back and just stood there. The fir trees towered high into the sky and the air smelled like pinesap.

"Look at those stars," she whispered.

Gage tamped down his impatience. He glanced at the sky. Then he looked at Kelsey and felt a stab of worry.

"We used to come here." She looked at him, and her brown eyes were luminous in the moonlight. "Well, not *here* here. But this part of the state. Back when my dad was alive, we'd load up the car and go camping. Sometimes Joe would come if he had leave." She looked up at the sky again. "I used to lie in the tent and listen to the grown-ups talk after they thought I'd gone to sleep. I can't believe he's gone. And Blake—"

Her voice caught and she turned away. Gage gritted his teeth. Even in the dimness, he could see her shoulders shaking.

Gage wrapped an arm around her and pulled her close. She pressed her face against his chest and he felt warm tears seeping through his T-shirt.

"Hey," he said. He hated when she cried. He shifted her closer until her breasts flattened against him. She felt good. She smelled good. It had been months since he'd touched her this way. It was a turn-on, even though she was standing here grieving over another man—which made him either an idiot or an insensitive jerk. Maybe both.

She twisted out of his arms and wiped her cheeks.

"Sorry."

"It's okay." He watched with annoyance as she took another step away from him. "Kelsey, you need to tell me what's happening."

She looked off into the dark woods. "It's been so crazy. I don't know where to start."

"How about Friday, when you walked out on me at the pub?"

She shot him a look. He'd ticked her off, which was good because at least he'd succeeded in making the tears stop. She took a deep breath.

"I'll start with Monday," she said.

Gage shoved his hands in his pockets and listened, growing more alarmed by the second as she recounted everything from the moment she left the San Antonio airport to the moment she drove off of Hal's Used Car Lot in a piece-of-shit car that had cost half her bank account.

"So, that's it," she said. "I needed a place to go while I sort this out. My cash is limited and I didn't want to use a credit card, so I decided on the cabin. I thought no one knew about it."

"Everyone knew about it. There're no secrets in the teams."

The lack of privacy took some getting used to, but it was simply reality. A guy was having money problems, word got around. Someone's wife was having an affair, everyone knew. It was one reason his breakup with Kelsey had sucked. Everyone on his team—including Joe—had known about it almost the instant it happened.

"My grandmother said Joe went there to get away."

He looked at her. "I didn't say we bothered him there—just that we all knew about it. Fact, I'm pretty sure he had a woman there."

Her jaw dropped. "*Joe* did?"

"It's not like he was a monk." Gage smiled. "SEALs are chick magnets—even older ones."

The comment pissed her off, as he'd intended. It was easier to see her mad than sad.

"You know, I can read your mind." He stepped closer and gazed down at her in the dimness. "You're thinking about that girl back at O'Malley's. I didn't take her home with me, in case you were wondering."

She scowled and looked away. "I wasn't."

"Yeah, you were. Admit it."

"I couldn't care less what you do."

He eased closer. She wouldn't look at him. He touched his finger to her chin and lifted it. "Liar."

She tried to pull away, but he leaned down and kissed her.

CHAPTER 7

She felt an instant of pure shock, followed by a rush of heat. His tongue swept into her mouth and his strong arms wrapped around her. Without even thinking, she slid her hands around his neck and pressed against him. She tasted the hot inside of his mouth as his hands dropped down and molded her body to his. God, she'd *missed* him. Missed *this*. She felt his hair between her fingers, felt his stubble scraping against her chin as he changed the angle of the kiss. His mouth was strong and eager and she could tell he wanted to pull her to the dirt and take her clothes off right there.

And she wanted him to. All he had to do was touch her and she was ready to go for it. She dug her nails into his scalp. She pressed her breasts against him and kissed him with that heat, that *urgency* they'd always had together.

Through the lustful haze, she felt a twinge of pain as a barely healed wound started to tear open. For months she'd resolved never to let this happen again, never to put herself back in this position. And even as she kissed him and absorbed his intoxicating taste and moved against him, she was thinking of all the phone calls she'd resisted making, all the e-mails she'd written and deleted. She thought of all the impossible steps she'd forced herself to take to get *over* him. And now with one hot kiss, her willpower evaporated.

Panic bubbled up at the thought of going through that pain again.

She jerked away. She blinked up at him in the moonlight and they were both breathing heavily.

He bent his head down again, and she stepped back. "Let's not . . . complicate things."

"Kelsey, come on." He reached for her and she stepped away.

"I'm not doing this." She walked back to the truck and climbed in, then pulled the door shut with maybe a bit too much force. She needed to calm down. She needed to be objective, not emotional. After eight months of agonizing self-discipline, she couldn't afford to let him know how much one kiss had shaken her resolve.

Gage slid behind the wheel. He turned to look at her in the dimness and his face was a hard mask.

"I appreciate what you did, back at the cabin." She was amazed how composed she sounded. "I didn't realize I'd made myself vulnerable by staying there. I think the best thing now would be for you to take me someplace where I can rent a car, and I'll go from there."

He started the engine and thrust the truck into gear. "Not happening."

"Gage . . . you've done enough. And I appreciate it."

The truck shot backward. He shoved it into drive and sped out of the gravel lot and onto the road.

"You don't need to involve yourself anymore, though."

"Too late." He pulled onto the highway. "I've been *involved* since Trent and his dickweed friend decided to frame me for Blake's murder."

She looked at him. "How did they frame you?"

"The combat knife. The broken neck. I'm surprised they didn't stick a SEAL pin on him just to make sure everyone got the message."

"Where did you hear that?"

"The rumor mill." He sped down the curvy highway and passed a road sign. FRESNO, 94 MILES; WOODLAND SPRINGS, 2. "But the FBI agents who came to visit me this morning make me think this particular rumor's got some truth to it."

Kelsey stared at him. He was completely serious.

"So you're a suspect?"

"Looks that way."

"Then shouldn't you be back in San Diego, in case they need to talk to you again?"

He didn't comment, and her stomach tensed. For days she'd thought she was being paranoid, that her conspiracy theories were far-fetched. But now those theories seemed all too real.

An FBI agent had killed Blake and tried to make it look as though Gage had done it. It seemed so outlandish, she could hardly get her mind around it.

And yet it had happened.

"I need to know something," Gage said now. He glanced at her, and she knew from his tone what he was going to ask. "What happened with you and Blake? Who broke things off?"

She looked away. "I did."

"Why?"

Because he wasn't you.

"Turns out we weren't suited for each other."

She gazed out the window at the trees rushing by, hoping he'd drop the subject. She didn't want to talk about this with him. It seemed . . . disrespectful somehow, now that Blake was dead.

She glanced at Gage behind the wheel, taking the dark curves in the highway with so much confidence. She could hardly believe he was here. She could hardly believe *she* was here, speeding through the forest in the middle of the night, on the run from some gunman.

"Do you have any idea why another agent would want Blake dead?" he asked.

"I don't know. I keep thinking it must have something to do with work."

"What was he working on?"

"Counterterrorism cases. I don't know the specifics. I'm checking into it, though. That's what I've been doing the last few days, with help from someone I trust at the Delphi Center."

"Maybe Blake was shopping information."

She turned to look at him. It was an ugly prospect, and she'd already considered it. Clearly, Trent Lohman was crooked. Maybe Blake had been, too.

"I don't have any reason to believe that," she said. "Maybe Trent is up to something and Blake found out about it. He might have threatened to blow the whistle on something."

"Maybe," Gage said, but she could tell he believed there was more to it. He'd never liked Blake.

Kelsey glanced out the window as they raced through

an intersection. They passed a gas station, a grocery store, all shut down for the night.

Conflicting emotions filled her. Part of her felt intensely relieved Gage had found her, because clearly her life was in danger, and Gage equaled safety—from a physical standpoint, at least. Her heart was another matter.

"The other man at Blake's condo," Gage said. "You recognize him from anywhere?"

"I'd never seen him before. And I never forget a face."

"You say he flashed a badge?"

"Yes, but not an FBI shield. It was silver. I only got a glimpse, but it looked to me like a police badge." She looked at him. "See why I don't trust anyone?"

He didn't answer as he veered off the highway and pulled into a small parking lot. Kelsey glanced around as he looped to the back of a long one-story building made of logs. The sign in the parking lot said TWO PINES LODGE.

"What are we doing?"

He rolled to a stop beside an alcove with a glowing red Coke machine. "I was up at 0300. I'm dead on my feet. We'll get some sleep, then tackle this tomorrow."

"I'm not sharing a room with you."

He cut the engine and looked at her. Kelsey reached into her purse for her wallet.

"Get two rooms." She held out some bills.

"Also not happening." He pushed open the door, and she felt a surge of alarm.

"I'm *not* sharing a motel room with you."

"And I'm *not* letting you out of my sight." He leaned

an arm on the door and peered in at her. "One room, two beds, babe. That's the best I can do."

"But—"

"Live with it," he said and slammed the door.

The conference room smelled like stale coffee and B.O. as Elizabeth took an empty seat between two men she didn't know.

"Frost with you?" Gordon asked from the other end of the table. His suit jacket was draped over the back of the chair, but he hadn't loosened his tie or rolled his sleeves up, even though it was nearly one in the morning.

"I saw him at ten," she said. "He told me he was headed home for the night."

Gordon checked his watch. "Okay, let's get started. We have new information on the whereabouts of Lieutenant Brewer." He folded his arms over his chest and nodded at the agent seated to Elizabeth's right. "Coffman, you want to fill us in?"

Elizabeth looked at Coffman. She hadn't met him, but then again, she had. He looked like so many other agents she knew: tall, good-looking, athletic. Maybe he'd been the quarterback in high school, then later decided to study law. When the novelty of working for some big firm wore off, he applied to the Academy. Of the six agents gathered here tonight, Elizabeth was the only female. Between this and the trip to the naval base, she was starting to get testosterone overload.

Coffman cleared his throat. "Prior to Lieutenant Brewer leaving his apartment, Agent Kimball and I installed a tracking device on his vehicle."

Elizabeth's gaze snapped to Gordon, but his focus was on the man speaking.

"After he eluded agents Frost and LeBlanc at Disneyland, he returned to his pickup truck and left the park. We allowed him to put some distance between us and followed him using the GPS."

As the words came out, Elizabeth felt sick to her stomach. She'd been a decoy. Gordon had known she'd botch this assignment from the very beginning. He'd planned on it. She glanced around the room, suddenly aware that no one was making eye contact.

"Unfortunately," Coffman continued, "it appears that Brewer discovered the tracking device when he stopped for gas."

"How'd he manage to do that?" one of the agents asked.

Coffman and his partner exchanged glances.

"We viewed the footage from the surveillance cam at the gas station," Kimball said. "He took a mirror out of his vehicle and used it to check the undercarriage. Then he slid under the truck and removed the device."

The room fell silent.

The agent sitting across from her leaned forward. "He checked under his truck with a *mirror*? Who the hell does that?"

"An explosives expert who's served in Iraq," Gordon said, then turned back to Kimball. "What'd he do with the GPS?"

"We don't have this on film, but it appears that he attached it to a motorcycle." He paused. "After tracking it for ninety minutes—not knowing about the switch— we recovered the device at a biker bar in Wasco."

Elizabeth giggled. Kimball shot her a glare.

"What's funny? We nearly got our asses handed to us in the parking lot."

She bit her tongue and looked down at the table.

"Fortunately, we have another lead on Brewer's destination." Gordon watched her as he spoke, and Elizabeth refocused her attention. "Turns out Kelsey Quinn's uncle—Lieutenant Brewer's former CO—has a fishing cabin up in Piney Creek. That's southeast of Fresno. We believe he was headed there. I spoke with the sheriff just a few minutes ago, and coincidentally, they just had an incident. Several shots fired on the property where this cabin is located."

Elizabeth sat up straight. "Was anyone hurt?"

"No injuries reported," Gordon said. "Just a few broken windows. But Kelsey Quinn is nowhere to be found, and the car she was using is still parked there."

Elizabeth sat back in her chair, digesting the news.

"We think Brewer is the shooter?" Coffman asked.

"We don't know," Gordon said. "We've got crime-scene techs headed up there first thing in the morning. They'll be combing the area for ballistic evidence."

"Sir?"

All gazes swung toward Elizabeth.

"I spoke with one of Brewer's teammates this evening. He tells me Gage was the one to end the relationship, not Kelsey. I think we should explore the idea that he's being set up here."

"We're looking into that."

"Just because Brewer dumped her doesn't mean he'd let go," Kimball pointed out. "Maybe he was jealous she was seeing someone else. We've got a combat knife, a broken neck. Now shots fired at her cabin. Sounds like a Rambo type to me."

"Maybe that's the idea," Elizabeth said, but no one seemed to be listening.

Gordon stood up. "Okay, that's it for now. Everyone report back here in exactly five hours. We'll renew the search. Remember, think aliases. Kelsey Quinn could be using one, and we know that Brewer habitually uses fake identities while doing covert ops."

Everyone stood and started to file out of the room, clearly eager to call it a day.

Gordon caught Elizabeth's eye and motioned for her to stay.

"This teammate you talked to," he said. "Who is he?"

"Lieutenant Junior Grade Derek Vaughn."

He flipped open a file on the table and skimmed some notes. "He was Brewer's swim buddy during SEAL training."

"That's right."

"It's a good angle. Keep working it, but don't get distracted."

She nodded.

"And you're riding up with me tomorrow," he informed her. "I want you to interview the caretaker at these cabins. Kelsey talked to her at length and convinced her to give her a key to her uncle's place. I'll want you to find out if this woman knows anything about what Kelsey was up to or where she might be going next."

"Yes, sir."

She looked him in the eye, almost certain he knew what she was thinking. He'd used her earlier. He'd counted on her inexperience and manipulated it to his advantage. The knowledge stung. She should have felt self-conscious, but instead she felt more determined than ever to prove him wrong about her.

"Grab a nap, LeBlanc. We need you sharp tomorrow. Any more screwups and I'm pulling you off this case."

CHAPTER 8

Kelsey awoke with a start. She kicked off the covers and stumbled across the darkened room to find her bleating phone. As she rummaged through her purse, she glanced over her shoulder at Gage, who was facedown on his bed, completely immobilized and wearing only jeans. Her heart did a little lurch. She grabbed the phone and took it inside the bathroom.

"Hello?" She eased the door shut and switched on the light.

"Too early to call?" Ben asked.

"No, it's fine."

She glanced at her watch. How had she managed to sleep past seven? She'd hoped to be up and out of here by now.

"Listen, a couple things," he said. "I took a closer look at Blake's phone records and spotted something interesting. Two days before his murder, he made several calls to his voice mail at work. First one was about seven in the morning, bounced off a cell tower in San Antonio. Second one, about four hours later, bounced off a tower in Denver."

"Denver?"

"Yeah, about eleven-fifteen."

She had a sudden vision of the roll-on suitcase in Blake's foyer. She remembered the luggage tag: SLC.

"He was going to Salt Lake City."

"Why are you whispering?"

She glanced at the bathroom door. "I'm not."

"Anyway, you're right. Turns out he booked a ticket to Salt Lake City from San Antonio. It was for a Saturday-morning flight with a plane change in Denver. He returned to San Antonio Sunday around noon."

Kelsey heard a noise in the bedroom. She peeked out just as the motel room door closed with a thunk. Gage was leaving, probably to go hunt up some coffee.

"Any other word on that Weber person?" she asked.

"Still working on it. Found out his first name's Charles, and I've got a P.O. box in Provo, but that's about it. This guy's hard to run down. Which says something."

"Says what?"

"I don't know. But there's something weird here. I shouldn't have this much trouble getting basic info. I'll keep digging."

"Thanks, Ben. You don't know how much I appreciate this."

"Don't mention it. Go back to sleep."

She ended the call and glanced at her reflection in the fluorescent light. A few hours of sleep had done nothing for her appearance. Her skin looked sallow and her eyes were puffy. She turned on the shower and set the water to molten hot, then stripped off the T-shirt she'd slept in and stepped under the spray, hoping it would rejuvenate her. Her freshly washed socks and panties were drying on the towel rack, but she could really use a new shirt today. Maybe she could convince Gage to stop by a Walmart.

What are you doing, Kelsey?

She was getting too close again. She could feel it. And she knew Gage well enough to know he wasn't going to be content with a platonic relationship for very much longer. It was completely counter to his nature.

She thought about him as the water sluiced over her. Instead of feeling relaxed, she felt edgy. And not just because of the mess she was in. She hadn't spent any significant time around Gage in months, and her instincts told her it wasn't going to go well. They'd either end up fighting or ripping each other's clothes off, and either way, she was sure to get her heart crushed. She needed to come up with a plan that didn't involve him.

The motel didn't have luxury amenities such as shampoo, so she settled for rinsing her hair. She wrapped a too-small towel around herself and stepped out of the tub just as a knock sounded at the door. It swung open.

"Hey." He leaned against the door frame.

"Yes?"

His mouth curled up at her curt tone. "Thought you might want some coffee."

"Thank you."

He handed over a cardboard cup, and she took a sip as he watched her, smirking.

"What?"

"Nothing, just . . . nothing." He handed her a small

paper sack. "Few things I grabbed at the convenience store across the way."

"Thanks. I'll pay you back." She peeked inside the bag. Shampoo, toothpaste, toothbrush. She glanced up, and he was eyeing her cleavage. "I'm almost finished in here." She moved to close the door, but he stuck his foot in the way.

"Hey, what happened to your arm?" He squeezed into the bathroom and lifted her elbow to examine the scab. "Did I do that?"

"It's from the other night. From when I jumped off the balcony and rolled."

Something sparked in his eyes. She'd activated his protective streak. She tugged her arm down, and all at once the room seemed steamy and much too small.

Kelsey hitched up her towel. "Could you give me a minute, please?"

He glanced over her shoulder. Then he seized her wrist and yanked her out of the bathroom.

"What—"

"Get down." He shoved her to the floor. "Someone's out there."

"Where?"

"Other side of the window. I saw a shadow."

Her pulse jumped. She envisioned the frosted-glass window above the toilet.

Gage crouched beside her and pulled out his gun. "Stay here. Keep away from the windows."

"But what are you doing?"

He held his finger to his mouth to shush her and eased out the door.

Kelsey waited, holding her breath, listening for any

hint of trouble. The fear spread through her system like novocaine and her skin started to feel clammy. For the third time in just a handful of days she was cowering on the floor, afraid for her life.

Correction: She was cowering on the floor *in a towel*. This was ridiculous. She stood up and yanked her clothes on. Then she grabbed the Mace from her purse and stalked over to the door just as it swung open.

"Maintenance guy." Gage looked her over and frowned. "I told you to stay put."

"Don't *do* that." She stomped her foot. "Stop leaving me behind while you rush off to fight bad guys! You're driving me crazy!"

He watched her warily as he took the Mace from her hand. "Whoa, relax. It was a false alarm."

A tear leaked out and she swiped it away.

"Hey." He tried to wrap an arm around her, but she ducked out of reach.

"You can't keep doing that."

He smiled. "What, hugging you or trying to keep you from catching a bullet?"

"Gage, this isn't going to work. Don't you have to get back to base?"

"I'm on leave."

"Well, then don't you have plans? Don't you need to go visit your family or something?"

He shoved the pistol in the back of his jeans and folded his arms over his chest. "Nope."

"I really think it would be best if you drive me to a place where I can rent a car. Then I'll lay low for a few days until I figure this out."

"Oh, yeah? And then what?"

"Then . . . when I have some idea what's going on and who I can trust, I'll reach out to the police. Or maybe the FBI."

He stepped closer and gazed down at her. "I'm not leaving you on your own with this, Kelsey. Get that through your head. Next plan."

She stared up at him.

"Why can't you just admit that you need me right now?"

A lump of frustration formed in her throat as she gazed up at him. Some of the frustration was from fear and lack of sleep. But some of it was because she knew he was right. She *did* need him. Her nerves were frayed, and she was only four days into this.

"I know a thing or two about personal security. You don't." His gaze dropped to her damp T-shirt. "Fact, I'm surprised you made it this far in one piece."

She was surprised, too. She wasn't accustomed to dodging bullets and people who wanted to kill her. That was his department.

"What's on the agenda today?" he asked. "And do I have time to shower first, or you want me to stink up the car? 'Cause I'm good either way."

She let out a sigh. She glanced at her watch, essentially conceding the battle.

"Make it quick," she said.

"Want to join me?"

"No."

He smiled. "Want to tell me where we're going?"

"We're taking a road trip."

• • •

Elizabeth made the three-hour drive to Piney Creek
with little help from Gordon and even less from his
vehicle's navigation system. The software was outdated
and didn't include all the narrow, winding roads in
this backwoods part of the state. So Elizabeth relied
on road signs and instinct, ignoring the curious looks
Gordon kept sliding her from the passenger's seat as
he conducted the investigation over the phone. He
wrapped up a call just as they were nearing the sign for
Piney Creek Cabins.

"Looks like the crime-scene techs beat us," Elizabeth
said as she squeezed the sedan into a space between a
pair of white vans.

They got out of the car. The air smelled like damp
pine needles—probably the result of the patch of
showers they'd passed through on the way up here.
The area was strangely quiet, except for the tapping of
a woodpecker high above them. Kelsey Quinn's cabin
was swarming with men in white Tyvek jumpsuits.
They looked out of place in the tranquil forest setting,
like storm troopers in the land of the Ewoks.

"Find the caretaker," Gordon said. "Find out everything she knows. I want descriptions, cars, clothing—
whatever she saw. We need to know who Kelsey's with
and if she's changed her appearance."

"Excuse me, sir?"

They turned around to see Coffman and Kimball
striding toward them. How had they beaten them here?
They must have left at five in the morning—no doubt
eager to redeem themselves after yesterday's biker bar
fiasco.

"We've been through the cabin," Coffman reported. "Looks like someone left in a hurry."

A woman stepped out onto the porch of the building near the road. She cast a worried look in Elizabeth's direction. This would likely be Joyce.

"I'll talk to the caretaker," Elizabeth said, but Gordon caught her arm.

"Wait. I want your take on the cabin first."

"My take?"

"You're the only female investigator we've got here. See if anything strikes you as important."

Elizabeth glanced at Coffman and Kimball and felt their annoyed gazes following her as she mounted the steps to the cabin. The window to the left of the door had been shot out. A technician crouched just inside the door picking up shards of glass with a pair of tweezers and depositing them into a cardboard box.

Elizabeth surveyed the door frame as she snapped on a pair of latex gloves. Dark smudges of fingerprint powder marred the woodwork. She guessed the prints had already been photographed and lifted because the photographer was on his knees now in the kitchen, which consisted of little more than a propane-fueled stove and 1960s-era refrigerator. The cabin's mismatched furniture looked to be about the same vintage. She stepped farther into the dwelling and noticed the unmistakable scent of Pine-Sol. The place had been cleaned recently.

Elizabeth crossed the living room in a few footsteps and poked her head into the bedroom. A neatly made double bed filled the space. She stepped into the bathroom, where she expected to find the most telling evidence. Careful not to touch anything, she spent a few moments looking around. Then she joined Gordon beside the stove.

"Where'd Kimball and Coffman go?" she asked.

"Up the hill to check out the sniper hide. Someone found flattened grass where it looks like the shooter camped out and waited."

Elizabeth peered through the kitchen window at the wooded hillside across the street.

"That's only about what, about fifty yards?"

"Sixty," Gordon said. "And you're right—doesn't look like our mystery gunman's much of a shot."

"Lieutenant Brewer—"

"I know, I know. Expert marksman. I don't think he did this." Gordon turned to the photographer kneeling on the floor. "You finished with that?"

The man nodded and handed up the spiral notepad he'd been photographing. Elizabeth saw a vertical list of words and numbers and a few more scrawled diagonally in the margin.

"You have your phone on you? Take a picture of this." He handed her the notepad. "I want you to run down these phone numbers, see what you get. The name Weber mean anything to you?"

"No."

Gordon pulled his phone from his pocket to check a text message as Elizabeth used her cell-phone cam to snap a picture of the notebook page. Kelsey Quinn's handwriting—assuming it was hers—was barely legible.

"What's your take on the bedroom?"

She glanced up, and Gordon was watching her intently.

"I agree with Coffman and Kimball," she said, trying to be diplomatic as the two agents stepped into the cabin. "Looks like she left in a rush. There's at least forty dollars' worth of cosmetics and toiletry items still sitting in the bathroom—everything brand new. I doubt she'd leave all that behind if she'd had time to pack."

"They're photographing a tire impression from the cabin two doors down," Coffman said. "Looks like someone was there, but the caretaker didn't see anyone."

"Whoever it was, she could have left with them in that vehicle," Kimball added.

"Have we checked the windows for latents?" Elizabeth turned to the CSI who was at the back door developing prints. He was using a Styrofoam cup to trap Superglue vapor around the doorknob. "Anything on the windowpanes?" she asked him.

"I got fingerprints on the doorknobs and throughout the kitchen," he said. "Also got a few in the bathroom."

"Goddamn it," Gordon muttered, scowling down at a message on his phone. He stepped out of the cabin, and Elizabeth returned her attention to the CSI.

"What about palm prints?" she asked him.

He stopped what he was doing and gave her an icy look—clearly not happy with her suggestion. Only the most thorough police departments took prints from the side of the hand, known as the "karate chop." But the Bureau was building an ever-growing database of those prints because research showed that many criminals cased a house by leaning the side of their palm up against a window and peering through.

"The palm database is growing," she said. "It's at least worth a try."

"I'll get to it," he said, and Elizabeth could tell he didn't appreciate being told how to do his job.

Gordon poked his head in. "LeBlanc, get out here."

She hustled onto the porch.

"That SEAL buddy of Brewer's," Gordon said. "Where is he?"

"Derek Vaughn? Uh, I'm not sure."

"Find him. Right now. Get him to tell you where Brewer is. Pay him a personal visit if you have to, but get the information."

"Actually, I already asked him and he wouldn't—"

"Make him talk." Gordon checked his watch. "And do it ASAP. I'm on the phone with the lab. They just ID'ed Gage Brewer's fingerprints at the homicide scene."

CHAPTER 9

"There's supposed to be a town here," Kelsey said.

"Think you're looking at it." Gage tapped the brakes as they approached the first of only two traffic lights on Main Street. The town of Briggs seemed to consist of little more than a dusty gas station and a few storefronts.

Kelsey glanced at her watch. Already seven-thirty. After leaving Gage's truck at the Bakersfield airport and driving across three states in a rented Explorer, they'd visited the address of every Weber in the Provo phone book. Three separate stops had netted them zero hits. No one had heard of Charles Weber.

They were down to their last possibility—a "Chuck" Weber living in Briggs, Utah, about thirty miles west of Provo. The neighbor at one of the addresses they'd visited had said Chuck moved away a couple years ago. She didn't have his new address, so the first order of business was to track down a local phone book and see if they could find him.

It was a long shot, but at the moment it was the only lead they had.

"What a wasted day," Kelsey muttered.

"Depends on how you look at it."

She glanced at Gage. "How else is there to look at it?"

"Well, you haven't been followed or shot at, so I'd say that's a win."

She tipped her head back against the seat and sighed. "Thanks for all the driving."

"No problem."

"Maybe we should look for a motel."

"Thought you'd never ask."

She glanced over her shoulder at the disappearing intersection. "There's not much here, though."

"I saw a sign a while back. There should be an Econolodge down the road."

"Fabulous."

He lifted an eyebrow. "Is that sarcasm? What happened to the fearless anthropologist who liked to spend her summers living in tents?"

"Campers," she corrected. "And I never said I *liked* living in them."

"Then why did you?"

"Part of the job. Same reason you jump out of airplanes and eat MREs."

He smiled. "You've never jumped out of an airplane, have you?"

"No. So?"

"So, you should."

"Why would I want to jump out of a perfectly good airplane?"

Gage turned into the parking lot of a cheap-looking motel and whipped into a space. "Because it's like sex, only better."

Kelsey bit her tongue. He was getting to her, and

he knew it. It was the way he looked at her with those warm blue eyes. It was his low voice, his two-day beard. Just the sight of his muscled forearm propped on the steering wheel right now was giving her a bone-deep craving for something she knew she shouldn't have. She should insist on separate rooms tonight. But instead of insisting on anything, she turned and looked out the window.

"This isn't an Econolodge."

"Local alternative." He pushed open the door. "SIG's in the glove compartment. I'll be right back."

Kelsey watched him saunter into the office of the Desert Rose Inn. The seventies-era building had white stucco walls and a Mexican tile roof. A courtyard beside the office had a lone yellow umbrella table. About a hundred yards up the highway was a diner. No bars, no nightclubs. With four cars in the parking lot, the grocery store looked to be the town hotspot.

Which meant there wasn't going to be much to do tonight except hang out in the room.

Her stomach fluttered. What was she doing? This was emotional suicide.

Gage reappeared with his cell phone pressed to his ear. She couldn't read his expression. He slid behind the wheel and steered the Explorer to a room at the very end of the row.

"Keep me posted on Hallenback," Gage said into the phone.

Kelsey collected her purse from the backseat, along with the shopping bag filled with items she'd picked up at the gas station where they'd stopped for lunch.

"Okay, man. Be good." He ended the call and

reached across her to retrieve his pistol from the glove compartment.

"Who was that?" she asked.

"Vaughn."

"Did you tell him where we are?"

"What do you think?"

She didn't know what to think. According to him, there were "no secrets in the teams." And yet he seemed to be taking every precaution to hide their tracks, from using a supposedly untraceable cell phone to renting the Explorer under a fake ID.

They got out of the SUV and Gage led her to a garish yellow door.

"Any news from Derek?" she asked his back.

"Not really."

Another non-answer answer. She should be used to it by now, but it irked her to be kept in the dark.

Kelsey followed him inside and surveyed the room. In contrast to the exterior, the interior had been updated with eighties-era mauve and turquoise. The evening sunlight slanted through the blinds, making stripes across the purple bedspread.

She looked at Gage.

"They didn't have a double."

She searched his face, almost certain he was lying.

"What?" he asked.

"I'm going to clean up."

She shut herself in the bathroom and took a luke-warm shower. She changed into a new T-shirt before calling Ben for an update.

"Hey, my favorite lab geek," he said cheerfully. "I was just about to call you."

"Tell me you have something about Weber."

"Just an address."

"First good news I've heard all day."

"Don't get too excited. It's another post office box, this one in a place called Briggs, Utah."

"That's where I am now. Someone gave us a lead on a 'Chuck' Weber who lives here, but they didn't have a street address."

"I don't, either, but I'm working on it. I'm searching postal records for whoever rented that box, but this firewall's surprisingly good. I'll call you when I get something."

"Thanks, Ben. I don't know how I can repay you for all your help."

"I do. This crazy woman showed up at my house tonight, and she's staging a sit-in in my kitchen until I let her talk to you."

Kelsey heard muffled sounds on the other end as he handed off the phone.

"Kelsey?"

The familiar voice made her heart squeeze. "Hi, Mia."

"*What* is going on? Are you okay?"

"I'm fine. Didn't Ben tell you?" Kelsey had asked him to get a message to Mia.

"Uh, *yeah*. He gave me your message, but since then I've had daily visits from the FBI. They really need to talk to you. Don't you want to come home?"

"I can't. Not yet."

"I'm so, so sorry about Blake. Are you all right? Tell me where you are and I'll come see you."

"You don't need to do that. I'm totally fine."

"Kelsey, I'm worried. Are you in Utah somewhere investigating this mess? Because you need to let the FBI handle it. This situation sounds dangerous."

"Really, I'm fine. You don't need to worry. Gage is with me."

Silence on the other end.

"He's just . . . looking out for my safety. While I sort out a few things."

"Kelsey . . . oh my God. Are you sure that's a good idea?"

Mia more than anyone knew the hell Kelsey had gone through after Gage broke up with her. Mia worked in the Delphi Center's DNA lab, so they saw each other every day and there was nowhere to hide. And unlike her other friends, Mia knew that her I'm-fine-and-this-is-for-the-better routine was all an act.

"I mean, I want you to be safe," Mia said, "but isn't there someone else you can call? What about one of Blake's friends at the Bureau? They could protect you from whatever you're worried about. And they could do it without tearing your heart to pieces."

"He's not tearing my heart to pieces. And I'm not going to sleep with him."

Mia snorted.

"I'm serious. And please, whatever you do, don't tell anyone at the FBI you talked to me. They'll be all over you. Pretend you haven't heard from me until I get back."

"And when is that?"

"Soon. Listen, in the meantime there's a way you can help. You know Dr. Froehler over at TCMEO?"

"Sure, he sends me DNA all the time. Why?"

"Would you mind calling him and asking for a copy of an autopsy photo?"

Pause. "Is this Blake Reid's autopsy? What on earth—"

"I need a photo of some trace evidence that was recovered from his clothing. Tell Froehler the request is for me, and he'll know which picture to send you. It's a human hair."

"What good is a picture? I can't run analysis on anything unless—"

"The evidence isn't available—just the photo. But we should at least be able to get some class characteristics."

The phone went silent.

"You there?"

"I'm happy to call Froehler. But Kelsey, I *really* think you need to reach out to the police here. Or the FBI."

"I will. Just not yet. I have to nail a few things down first."

"Are you sure you know what you're doing? Are you sure you're safe?"

"I'm perfectly fine."

Mia didn't sound convinced, but Kelsey managed to get off the phone. She wondered if Gage had been eavesdropping, but when she stepped out of the bathroom, he was sitting on the bed, talking on his cell.

"That's right. And double pepperoni." He looked her up and down, and she realized she'd left her jeans on the bathroom floor. She ducked out of sight to finish dressing as he ended his call.

"Are you sure no one can trace that?" she asked.

"Not a chance. It's part of my E and E kit."

She stepped out of the bathroom and eyed him warily. "E and E?"

"Escape and evasion. Don't worry, it's clean."

"What else is in that thing?"

"Compass, couple IDs, some first-aid stuff. I've got some PowerBars I could break out for dinner, case you don't want pizza."

"I definitely want pizza."

"Extra pepperoni, thick crust."

"Sounds good."

"See? I remember a few things." He got up from the bed and walked over to where she stood beside the dresser. Her pulse started to race. He eased so close she had to tilt her head back to look at him, but she held her ground.

"You know, I've been thinking, Kelsey . . ."

Her body tensed because she knew what he was going to say. He rested his hands on her shoulders. He brushed his fingers down the back of her neck and a shiver moved through her.

"Maybe we made a mistake before."

She held her breath and waited.

"I think we should give things another chance."

She'd expected this. Still, her heart pounded as the words reverberated through her brain. *Another chance.* Part of her desperately wanted to believe him and another part of her—the logical part—knew that this wasn't real. This wasn't about second chances. It was about habits that were hard to break and physical yearnings that got sharper with every hour they spent in close proximity.

"Tell me you're not thinking about it."

"Gage." She closed her eyes. When she opened them again he was staring down at her, his eyebrow cocked slightly as he waited for her to agree.

"Let's be honest here, Gage. This is about sex."

"So?"

She rolled her eyes. *"So?"*

"So, I want to have sex with you. What's wrong with that? Christ, I've been watching you walk around half-naked for two days. I've been listening to you sleep—"

"You can't *listen* to someone sleep."

"*Yes,* you can." He plunked his hands on his hips. "And those little sighing noises you make are driving me crazy."

"I don't make noises!"

"How would you know?" He glared down at her. "And what's wrong with me being attracted to you? You're attracted to me, too, you're just scared to admit it."

She stepped away and put her hands up "You know what? I'm not doing this again. All that's done."

He eased closer and the heat in his eyes made her insides tighten. She knew that look. She knew what he wanted. She wanted it, too. She just didn't want the misery she knew would come later, when he walked away from her again.

"Look me in the eye and say that again, Kelsey."

She didn't move.

"See?" He rested his hand on her shoulder and combed his fingers into her hair.

Emotion welled up in her chest. He leaned his head down to kiss her, but she stepped back.

"Did you happen to forget that *you* broke up with *me,* Gage? You told me it was over. That means finished. No replays just because you're in the mood and I happen to be available."

"That's not what this is."

"Oh, yeah? What is it, then?"

He folded his arms over his chest.

"I know about September, Gage."

As soon as the words were out, she felt a spurt of panic.

"What happens in September?"

"*Last* September."

He watched her, brow furrowed. And then his expression changed as realization dawned.

Kelsey's stomach knotted. She'd never meant to bring this up. She'd never wanted to talk about it. She'd never wanted to reveal to him how much he'd hurt her, and she'd been so proud of herself for keeping it inside and never letting him know. But now—inexplicably—she felt the overwhelming urge to just get it out there. Maybe she wanted to prove to both of them how screwed up they'd been.

"Do you have any idea how much I *missed* you all those months you were gone?" She heard the tremor in her voice. "Do you even have a clue?"

He looked down at the floor.

"Do you know how humiliating it was to find out from someone on *Facebook* that your tour ended early, that you'd been home two *weeks* without bothering to call me?" Her throat tightened as the words hovered in the air between them. "How do you think that felt, Gage?"

"Last summer . . ." He looked at the floor and rubbed the back of his neck. "Shit, last summer was bad, Kelsey. We lost three guys. When I came home, I needed some time." He looked up at her. "That was not about you."

Emotion expanded in her chest like a balloon. For months she'd thought she was over this, that she'd gotten past it, but now she was so furious she wanted to smack him.

"You have *no* idea what it's like to watch the news every night expecting your life to implode." She stepped closer, forcing him to look at her. "Every helicopter crash, every roadside bomb. Every *day* I was walking around dreading that phone call that would tell me you'd been hurt or killed. I used to count down the days until your deployments ended because then I could breathe again like a normal person."

He looked at the floor. "I needed some time. I needed to get my head on straight."

"You ever think *maybe* I might have liked to be there for that? That maybe I cared about you and wanted to help you go through things? I wanted a chance to be your friend, Gage. Not just some plaything you turn to when you're on leave and want to blow off steam."

He shook his head. "I didn't mean to hurt your feelings. I just had to be alone."

"Hurt my feelings? Gage, I was in *love* with you! I was ready to spend my life with you, and you stabbed me through the heart!"

He blinked down at her. The shock on his face made her sick to her stomach. God, he had no idea.

"Kelsey." He reached for her and she jerked away.

"Forget it. It's over."

"Kelsey, come on."

"I don't want to talk about this. Ever again." She glanced around the room, at the stained carpet, the ugly purple bedspread—anything but him.

"Obviously, it's not over, or you wouldn't be so upset."

"I'm not upset."

Her phone buzzed from across the room and she moved to answer it.

"Yeah, you're not upset, you just won't even look at me."

She glared at him now as she yanked her phone from her purse and answered it.

"What?"

"Whoa. Bad time to call?"

She took a deep breath. "Sorry." She turned her back to Gage and closed her eyes. "What's up?"

"I've got that address," Ben said. "You have a pen?"

"Yes." She took a notepad from her purse and jotted the address down. "Thanks."

"I don't know if this is current, but it's worth a try."

"Thanks."

"Kelsey—" He paused. "Are you all right?"

"I'm fine. Thanks for helping me."

"No problem. Just . . . I've got a weird vibe about this guy. Whatever you've got planned, be careful."

She hung up and turned around, and Gage was sitting on the bed, shoving his feet into sneakers.

"When does your leave end?" she asked.

"Tuesday. Why?"

She walked over and stood in front of him. "Because I think you should get back to whatever it is you had planned. I can drive you to the airport in Salt Lake City tonight."

He tied his shoes, his movements jerky with anger. He stood up.

"Forget it."

"Gage—"

"Forget it, Kelsey." He grabbed his wallet off the dresser and stuffed it into the pocket of his cargo shorts.

"Don't we have a pizza coming?"

"Fuck the pizza. Where are we going?"

Kelsey gazed up at him. He had that hard look on his face that reminded her of her uncle, and she knew there was no arguing with him when he got this way.

"You don't have to do this."

"Where are we going?"

"I've got an address for Weber. I was thinking he's most likely to be home at night."

He grabbed the rental car key. "Let's go."

Elizabeth trudged over a sand dune and surveyed the people jogging along the shore. It took her no time to spot him. His tall, muscular body stood out, even on a beach filled with exercise fiends. He wore athletic shorts and running shoes. A T-shirt hung from the waistband of his shorts.

Elizabeth slipped off her shoes and turned them upside down. Sand cascaded out. She hooked her fingers in the heels and strode across the beach toward him. His pace didn't change, but she could tell he'd spotted her because something in his face shifted.

"Howdy," he said, stopping in front of her.

"Howdy yourself. Where have you been all day?"

"Here and there."

He lifted his arm to wipe the sweat from his brow, and Elizabeth glanced away. She was much too level-headed to get distracted by some glistening pecs, but *Oh my Lord*. The way the sun shimmered off him made him look like some kind of Greek statue.

"I need to interview you," she said. "In connection with the Blake Reid case."

He smiled slightly. "Sounds pretty important. Do I need to call my lawyer?"

"That's completely up to you."

His smile faded and he looked at the surf crashing against the sand. He checked his sports watch.

"Tell you what, why don't we keep this informal." Derek started walking, but away from the lot where she'd seen his car parked.

Elizabeth fell into step beside him. "I'm not joking around here. I need—"

"I need to eat," he cut in. "What about you? You hungry?"

"No."

"Well, I could use a taco."

"Get it later, then. I need to talk to you."

"Talk while we eat."

She had to stretch to keep up with his long strides, and she could feel her blouse getting damp beneath her blazer. She knew she looked ridiculous out here in business clothes, but as of last night, she'd decided she'd put up with any amount of embarrassment if it meant delivering Lieutenant Brewer into custody. Gordon was counting on her, and this time she could tell it was for real.

"How'd you find me?" Derek asked.

"I talked to your neighbors."

She spotted a wooden hut on the side of the highway. It was surrounded by picnic tables and had a weathered blue sign out front that said ERNIE'S TACO SHACK. Surfboards were propped up against the side of the building, and a pair of bikini-clad girls stood at a window ordering.

Elizabeth glanced at Derek, and he was smiling.

"So you flashed your badge around, huh? You trying to tarnish my rep as an upstanding citizen?"

"I bumped into your neighbor, Mr. Waugh," she said. "He was more than happy to talk to me."

"Better watch out for Waugh. He's a sneaky old bastard." Derek stepped up to the window. "Three beef-and-cheese and a large Coke." He looked at her. "You?"

"Nothing, thanks."

"Six beef-and-cheese, two Cokes." He dug a bill from the mesh pocket of his shorts and handed it over.

"I can't eat *three* tacos."

"Sure you can." He dropped his change in the tip jar. "You've got a healthy appetite." He walked over to the picnic table and straddled the bench, and Elizabeth tried not to notice his muscular thighs. They were like tree trunks. She glanced at his running shoes and decided they had to be thirteens, at least.

She looked out at the surf. It glimmered in the evening sunlight. The seagulls' high-pitched cries reminded her how far she was from home. Such an idyllic setting should have relaxed her, but instead she felt edgy.

"Rob, your order is now available," droned a voice over the microphone.

"Take a load off, Liz. You seem tense."

She shot him a look. He'd pulled on his T-shirt, at least. That was marginally better. Elizabeth took a seat on the opposite side of the table and dropped her shoes onto the bench.

"I need to know the last time you spoke with Gage Brewer."

"Well, let's see . . ." He squinted up at the sky. "That would have to be 'bout 1800."

"You talked to him *today*?"

"Yep."

"Where is he?"

"Now, that I can't tell you."

He'd said almost those exact words yesterday, and she felt her temper bubbling up.

"Cut the crap, Derek. This is a murder investigation. The FBI needs to know where Lieutenant Brewer is, and they need to know now."

"Derek, your order is ready. Derek."

He got up to retrieve two plastic baskets filled with foil-wrapped tacos.

"I'm not playing around here," she said when he returned. "Things have escalated."

He chomped into a taco and seemed to be listening intently. "Is there a warrant out for him?"

"Yes."

He froze. But then he resumed eating as if she hadn't said anything. She dropped her next bomb.

"If you refuse to cooperate with the investigation, I

can have you arrested and charged with obstruction of justice."

He lifted an eyebrow at this and then took another bite. She sat there, sweating, feeling like she was playing a game of chicken. There was simply no way he could be this nonchalant about something so important.

He unwrapped the second taco and nodded at her basket. "Try your food. It's good."

Elizabeth reached for her drink, refusing to be bullied. She took a long pull through the straw and let the Coke cool her throat. She felt hot under her blazer, and it wasn't just the summer air—it was the way this man seemed to know just how to push her buttons.

He balled up a piece of foil and dropped it in the basket. "He's with Kelsey."

Her heart skittered. "Where?"

"I honestly don't know."

She studied his expression, looking for signs that he was lying again. But he was a trained operator, and she had no doubt he'd gotten rid of any tells years ago. Evasion wasn't just a tactic he'd learned, it was a conversational skill, as exemplified by the fact that he'd shared this bit of information with her. Kelsey Quinn was alive. Elizabeth hadn't known that for certain until just that moment. He probably thought she'd be so distracted by this news that she'd lose sight of her objective.

"What evidence have you got to back up that warrant?" he asked.

"It's rock solid, and that's all I'm saying about it." She watched that sink in. "If you care about your friend's welfare, you'll help us locate him before this becomes a nationwide manhunt. *That* would be something that could tarnish his rep."

Something flared in his eyes. She could tell she'd struck a nerve. But then he shook his head with more of that country-boy attitude that she wasn't buying at all. He was scared for his teammate.

"Tell you what," he drawled. "Let me give him a call, see what I can find out. Maybe he's on his way home."

"Call him now." She pulled the BlackBerry from her pocket and plunked it on the table.

He gazed at her for a long moment. Then he picked up the phone. He glanced down at it and dialed a number with his thumb.

Elizabeth watched him and listened to the tinny sound of ringing on the other end. Someone answered the phone.

"Evergreen, Illinois," he said. "I need a Thomas Davenport."

Derek held her gaze as the call connected. Meanwhile, her mind raced. Gage had a sister in Evergreen. She'd seen the woman's name in the file but couldn't remember it now.

"Brooke?" Pause. "Hey, it's Derek Vaughn." A smile spread across his face. "Pretty good. Can't complain. How 'bout y'all? . . . What's that?" He pressed his finger in his ear. "Sorry, the reception's bad. Say that again?"

Elizabeth watched him talk as she tried to recall Gage's background. He was the oldest of four, and his two brothers—along with his parents—lived up in Chicago, where Gage had grown up.

"Carrie, your order is now available. Carrie."

"What's that?" Derek stood up and stepped around the side of the restaurant. Elizabeth strained to listen. "Yeah, sounds good. Hey, listen, I'm looking for Gage. He shown up yet?" Pause. "Yeah, he told me he might drop in on you guys."

Elizabeth glanced at her watch and considered the timeline. Could he have driven all the way to Illinois by now? They'd been monitoring the airlines but had no sign of him taking a flight, either domestic or international.

"Cole, your order is ready. Cole."

Elizabeth strained to eavesdrop on the call. The skin at the back of her neck prickled. She jumped to her feet and rushed around the side of the building.

Her BlackBerry sat on an empty picnic table. Derek Vaughn was gone.

CHAPTER 10

The sun was setting over the mountains as Gage sped down the desert highway. He looked at Kelsey in the seat beside him. She hadn't said a word since leaving the motel.

"What's your obsession with this Weber?" he asked.

"I'm not obsessed."

"I've put five hundred miles on this car today."

Kelsey looked away. After a moment she said, "I don't know. I just think he's the key." She turned to face him. "Don't you ever get an inkling about something? Something that could just be nothing?"

Gage did. He was known for his inklings, in fact. His teammates called it his frog vision—that inexplicable sixth sense that had kept him and every other frogman on his team alive on more than one occasion.

"Anyway, this could be a wild-goose chase, but I don't think it is," Kelsey said. "The phone calls, the last-minute plane trip . . . The timing of everything on the weekend of Blake's murder. I think it's possible it's all connected, don't you?"

He didn't answer. He'd learned a long time ago that

possible and probable weren't nearly the same thing. But either way, he wasn't sorry to be here. Kelsey was safer when she was with him, and his chief objective at the moment was to keep her bullet-free, even if that meant spending the first leave he'd had in months driving through Bumfuck, Utah, with a woman who was treating him like a leper.

He glanced over at her. She looked good. Healthy. A little heavier than when he'd last seen her a few months ago. He hadn't mentioned it because he knew she was touchy about stuff like that, but he liked her with a little meat on her bones. When he'd seen her at Joe's funeral, she'd just come from a Third World country where she'd been digging in the dirt for a month, probably subsisting on rice and bananas.

She glanced at him. "What?"

"Nothing."

She looked out the window at the sun, which was quickly vanishing behind the mountains. "What's your best guess? What do you think he's mixed up in?"

Gage gazed ahead at the dusty highway. "Could be anything. Trafficking, maybe. Weapons, people, drugs. Possibly a combination."

"Or it could be he's some kind of protected witness."

He glanced at her. "So, what are you planning to do? Knock on the door and tell him you're with the Census Bureau? Ask him if he runs dope for a living?"

"Any cars on the property might tell us something," she said, ignoring his sarcasm. "I can get a friend of mine to run any plates we see to find out who he associates with. And then, I don't know, maybe we can observe him for a while and see what he's up to." She looked down at the map and then glanced around. "Turn here, up at the juncture."

Gage rolled to a stop. "Which way?"

"West."

He turned toward the fading daylight. "What makes you think he's a protected witness?"

"My friend at Delphi told me his background seems slippery." She sighed. "On the other hand, maybe Charles Weber has nothing to do with anything and we're wasting our time."

"Anything that helps get me out of a murder rap is a good use of time."

She didn't respond. He glanced at her, and she looked stricken.

"They're not really serious about that, are they?"

"Seemed serious to me."

"But I thought you had an alibi."

"I do, but it's not perfect."

She gazed out the window. "I'm really sorry you're involved in this."

For a few minutes, they drove in silence. The tires rattled over the old road. Gage looked at her.

"You know, you could have just told me," he said.

She glanced at him and then turned away.

"That's what was wrong, wasn't it? When you slapped me with that ultimatum about leaving the teams?"

She flipped the map over. "You should check the odometer. This is showing two point five miles until the next driveway. That should be his."

He fixed his attention on the road. Clearly, she didn't want to talk about this, which was pretty ironic since she was the one who had brought it up. Of all the women he'd known, Kelsey was the least woman-like when it came to talking about relationships. She avoided it. Maybe it had something to do with her dad dying when she was little—he wasn't really sure. But in the two years he'd known her, she'd never been much for talking about her feelings.

Which made her little outburst earlier all the more startling.

I was in love with you. I wanted to spend my life with you . . .

Gage had picked up on the past tense—kind of hard to miss. The "was" she'd thrown out there didn't bode well for his chances of getting her back into bed.

He'd also picked up on the fact that she'd been hoping for a marriage proposal. That came as a surprise. Obviously, he'd realized she'd wanted to get married—her engagement five minutes after their breakup had tipped him off to that. But he'd never really thought she wanted to marry *him*. Kelsey was devoted to her career. So was he. It was understood that for both of them, the job came first. Working for the Delphi Center, she had one of the top positions in her entire field, and the idea of asking her to pull up stakes and move to California—one of only two places in the country where SEALs were based—had never seemed realistic. Hell, the whole idea of *marriage* had never seemed realistic. Someday down the road, maybe, but not now. And definitely not eight months ago when they'd had the big fight that ended their relationship.

A fight that Gage now thought had been carefully orchestrated to do just that.

He'd hurt her feelings, so she'd lashed back at him. *Me or the teams, Gage. It's your decision.* It had been like a declaration of war. He'd been so pissed off over it that he hadn't ever stopped to think about what was behind it. Looking at her now, he realized maybe she was right. Maybe he should have tried to talk to her about all the shit he'd been through that summer. She'd been in war zones before. She'd been to Iraq and Rwanda and Sudan as part of her humanitarian work. She'd seen death up close.

But talking about stuff like that had never been easy for him. He preferred to pop open a few beers with his friends and let it fade to the background. Or when Kelsey was around, he preferred to peel off her clothes and forget about everything.

"Hey, that's it," she said as he sailed past a turnoff.

Gage took his foot off the gas. "You sure?"

"Number Four Cactus Ridge. There was a four on the mailbox. And there isn't another house for miles."

Gage glanced in the rearview mirror at the wooden structures—a house and several small outbuildings, plus a large barn that was the same weathered gray color as everything else.

"I wonder why he needs a mailbox and a P.O. box."

"Who knows? Maybe he's paranoid about privacy." She glanced around. "I doubt it's a ranch. I haven't seen so much as a cow in the last half hour. I've barely seen a car since we left Briggs."

He sped up again.

"Don't you want to circle back and do a drive-by?"

"I want to do a walk-by."

She looked surprised.

"Boots on the ground," he said. "Best way to get intel. But I think I'll wait until sundown just in case he's skittish about visitors."

He drove another minute and found a wooden sign advertising a copper mine two miles ahead. The sign was practically falling down, and he'd bet the mining operation was in similar disrepair. He parked the SUV behind the billboard and rolled down the windows before cutting the engine.

"What are we doing?" Kelsey asked.

"Waiting for dark."

She glanced over her shoulder and then turned to look at him. "We're just going to sit here?"

"'Less you want to fool around." Gage pulled the pistol from the holster at the small of his back. He checked the magazine. He glanced at Kelsey, who looked annoyed, as he'd intended. He figured if she was ticked off at him, she'd put up less of a fight about staying in the car.

They said nothing as dusk settled over the arid landscape. He closed his eyes and listened, letting his brain acclimate to the native sounds. No cars. No people. The aging billboard beside them creaked and moaned with every gust of wind. Then the gusts died down and all was silent except for the distant, tambourine-like noise of a rattlesnake.

"How many surgeries did you have?"

He glanced at her. He'd known she'd ask about it eventually, but he hadn't expected her to talk about it now.

"Two," he said. "One on the ship. That one was pretty hurried, left a big scar. Second was after I came home."

"May I see it?"

"You won't sleep with me, but you want me to strip for you?"

She sighed and looked away. "Don't you ever think about anything besides sex?"

"That's a rhetorical question, right?"

She turned toward him and her face was serious in the dim light.

"Okay, fine, but try to control yourself. I've been working out a lot since you last saw me." He shrugged out of the button-down he'd been wearing to conceal his holster and pulled the T-shirt over his head.

She scooted closer and her gaze zeroed in on the scar. "Turn around."

He turned in the seat and showed her his back, where the bullet had exited. "Looks worse than the front."

"It fractured your acromion?"

"Yeah. Healed up pretty quick, though."

"And your range of motion?"

He felt the light pressure as her fingers palpated the skin around the scar tissue.

"It's all right. Not a hundred percent, but close enough."

He turned around and sat back. Still not meeting his gaze, she pressed her fingers against the entry wound. His pulse sped up, and he resisted the urge to pull her into his lap.

"You're lucky." She glanced up and her eyes were somber. He didn't answer. It had been a strange experience. He'd spent years living with the prospect of taking a shot, but thinking about getting shot and actually *getting* shot were two different things.

She looked away, and he pulled his clothes back on. He surveyed the sky and saw the first wink of a star. He pushed the door open and switched off the interior light.

"I'm guessing fifteen minutes in, fifteen out," he said. "Plus twenty to look around. If I'm not back in an hour, drive back to the juncture and wait for me."

"Nice try." She shoved open the door and hopped out.

Gage muttered a curse and followed her. "You need to stay here."

"This was my idea. I'm coming."

"This is a straight recon mission. I could do it in my sleep. I'll be in and out of there in no time."

"*We'll* be in and out of there."

"No, we won't."

She crossed her arms. "Two pairs of eyes are better than one."

"Kelsey." He used his lieutenant's voice. "Get back in the car."

She set off in the direction of the road and Gage cursed again. He hadn't counted on her staying back, but he'd hoped for it. He grabbed the car key and caught up to her.

"Stay behind me," he ordered. "And no talking until we see if anyone's there. Place like this, voices carry."

"Got it."

"If you see or hear anything, signal. Keep a lookout for dogs. I'll try to approach downwind, but any dog will probably hear us coming. There are plenty of animals out here, so a few barks shouldn't raise too much alarm, but try not to squeal."

"Squeal?" Her teeth flashed white in the dimness. "They teach you that in BUD/S? Try not to squeal if you see the enemy?"

"You want in on this or not?"

"Yes sir, Lieutenant. I want in."

"Then quit being a smart-ass and follow me."

Gage ducked through a barbed-wire fence and set out for Weber's house, choosing a route that had them approaching from the west, where he'd be less likely to expect visitors. He picked his way carefully over the desert terrain. The ground was flat and dotted with cacti. Vegetation was sparse and low, but Gage used what little there was to help conceal their movements as they neared the buildings.

He'd noted three small structures on the way in, but now he counted four—three outbuildings and a modest-size house. There was also a barn, but as Kelsey had pointed out, there didn't seem to be any livestock nearby. Whatever Weber was doing here, it wasn't ranching.

They neared the buildings. No barks, no slamming doors, no distant cars approaching. Everything was dark, except for the yellow lightbulb glowing above the back door. No cars or trucks that Gage could see.

Kelsey moved along behind him with surprising stealth. She wasn't bad at this, but her presence was distracting. Gage didn't want to be thinking about her when he needed to be focused on gathering intel. His senses were on high alert. There was something odd about this setup. What was Weber doing out here that had attracted the attention of a federal agent? If he was trafficking something, Gage saw no hint of it. From what Gage had observed, this was a shitty location for smuggling anything. They were more than fifty miles from the nearest interstate, so any regular back-and-forth of people or vehicles would likely attract the notice of area residents, not to mention the local sheriff.

But maybe the sheriff was on the take. Stranger things had happened. They wouldn't be here at all if Kelsey hadn't witnessed an FBI agent snuffing out one of his own.

By the time they reached the first outbuilding, Gage was almost certain no one was home. The structure looked like a storage shed. The door was held shut by a rusty padlock, but the hardware was a joke and it would have taken one swift kick for Gage to bust through it. Not a likely hiding spot for anything valuable.

The second building was a greenhouse, and Gage stopped to peer through a dusty windowpane as they crept past. In the faint glow from the porch light, he saw a tangle of leafy plants that were obviously being watered on a regular basis.

Gage motioned for Kelsey to stay in the shadow cast by the third outbuilding. She obediently melted into the darkness. He walked the perimeter of the house and returned to the back porch, where he paused to listen. No cars. No dogs. He looked through a window into the kitchen, where a light shone down into a sink filled with dishes. On the floor were several large garbage bags overflowing with trash. He took out his pocketknife and checked the window, and was surprised once again when it opened with a faint *pop*.

Kelsey emerged from the shadows and gave him a *what are you doing?* look. He shoved the window up. Then he hoisted himself onto the sill and slipped inside, easing the window down behind him.

The air in the kitchen felt cool, as if someone had been running the AC all day. Gage had noted several window units when he circled the house, but they weren't running anymore, so someone must have left fairly recently. He glanced around at the counters littered with dishes, beer cans, plastic water bottles. Despite the trash everywhere, something about the place reminded him of his grandmother's kitchen. It was the smell, he realized—the lingering aroma of a thousand bacon-and-egg breakfasts cooked over a gas stove.

Gage moved into the living room. It was dark, so he took out his flashlight and darted it around. He was looking for a desk, some papers, maybe a stack of mail—anything that would give him a clue about this guy's life. The room contained two well-worn sofas and a coffee table blanketed with newspapers. Gage stepped over and read a few headlines.

A floorboard creaked and he spun around to see Kelsey behind him.

"Find anything?" she whispered.

Squawk.

They turned toward the fireplace in unison. Kelsey moved toward the noise but Gage caught her elbow.

"Give us a kiss!"

"A fucking parrot." Gage released her arm, and

she walked over to lift the corner of a blanket that was draped over a birdcage.

"It's a macaw," she said, and her words were cut off by a chorus of chirps from the opposite corner of the room. Yet another chorus went up from a different corner.

He turned around. "Damn, he's got an aviary in here."

Kelsey dropped the blanket over the macaw and checked out the second cage. Gage aimed his flashlight beam at the small green bird now poking its beak through wire mesh.

He spotted a stack of papers on a table near the door and walked over to comb through. Junk mail, mostly. He flipped over one of the mailers and saw Charles C. Weber on the address label.

A gasp from Kelsey. He turned around as she dropped to her knees beside the coffee table.

"It's about Blake," she said.

"What is?"

"This newspaper article. He's reading about Blake's murder."

Gage peered over her shoulder to read the headline, and he knew this was no wild-goose chase. Or parrot, whatever. Whoever this guy Weber was, he was connected to Blake and keenly interested in his death.

Gage's head snapped up at the sound of an approaching car.

"Someone's coming!" Kelsey said as Gage pulled her to her feet and hustled her down the hall and into the bedroom, where they'd be less likely to bump into Weber while making their escape.

Gage glanced around. The only window in the room had an air-conditioning unit attached to it. Kelsey rushed into the bathroom, where he spotted a window above the toilet.

She tugged at the latch and shot him a frantic look. "It won't budge!"

The back door creaked open.

Gage forced the latch, then shoved up the windowpane. Kelsey turned and stuck her foot through, and Gage caught her under her arms and helped her balance as she stuck her other leg through and dropped down.

Footsteps in the living room.

The instant Kelsey disappeared, Gage poked his head out. All clear. He dove through the window and rolled onto his shoulder to break the fall. A bolt of pain shot down his arm as he got to his feet, and he rushed back to help Kelsey pull the window closed as a light went on in the hallway.

They crouched beneath the windowsill and pressed their backs flat against the siding, breathing heavily. Footsteps sounded in the bathroom. Gage heard the thunk of a toilet lid, followed by a loud waterfall of piss that seemed to go on forever. It sounded like he'd downed a full keg of beer. At last it subsided to a trickle. But then it came back again, and Kelsey turned and gave Gage a bug-eyed look. He nudged her ribs. She stifled a squeal and he clamped a hand over her mouth, but she pulled away from him and hunched into a ball to keep from laughing. Gage had the sudden urge to tackle her right there in the dirt and kiss her, even if it meant getting his ass shot off.

Finally a flush, and the bathroom light went off. Footsteps receded down the hall.

Gage looked at Kelsey and jerked his head in the direction of the barn. She followed him to the back of the house. Gage stuck his head around the corner and saw the white sedan that had pulled up while they were inside snooping around. Keeping well away from the halo of yellow created by the porch light, he led the way toward the greenhouse, which would provide cover.

Kelsey halted. She shot him a fearful look and pointed at the house.

The back window was open a good two inches. *Fuck.* Gage looked at Kelsey and saw the guilt on her face. She'd no doubt assumed they'd leave the same way they'd come. Rookie mistake, and it was too late to do anything about it now.

Gage tugged her into the shadow of the greenhouse. They needed to get out of here, ASAP. Once in the shadows, Gage stopped and listened. He heard the faint noise of a TV coming on. Maybe Weber wouldn't notice the kitchen window until they were way the hell away. As a precaution, he slipped the pistol from his holster and took Kelsey's hand to pull her deeper into the darkness. The moon was covered by clouds, which was good for cover. What wasn't so good for cover was the lack of plants or rocks or man-made structures above eighteen inches tall within a mile of the house. Until they reached the truck, they were more or less out in the open.

Gage remembered the beer cans lining the counter. Any minute now, Weber would head into the kitchen to grab a brew, and unless he was falling-down drunk, he'd notice the window. Gage pulled Kelsey along quickly, choosing speed over stealth.

The back door creaked open. Gage lunged for the barn. They crouched low beside it.

Kelsey leaned into him, and he felt her breath on his neck. "Think he knows we're here?" she whispered.

Gage didn't answer. The next instant, a beam of light swept over the dirt right in front of them. Kelsey scampered away and ducked into a door at the back of the barn. Gage darted after her.

The barn was cavernous and smelled like garbage. His eyes adjusted to the darker surroundings, and he could make out the vague outline of an old-fashioned pickup truck.

Psst!

He glanced at Kelsey, who was little more than a shadow. He picked his way through a minefield of junk and debris and joined her on the far wall, where she was watching the house through a gap in the wooden slats.

Outside the barn, a low voice.

Shit, were there two of them? Gage had only noted one set of footsteps. He shifted Kelsey aside to take a look and saw a medium-built, dark-haired man—presumably Weber—talking on a cell phone.

In his other hand was a pistol. Which meant he'd probably noticed the window.

"I've seen him somewhere," Kelsey whispered.

"Where?"

She shook her head.

Chirp.

Gage spun around.

Chirp. Chirrrrp.

It was too dark to see the location of the birdcage, but it didn't matter. Gage glanced through the gap in the boards again and saw that the man was now equipped with both a pistol and a flashlight as he tromped toward the barn.

Gage glanced around for cover, but he could hardly see. He pulled Kelsey toward the center of the room, where the truck was a hulking shadow.

Chirrrrp.

Kelsey tripped over something and stumbled into him as one of the barn's big front doors squeaked open on rusty hinges. They ducked low beside the pickup. The man stood in the doorway, silhouetted by the yellow glow from the porch light.

He stepped into the barn. Beside Gage, Kelsey tensed. Gripping his SIG securely, Gage rested his hand on her thigh to remind her that he was armed.

Chirp. Chirrrrrp.

The man moved into the far corner and aimed his flashlight at yet another birdcage. This one sat on the ground amid a collection of rank-smelling trash bags.

Chirrrrrp.

He opened the cage and reached in. Gage heard the flap of feathers.

Chirp!

With the flick of his wrist, he snapped the bird's neck, then flung it on the ground.

Gage stayed utterly still. Kelsey was still, too, except for her ever-tightening grip on his forearm.

The man made another sweep with his flashlight

and walked out, leaving the door open behind him. Footsteps on the back porch. A slamming door.

Gage glanced at Kelsey as they rose to their feet. She still had his arm in a vise-like grip.

"Do you smell something?" Her voice was barely audible.

"Trash."

"Yeah, but something else, too."

"Trash and bird crap. Come on, let's go." He pulled her, but she wouldn't budge.

"Gage, I know that smell."

The tone of her voice sent a chill down his spine.

"You mean . . . ?"

"I smell a corpse."

CHAPTER 11

Gage whipped out his flashlight and swept it around. Bulging bags of garbage, tires, car parts. On the wall behind him was a row of empty metal cages in various shapes and sizes.

But no corpse.

"You sure it's human?"

Kelsey didn't answer him as she approached the pickup. Gage aimed the flashlight inside and illuminated a seat with ripped upholstery. He checked the floorboards. Nothing.

"Try this," Kelsey said, reaching into the truck bed for a tarp that was draped over something bulky.

Gage grabbed her arm. They exchanged glances. He held his breath against the stench, which was impossible to ignore now that she'd identified it. Slowly, he peeled back the tarp.

And revealed a rusty bicycle frame.

Not even pausing to breathe a sigh of relief, Kelsey moved to an unexplored corner of the barn.

"It's time to bug out," he said. "He knows someone broke in while he was gone."

Ignoring him, she bent down and peered under the truck. "Shine the light under there."

Gage did. Nothing. He swept the narrow beam around and a sickening thought occurred to him as he once again noticed all the trash bags.

Kelsey was already approaching one of the piles.

"Oh my God."

He joined her by a mound of bags that had been heaped on top of something. Or some*one*.

At least it used to be someone until another someone decapitated it.

Gage fought the urge to retch as Kelsey calmly took the flashlight from his hand and aimed it at the corpse.

"Shotgun blast," she said softly, studying the body. Gage tried to pull her away from it, but she swatted his hand.

"That medical kit," she said. "Does it have any bandages?"

"Think it's a little late for that."

"I need to collect some things."

Gage shook his head. Any other woman he knew would have run screaming from this place, but Kelsey wanted to hang around and collect evidence.

"Do it fast," he said, digging into his pocket for his E & E kit. He took out a sterile bandage and ripped open the package. "Here."

"Is that your only one?"

"Yep."

She tore it in half and began shining the flashlight around, collecting specimens of some sort. Clearly, she was on a mission. Having seen her at work before, he knew better than to get in her way. He stepped to the side door to make sure Weber wasn't coming out again.

Unless this *was* Weber.

Gage looked at Kelsey kneeling beside the mangled body. For the first time he noticed how shriveled the skin was. It looked like beef jerky, and he could see yellow bones protruding around what was left of the neck.

"I wish I could take a tissue sample," she muttered.

"He won't mind."

She darted a glare at him. "This is a crime scene. I can't touch him. I shouldn't even be taking this sample."

"Whatever you're taking, do it quick. It's time to get out of Dodge."

She tucked the evidence into the pocket of her Windbreaker as the sound of another car neared the house.

"Shit, more company." Gage pulled her to her feet. He hustled her to the side door and peeked out to see where the headlights were moving. The driver pulled up to the front of the house and cut the engine.

"Now." Gage tugged Kelsey through the door and positioned her ahead of him, keeping his body between her and the house. "Get low. We're going due north until we put some distance between us."

They moved swiftly through the darkness, with Gage checking over his shoulder every few seconds. The back door opened again. Two men stepped out this time—the dark-haired guy they'd seen earlier, plus someone taller with light brown hair. Gage immediately zeroed in on the weapons—a couple of M-16s with custom sights. The tall guy held his awkwardly at his side, but the dark one had his gun slung casually across his body in a posture Gage had seen many times before.

Gage pushed her faster. They were almost running now and he hoped to hell they didn't step in a hole or turn an ankle.

She glanced over her shoulder and stopped dead. "Oh my God, *look*," she said breathlessly.

He turned around. The taller guy was pouring something from a metal can around the door of the barn.

"Bet that's gasoline," he said.

"Gage, that's *Trent*. What's he doing here?"

"Looks to me like he's torching your crime scene. Come on." Gage grabbed her hand and towed her behind him. He picked up their pace. Trent looked distracted, but Gage wouldn't be comfortable until they were well out of bullet range. Those rifles had a much farther reach than Gage's pistol. He and Kelsey had darkness in their favor, but a simple nightscope or a pair of NVGs would make them easy targets in this wide-open field.

Gage spotted a familiar boulder in the distance and shifted direction. In a few more minutes, they'd reach the sign where they'd left the SUV. Another glance over his shoulder. The barn was on fire now, orange flames licking up around the door. Trent and his buddy were nowhere in sight.

"Look." Kelsey stopped and pointed at a car racing across the field, no headlights, straight for the highway. Gage scanned the area and spotted the other sedan—a dark shadow bumping over the terrain. If either one of them swung north, he and Kelsey would be roadkill.

A deafening *boom* as the house fireballed. Kelsey pitched forward into the dirt. Gage leaped on top of her, trying to shield her with his body as debris shot into the air and then rained down. Dust billowed around them. Gage lifted his head to see flames curling up into the night sky. Beneath him, Kelsey wheezed and coughed.

He rolled off of her. "You okay?"

"Holy *shit*," she croaked.

He'd never heard her use that particular phrase, and he took it to mean she wasn't injured as she stared with astonishment at the house. Twin flames were reflected in her shocked brown eyes.

"Was that a *bomb*?" she asked.

"Gas explosion, more likely. Maybe they turned on the stove. Come on."

He hauled her to her feet and pulled her toward their vehicle. She stumbled along behind him, gasping for breath. She seemed dazed and confused as they finally reached the barbed-wire fence.

"Careful." He held the wire for her as she ducked through. He followed. The black Explorer was a welcome sight, and Gage wanted nothing more than to get down the road, well away from the emergency vehicles that would no doubt be racing to the scene soon.

He climbed behind the wheel and looked at Kelsey. "You all right?"

She stared at him blankly. She had a red scrape on her chin and debris in her hair. The front of her T-shirt was coated with dust.

"Nod if you understood the question, Kels."

She gave a slight head bob. Okay, maybe she was in shock. She wasn't used to seeing things go boom like he was. She needed a minute to recover.

Gage nestled his SIG in the cup holder between them, within easy reach in case an unfriendly car should pull up alongside them. He started the engine and turned west onto the road.

"Where are you going?" she asked in a wobbly voice.

"Right now anywhere besides Briggs is a good bet."

Gage pressed the gas until they were going just under the speed limit. Kelsey started coughing. Gage reached into the back and grabbed a bottle of water for her, and she took a long swig.

"Better?"

"Yeah."

He wasn't sure he believed her, but he let it go. She put the water bottle away and took out her phone.

"Whoa there. What are you doing?"

"We've got to call this in."

"No, we don't."

"Gage, that was a *homicide* scene they just tried to destroy."

"They did destroy it. It's blown to smithereens."

"Not the barn," she said. "The barn only burned. Arson investigators will find those bones and probably bring in a forensic anthropologist to identify them."

Gage fixed his attention on the highway that stretched endlessly into the desert.

"You need to think about that, Kelsey. That's the second homicide scene you've run away from in less than a week. How do you plan to explain that?"

She gazed down at the phone in her hand.

"You probably won't even get a signal way out here, anyway."

She bit her lip as she stared down at the phone, and

he could feel the tension created by her dilemma. She wasn't used to being on the wrong side of the law. Her whole career, she'd considered herself on the side of justice.

She tucked the phone in her pocket and gazed out the window, probably contemplating this latest addition to their unbelievably crappy run of luck.

Gage drove through the darkness, on alert for any sign of the vehicles they'd just witnessed leaving the scene. Both were sedans, one white and one dark— maybe gray or navy blue.

"That guy back there—I know him."

Gage glanced at her. "You mean Trent?"

"The other one, too. I recognize him from some-place." She shook her head. "I can't pinpoint it."

"Try."

"I am. I keep picturing him . . . I think it was something recent."

Gage checked the mirror. No sign of a tail.

"Oh God, the video."

He looked at her. He couldn't see her expression in the darkness, but her voice was filled with alarm.

"Gage, he was in the *video*!"

"What video?"

"The one I told you about—at Blake's place the night he died. The terrorist training video. Gage, what is this *about*?"

Gage glanced at her, then back at the road. He had no fucking idea, but it wasn't good.

But how could she be sure it was the same man? She'd seen him from a distance. Maybe she was still rattled from the explosion. Maybe she'd hit her head.

The Explorer slowed abruptly and made a choking sound. Gage tapped the brake. He noticed the light glaring up at him from the dash.

"Shit, no way." He pressed the accelerator, but they continued to lose speed. "It says we're out of gas."

"But we just filled up. I gave the attendant three twenties back in Provo. Didn't you fill it?"

"Hell yeah, I filled it."

The engine continued to sputter. Gage steered onto the shoulder and coasted to a stop. Alarm bells were going off in his head as he thrust it in park and cut the engine.

"Stay here."

He grabbed his gun and listened intently for the sound of an approaching car before going around to check the fuel tank. Cold fury filled his chest as his flashlight beam illuminated scrapes on the paint. Someone had jimmied open the hatch.

He jerked open Kelsey's door. "Come on."

"Where are we going?"

He reached around her and grabbed everything he could—water bottles, map, the baseball cap he'd left on the floorboard. He checked the glove compartment for anything useful, but the only thing inside it was the rental agreement with his fake name on it. Gage grabbed it and stuffed it in his pocket.

He checked up and down the highway again.

"What is it?" she demanded.

"They siphoned our gas."

"Who did?"

"Trent. Guy at the house probably called him after he noticed the break-in and told him to look for a vehicle on his way in."

Gage shoved a water bottle in Kelsey's hand. He pulled the keys from the ignition and stuffed them in his pocket.

"But why would he do that?"

"Who knows? Maybe to get us stranded on a deserted highway so he can roll up and hose us down with bullets." He took her arm and pulled her away from the Explorer.

"Where are we going?"

"I don't know, but we're not just going to sit out here and wait for an attack."

"But it's pitch dark! We can't see!"

"I do my best work in the dark. You should know that."

"Gage, I'm serious."

"So am I."

He glanced back over his shoulder, looking for any sign of approaching traffic. No headlights in either direction. Maybe he was being paranoid.

Kelsey halted. "You hear that?"

Sure enough, the sound of tires on asphalt echoed across the landscape. The car was coming from the east, moving closer, and the lack of headlights told Gage that it was wasn't friendly.

"Come on." He broke into a jog, pulling Kelsey with him. "See that line of rocks in the distance?"

"I don't see anything!"

"Hold on to me, then. And run like hell."

Kelsey stumbled through the darkness, expecting at any moment to feel the sting of a bullet in her back. They'd been moving briskly for what seemed like hours, pushing deeper and deeper into the empty desert.

"Another quarter mile, we'll take a break." Gage's voice was little more than a murmur beside her, but the familiar sound of it reassured her, even though they were out here running for their lives.

She couldn't even see him, and yet he seemed to cut through the blackness with complete confidence. She knew he was accustomed to moving around at night. Maybe he even preferred it. SEALs were trained to move stealthily through the dark, using the shadows and the dead space to conceal themselves. They were trained to slip through forests and jungles and deserts in any light conditions without making a sound.

Kelsey, not so much. And with every crunch of rocks beneath her feet, she shuddered at the possibility that she'd just betrayed their location to a determined killer with an automatic rifle and a pair of night-vision goggles.

She touched Gage's arm again and eased closer. So often, his cocky confidence had driven her crazy— he acted like he was bulletproof. But she needed that confidence right now. She needed that unstoppable determination that told her he was going to keep them both safe, no matter what, and they'd make it out of here alive.

Gage's grip tightened, and a moment later the ground sloped down beneath her feet. They'd worked out a communication system: He gently squeezed her arm whenever the terrain was about to shift. She wasn't sure how he knew—only that his silent warnings had kept her from falling on her face at least a dozen times.

She glanced up at the sky, where a sliver of moon did almost nothing to help them.

Or maybe it *was* helping. If the moon had been full tonight, they might have been riddled with bullets back at the house.

Gage slowed his pace and then halted beside a boulder she hadn't even noticed. He took something out of his pocket and looked at it.

"What's that?" she whispered.

"Compass."

His voice was normal and her shoulders drooped with relief. For the first time in hours, he wasn't worried that anyone was close enough to hear.

"Are they still behind us?" she asked.

"We lost him."

"Him?"

"It was only one. We shook him loose in the first half mile."

A wave of relief crashed over her. Her knees wanted to give way. She reached out until her hand encountered the cool hardness of the boulder and then she sank onto it.

He sat down beside her. "How's the chin?" His warm fingers cupped the side of her face.

"How'd you know about that?"

"Noticed it in the car." He shuffled around for a moment, then folded something damp into her palm. "Antiseptic. I'd give you a hand, but you know better than I do where it hurts."

Kelsey dabbed the cool cloth against her chin.

"You need any of this?"

"I'm good."

She used the remaining moisture to wipe the scraped heels of her hands. Her jeans had protected her knees at least, but that wasn't saying much. Every part of her body either stung or ached, and now that she was no longer moving, her thighs had begun to quiver from fatigue.

"How long have we been out here?" she asked.

Gage consulted his watch, and the faint green glow gave her her first glimpse of his face since they'd fled the Explorer.

"Three hours, twenty minutes."

She absorbed the number, a little dazed. "How far is that?"

"Fourteen miles."

"You're kidding."

"Not in a straight line, though. We did some looping around at the beginning to cover our tracks."

Kelsey glanced around at their surroundings. The ridge to one side of them was a dark line, but other than that, she couldn't discern a single landmark.

"Shouldn't we have hit a town by now? I thought the map showed the town of Spur about five miles away from where we started."

"We're northwest of there. And anyway, we're heading to Copperville."

"But that's got to be another five miles."

"More like seven. But it's our best bet. We should be there by sunrise."

She felt a twinge of frustration. Seven more miles in the pitch dark? She wasn't sure she could do seven more minutes. Just the thought made her want to collapse into a heap on the desert floor.

"Spur is too obvious," Gage stated.

"Never go where the enemy expects you to be."

"Exactly."

"The only easy day was yesterday."

He laughed softly in the darkness. "Where'd you hear that one?"

"Something Joe used to say."

Kelsey closed her eyes and swallowed down all the whiny, self-pitying things she wanted to say. She hugged her arms around herself and tried to count her blessings. First and foremost, they were alive. Also, she had a skilled guide and a lightweight jacket to fight the chill. But she was hungrier than she'd ever been in her life and the thought of walking another seven miles seemed utterly impossible.

Gage sighed. "I'd trade my left nut for a slice of that pizza we ordered."

Kelsey whimpered.

"How about a PowerBar?"

"Gage! You have food and you didn't tell me?"

"It's a little squished." Paper crinkled as he tore open a package. "Here."

"You first."

"Nah, I'm good."

"You were ready to castrate yourself for a slice of pizza." She broke the bar in half and handed him what felt like the bigger chunk. She downed her share in two bites, then shook the water bottle. It sounded nearly empty. "We should probably save the rest of this."

"Go ahead. I've got enough sweat in my socks to last us for days."

His tone was joking, but she knew he wasn't completely kidding. He'd been through some intensive survival training.

"Seriously, drink up." He nudged her arm. "I've got another bottle in my pocket."

"Where'd you get that?"

"While you were busy arguing with me, I cleaned out the car."

She shared the last of the water with him and pushed off the rock. He seemed to understand that sitting around for very much longer was going to make it impossible for her to keep going. Her legs still felt noodly, but the food had already started to hit her bloodstream.

He took her arm again, and they resumed the trek.

"That stuff you collected from the dead guy. What's that for?"

She was glad for something to think about besides sore muscles.

"The insect casings will help us determine PMI. And the dirt sample includes dried blood, which gives us DNA. Maybe he's in a database somewhere."

"PMI?"

"Postmortem interval. Time elapsed since death. Also, on my way through the kitchen I swiped a crumpled beer can. It might yield prints or biological material."

Gage sighed.

"What?"

"You can take the girl out of the crime lab, but you can't take the crime lab out of the girl."

"It's my job."

"I'm aware of that. So, what are you going to do with that stuff?"

"Take it to someone at Delphi who can run the analysis for me."

"*Take* it?"

"Or send it. Depends on how the rest of tonight goes. We could be dead by morning. And even if we're not, what if we stagger into town and get arrested by the local sheriff?" Her stomach churned thinking about the degree of trouble they were in now.

"I'm thinking the body might be Charles Weber," she said.

"I'm thinking that's a strong possibility."

She waited, sensing there was more on his mind.

"Blake's plane trip last weekend," he said. "You think it was a murder mission?"

She tensed at the prospect. "The timing doesn't work. That body was in a more advanced stage of decomp." She kept the rest to herself—that no matter what Gage thought of him, Blake wasn't a murderer. Kelsey simply didn't believe, deep down, that the man she'd known for years could do something like that.

And yet a week ago, she would have said the same thing about Trent Lohman. As long as she'd known him, he'd seemed like a model federal agent. And yet he was a murderer who consorted with terrorists. Kelsey never would have believed it if she hadn't seen it with her own eyes.

She doubted anyone else would believe it, either. At least not without evidence. She patted the pocket of her jacket to make sure the items she'd collected at Weber's were still there. And then there was the hair that had been recovered from Blake's clothing at autopsy. Did it belong to Trent? His accomplice? One thing she knew for sure: It didn't belong to Gage. If nothing else, its existence should raise doubts about the circumstantial evidence pointing to Gage as a suspect.

Kelsey trudged through the darkness. All of this felt so surreal—Blake's death, Trent's involvement, Gage's presence next to her in the middle of the desert.

What, exactly, was this about? She kept trying to put the pieces together, but her brain didn't seem to want to work tonight. Exhaustion was taking a toll.

So was Gage. For the past three hours he'd been touching her, guiding her through the darkness. What had started out as something purely helpful now felt charged with meaning. With every shift of his grip or brush of his body, she felt a jolt of sexual awareness. She knew he felt it, too.

Wind gusted around them, and she blinked dust from her eyes. She was beginning to get the shivers. It had to be at least fifty degrees out, but for some reason she couldn't stop shaking.

She distracted herself by letting her mind wander to another place. She thought of her house back in San Marcos. She thought of her stocked pantry and her comfy sofa and the baskets of unwashed laundry that a few days ago had seemed like such a problem.

She thought of the unmarked car that was probably

parked on her street right now, and the pair of agents inside it who were probably downing gallons of coffee to stay awake.

She was a fugitive now. So was Gage. They had the world's top law-enforcement agency searching for them, not to mention a pair of heavily armed men.

Kelsey shuddered. Thinking about her quiet little house under surveillance made her sad, so she reached for another image.

Joe's cabin. She didn't focus on the flying bullets or shattered glass, but rather the cabin as she'd first known it, back when she was a kid. It had been a cozy, happy place, and she remembered sitting around the kitchen table with her parents as Joe lectured her on the basics of Texas Hold 'Em. Joe had been an accomplished poker player, and he'd taught Kelsey everything he knew— enough tricks, in fact, that she had whipped Gage's butt the very first night they'd played together.

She hadn't beaten him since, though, and looking back, she'd often wondered whether Gage had given the game away to put her in a good mood so he'd get lucky in other areas.

She hadn't caved into temptation that night, but it hadn't taken long. The chemistry had been there from the very beginning. In some ways, Gage was like an addiction. It had taken multiple lonely deployments followed by a gut-wrenching rejection to cure her of the habit.

"Let's take a break," he said, startling her out of her thoughts.

"I'm okay."

"No you're not—you're shaking." His hand slid around her waist and pulled her against him. His warmth seeped into her and she realized she was freezing.

"I don't know why I'm so cold."

He led her to a large boulder at the base of the ridge they'd been following. "There's a wind. And you're probably dehydrated, too. Here." He handed her the flashlight. "Check the area."

She thumbed on the switch and darted the narrow beam around. They were at the base of a low cliff, where a pile of large rocks formed a windbreak. The desert floor was hard and gravelly, which explained her sore feet. She moved the light around, looking for snakes or scorpions or whatever else might be lurking in the vicinity. Then she aimed the light at Gage, who was shrugging out of his loose-fitting shirt.

"Sit on that for a minute."

Kelsey wanted to protest. She was pretty sure that if she stopped now she'd have a hard time starting again, but her legs needed a rest. She lowered herself onto the soft fabric and leaned gratefully against the rock.

Gage handed her the water.

"Thanks." She took a swig and passed it back.

He sat down beside her and pulled her onto his lap.

"Hey."

"Get warm." He moved his legs apart and settled her into the space between them. She resisted for all of three seconds and then the heat of him was too much. She leaned against the solid warmth of his chest and sighed.

"Drink some more."

He passed her the bottle, and when she lifted it to her lips, he slid his arms around her waist.

She offered him the bottle, and he took a small gulp before passing it back.

"More," he said. "You're dehydrated."

"We should save it."

"Do you ever do anything without an argument?"

"Not if it means wringing water out of your socks in the morning." She took a small sip and then screwed the lid back on. The warmth of his arms flowed into her, melting away the chills but also making her heart beat faster. He rested his palms on her knees.

"I'm proud of you."

She turned to look at him, although she could barely see him in the darkness. "You're *proud* of me?"

"You did good tonight."

"I left the window open."

"True, but you also found some valuable evidence."

She turned around again and settled back against his chest. "We hope."

"This trip was your idea. You brought us one step closer to figuring out who framed me for Blake's murder."

"That's an interesting take on it, because I don't feel like I've figured out anything. I'm more confused than ever."

"It's not that confusing. I've been thinking about it." He settled his arms more snugly around her body, and she felt a niggle of suspicion that this whole conversation was an elaborate distraction. "It's clear that this Weber—whether he's the dead guy or the one we saw walking around—is mixed up in something illegal.

Blake knew about it and somehow it got him killed. Trent Lohman knows about it, too."

"The question is *what* is the something illegal?"

"That's only part of the question," he said. "The bigger question for you and me is, who can we trust enough to tell about all this without getting arrested?"

Kelsey stared glumly into the darkness. It was the same dilemma she'd had before, only now the stakes were higher. Gage was involved, which automatically put his career at stake. Her career was at stake, too, if she didn't figure out a way to keep this whole debacle from destroying her reputation in law-enforcement circles.

And then there was the victim in the barn. Who killed him? Why did he die? Was he some innocent homeowner caught in the wrong place at the wrong time? Had he seen something he shouldn't, as Kelsey had? Or was he involved in something illegal that had caused him to be decapitated with a shotgun?

"I'm proud of you," Gage said again, but this time his voice was warm against her ear. "Joe would have been proud of you, too."

Tears sprang into her eyes at the words. She turned her face upward and gazed up at the thin sliver of moon.

"I miss him."

His arms tightened. "I do, too."

She stroked her hands over his muscular forearms and cupped them over his big fingers. His entire body was big, and she'd always loved that about him. She wasn't self-conscious around him because he'd always made her feel feminine.

She looked out and listened to the desert. "You

know, when I first got the call—when I was in the Philippines—I thought it was about you."

He didn't say anything as she traced her finger over his knuckles. Did he have any idea how hard it was always expecting a call like that? Joe's death had been so awful, and throughout the funeral she'd kept thinking that at least he hadn't been married. At least he hadn't left behind a wife and kids. She'd looked at all those strong young men in the pews and thought about *their* families—their wives and girlfriends and parents and siblings, all dreading phone calls like the one she'd received. The potential for heartbreak was immeasurable.

Gage shifted her closer. She looked up at the sky. She tried to focus on the faint, barely perceptible sounds of the night rather than the low buzz of warning in her head.

His hands slid down her thighs, and she tensed.

"Relax," he whispered, and his breath tickled the back of her neck.

She didn't relax. Her pulse sped up as his hands moved slowly over her thighs, gently kneading them through the denim of her jeans.

"You know what we've never done together?"

She turned to look at him. "What?"

"Gone camping."

She settled back against his chest. "Well, if tonight is your effort to convince me, I'm not sold."

"It'd be fun. There're a lot of things we haven't done together."

She didn't respond, wanting to hear what he'd say next.

"Skydiving, for instance."

"Actually, that I might like."

"Really? You'd try it?"

"Maybe," she said. "If we were strapped together or something."

"That can be arranged."

She gazed up at the stars and pretended they were somewhere else. Beneath the redwoods, maybe. Or camping on the beach.

Anywhere but lost in the desert, running for their lives. Only they weren't running anymore. She was acutely aware of the fact that he thought they were safe enough to take a break.

And she was acutely aware of his hands stroking over her legs, warming her skin. Warming her everything.

"Kelsey." He kissed her neck. "Let me make you feel good."

Her pulse skittered. She should be resisting this, telling him no. But she didn't make a sound. The only sound she could hear now was the wind whistling around the rocks and the thump of her own heartbeat.

He took her silence for a yes and moved his hands slowly down until they rested on her hips. Then they slid up her rib cage to cup her breasts, and he made a groan deep in his chest.

"Damn, I missed you."

She'd missed him, too, but it wasn't just sexual—it was a cold, bone-deep ache that she'd fought hard not to think about for eight long months. And now here she was, surrounded by his body, letting him stoke the fire back into her with his knowing hands.

"Relax," he said again, and his thumbs made slow

circles over the tips of her breasts. She couldn't relax. Heat pooled low in her belly and her nerves fluttered with anticipation.

She was going to regret this tomorrow. Assuming they lived to see another sunrise. Which she *did* assume, because he wouldn't be sitting here touching her this way if he thought they were in imminent danger.

At least she didn't think he would. He was on a mission to protect her, but she knew part of that mission included getting her to sleep with him. For days now, he'd been watching her with that glint in his eyes, making no secret of what he wanted. It was no secret now, either, as one of his hands slid down to settle between her legs.

She squirmed, and he responded with a hot kiss just under her ear. Heat jolted through her.

Tomorrow she'd be sorry. But even that realization brought a rush of excitement, because it meant she was going to do it. She was going to break eight long months of forced aloofness and open herself up to him again.

She took a deep breath. "This doesn't change anything."

He went still. It was her moment of surrender, and they both knew it. He wrapped his arms around her waist and squeezed tightly.

"I mean it." She twisted around to face him. "Nothing changes."

He made a grunt of what could have been agreement as he shifted her into his lap, facing him, and went after her mouth. The kiss was hot, impatient. Her sudden change of heart seemed to trigger some insatiable need he'd been keeping locked down. He pulled the jacket from her arms and shoved her shirt up, then fastened his mouth over her nipple. She tugged the shirt over her head and tossed it away as he splayed his hands behind her back and pulled her against him. The breeze tickled her skin, but his hands were warm as they stroked over her. He pulled the straps of her bra down her arms and pushed the lace aside.

"God, you're pretty."

She smiled. "You can't even see me."

"I can feel you."

He kissed her and licked her, and she arched her back and let his heat spread into her. She missed this. She'd missed this so much she couldn't quite believe it was happening, but she combed her fingers into his hair and dug her nails into his scalp to confirm it was real. He kissed his way up her throat and went for her mouth.

She pulled back. "My chin."

"I'll be careful."

He threaded his fingers into her hair and angled her head so he could kiss her. His lips felt gentle against the side of her mouth, and the tenderness of it made her chest tighten. Their tongues tangled together and he tasted so good—so hot and male and *familiar*—and she wanted to freeze the moment so she could look back on it later when he was halfway around the world and the horrible loneliness set in again.

But she didn't want to think about that now. She wanted to think about *this* moment only, and the fact that they were completely alone together, completely focused on making each other feel pleasure. She reached for the hem of his shirt and pulled it over his head. She slid her palms over his broad chest, loving the texture of his hair, the definition of his abs. He'd once told her that abs were the bedrock of a fighting man's strength—they were good for climbing and rowing and lifting and swimming. She stroked her hands over his muscles now, loving his body and the way that he took pride in keeping it in such peak condition. She trailed her fingertips down and went to work on his belt.

"Your gun," she whispered.

He shifted her off his lap so he could get rid of the holster as she sat back and waited. The breeze kicked up and she glanced around at the surrounding darkness. The moon was hidden behind a cloud, making the darkness even more complete.

His hands slid around her. He unhooked her bra and tossed it away. One hand cupped her breast as the other glided down to unbutton her jeans. She eased away from him to kick off her shoes. As she wriggled out of her jeans, she heard the thump of his sneakers hitting the ground beside the ever-growing pile of clothes and gear.

He trailed his fingers down her arm and found her hand. He started to pull her onto him, but she resisted.

"I want to lie down," she said.

"This ground's pretty hard."

Instead of arguing with him, she felt around for her jacket. She spread it out beside his shirt and stretched out on top of it.

His hand traced over her body and came to rest on her hipbone.

"Honey . . . you're not going to like that."

"Shows what you know."

Silence.

She closed her eyes and waited, tingling. Soon she felt the warm slide of his hands over her thighs.

"I know what you like." His voice was low and dangerous, and a shiver of excitement moved through her. He *did* know. He was so physical, so intuitive—he'd always seemed to know her body even better than she did.

His fingers became feather-light as he reached her breasts, then skimmed over her navel. Up and down, lazy circles that made her dizzy with lust. He nudged her legs apart with his knee and bent over her.

"Cold?" he asked, gliding kisses over her.

She shivered again. He dipped his head down and nuzzled her rib cage, and her hands went into his hair. His stubble rasped her skin as he kissed his way down her body. She arched back.

"Gage."

But he wasn't listening—at least not to her words. He was completely focused on showing her with his mouth and his hands that he knew exactly what she craved— what she'd been craving for months and months. She moved under him, feeling the heat build, feeling the excruciating pressure until she felt like she'd shatter.

"Gage."

He sat back and pushed her legs apart, and she braced herself for that bittersweet *joining* she'd been yearning for ever since that kiss in the forest—the one that let her know she'd been fooling herself all this time by telling herself she didn't want him. She did want him, with every cell in her body. And in this moment, she had him. She wrapped her arms and legs around him and pulled him as close as she possibly could, so close she couldn't breathe.

He supported his weight on his palms and moved against her, setting a powerful rhythm that she strove to match. All that energy poured into her. His muscles grew slick under her hands and she felt him struggling to keep his weight from crushing her as he gave her exactly what she wanted, exactly what he knew she needed. She tipped her head back as everything started to swim. The pain and the pleasure converged into a single bright pinpoint. Her world exploded in a blinding burst of light, and then his did, too.

She lay there, shuddering, until the last bright flash faded into a dim afterimage. She opened her eyes and blinked up into the inky darkness.

Gage rolled onto his side, leaving her naked and exposed in the desert chill.

"Damn, Kelsey."

She turned to look at him, oddly pleased to hear his labored breathing. "Damn what?"

"Just . . . damn."

She rested her hand on his sternum and felt his heart pounding. Knowing she'd done that to a man who could run marathons gave her a surge of pride. She scooted over and nestled her head against his side.

For a long moment they just lay there, listening to the sounds of the desert. Wind howled through the rocks. She shivered. He nudged her onto her side and pulled her back against him, so that her backside was snug against his groin.

"Was that so bad?"

She glanced over her shoulder at him. "What are you talking about?"

"You and me."

She jabbed an elbow into him.

"Ouch! Hey." He trapped her arm against her chest.

"Of course it wasn't *bad*. It was never bad. It was just—"

Terrifying, she wanted to say. That was exactly the word for it. Because every time they got close like this, all she could think about was how beautiful he was, how perfect. And no matter how beautiful or perfect, or strong or well-trained, he still wasn't bulletproof. Looking at his scar earlier had underlined that fact. He could be ripped away from her in the blink of an eye.

"Amazing?" He nibbled her neck. "Hot?"

"Amazingly hot."

He made a low growl. "I knew it."

"But this doesn't change anything."

"You said that already."

"I meant it."

He filled his hand with her breast and pulled her in closer.

"Gage?"

He gave a contented sigh and his body went lax around her. "Take a nap, Kelsey. We can argue about it later."

CHAPTER 12

Kelsey awoke to the sound of voices. She sat up.

Correction—*Gage's* voice. He kneeled beside a boulder, talking on his cell phone as he scanned their surroundings with an eagle eye.

She rubbed her eyes and looked around. In the predawn light the desert looked otherworldly, like some sort of moonscape. Kelsey shifted and the jacket she'd been using as a blanket slid off of her hips. She pulled it around her shoulders and searched for the rest of her clothing as her sluggish brain tuned into the conversation.

"About four, maybe five clicks."

She found jeans and panties and wiggled into them. She glanced at Gage. He was watching her intently, but his thoughts looked to be a million miles away.

"Say again? You're cutting out." He stood up and glanced around, as if looking for a cell tower. Kelsey looked, too. She saw nothing in any direction except miles of desert.

Gage mumbled a curse and stuffed the phone in his pocket.

"That was Derek," he said, crunching over the rocks to stand beside her. He had on cargo shorts and worn running shoes, but he was bare-chested, and her gaze went to the mark on his shoulder.

"Derek Vaughn?"

"He's meeting us in Copperville."

She blinked up at him. "He's coming *here*?"

"He already is here." He looked out over the horizon. "Actually, he's in Briggs. He drove up last night, said he has something urgent he wants to talk about."

Kelsey glanced around, trying to process everything at once. Her head throbbed. Her mouth was parched. She felt as though she had the mother of all hangovers, only she couldn't remember the last time she'd had a drop of alcohol.

She pushed to her feet and pulled the Windbreaker closed over her bare breasts.

"What is it?" she asked.

He gave her a questioning look.

"The something urgent?"

"Don't know," he said. "The signal dropped. He's meeting us in town, so we'll find out soon enough."

"Are you sure that's a good idea?"

"It's a great idea. He can drive us back to the rental car with a jug of gas."

"Trusting him, I mean. How do you know he won't turn you in?"

"This is Derek we're talking about. He'd jump on a grenade for me."

Kelsey shook her head.

"What, you don't believe me?"

"I don't get this whole brotherhood thing you guys

have together. And anyway, it doesn't apply to me. What if he turns *me* in?"

"No one's turning anyone in. At least no one I know."

"What's that supposed to mean?"

Gage gave her a hard look. He picked up the holster and belt he'd shed last night, and Kelsey remembered straddling his lap, unfastening it.

"You've been spending a lot of time on the phone with Ben," he said.

"Ben's helping me. If it weren't for him, we'd never have tracked down Charles Weber."

"And look how that turned out."

"What's that mean?"

He shrugged. "Nothing."

"Bullshit. You have something to say about my friends, say it."

"Fine. I don't trust a lot of people right now besides you and Derek. Ben, Mia, all your lab rat friends aren't high on my list. How do we know they won't hand us over to the feds?"

"You *know* Mia! I can't believe you'd even say that."

He picked up the SIG that was sitting on the rock near where they'd slept. Kelsey noticed the condom wrapper beside it. Gage picked it up, too, and slipped it in his pocket.

"She's engaged to that cop, right?" he asked.

"So?"

"The one whose brother's an FBI agent."

She gazed up at him. Her stomach knotted as she realized what he was suggesting.

"We can trust Mia. And Ben."

"I hope you're right."

"And I hope you're right about Derek."

"I'd bet my life on it," he said.

"I think you already have."

They looked at each other for a long moment. He stepped closer, and all the memories of last night flooded back. He slid his hand into her hair. When she didn't say anything, a spark of heat came into his eyes.

"What?" she asked.

"Want to go for round two?"

"No more rounds. I told you last night, that was a one-off."

He gave her a *get real* look.

"It doesn't change anything."

He dropped his hand and looked down at her. "Why are you so dead set against giving us another chance?"

"Because."

He lifted his eyebrows.

"I have no interest in going there again."

"Would it help if I told you I'm sorry about September? I didn't mean to hurt your feelings and I apologize."

"Apology accepted."

"But you don't believe me."

"I totally believe you."

"No, you don't."

"I do," she said. "But it's not just about September. It's about us being different people. I've realized a lot of things about myself this year, and there's nothing you could say or do to convince me it makes sense to go down this path again." She folded her arms over her chest. "Why are you smiling?"

"That sounds like a challenge."

"It's not. It's a statement of fact."

He reached down and snagged his T-shirt off the ground. "*Sounded* like a challenge. You want to give our relationship another chance, but you need to be convinced."

"That's not what I said."

"No, it's good." He pulled the shirt over his head. "I like a challenge."

She blew out an exasperated breath. "Clearly your brain is warped. It's from being around too much macho all the time. I am *not* challenging you. I don't need you to convince me of anything."

He scooped up the white bra that was draped over a rock. "Step one, convincing you that I care about more than just sex." He held out the bra, and she snatched it away from him.

"Good luck with that."

"Which is why—" He checked his watch. "You're right—we don't have time for round two. Hurry up and get dressed. We need to move."

Derek sat in a corner booth with his back to the wall— the same spot Gage would have chosen if he had arrived first. Gage slid into the arc-shaped seat, which gave him a clear view of the motel lobby.

Derek looked him over. "You look like crap."

"Thanks."

"Where's Kelsey?"

"Showering."

He arched his eyebrows.

"I left the SIG with her."

A waitress appeared and Gage ordered only coffee. He'd wolfed down a breakfast sandwich half an hour ago, the minute he and Kelsey had set foot in town. After meeting up with Derek and retrieving the rental car, it hadn't taken them long to find lodging—such as it was. Even by Gage's standards, the motel was a dump, but the bustling metropolis of Copperville hadn't offered a lot of options, and they'd needed a place where they could clean up and formulate a plan.

"You're in some serious shit, man," Derek said now.

"I'm aware."

"You aware there's a warrant out for you?"

Gage stared at him.

Derek leaned back in the booth and sighed. "Didn't think so."

"Where'd you hear that?"

"FBI agent I know."

That solved one mystery. Gage had known Derek wasn't crazy about him getting back together with Kelsey, but he'd also known his friend hadn't come all the way here to dole out relationship advice.

Derek watched him silently, waiting for a reaction. The waitress delivered Gage's coffee. She topped off Derek's cup and scuttled off.

"Seems like you might want to get your ass back to base, clear some of this up."

"What am I supposed to say? Any so-called evidence they have against me is bullshit."

"Yeah, that's what I thought, too, but turns out they've got your fingerprints."

Gage scoffed. "Where?"

"Blake Reid's apartment."

"That's crap."

"Yeah? Well, that's not what Christina says. Fingerprint evidence is pretty impossible to refute. I'm telling you, first thing you need to do when you get back to SD is hire a lawyer."

Gage stared at him. Christina was some FBI agent Derek had dated more than a year ago. She was hot, young, and aggressive—which was why Derek had dated her. But the young part meant she wasn't that high up in the organization. Maybe she had her facts mixed up.

"That's got to be a mistake," Gage said. "How could my prints turn up at his apartment?"

"Good question."

"Shit, you think I did it."

Derek didn't say anything.

"You can't be serious. I've never even been there."

Derek just looked at him.

"I'm fucking serious."

Derek held up his hand. "Listen, I know you didn't kill the guy. Jesus. But in case you forgot, I was there when you found out about him and Kelsey, and you were severely pissed. So, maybe you paid him a visit."

"I didn't."

"Hey, I don't blame you. From what I hear, he was a first-class prick. All I'm saying is, you need to think about getting your ass back to California. And you need to think about hiring a lawyer to help you answer some of this shit before it gets out of hand."

Gage gritted his teeth and looked away. The lobby was clear. No new cars in the lot. He checked his watch. He'd been gone twelve minutes, and he needed to get back to Kelsey.

He looked at Derek, who was still watching him.

"I'll get there," Gage said. "But I have to go to Texas first."

"What the fuck's in Texas?"

"Kelsey's got some stuff to take care of at the Delphi Center. I told her I'd drive her down there."

Derek leaned forward on his elbows. "Are you fucking *aware* that our leave ends in seventy-two hours? We're wheels-up on Tuesday, and if you go UA on Hallenback, there's not a lawyer in the world who can dig you out of that shit."

"I'll handle it."

Derek shook his head. "Right."

"What's your problem with Kelsey?"

"I don't have a problem with Kelsey. But the two of you together—that's a goddamn train wreck. Have you forgotten that less than a year ago she asked you to leave the teams?"

Gage looked away, uneasy with the memory. He'd known when he told Derek that, Kelsey would be on his blacklist forever.

"Gage, come on."

He thought of the countless beers Derek had bought him in an effort to snap him out of the funk he'd been in for months now.

"I know better than anyone how hard you busted your ass to get through BUD/S," Derek said. "It was something you wanted since you were a kid, and you *got* it, and you helped *me* get it, too, and any woman who would ask you to walk away from that . . . Shit, she doesn't know you. She doesn't know you, or she wouldn't ask."

Gage looked at him and felt the ball of frustration

in his gut that he felt every time he thought about that damn ultimatum. There was some truth to what Derek was saying.

But another more important truth was that a line had been crossed back at Joe's cabin. Gage was in the thick of this now, no matter what.

He leveled a look at Derek. "In the last week, Kelsey has been stalked, shot at, and stranded in the desert. She's lucky to be alive. And I'm not going to California to answer charges or questions or *any* damn thing until the threat to her is taken out."

Derek watched him for a long moment. If the situation were reversed, he'd feel the same way—no question about it.

Gage slid out of the booth. "I need to go."

Derek stood, too. They looked at each other.

"Tuesday, man," Derek said. "Don't fuck this up."

Elizabeth LeBlanc got Derek's blood going, and he wasn't sure why. Maybe it was the haughty attitude. Or the conservative suits. Or the prospect that a woman her size knew how to handle a serious gun. He'd been puzzling over it for days, and as he pulled into the parking lot of the Desert Rose Inn, he decided it was all of the above.

She was standing at the entrance to Room 112 with her Glock plastered to her hip and a BlackBerry pressed to her ear. Her body language told him she was arguing with someone. He watched her for a minute, taking in the scene as crime-scene technicians streamed in and out of Gage's abandoned motel room.

Derek got out and slammed the door. Elizabeth

glanced in his direction. Her gaze turned arctic as he sauntered over. She ended the call and shoved the phone in her pocket.

"What are you doing here?" she demanded.

"A little sightseeing. How's it going?"

"You *fled* the interview! I should have you arrested and charged with obstruction of justice."

"Hey, didn't I warn you about snacking on the job? Gotta keep your eye on the ball, Liz. At all times."

She glowered up at him, and Derek's heart gave a kick.

"Is everything a joke to you? Do you have any idea how many man-hours have been spent trying to locate this suspect?"

"Looks like you just missed him." Derek stepped back as a crime-scene tech passed between them carrying Gage's battered leather work boots. He glanced into the motel room and saw another item he'd come to retrieve—the keys to Gage's pickup—being dropped into an evidence bag.

"Well?" Those ice-blue eyes sparked up at him. "*Where* is he?"

Derek stood silent.

"No more games. I need his current location."

"I'm sorry, ma'am, but that's classified."

Elizabeth's gaze narrowed, and he knew she would have liked nothing more than to scalp him right there in the parking lot. She took a deep breath.

"Fine." She turned her attention to the agent standing nearby. "Frost, cuff this man and put him in a vehicle."

Derek smiled.

She turned her back on him and whipped out her phone.

"Liz, come on."

But Frost already had the cuffs out. He took Derek's wrists and pulled them behind his back.

Un-fucking-believable. She was serious. Gage was going to owe him for life.

The first bracelet clinked.

"Hey," he said to Elizabeth's back. "Don't you even want to do the honors?"

Without a backward glance, she strode away.

CHAPTER 13

Marissa Ramli tipped her head back to let the sun warm her face. Another beautiful Saturday in the city she loved. A gleeful squeal reached her and she looked over at her daughter on the swing set. Leila was hanging stomach-down on the swing's rubber seat and using her feet to twist herself in circles so she could let go and spin like a top.

"You used to do that."

She glanced over her shoulder, and her sunny mood evaporated.

"I didn't think you'd come," she told her brother. "You've stood me up twice now."

He walked around the bench and took a seat beside her, but not too close. Marissa skimmed her gaze over him, cataloging every detail. He wore jeans, sneakers, and a white polo, which reminded her of the preppy phase he'd gone through back in high school. He'd gained weight since she'd last seen him and trimmed his hair. But the biggest difference was his clean-shaven cheeks, which made him look like a kid.

He stretched his arms out on the back of the bench

and smiled at her. "It's an odd thing, but anyone who disappears is said to be seen in San Francisco."

She eyed him curiously.

"Oscar Wilde," he said.

Marissa shook her head and gazed at Leila. She was spinning again, laughing with delight, and Marissa resented her brother's intrusion on one of their few pockets of quality time together. Every moment of the workweek was spent shuttling Leila to and from day care, putting in long hours, and catching up on chores at night. Outings to the park were strictly reserved for weekends.

Until recently.

She took a deep breath. "What do you want, Adam?"

"Just checking in."

She gave him a sour look because they both knew that was a lie. She picked up the purse at her feet and took an envelope from it.

He frowned as she handed it to him. "What's this?"

"It's from Mom."

"You talk to Mom?" He definitely sounded surprised to hear that.

"Only occasionally. She calls on Leila's birthday." She paused. "Which was last month."

Did her brother even know his niece's birthday? Probably not. She glanced at him as he thumbed through the bills.

"Three hundred dollars," she said.

"I don't want it."

"Just keep it, okay? It'll make her feel better."

"You keep it." He tucked it back in her purse. "Buy something for Leila."

Marissa simmered. Fine, she *would* keep it. She was up to her neck in bills. Groceries and gasoline and ballet lessons didn't come free in this town. But she loved it here, had since she'd first arrived at the ridiculously young age of twenty. She never wanted to leave. She wanted to raise her daughter here, and she planned to work her fingers to the bone to make that possible.

She looked at her brother now. "She worries about you, you know."

He glanced away, toward the chess players who liked to gather at Sandburg Park. Marissa remembered her father and brother playing chess another lifetime ago. Her father had been good, but Adam had been better. Always ten moves ahead.

"I worry about you."

He looked at her. "That is energy wasted."

Another lie. She was getting annoyed now.

"What brings you to town?" she asked. Her stomach knotted as she awaited the answer.

"Business."

The knot tightened. She gazed out at her daughter and felt a wave of bitterness. In four short weeks he'd managed to turn her life upside down. *He* was the reason she couldn't sleep at night. *He* was the reason her nails were bitten down to the quick. *He* was the reason she'd spent her last three lunch hours race-walking to the public library to use the computer, because she was afraid of the one at her own desk. *Her own desk.* She couldn't even be comfortable at work now.

She looked at her brother. Did he have any idea that she'd spent the past week researching David Kaczynski?

Did he have any idea how much legal wrangling that man had gone through to save his brother from the death penalty? As it was, the Unabomber would be spending life in prison because David Kaczynski had hired a top lawyer to negotiate with the FBI before turning his brother in. Marissa couldn't afford a top lawyer. And she sure as hell didn't want her name, and Leila's name, to go down in history in connection with a monster.

But Adam was oblivious to her turmoil because the prospect of her turning him in had clearly never entered his mind. All their lives, they'd trusted each other. He trusted her now.

What he didn't seem to realize was that this thing— whatever it was—was a bit different from him covering for her so she could sneak out of the house and meet her boyfriend.

"What do you want, Adam?" she said, and heard the tremor in her voice. He wasn't here for money, obviously. And he couldn't possibly think she'd help him in any way.

"I need a favor." He looked at her with calm dark eyes, and she felt a shiver of fear. "It's very simple, really."

It was high noon when Elizabeth finally emerged from the motel lobby. Her gait was as businesslike as ever, but her eyes looked tired. She walked over to the car where Derek had been sitting for the past four hours, listening to Frost clack away on his laptop.

She opened the door and waited.

Derek slid out. He shook his stiff legs as Frost buzzed down the window and reached over from the driver's seat to hand her a key.

"You know, it's a good thing I like handcuffs," he said.

She took his arm. With a quick *snick,* she removed the cuffs.

"You're free to go," she said, then turned and passed a crisply folded paper through the window to Frost. "Your itinerary. I booked you on the four-thirty to San Diego."

Derek flexed his hands. Then he planted them on his hips and glared down at her.

"That's all?"

"I said, you're free to leave."

He didn't move.

"Unless, of course, you want to tell me where Lieutenant Brewer is. Won't save my ass, but it would help the investigation."

Derek looked her up and down. Some of her hair had come loose from her ponytail and the sleeves of her white blouse were rolled up. The middle button had come undone, but it looked as if she'd been too busy to notice.

"That's what I thought." She ducked her head down and peered into the car at Frost. "You want anything from the vending machine before we go? I'm going to grab a Coke."

"I'm fine, thanks."

She turned away, but Derek caught her arm.

"Where are you going?"

"Salt Lake City." She shook off his grip. "I've got a five-fifteen flight to San Antonio."

"What's in San Antonio?"

"My home office. I've been pulled off the case." Something flickered in her eyes, and he could have sworn it was shame.

"So that's it?" he asked.

"That's it." She brushed a lock of hair out of her face and gazed up at him. "That's what happens when you drop the ball one too many times. You get benched." She looked off into the distance. "But, hey, I'm lucky I didn't get fired."

He felt a surge of annoyance. Four damn hours he'd spent in the back of that car, cooling his heels and absorbing the air-conditioning just so she could prove a point. Why the hell should he feel bad about this? He shouldn't. If she'd been better at her job, they wouldn't even be here. And he was supposed to be on leave, for Christ's sake. Instead, he'd spent the past three days tangled up with this woman. It made no sense, but he couldn't seem to untangle himself.

"I'll drive you to the airport." He took his keys from his pocket and watched the shock come over her face. "Come on, let's go."

"Uh, *thanks,* but no."

"Why not?"

She shook her head and jerked the car door open. "You know something? You SEALs, you have so much pride about this loyalty you have for each other, but you take it too far."

"Is that right?"

"That's right. Your friend is wanted for *murder,* Derek, not a fraternity prank."

"Gage didn't murder anyone."

She tossed her head. "He had motive, means, and opportunity, and his prints were recovered from the crime scene."

"That doesn't mean he did it. This thing is a setup."

She scoffed. "How would you know?"

"Because I know Gage. I know him better than I know my own brother. Look at your evidence again. You guys got something wrong. And meanwhile, while y'all are busy chasing your tails, the person who really did this is getting away with it."

She shook her head and looked away. "Blinders. It's amazing."

He waited for her to meet his gaze again.

"Let me take you to the airport."

She smiled and shook her head. "God, you're stubborn."

"Let me take you."

The smile disappeared. "Thanks, but I'll pass. Have a safe trip home."

Gage had spent most of his career trying to avoid ending up in a body bag, and the reality was even worse than he'd imagined.

He'd always figured if he ever ended up in this situation, he wouldn't really be aware of his environment. At the moment, he was not only aware of it, but pretty damn creeped out by it. He couldn't stop thinking about the stale air surrounding him, the utter darkness, the smell of hot plastic. The fact that he was on his way to get tossed into a shallow grave wasn't helping.

"Are we there yet?"

"Quiet!" Kelsey snapped from the front seat. "We're approaching the gate."

From the cargo space of the Explorer, Gage heard the window buzz down, followed by Kelsey's muffled voice as she exchanged pleasantries with the guard. Gage held his breath. This was the moment of truth. If the guard decided to check out her cargo, they were blown. If the guard decided to give her crap about her vehicle—which lacked a Delphi Center parking tag—they were blown. If the guard happened to know she was wanted for questioning by the FBI, they were blown.

There were at least a dozen different ways today's little covert op could get blown to hell, but Gage had been willing to risk all of them. Kelsey felt adamant that the evidence in her possession would not only clarify what was going on, but exonerate Gage of Blake's murder.

And Gage felt adamant that he wasn't letting Kelsey out of his sight right now, which meant she wasn't going anywhere—even her own workplace—without him.

And so here they were, sneaking into a crime lab, with Kelsey playing the role of herself and Gage playing the role of a donated cadaver. Gage hoped that because it was Sunday they stood a better chance of getting away with this crazy scheme.

The SUV moved forward, and Gage waited a good thirty seconds before opening his mouth again.

"Did it work?"

"I told you it would," she said. "They're accustomed to seeing me come and go with bulky deliveries. They used to check everything, but they got burned once, so now they pretty much wave me through."

"Burned?"

"What's that?"

He lifted the corner of the tarp Kelsey had meticulously folded and taped around him to resemble a body bag. She'd even stenciled the initials of the local ME's office down the front to make it look authentic.

"How'd they get burned?" he asked.

"Well . . . you probably don't want to hear this. It's a bit macabre."

"I've spent the last forty minutes impersonating a stiff, Kelsey."

"Well, I would have thought the skeletons would gross them out. I bring them in from time to time after I do recoveries. But that didn't seem to bother them much. I guess they figured it was part of what they signed on for when they applied to work here. I mean, we're a full-service forensic lab, but locals know us best as a body farm. Anyway, it was the fingerprint workshop that did it."

They hit a bump and Gage's head knocked against the side of the SUV.

"Sorry. You okay?"

"Tell me about the fingerprints."

"I was driving up from the ME's office and our fingerprint expert asked me to bring up some samples she needed for a training workshop. So I loaded them up in the cooler."

"You're talking severed hands?"

"Three of them. I tried to warn the guard, but I think he thought I was kidding. He lost his lunch right there on the sidewalk."

"I don't blame him."

"I think it was the number that freaked him out. You know—*three* instead of two or four."

"Yeah, I doubt that's what did it."

"Well, I don't know. Maybe I'm wrong about that, but he hardly even talks to me anymore, just waves me through. Okay, we're here."

She rolled to a stop and Gage waited for her to open the cargo door and give him the all clear.

Patience, he told himself. His patience had been stretched thin since yesterday, and getting almost no sleep and even less sex in the past twenty-four hours had done nothing to improve his mood. They'd spent all of last night on the road.

The door squeaked open. "Looks like we're clear. Hold still, though—I don't want to cut you."

He heard the tear of duct tape as Kelsey sliced open the makeshift body bag with the box cutter she'd purchased this morning at Home Depot, along with the rest of their supplies. She had insisted on buying everything alone, while Gage waited—again, patiently—in the SUV. She didn't believe it was smart for a man suspected of murder to be seen buying a box cutter, a tarp, and a roll of duct tape, and Gage had to admit she had a point.

Now she peeled back the thick layer of plastic. Gage sat up and took a deep breath.

"Damn, it smells worse out here."

"We're in the bone yard."

He got out of the SUV and stretched his arms over his head as he looked around. They were on a dirt road in a wooded area. Through the trees he glimpsed the imposing Greek-style building he'd seen only in photographs. With its tall white columns, the Delphi Center looked impressive, but Gage knew from Kelsey that even its massive size was misleading. The center was actually twice as big as it looked because of underground levels that housed a ballistics lab, a microbiology research center, and Kelsey's domain—the Bones Unit.

"Here." She handed him a pair of dirt-caked work gloves. "Put these on."

Gage followed directions as he glanced around. She'd pulled up to a ditch, which would account for the smell. He was pretty sure he could guess what had been unearthed from the hole there recently, probably using the various shovels and trowels he saw littered around the area.

"Grab some equipment," she said, picking up a spade and a tackle box that someone had left near the pit. "If anyone notices the security cam as we walk in the back door, they'll assume we've been out here digging all morning."

"Long time no see."

They turned around. A man was leaning against a nearby tree.

CHAPTER 14

"Hi!" Kelsey was chipper. "How's it going?"

The man stepped into the sunlight, and Gage immediately recognized him. This was Kelsey's lanky field assistant, Aaron. Gage had met him several summers ago, and he could tell that the guy's opinion of him hadn't improved.

Gage stepped forward and nodded. "Aaron, good to see you again."

The guy looked him up and down, then turned to Kelsey. "Where have you been?"

"Oh, you know. Around." She was still doing cheerful. "What brings you in on a Sunday?"

"Setting up a few things for a class tomorrow." He eyed Gage suspiciously.

"How long have you been standing there?" Kelsey asked him.

"Long enough. Can I talk to you a minute?"

Gage leaned against the SUV and watched silently as the guy led her a few feet away to have a private conversation, which he no doubt expected Gage to overhear.

"A phone call would have been nice, Kelsey."

"I'm sorry." She squeezed his arm and Gage's gaze narrowed. "I didn't mean to worry you."

"Yeah, well, you did. I've been taking my cues from Mia, though. She suddenly stopped worrying, so I figured you were okay."

"I'm fine. It's just been crazy lately. A lot of unexpected travel."

"What's with Lazarus Man?"

Kelsey turned to look at Gage. "Nothing, he's just visiting for a few days."

Aaron gave him a hostile look over Kelsey's shoulder. Not for the first time, Gage wondered if they had a history together. The man didn't strike him as Kelsey's type, but he was around a lot, which was more than Gage could say.

"Listen, I need to get going," she said. "Do me a favor, would you? Don't mention that you saw us here."

"What if someone asks me? Such as Special Agent Lohman?"

Kelsey froze. "Who?"

"Trent Lohman, with the FBI? He was here twice last week looking for you. He gave me his business card."

Gage walked over. "You still have it?"

Aaron looked at Kelsey. He took out his wallet and handed her the card.

"Thanks, I'll give him a call." She glanced at Gage. "You ready?"

He picked up a shovel and followed her up a narrow dirt path leading to the back of the building.

"As insertions go, I'd say that was a bust."

She gave him an annoyed look. "Are you blaming me?"

"Nope—that was my bad. I should have seen him there." The fact that Gage hadn't even though he'd checked made him think the guy had been hiding. Had Aaron spotted them coming and then ducked behind a tree to spy? The encounter didn't sit well with Gage. Even though Kelsey trusted the people here, Gage had his doubts. With the exception of Kelsey, the only people Gage trusted right now were his SEAL teammates.

Kelsey swiped her ID badge and opened the door. Once inside, she flattened her palm against a biometric panel to open yet another door.

"Maybe we'll have better luck inside," she said.

"Let's hope. We're both risking our necks to be here, and if this doesn't work, we'll have to cut over to Plan B."

"Which is?" She led him down a short staircase and through yet another door into a frigid hallway.

"Damn, it's freezing in here."

"What's Plan B?"

"I don't know," Gage said. "I'll keep you posted."

She stopped in front of a door and did another palm-press thing to open it.

"Here we are. The Bones Unit."

He nodded at the little black pirate flag pinned up beside the door. "Cute."

"A little geek humor."

Gage stepped into the room as she switched on the light. Far from the high-tech laboratory he'd imagined, the room looked like any other shared office space. It was crammed with desks, computers, and bookshelves filled with clutter.

"I just need to grab a few things." She shrugged into a lab coat. Then she took a clip from her desk and eyed Gage suspiciously as she pulled her hair into a ponytail. "What's that look?"

"I ever tell you about my nurse fantasy?"

She rolled her eyes and strode into the next room.

"Doctor works, too." He followed her. "I'm open-minded."

She crossed the room and opened a cabinet as Gage glanced around. The room contained several stainless steel tables. He noted the hanging scales, the sinks, the stove with the giant pot sitting on top of it.

Gage turned away and noticed the bulletin board covered in color photographs. He read one of the labels and stepped closer.

"These are from Basilan Island?"

She glanced up from her work. She'd put on latex gloves and eye shields and was transferring the evidence she'd collected at Weber's into glass vials.

"That's the skeleton I told you about. James Hanan."

Gage studied the bones. "The guy who started all this mess."

"Maybe," she said. "We don't know that for sure."

"I do. It's too much of a coincidence that Blake was helping you on this case at the time he was killed, and now you're being targeted. Plus we just bumped into one of Hanan's comrades-in-arms out at Weber's place." Gage squinted at one of the photos. "What are these little pouches?"

"Cheek implants. They were my first tip-off he'd had plastic surgery." She came to stand beside him and pointed at a view of the skull. "Also, see the scratch marks on the mandible? And here, just above the eye orbit?"

"I don't see anything."

"Well, it's very obvious under a microscope. He underwent extensive plastic surgery."

Gage looked at her standing there in her lab coat and eye shields and felt a wave of regret. This was a side of her he'd never really known, only glimpsed. How many times had she flown out to California to visit him on his turf? She'd met his friends, she'd been to his favorite hangouts, she'd toured the naval base. He'd only been to visit her in Texas twice, and she'd never brought him to see this place that was so important to her. Seeing her here made him realize she'd been right—he *had* been pretty focused on the sexual side of their relationship to the exclusion of everything else.

And to top that off, he'd broken up with her. She was understandably gun shy.

But she still cared, he knew. He could read her. The challenge was going to be getting her to admit it.

She glanced up at him. "What's that look?"

"What look?"

"I am *not* playing doctor with you, so just get that out of your head."

"Hey, I didn't say anything."

"You were thinking it." She pocketed the vials of evidence and led him back into her office, where she rummaged through a desk drawer. "Here's a visitor's badge. It's old, but it should work."

Gage clipped the badge to the lapel of the shirt he'd been wearing for four straight days now to conceal his holster. He followed her out of her lab and to an elevator bank.

"First stop, Spiderman—but I doubt he'll be in on a Sunday."

"Spiderman?"

"That's what they call our entomologist—although the nickname is really a misnomer, because spiders aren't actually insects."

Gage shuddered.

"Don't tell me you're afraid of spiders?" She smiled as she stepped onto the elevator.

"Hate the damn things."

"You're kidding."

"Nope."

"You'll pit yourself against bombs and terrorists and soldiers who are trained to kill you, but you're scared of arachnids?"

"I understand bombs and terrorists and people who want to kill me. Arachnids freak me out."

The doors dinged opened and they stepped into a long carpeted corridor. Kelsey stopped at the first door and knocked. No one answered, and she used her palm print to gain access.

"That work everywhere?" Gage asked.

"Just the sections I frequent on a regular basis—Entomology, Serology, Osteology." She flipped on the light and he found they were in a large room with a tall slate table in the center. On it were several microscopes.

"Okay. Exhibit A." She collected some items from a drawer and began preparing slides.

Gage glanced around and immediately noticed the terrarium on the counter. The tarantula inside it was as big as his hand.

"That's Aragog," Kelsey said. "Don't worry, he's friendly."

Gage stepped over to a computer station. On the wall behind it was a series of photographs, and he leaned closer for a better look.

"Are these maggots?"

She glanced up from the microscope. "Blowflies, in various stages of their life cycle. He keeps those on display as sort of a cheat sheet for when he's out of the building. Here, tell me what you think."

He stepped up behind her and peered over her shoulder into the microscope.

"These are pupal casings."

Gage glanced back at the photographs. "So, that's the fifth stage, which he conveniently labeled for the rest of us poor saps who don't have a doctorate in bugs."

"The presence of pupae indicate that the corpse is at least six days old. But did you notice how in several of these specimens, the end appears to be cut off? That tells us the flies have already emerged, which means time since death is longer."

"How much longer?"

"A lot depends on conditions, but given what I saw of the body, plus the most likely weather conditions, I'm going to guess about eighteen days since death." Kelsey sat down at a workstation and brought the computer to life with the tap of a mouse. "Let's corroborate that with the ADD software. That's Accumulated Degree Days, which is something forensic anthropologists use to help determine postmortem interval."

Gage watched as she clicked on a skull and cross-bones logo to open a new program. Several blank fields popped up, and she entered yesterday's date and the zip code of Charles Weber's property.

"So, number of days times the average temperatures on each of those days in that zip code. The software factors in climate conditions such as moisture levels and translates that to a specific phase of decomp . . ." Her voice trailed off as the little hourglass turned in a circle on the screen. After a few moments, a line of text appeared.

"'Advanced putrefaction / mummification,'" Gage read.

Kelsey's shoulders slumped. She buried her head in her hands and looked to be on the verge of tears.

Gage didn't get it. What was she upset about?

"So . . . mummification?" he asked.

"The hot, dry air up there. The body showed some signs of heat desiccation. I was worried my time-of-death estimate might be off."

"But it's what you thought, right?"

She nodded.

"So, what's the problem?"

"I just needed to confirm everything." She stood up and squared her shoulders, and Gage understood. She'd needed proof of what she'd insisted on back in Utah—that Blake wasn't there when the murder occurred. She'd needed proof that her ex wasn't a cold-blooded killer.

She collected the slides and dropped them into an envelope, then slipped them in her pocket. Tears glistened in her eyes, and he felt a fresh wave of jealousy over how much she'd obviously cared about a man Gage couldn't stand.

"So, we've established that Blake didn't kill him," she said crisply. "Now, let's find out who did."

Elizabeth stepped into the condo and smiled at Officer Resnik. "This shouldn't take too long."

"I'll wait right here. Holler if you need anything."

For the second time that week, Elizabeth stood on the square of butcher paper and traded her shoes for paper booties. For the second time, she pulled on latex gloves. For the second time, she walked into the foyer and gazed down at the spot where a fellow agent had died.

Or where she *assumed* he'd died. Crime-scene investigators had found no sign that the victim had been killed elsewhere and transported. And yet Derek's words kept going through her head.

You guys got something wrong.

Elizabeth crouched beside the dried puddle of blood and examined the stained grout. She stood up and glanced around. She looked at the front door and once again saw no sign of forced entry. She looked around the living room. Her gaze fell on the evidence tags sitting on the coffee table, marking the spots where a beer bottle and a computer had been removed. Those two critical pieces of evidence had shaped the working theory of the case: Blake had been at home Monday night, working on his computer, when someone knocked on his door—

without leaving fingerprints. Blake had gone to the door and likely recognized the person—Gage Brewer— whom he'd met two summers ago during a terrorist incident in West Texas.

Maybe Blake had been surprised to see him, maybe not. Gage had come in for a beer and maybe a little talk about the woman they both knew, which was of course when things escalated. The conversation moved to the foyer, possibly as Blake tried to get Gage to leave. The SEAL grabbed him from behind, broke his neck with a quick twist, then whipped out his combat knife and stabbed him through the kidney.

Derek's words echoed through her mind again: *Why'd he kill him twice?*

She couldn't get past that point because he was right—it didn't make sense. It also didn't make sense to her that someone who had clearly premeditated the crime by coming all the way from California and showing up armed with a silent weapon would be careless enough to leave fingerprints on a beer bottle.

Then again, violent people did dumb things all the time—particularly in the heat of the moment. Maybe he'd been overcome by emotion. He'd certainly been emotional enough when Elizabeth first met him on the naval base.

Elizabeth thought of Kelsey. The woman was the key to all of this, she felt certain.

What had spooked her into running away? Had she known what Gage had planned? Had she helped plan it? Had she witnessed something, and now she was running for her life?

Derek had said that Gage was protecting her. *Protecting,* not threatening.

Elizabeth firmly believed Kelsey had been in this apartment on the night of Blake's murder, although she had no physical evidence to back up that theory. What she had was a lack of evidence in key areas.

She moved down the hallway now and into the bathroom, where, strangely, no fingerprints had been recovered. CSIs had dusted the doorknob, the faucet, the toilet, the cabinets. No prints had turned up, not even the maid's. How was that possible? According to her original interview, the maid who found Blake's body came every Tuesday and cleaned the condo top to bottom. If she was the last person to wipe down this room, that meant Blake hadn't used the bathroom closest to his living area in a week. So every evening, he'd gone all the way downstairs to use the restroom?

The lack of fingerprints had puzzled the entire team at first, but after tossing the topic around awhile, everyone had dismissed its importance. Maybe Blake didn't use his living room much and preferred to spend time in the master suite downstairs, which had a larger TV. Or maybe he was just quirky about his bathroom habits.

But Elizabeth didn't believe either of those explanations. She felt almost certain someone else had been in this bathroom on the night of the murder and carefully wiped away all the prints.

Elizabeth glanced in the mirror and was startled by what she saw. She looked tired. Disheveled. More than anything, she looked overwhelmed. She *felt* overwhelmed, even though she shouldn't because she'd been kicked off the case and sent home with her tail between her legs. She was back to her regular duties, back to tasks she could handle. But instead of handling them, she was secretly still working on the very case that had almost cost her her job.

She couldn't let go of it.

She didn't know why, but this crime scene kept pulling at her. Maybe because it was her first real murder scene, or maybe because she'd known the victim. Whatever the reason, Elizabeth hadn't been able to stay away.

She made a trip down to the master suite to complete her walk-through. She stood in the doorway and gazed at the bare mattress. She glanced down the hallway. The light near the stairs shone into the utility room, illuminating another pair of evidence markers where CSIs had collected a T-shirt and running shorts, which were presumed to be Blake's. The clothes were currently being tested for DNA.

Elizabeth looked at the dryer and tried to imagine Blake doing his own laundry. Or did his maid do it? She pictured him dumping a load of clothes in the machine—probably mixing all the colors and whites together—before going to bed. She stared at the laundry room for a moment and then walked down the hall to examine the doorway.

No door.

No barrier to close off the loudest room in the home from the master bedroom. She flipped on the light and looked at the marks in the wood where hinges had once been. She noted a scuff on the baseboard. She crouched down and ran her gloved finger over the slight indention in the wood where a door stopper had made its mark over the years.

Elizabeth's pulse sped up. She took the stairs two at a time and returned to the upstairs hallway. The bedroom door got stuck on the carpet and she had to use her shoulder to open it, just as Gordon had done when they'd first toured this scene. Elizabeth examined the wood. She dropped to her knees and checked out the rubber doorstop. On the wall nearby was a corresponding scuff mark. Elizabeth pushed the door back.

The marks didn't line up.

Someone had changed out this door. But when? And why? Explanations poured into her head. Maybe it had been damaged during a confrontation. Maybe it had evidence on it—blood, prints, possibly DNA from someone's fist.

She stared at the doorknob and tried to imagine it. She got on her hands and knees and searched the carpet for splinters, blood, anything the CSIs might have missed. Slowly, she crawled around, examining the beige fibers. As she reached the bare mattress, her finger brushed over a depression in the carpet.

"No way," she murmured.

She reached for the lamp on the bedside table and turned it on. She pulled it to the floor and dragged it close to the spot. Metal glinted.

An embedded slug.

Elizabeth sat back on her heels and held her hand to her chest. Her heart pounded. Her breathing was shallow. An armed confrontation involving someone— presumably Kelsey—had occurred right in this room. And someone—presumably Kelsey—had managed to get away. The CSIs had missed this, but she had the evidence right here.

Elizabeth's mind reeled. She thought about combat knives and alibis and a beer bottle that never should have been left on that coffee table.

She pulled the phone from her pocket and made a call.

"Moore," came the brisk answer.

"Sir, it's Elizabeth LeBlanc."

Silence.

"I'm calling from San Antonio. I'm at the crime scene, actually."

"You're no longer on this case, LeBlanc." His voice was laced with irritation.

"Yes, I know, but I was free today, so I decided to follow up on a few questions. I'm glad I did, because I've found some critical evidence that was apparently overlooked by the CSIs." She cleared her throat, which suddenly felt dry as sandpaper. "Sir, I think this crime scene was staged."

No response. Elizabeth knelt on the floor in the silent bedroom, holding her breath and waiting.

"Let me make myself clear, LeBlanc. As of noon yesterday, you are no longer associated with this investigation. Is that understood?"

"Sir, I—"

"You are to go home, right now. Do not stop by your office. Do not make any phone calls. Do not, under any circumstances, repeat a word of what you just told me to anyone. I'll call you later. Are we clear?"

Elizabeth tried to speak, but her voice wouldn't work.

"Are we clear, LeBlanc?"

"We're clear, sir."

Kelsey spent most of her time at Delphi in what she thought of as the catacombs, while Mia inhabited the top. As the Delphi Center's crown jewel, the DNA laboratory occupied the sixth-floor penthouse.

Kelsey led Gage down the glass hallway leading to Mia's office. The windows on one side offered views of the Texas Hill Country while the other gave a glimpse into the center's cyber-crimes lab.

"Impressive," Gage said, looking around.

Kelsey felt a surge of pride. He'd never been to the lab before, and it *was* impressive. Just being here gave her a sense of comfort. It wasn't just the familiar surroundings that made her feel that way, but her confidence in what they did here. Investigators from all over the world turned to Delphi for help with their toughest cases.

"This floor is our showcase," she told Gage. "The DNA research is really the guts of what we do, and it generates most of the private funding, so this is where they take all the VIPs."

"No one visits you in the bone basement?"

"I don't mind. I'm not there that much, anyway. When the weather's not too terrible, I prefer to be outdoors with students or out on a recovery."

Kelsey stopped in front of Mia's office. The door was open and Mia stood at a tall worktable, tapping away on her computer.

"Hi there."

Mia glanced up. "Hi! When did you get here? I was

getting worried." She crossed the room and pulled Kelsey into a hug.

Gage stepped through the doorway, and his enormous size made Mia's office seem even smaller than it actually was.

"Mia." He nodded at her.

"Gage."

Her cool tone told Kelsey exactly where she stood on the Gage question. In an effort to cut the tension, Kelsey walked between them and placed her evidence on the counter. It consisted of a glass vial and a sealed paper bag.

"Thanks for meeting us on a Sunday," she told Mia. "I've got several things for you."

Mia switched on an overhead lamp that was bright enough for a dentist's office. She adjusted the metal arm and held up the vial to the light.

"Dirt sample?"

"Mixed with blood," Kelsey said. "We're working on the premise that the victim is someone Blake knew. We believe his name is Charles Weber, but that's about all we know about him."

"Victim?" Mia looked at her.

"It looked like he died from a shotgun blast to the head, but we haven't confirmed that."

Mia put the vial on the counter and regarded it skeptically.

"What? Didn't I get enough?"

"No, that's plenty here to run tests," Mia said. "I can use PCR to amplify the sample."

"PCR?"

Mia glanced at Gage. Kelsey wasn't sure whether he

really cared about the process or was simply trying to draw Mia out of her shell.

"A polymerase chain reaction. It's a technique we use to get what's essentially a Xerox copy of the DNA we need from a very small sample. It even works on old or degraded samples, so that shouldn't be a problem." She turned to Kelsey. "But what makes you think he'll be in a database? You said he was a victim. Does he have a criminal record?"

"We'd like to find out."

"What's this?" Mia donned a pair of latex gloves and used an X-ACTO knife to unseal the bag. She pulled out an aluminum beer can. It had been crushed by someone into a nice portable size, which was one reason Kelsey had snatched it up and stuffed it in her pocket on her way through the kitchen.

"This was recovered from the crime scene," she told Mia. "It seemed like the killer was staying there, so you might be able to get some DNA from the can."

"Or prints," Gage added.

"I'll swab the can here first, then run it down to Ident to see if they can get anything. I've got to be honest, your chances with them are better."

"You don't think you'll get DNA?" Kelsey asked.

"No, I will. But AFIS includes far more records than CODIS—about seventy million."

"When you're dropping off the can, give them this, too," Gage said, pulling out the business card he'd wanted from Aaron. He held it by the edges. "We're interested to see if any prints from the can match the ones on this business card."

Mia read the name and lifted an eyebrow. "Special

Agent Lohman." She gave Kelsey a pointed look. "He was here last week."

Kelsey's phone rang again and she pulled it out to check the number.

"Hey, Aaron, what's up?"

"Thought you'd want to know," he said, "I just left the lab, and as I drove through the gate, the feds were pulling in."

CHAPTER 15

Gage watched from behind a storage shed as the gray Taurus circled the Delphi Center's employee parking lot.

"What are they doing?" Kelsey asked.

"Probably looking for the SUV. Maybe they talked to the guard."

The Taurus made another slow loop. Because it was Sunday, the lot wasn't full. Many of the cars looked to be unmarked police vehicles, probably belonging to detectives who were dropping off evidence. At last the Taurus pulled into a space.

Gage gripped his SIG in his hand as he waited to see who would emerge. If Trent Lohman got out, he was going to have a tough time resisting the urge to take him out right now.

The driver's-side door opened, and an FBI agent got out.

"That's not Trent," Kelsey said.

"Supervisory Special Agent Gordon Moore."

She turned to look at him. "You know him?"

"He interviewed me back at base. Where's your phone?"

"Right here."

"Call Mia," Gage said. "Ask her to intercept him in the lobby and get his cell number. She can tell him anything she wants—she's expecting to hear from you, she'll let him know when you call—whatever she needs to say to get his number."

"Why do we want his number?"

Gage watched as the agent walked up the white marble steps to the Delphi Center's front entrance. He hoped to hell he hadn't misread this guy.

He turned to Kelsey. "Because it's time for Plan B."

Kelsey fidgeted with the Mace inside her pocket. It was pretty useless, considering who she was up against, but Gage had insisted that she have it ready, just in case the plan went sideways.

A child squealed, and she glanced over her shoulder. A little boy of about five or six stood on tiptoes, peering over the outer wall of the elephant habitat where a mother elephant was giving her baby a bath. Kelsey glanced over her other shoulder. More children, more parents, a cotton candy vendor. Her nerves jangled as she thought of the many things that could go wrong.

And then she spotted him. He'd traded the suit and tie for khakis and a navy blazer—which made him only slightly less conspicuous in the late-morning heat. The agent's gaze zeroed in on Kelsey, and she made an effort to appear calm as he strode toward her.

He glanced around, then stopped in front of her and gave a crisp nod. "Dr. Quinn."

She waited a beat, then offered a handshake. "Agent

Moore. Greg, is it?" She held on to his hand and leaned forward to hear the answer.

"It's Gordon."

Gage appeared behind him and clamped a hand on his shoulder. "Gordon. Nice to see you again." Gage snaked his hand inside his blazer and relieved him of his pistol. It happened so fast that Kelsey would have missed it if she hadn't been standing there, gripping the agent's hand.

"No offense," Gage said, "but we'd like to keep this friendly."

"None taken," he said tightly.

Kelsey settled back against the low stone wall beside Gage. Moore watched them, clearly seething.

She smiled. "Did you come alone?"

"He did," Gage confirmed.

Moore looked at Kelsey, then at Gage, then at the Saharan backdrop they'd chosen as a site for their meeting.

"I'm sure you're busy investigating, so we'll keep this brief," Gage said. "Kelsey wants to set the record straight on a few things."

The agent's attention shifted to Kelsey, but she could tell he still considered Gage very much a threat.

"I'm listening."

"Over the last six days," she said, "it's become painfully obvious that your investigation has taken a wrong turn."

She took him through what she'd seen on the night of Blake's murder, then followed up with the shooting incident in Piney Creek. Moore listened without interrupting.

"The next time I saw Trent Lohman," Kelsey told

him, "was in Briggs, Utah. I understand you've had agents up there recently."

He nodded.

"Trent was at the home of Charles Weber. He was with an accomplice. I believe one or both of them killed Weber before setting fire to the crime scene."

Moore gave them a long, hard look. "How can you be sure who killed him?"

"We can't," Gage said.

"We're not even certain it was Charles Weber we saw in that barn," Kelsey said. "I collected some evidence from the crime scene that's now destroyed, and I'm hoping to get something through DNA. But you're right, we don't know for sure. What we *do* know for sure is that Trent Lohman is directly involved in one murder, and directly involved in the cover-up of another. Whether the victim was Charles Weber or not—"

"It wasn't."

Kelsey stared at him. "It wasn't?"

The agent looked at Gage, then back at Kelsey. He gazed out at the elephants again and seemed to be struggling with a decision.

"Charles Weber is an alias. The remains you found in the barn belong to Dr. Robert Spurlock, who started his career at the University of Cincinnati. Fifteen years ago he went to work for the government."

A cold ball of dread formed in Kelsey's stomach. "Doctor of what?" she asked.

Moore gave her a grim look. The dread expanded.

"Microbiology," he said. "He's one of the country's foremost experts in *Bacillus anthracis*."

CHAPTER 16

The color drained from Kelsey's face. Gage looked at Moore.

"Anthrax?" Fury bubbled up in his chest. "You're telling us he was making anthrax?"

"I don't know what he was making."

Kelsey made a strange noise and bent over, looking sick. Gage crouched beside her and squeezed her knee. "Kelsey, listen to me. When was your last shot?"

She just stared at him. The stark look on her face made him feel like someone had him in a chokehold. Just a few grams of weapons-grade anthrax could kill hundreds of people.

"Before you went to Iraq with that human-rights group," Gage said, "you had a round of shots."

She nodded.

"When was your last booster?"

She closed her eyes. "November. No—December, right before Christmas."

"What about you, Lieutenant?" Moore turned to Gage. "I assume you've been vaccinated?"

Gage studied Kelsey's face. "Are you sure it was December?"

"Lieutenant Brewer? You've had the vaccine?"

Gage shot him a glare. "I've been in a fucking combat zone for ten years. Of course I've had it." He turned back to Kelsey. "You're sure it was *last* December and not the year before?"

"It was. I remember because it was just before the holiday, and I went on my lunch hour . . ." She jumped to her feet. "Oh my God, *Mia*! I took her that evidence. What if it's contaminated?"

Gage stood up and looked at Moore.

"What evidence?" the agent asked.

"A soil sample from the barn. It included Weber's blood. Or Spurlock's. Whoever he was. Oh my God, *Gage*!" She gripped his arm. "What about the firemen? The first responders? Think of all the people who might be exposed!"

"Spurlock wasn't infected," Moore said calmly.

"How do you know?" Kelsey asked.

"Our Salt Lake City field office keeps tabs on former Dugway employees who live in the area. Within minutes of hearing about the explosion, we had a hazmat team on the scene, testing for anything unusual."

"*No* trace of anything?" Gage asked. "You guys are sure?"

"No trace. And we used the most sensitive equipment known to man. No hazardous material was detected on his property. But that's not to say he's never had any there. We have reason to believe he might have contracted with an outside party to cultivate the virus."

"What's Dugway?" Kelsey asked.

"Dugway Proving Ground," Gage told her. "A military testing facility. I didn't even think of it. It's due west of there."

"He worked there for eight years until he was let go in 2005. The FBI's been keeping tabs on him since then."

Kelsey stared into space. "The *birds*." She looked at Gage. "That's what they were for."

"Birds?"

She looked at Moore. "He had cages everywhere. Like that saying, 'the canary in the coal mine.' He kept all those birds around to make sure the air was safe."

"I bet you're right," Gage said. "And every one of those damn things was alive. I didn't see any dead ones. Did you?"

"No."

"Let me reiterate—Spurlock was *not* infected," Moore said. "There's almost no chance that soil sample contains anthrax. The man was killed by a shotgun, not a virus. Your friend in the lab is not at risk."

"Still, I need to call her," Kelsey said.

"First, I need to know more about this accomplice. The man with the dark hair. Was he the person who went after you in San Antonio?"

"Definitely not." She shook her head. "The guy with the badge was short and stocky. This other man was taller and slender. I told Gage, I think I recognize him from that training video Blake showed me at his house."

Moore's gaze narrowed. "The Asian Crescent Brotherhood?"

"The footage from the training camp. It's on Blake's computer. I'm almost certain he's the man in the final frame who sets fire to the American flag. Review the video and you'll see. He's the one with the lighter."

Moore reached into his jacket. Gage seized his wrist.

"Easy there."

"I need to make a phone call," Moore said.

Gage reached into the blazer pocket and pulled out the phone. "Before you call anyone, I need a few questions answered. We just spent the last fifteen minutes telling you how one of your agent buddies is a murderer who hangs out with terrorists. And you know what I notice? You don't look surprised. Why haven't you guys arrested the son of a bitch?"

"Trent Lohman is not my buddy," Moore said flatly. "For the past forty-eight hours he's been at the top of my suspect list in Blake Reid's death."

"Then why is there a warrant out for me?"

He hesitated. Again, he seemed to be debating how much to tell them, and Gage's temper festered.

"I've been investigating violent crimes for the Bureau for sixteen years," Moore said. "I always start with people close to the victim, which is why I looked at you," he told Kelsey. "And that led me to you." He nodded at Gage. "But I also looked at Reid's closest colleague on the counterterrorism team."

He paused for a moment and gazed out at the elephants. "Trent Lohman has an alibi for the night of Reid's murder. He was in Washington, D.C., at a late-night meeting with Rick Bolton, the director of counterterrorism."

The news was like a sucker punch. Gage stared at the man, thinking maybe he'd heard wrong. But then he looked at Kelsey and knew she'd heard exactly the same thing.

Gage tipped his head back and looked at the sky. His career was over. His fucking *life* was over. This setup went to the highest levels of law enforcement and there was a serious chance Gage was going to spend the rest of his days rotting in prison for another man's crime. He closed his eyes and tried to swallow the lump of rage that was lodged in his throat.

"You see my challenge here?" Moore said. "And I probably don't need to spell out for you the sort of power someone in Bolton's position has. So that's the reason for the warrant. While that warrant is in place, certain people can rest assured that our investigation is on the wrong track."

"That's unacceptable."

Gage looked at Kelsey. Her eyes blazed. She had a fierce expression he'd never seen before.

She stepped forward and jabbed a finger at Moore's chest. "If you don't have the evidence you need, you *do* something about it. You do your *job*. You do not destroy a man's *life* just to save your own ass."

Moore eased back from her. "It's not about my ass. Or even his." He looked at Gage. "This is much bigger than that. If you've got your facts right, that means there's a terrorist *inside* our borders with access to a biological weapon. And if I've got *my* facts right, there's a conspiracy in place not only to protect him, but to help him. This thing's a minefield, and I'm trying to navigate it without getting blown up."

Kelsey still looked pale. "Do you have any idea what weaponized anthrax can do?"

"It can kill thousands of people. Maybe hundreds of thousands," Moore said. "Believe me, I'm well aware. I've hardly thought about anything else since I found out about Spurlock."

The phone in Gage's hand buzzed, and he looked down at it. The caller ID said US GOV. Gage smiled bitterly at the irony and held out the phone. "It's for you."

Moore took it. He gave Gage a stony look. "I'll do what I can about the warrant, but not now. In the meantime, you should think about using one of your phony passports and taking that dive trip you had planned."

Gage glanced at Kelsey.

"Take her with you," Moore said, and answered the phone. "Gordon Moore." Pause. "Let me call you back." He hung up and held out his hand. "I'd like my gun back."

Gage smiled ruefully and shook his head. He and Kelsey were in a world of shit and he had no idea how he was going to dig them out. He held up the key fob he'd lifted when he reached into Moore's pocket. The agent frowned as Gage unclipped the key from the remote locking device.

"I'd just as soon not walk out of here in handcuffs." Gage gave him the key. "Take your phone call. I'll leave your gun and the rest of your keychain in your trunk."

Kelsey checked the peephole and pulled open the door.

"Wow." Mia stepped into the motel room. "You look awful."

"Thanks." Kelsey shut the door behind her. "I really needed to hear that today."

Mia set her purse down on the table and glanced around at the latest in this week's series of dingy motel rooms. Her gaze lingered on the pistol atop the dresser.

"Where's Gage?"

"Across the street getting food." Kelsey sank onto the bed. "Although I told him I can't eat anything. I feel terrible."

Mia walked over and gazed down at her with a worried look. "*Physically* you feel terrible? Or emotionally?"

"Physically, I'm fine. I think it's just all the stress catching up with me." She laughed without humor. "I mean, it's pretty unbelievable. The last seven days have been one catastrophe after another and I couldn't *imagine* how things could get worse, and now suddenly I think the worst catastrophe is yet to come."

Mia tipped her head to the side and looked concerned. "How's Gage?"

Kelsey laughed, even though nothing was funny. Tears burned her eyes and she blinked them back. "He says he's fine, but I know he's lying. God, I'm so worried about him. I can't believe I did this to him."

"Hey." Mia sat down beside her. "You didn't do anything to him. This is someone else's doing."

Kelsey took a deep breath and nodded. "I know that logically, but I still feel responsible. This murder investigation could end his career."

"I thought you didn't like his career."

"I don't," Kelsey said. "I hate it. I hate that he puts

himself in danger all the time. But Gage loves being a SEAL. He wouldn't trade it for anything—not even me—and the thought of that being taken away from him . . . It makes me so angry, I want to hurt somebody."

Mia watched her for a long moment. "How are you and Gage relationship-wise?"

She was talking about sex—one of their frequent conversation topics. Kelsey looked at her lap and warmth flooded her cheeks as she recalled Gage's kisses, his body, the feel of his hands on her.

"Mia." She closed her eyes and sighed. "It's so good. He's just . . . amazing. You have no idea."

"I think I might. Ric's pretty amazing."

She glanced up, and Mia was grinning at her.

"It's just that, besides the physical, I don't know what we really have together. There are things I want that I'll never be able to have with him."

"Such as?"

She looked at Mia, uncomfortable with the idea of saying it out loud. She wanted simple things, things she'd lost when her dad had died suddenly and her mother had become cold and withdrawn and stopped being a mom. She wanted a family. She wanted aunts and uncles and cousins and big Christmas mornings with children underfoot. She wanted things she would never have if she devoted her life to a man who was overseas all the time and defused bombs for a living.

But it wasn't only Gage's career that got in the way. It was hers, too. She'd never seriously considered leaving her prestigious job at the Delphi Center to be close to a naval base. And for the past four years, she'd spent her summers in remote locations digging up bones. *Her* career wasn't exactly conducive to family, either.

"I don't know, Mia. Maybe I'm being unrealistic."

"Don't be ashamed of what you want." Mia looked at her pointedly. "You deserve to be happy."

The door swung open. Gage stepped into the room with armload of bags. He looked from Mia to Kelsey and narrowed his gaze.

"Uh-oh. What'd I miss?"

"Nothing." Mia popped up.

Gage put all the bags on the table and shot Kelsey a suspicious look. "I interrupted something."

"I was just telling Kelsey about the delivery I brought you." Mia unzipped her purse and pulled out a white paper bag. "I had a doctor friend of mine write a script for an antibiotic."

Kelsey walked over. "I thought you said we were in the clear?"

"You are." Mia opened the bag. She handed a small brown bottle to Kelsey and one to Gage.

"Seprax." Kelsey looked down at the label, which had Mia's name on it. "I've never heard of it."

"You've heard of Cipro. This is just a knockoff. You're both vaccinated, and you weren't even really exposed, so this is totally unnecessary. It's for peace of mind. The script was actually written for me. I figured you wouldn't want your names popping up on some computer system. Anyway, I hope it will help dial down the stress level a little."

"Thank you." Kelsey reached over and squeezed her hand. She realized how much she'd desperately needed the very brief bit of girl talk. "I'm glad you came by."

"Anytime. You take care."

"I will."

"Gage." She gave him a curt nod and walked out.

Kelsey glanced down at the medicine in her hand. She looked up as the door opened again and Gage stepped out. The door thudded shut and she stood there, staring at it. What now? She went to the window and shifted the curtains. Gage stood in the parking lot, hands on hips, towering over Mia. He was at least a foot taller than she was, but Mia had her arms crossed over her chest and didn't look at all intimidated. Kelsey couldn't hear the words, but clearly they were arguing.

Kelsey watched, astonished, as Gage leaned down and kissed Mia's forehead. Mia looked equally surprised.

She stepped away from the window. Gage reentered the room and started unpacking food. The scent of French fries filled the air.

"What did you say to her?" she asked.

"Nothing."

"Nothing?"

"I told her to put the claws away."

Kelsey stared at him.

"She cares about you. I get it. But I'm sick of being treated like I'm pond scum." He glanced up at her. "And I don't want her bad-mouthing me while I'm trying to make things right with us."

"You are?"

He plopped an enormous order of fries in front of her. "I told you that. What, you didn't believe me?"

Kelsey didn't know what to believe. And she didn't know how she felt about his effort to sweet-talk her friends and "make things right" when she was almost certain it meant starting up a relationship he didn't really want.

Kelsey distracted herself by addressing the deadly illness they'd almost been exposed to. She took out a pill from each of the brown bottles and set them on the table.

"Take one a day," she instructed. "It'll give you peace of mind."

Gage sneered. Kelsey popped her pill and washed it down with a slurp of syrupy-sweet Coke. Gage handed her a cheeseburger.

"Thanks, but I don't feel like eating," she said.

"You stressed?"

"Just a little."

"Why don't you take a hot bath?"

"That sounds really good." She stood there, waiting for the innuendo.

He continued to unpack food.

"I'll just soak in the tub for a while, see if I can get some of these kinks out." She waited. No suggestive look. No lewd comment. "Are you feeling okay?" she asked.

"Considering my career has gone to shit? I'm feeling pretty good, actually." He sank into the chair in front of what appeared to be two super-size meal deals. "Why?"

"Nothing."

"Okay, here's the plan." He unwrapped his burger. "You go have your soak. I'll have some of this food. And then we're going to sit down at the table and map this thing out, because I'll be damned if I'm going to sit around and wait for any more shit to come down. It's time to make a battle plan."

　　Kelsey's ring tone sounded and she crossed the room to dig the phone from her purse. After a brief conversation, she turned to Gage.

　　"We'll have to postpone the battle plan. That was Gordon Moore."

　　His eyebrows arched. "How'd he get your number?"

　　"No idea. But I'm urgently needed back at the Delphi Center."

CHAPTER 17

By the time Kelsey got things into position and arrived at the lab, everyone else was already gathered in the visitors' conference room on the ground floor. Moore stood up when she walked in, and the impatient look on his face told her they'd been waiting on her.

"Sorry I'm late." She looked around the table and was startled to see not only Ben Lawson, but his boss, Mark Wolfe, who ran Delphi's cyber-crimes division. Mark had a laptop open in front of him. Kelsey sent Ben a questioning look as she took a seat at the table.

"Where's Lieutenant Brewer?" Moore asked.

"Close by." Kelsey smiled to mask the threat behind the words.

Moore glanced at the door, then at the conference room window, which had a view of the woods behind the building. Kelsey pretended not to notice the agent's look of irritation.

"I'd hoped you both could weigh in on this, Dr. Quinn."

"It's Kelsey," she said. "And I don't think you're

going to be seeing much of Gage until you drop the warrant for his arrest."

Moore gave her a hard stare, and she knew he was debating whether to take up this topic in front of the others.

"Call me Gordon," he said. He glanced at the window. "And maybe you'll be able to give us what we need without him."

"Hi!" Mia breezed into the room, looking windblown and frazzled. She dropped into the chair beside Ben, and Kelsey could tell she wasn't surprised to see the other people here. Obviously, she'd been told more about this meeting than Kelsey had.

"Let's get started," Gordon said. "Mia, you want to share the results?"

"I'm still running the DNA on the beer can from the house in Utah," Mia said. "But after swabbing the can, I took it down to the fingerprint lab and they came back with a hit almost immediately."

"That was quick," Kelsey said.

"That's because the print belonged to someone we know well," Gordon said, and she caught the edge in his voice. "Mark knows him, too, from his days with the FBI. Mark?"

Kelsey held her breath. This was going to be the proof they needed of Trent's involvement. Maybe it would corroborate her story enough for Gordon to drop the warrant for Gage and arrest Trent instead. She slipped her phone from her pocket to make sure the line was open. She wanted Gage to hear this.

Mark cleared his throat and looked at the faces around the table. With his dark good looks, the former criminal profiler had always reminded Kelsey of George Clooney. Mark was somewhat new to the Delphi Center, but he'd already established an impressive reputation by spearheading the lab's new cyber-profiling unit.

"When I worked at the Bureau, I did consulting for various law-enforcement agencies both here and overseas," Mark said. "They brought me in on the Bali market bombing of 2009, which killed thirty-three people, including four Americans. I helped develop criminal profiles on some of the suspects."

Kelsey leaned forward, puzzled by his lead-in.

"One of the people I profiled in that case was this man." Mark tapped his computer mouse and turned to face the screen at the end of the conference room. An enormous photograph of a smiling boy in a football uniform filled the screen.

"Meet Adam Ramli aka Asmar Husin."

Kelsey gaped at the image. The kid in the photo couldn't have been more than sixteen. He had dark, tousled hair, braces, and a slender build that was dwarfed by his bulky shoulder pads.

"Where's he from?" Kelsey asked.

"Peachtree, Georgia." Mark looked at her. "Here's a more recent photo."

The next image showed the same person, but all the features had matured: elongated nose, full beard, deep-set eyes. But the real difference was the facial expression. The youthful smile had been replaced by a defiant stare. And instead of holding a football, he held an assault rifle.

"Adam played wide receiver for his high-school football team," Mark continued. "He was on the debate squad. He was elected president of his senior class. He's smart, charismatic, and five years ago he became a committed member of the Asian Crescent Brotherhood, a terrorist organization headquartered in Indonesia."

Silence settled over the room.

"How old is he?" Mia asked.

"Twenty-four."

"And he's American?" Kelsey still couldn't believe it.

"Born and raised," Mark said. "He speaks English with a Southern accent. He's got an American birth certificate. A U.S. passport. Without the beard and weaponry, he looks like the kid who might take your order at Applebee's. He's the jihadist next door. In short, he's our worst nightmare."

A new photo appeared on the screen, this one showing Adam Ramli crouched in the dirt beside what looked like a homemade bomb. Again, he held an assault weapon in his hand, and on either side of him were heavily armed men. Adam looked straight at the camera.

"Can you confirm that this is the man you saw in Utah two nights ago?"

Kelsey glanced at Gordon and realized the question was directed at her. She looked at the photograph again.

"That's him."

The room went quiet.

"He was using a white sedan," she added. "A Buick or maybe a Ford, late model. It looked to me like a rental car."

"It's good information." Gordon looked at Mark. "Fill us in on the rest. Whatever you know."

"Well, the Bureau's case file on this guy is probably

a foot thick, but I'll hit the highlights. Adam's father was born in Indonesia. He was raised Muslim but hasn't practiced since he came to American thirty years ago to attend medical school."

"What sort of doctor?" Kelsey asked.

"Orthopedist." Mark smiled. "Another bone doc, like yourself. His mother is from Atlanta. Used to work as a nurse, which was where she met her husband. Jennifer Ramli is a strict Southern Baptist and took her kids to church while they were growing up."

"Kids?" Mia asked.

"Adam has a sister, Marissa. She's a file clerk at a law firm in San Francisco. Anyway, shortly after Adam graduated from high school, he took a trip to Jakarta to visit relatives. Within months of that trip, during his freshman year of college at Georgia Tech, he started going to a local mosque. About this time, Marissa left home and moved to the Bay Area with her boyfriend. She'd had a falling-out with her parents, from what we can gather. Adam did, too. In April of his freshman year, he withdrew from school, cleaned out the checking account his parents had provided for him, and bought a plane ticket to London. Our investigation shows that this was when he met face-to-face with some people he'd previously only known online. He started visiting a mosque headed by a man on the Bureau's terrorist watch list."

Mark tapped a button and a video appeared on the screen. Kelsey recognized the footage she'd seen at Blake's place.

"When Adam Ramli turned up at this Al-Qaeda training camp in Indonesia, he himself was placed on the watch list."

"So, he's Al-Qaeda or Asian Crescent Brotherhood?"

"Now he's ACB," Mark said. "Which is just as bad—maybe worse, because we know less about their operations. This offshoot of Al-Qaeda is extremely violent. Not long ago they kidnapped a group of missionaries in the Philippines. Thirty-one people were beheaded. All the female victims in the group showed signs of brutal sexual assault."

Kelsey had heard about the attack while she was working in the Philippines. She watched the men on the screen as they conducted target practice.

"Stop the video." She leaned forward. "That man there." She looked at Gordon. "That's James Hanan, the man whose bones our team recovered in the jungle on Basilan Island."

"That's correct," Gordon said. "Our investigation shows that the week before Blake Reid's death, he took a phone call from one of our lab technicians at Quantico, where he'd sent a sample for analysis. The technician confirmed the identity of those bones."

Kelsey sat back in her chair. A sick feeling washed over her. The favor she'd asked Blake to do may well have gotten him killed.

"What is Hanan's connection to Adam Ramli?" she asked.

"Besides being Asian Crescent Brotherhood? They're both Americans. We're seeing an increase in Americans joining some of these groups, and it's very alarming. The groups gain an advantage because American membership helps them spread their message in English-speaking countries. Also, these guys possess U.S. passports, and if we don't know they've been radicalized, they can move in and out of our borders with little or no trouble."

"Hasn't his passport been flagged?" Kelsey asked.

"Absolutely," Gordon said, "but the border's porous. Or he could have come in on a fake passport. Or a stolen one. Someone with his accent and knowledge of the culture would be able to blend in easily and not draw attention to himself."

"So, with Kelsey's eyewitness account, plus the fingerprint evidence from Utah, we have to believe he's here now," Mia said.

"Which brings us to our next problem," Gordon said. "Dr. Richard Spurlock. Until his recent death, the retired microbiologist was one of our country's foremost experts in anthrax."

A new photo appeared on the screen, and Kelsey got her first look at Richard Spurlock alive. He appeared thin, bald, and nervous behind a pair of wire-rim spectacles. He gazed straight ahead at the camera.

"This is a driver's license picture?" Mia asked.

"It's from his employee badge at Dugway Proving Ground, which is a high-security biological and chemical weapons testing facility in the Utah desert. Spurlock worked there for eight years and handled some of the most sensitive biological research ever conducted by the U.S. government."

"Retired?" Mia asked.

"He was let go in 2005," Mark said, "after a series of minor security infractions. Entering the lab at non-designated hours, failing to turn in routine reports, that sort of thing."

Kelsey looked at Mark. "You profiled him, too?"

"Someone on my team did. As part of the anthrax investigation of 2001, we were called in to profile every researcher who may have sent those letters. We looked at several key factors to put together our suspect list: scientific ability, lab access, proximity to the mail sites, and suspicious behavior. Spurlock fit all of our criteria except proximity to the sites where the anthrax letters were mailed. He was high on our suspect list for months. But ultimately the FBI lab was able to genetically trace the strain used in those attacks to a particular flask in a particular refrigerator in a particular research laboratory on Fort Detrick, Maryland. Spurlock was crossed off our list, but he'd raised some red flags, so we continued to keep an eye on him. After a few years, he'd racked up a number of minor violations, so the lab let him go. Until we officially closed the anthrax investigation, he was still getting occasional media attention as a possible suspect, which is probably why he decided to change his name."

"The anthrax doc and the jihadist," Ben said, speaking up for the first time. "What a duo."

"An extremely deadly duo." Mia looked around the table. "I realize I'm the only microbiologist here, but do you all grasp the gravity of this situation?" She leaned forward. "Imagine a five-pound bag of sugar. If you spread that amount of weaponized anthrax over a city the size of Washington, D.C., you could wipe out half the population."

A chill slithered down Kelsey's spine. She looked at Gordon. "Don't they keep track of the samples in the lab? Did he steal some before he left?"

"They keep very close track, and no, there's no evidence that he stole any. There's none missing."

"So what do we think was going on?"

"We don't know," Gordon said. "And I, in particular, am not in a position to know because I'm not part of the FBI's counterterrorism division. I investigate violent crimes."

"I'm still not seeing it," Kelsey said. "If there's none missing, then where would Ramli get it? How could some twenty-four-year-old commando get hold of one of the most tightly controlled substances on the planet? That seems like a major stretch."

"You might not think so if you'd been on the investigative side," Mark said. "Literally hundreds of scientists have had access to the material at some point in their careers. If it didn't come from Spurlock, it could have come from someone else."

"And he might not have gotten it here," Ben said. "Think about Iraq, Libya, Egypt—all the places that were probably developing this stuff whose governments have fallen apart post–Arab Spring. There're all kinds of weapons on the black market now, from rocket-propelled grenade launchers to mustard gas."

Kelsey's chest tightened. She'd heard through the rumor mill that the missile that downed Joe's helicopter had been traced to an arsenal in Libya.

She touched the phone in her pocket and wondered if Gage was still listening.

"Ben could be right," Mia said. "Non-weaponized forms of the virus are much easier to obtain and transport." She looked at Kelsey. "That means a liquid form, such as a slurry. The trick is to dry it out successfully, which is a much more complicated task involving special expertise and equipment. When it's deprived of liquid, the virus forms durable spores. And here's the part that's hard to pull off: It becomes weaponized when the spores are milled into extremely fine particles, small enough to enter the lungs. The disease itself is not contagious, but a mass release of *weaponized* spores could kill thousands and thousands of people."

"Once it's in a fine-powder form, it's not difficult to disseminate," Mark added. "All he'd have to do is put it in a fragile container—a bottle, a jar, a lightbulb—and drop it in a public place. Once the container shatters, the spores take to the air."

Across the table, a phone chimed.

"Excuse me," Mia said, standing up. She slipped out of the room.

"So, it's possible Adam Ramli or someone provided the raw materials, and probably the funding," Kelsey said, "and Dr. Spurlock provided the expertise."

Mia slipped back into the room. "It's for you."

Kelsey took the phone, startled. "Hello?"

"Tell everyone to quit dicking around with the science lesson," Gage said. "We've got a fucking weapon of mass destruction inside our borders. What is Moore doing to *locate* Ramli?"

Kelsey glanced around the table, and all eyes were on her. "Gage wants an update on the manhunt. Where is Adam Ramli?"

"And Trent Lohman," Gage added.

She put the phone on the table and switched it to

speaker mode. "And Trent Lohman. Where is he while all this is going on?"

Gordon glanced uneasily at Mark. "We have reason to believe one of our agents is involved in this plot."

"We know it for a *fact*." Gage's angry voice joined the conversation. "Kelsey and I saw him with our own eyes. He needs to be brought in. He can tell us where Ramli is."

"Lohman is being protected by someone very high up in the organization," Gordon said. "It's not as simple as just asking him."

"Oh, yeah? Give me ten minutes in a room alone with him, and I'll ask him," Gage said. "I bet I get some answers, too, before he murders a hundred thousand people."

Mark leaned forward on his elbows and looked at Gordon. "How high up?"

"The assistant director for CT," Gordon said.

No one spoke. Kelsey glanced at the phone, where even Gage had gone quiet.

"You see why my hands are tied. I'm investigating a potential terrorist attack without involving counter-terrorism."

"Who are you using?" Mark asked.

"Two trusted agents, people I've known for more than a decade. One of them is surveilling Ramli's parents down in Atlanta, hoping he'll make contact. The other was just in San Francisco, interviewing the sister, but she claims not to have had any contact with him in five years."

"So, what's Lohman's role in this?" Mark asked.

"He was a brand-new agent in 2001 when we started the anthrax investigation," Gordon said. "That was one of the most heavily staffed investigations in our history, and Lohman was part of it. He had access to the FBI's suspect list, so I think his role in this was to connect Ramli with a scientist who had the expertise to help him make a biological weapon. I doubt Lohman would involve himself in an actual attack."

"Where is Trent Lohman now?" Kelsey asked.

"I don't know," Gordon said. "But he's supposed to be in some meetings in Washington tomorrow afternoon."

"He might know where Ramli is," Mia said. "And we obviously need to find him and get control of this material."

"Talk to Ramli's sister again," Gage said. "She's a better bet than the guy's estranged parents."

"We're doing everything we can."

"Using only three people, including yourself?" Kelsey asked. "You're not taking this seriously!"

Gordon's face hardened. "Do you have any children, Dr. Quinn?"

She drew back, affronted. He knew damn well she didn't have children.

"Do you?"

"No."

"Any nieces or nephews?"

"No."

He leaned forward and looked her squarely in the eye. "I have two daughters, ten and twelve. They live in our nation's capital. You'd better believe I take this seriously."

"What can we do?" Mark asked, breaking the tension. "You obviously need as much help as you can get from outside the Bureau."

Gordon looked around. "That's why I'm here. Ben is investigating all digital activity related to Adam Ramli, his family, and also Trent Lohman. Your lab has helped expedite the physical evidence and provided a criminal profile."

Kelsey turned to Mark. "Do you have any predictions about this guy? Anything that might help determine where he is now or what he's planning?"

Mark nodded. "I can tell you about his Achilles' heel. The man's a narcissist, which is good and bad. Bad, because I can almost guarantee he's planning something big, something that makes a splash and gets lots of media attention. The good part, though, is that he'll want to survive the attack and bask in his achievement. This man isn't suicidal. And despite all his rhetoric, he's not even that religious, when it comes down to it. He's egocentric. He thrives on attention. He doesn't want to die for his cause, he wants to shine a spotlight on it, as well as himself. This means he has an exit strategy, and that involves planning—travel arrangements, documents, funding."

"I'll check it out," Ben said.

"So, the main question now is, are we searching for the right person?" Gordon looked at Kelsey. "You're one hundred percent sure the man you saw in Utah is Adam Ramli?"

Kelsey looked at the screen again. The video was paused on an image of Ramli standing in front of a group of armed men, and he looked to be giving a speech. He stood taller than the others. She studied his face.

"I'm looking at the pronounced cheekbones, the orbital ridge, the bump on the nose," she said. "Disguises come and go, but without plastic surgery, those features stay the same." She paused for a moment. "Push play again."

The scene changed. He was leading a group of commandos now, walking over rocky terrain, his weapon slung casually across his body. Kelsey remembered the same face, the same posture, the same gait from the encounter in Utah.

"I'm sure," she confirmed. "It's definitely him."

CHAPTER 18

Kelsey cast a worried look at Gage in the driver's seat. She could practically feel the anger seeping from his pores.

"Three agents." He pounded the steering wheel. "How can he conduct a manhunt with fucking *three* people?"

"He's got us, too. And Ben and Mark."

"Yeah, the Geek Squad. I'm sure they'll scoop him right up. What he needs is some SEALs. We'd bag this guy in a minute."

She rolled her eyes.

"You don't believe me? We find people in mountain ranges the size of Texas. Jungles. Deserts. You don't think we could locate some guy strolling through Times Square with a bomb strapped to his chest?"

"He's not going to have a bomb strapped to his chest. Did you listen to Mark? He's interested in self-preservation."

Kelsey's phone vibrated in her pocket and she pulled it out to look at the screen.

"What's up, Ben?"

"Is Gage with you?"

"Yeah. Why?"

"We need to talk. Meet me at Randy's in fifteen minutes."

Gage shot her a questioning look and she muted the phone. "He wants to meet us at Randy's Pool Hall. He's got something on his mind."

"That's the bar where we went with Mia that time, right?"

"Yeah."

"No dice. Never go—"

"—where the enemy expects you to be. I got it." She un-muted the phone. "Not Randy's. How about Smoky Joe's?" she asked him.

"I thought you hated barbecue."

"I do."

"Okay, whatever. But don't be late. I've got about a thousand things I have to follow up on today after we talk about this."

"Talk about what?"

"I'll tell you when we get there."

The sedan whipped into a parking space in front of the motel. Elizabeth watched for a moment, then eased closer. As the driver reached for something in the backseat, she jerked open the passenger door and slid inside.

"Goddamn it, LeBlanc!" Gordon glared at her, and she noted his hand on his weapon. "What the hell's wrong with you?"

"A little jumpy lately?"

He turned around in his seat and scanned their

surroundings. Then he looked at her. "I thought I told you to go home and stay there."

"You also told me you'd call me." She checked her watch. "It's four o'clock. That was six hours ago."

He looked out the window and once again surveyed the area. Clearly, he didn't care to be sitting in this parking lot with her. On the other hand, he probably didn't like the idea of asking her into his motel room, either.

"Why haven't you arrested Lieutenant Brewer?" she asked.

His gaze hardened. "I don't know where he is."

"Not true. He's at the La Quinta on I-35. He checked in using the same phony ID he used at the rental car counter in Bakersfield."

He responded with a stony look.

"This isn't a love triangle," she said. "You're investigating something else and I'd like to know what it is."

"You've got an attitude, you know that?"

"I don't like being lied to."

He shook his head and looked out the window. The man had about fifteen years on her, but he knew he was trapped. He was going to have to tell her something, and although she doubted it would be the truth, she wanted to hear it.

She watched his profile, almost certain he was trying to come up with a plausible story.

Elizabeth reached into her purse. "Something came through our office that I thought might interest you."

"I told you not to go by the office."

She unfolded a piece of paper and handed it to

him. The color copy showed a head-and-shoulders photograph of a man lying on an autopsy table.

"Manuel Artigas. Killed last Tuesday night in San Antonio in a hit-and-run accident, just a day after Blake Reid was killed." She watched his face, but he didn't react to the name or the photo. "SAPD gave us a heads-up because Artigas had one of our agents' cell numbers programmed into a mobile phone collected at his apartment."

Gordon glanced up.

"Trent Lohman," she said. "Police figured maybe Artigas was one of our confidential informants. He had a long criminal history."

Gordon studied the picture again. "Was he?"

"One of our CIs? No," she said. "At least not that anyone's told me."

She watched him for a long moment. "That's two people with a connection to Trent Lohman who have turned up dead in the last week. Odd coincidence. Another odd coincidence happened while I was up in Utah looking for Gage Brewer."

Gordon folded the paper and tucked it into the pocket of his blazer. He took a deep breath and seemed resigned to whatever she was about to say.

"On our way to the Salt Lake City airport after being *removed* from the case, Frost and I pulled into a gas station. We bumped into several members of an FBI emergency response team. They were coming back from investigating a gas explosion about half an hour away."

Gordon didn't say anything.

"Funny thing, though, I also noticed a hazmat team

trucking through town." Elizabeth folded her arms over her chest. "Which sounds to me like something a *bit* more serious than a gas explosion."

"LeBlanc . . ." Gordon closed his eyes and rubbed the bridge of his nose.

"I know I'm new. I know I'm inexperienced," she said. "But I'm observant. And I'm *not* an idiot."

He looked at her. "What is it you want?"

"I'm a good agent," she said, trying to sound more confident than she felt. "I want you to give me a chance."

Country music and the spicy aroma of barbecue greeted them when they stepped through the door. Kelsey glanced around, looking for Ben.

"He's not here yet."

"Yeah, he is." Gage nodded at a corner of the restaurant, where Ben sat at a picnic table. "Damn, I never met a guy who brings a computer to a bar."

"It's a restaurant," she said. "And what's your beef with him?"

"I don't have a beef."

"Every time his name comes up, you say something negative."

Gage put his hand on her waist and steered her toward the table. "Okay, you're right. I don't like him. He's had the hots for you since I can remember."

"What are you talking about?" She looked over her shoulder at him.

"You know exactly what I'm talking about."

Kelsey bit back a retort as they neared the table. She sat down on the bench across from Ben.

"I ordered us a bucket of beer," he said. "Figured you'd be thirsty after your trip to Utah. Pretty dry up there, from what I hear."

"Thanks, I could use a beer," she said. "Talk about a disillusioning day. I'm still having trouble believing everything we heard in that meeting."

"Really?" Ben said. "I'm having no trouble at all. Government agents have been switching sides since the beginning of government."

"That's right, I forgot—you're a conspiracy theorist."

He shrugged. "Some conspiracies are real. I mean, think about it. Now that Bin Laden's dead, the Department of Homeland Security has to justify its existence—along with its very big budget."

Kelsey shook her head. "That's depressing."

"That's reality."

"What's with the laptop?" Gage asked, clearly ready to get to the point. She could tell the stress, the driving, and the lack of sleep were catching up to him.

"I noticed something you said back in the meeting," Ben said. "You were talking about Marissa Ramli."

"What about her?"

"You said you think she's a better bet than the parents. Why is that?"

He shrugged. "Sibling stuff." He looked at Kelsey. "Well, you don't have siblings, but I do. Anyway, she ran off with her boyfriend about the same time Adam started going to a mosque."

"And becoming very religious," Kelsey added. "I wouldn't think they'd have much in common at that point."

"They've got their childhood in common," Gage

said. "And problems with their parents. That goes a long way. Why, did you find something?"

"Not really," Ben said. "Gordon thinks there's nothing there. The FBI's had an eye on this woman ever since her brother was added to the watch list. They even had a phone tap there for a while. By all accounts, she hasn't seen or heard from her brother in five years, just like she said. Also, Gordon had that agent interview her, and didn't get anywhere."

"But you think she's a lead."

"Maybe." He turned the laptop around, and Kelsey was looking at a Facebook profile page for Marissa Jane Ramli.

"How'd you get into this account?" Kelsey asked.

Ben gave her a baleful look.

Gage leaned closer. "She's friends with him on Facebook?"

"No." Ben tapped a few keys. "However, she *is* friends with Amanda Lawrence." Ben brought up the profile page for a twentysomething blonde who was mugging for the camera with a cat in her arms.

"You think Amanda's him?"

"Maybe, maybe not. She's supposedly from Atlanta. She doesn't check in often, hardly uses the account—which doesn't really mean much. Some people open an account and let it sit idle."

"So?"

The bucket of beer arrived, and Kelsey wasted no time popping one open as she waited for Ben to get to the point.

Ben didn't reach for a beer, he just stared at his computer and drummed his fingers on the table.

"This could be nothing, but whenever these two exchange messages, it's about baseball. They're both Braves fans."

"Makes sense if they both grew up in Atlanta," Gage said, helping himself to a beer.

"Yeah. But I don't know." Ben looked at Kelsey. "What do you talk to your girlfriends about?"

"Oh, you know. Shoes, shopping, fingernail polish."

"I'm serious."

"Lots of stuff. People we know, our careers, relationships."

"But not sports, right?"

"Not usually."

Ben looked at Gage. "These two have exchanged four messages in the past five weeks, and they read like code. 'Braves versus O's tonight at the Yard. You watching?' Stuff like that."

"Sounds like Braves playing the Orioles at Camden Yard," Gage said.

"Yeah." Kelsey frowned at Ben.

"*Or* meet me somewhere tonight," Gage added.

"Exactly. The last message was two days ago. 'Hey, Braves are playing Phillies at the park. Don't miss.' Which could be Citizens Bank Park, where the Phillies play, right?" He looked at Gage. "But there was no game that night."

Gage tipped back his beer. Then he looked at the computer and rubbed his chin. "Do you have Google Earth on that thing?"

"Sure."

"Pull it up. See if there's a park anywhere near this girl's house."

Ben pulled up the program and entered Marissa's address in a blank on the screen. Kelsey watched the satellite view zoom in on California, then the Bay Area, then a densely packed neighborhood in San Francisco. They zoomed right on top of a concrete roof.

"That an apartment?" Gage asked.

"Yep. She's renting. The building's an old walk-up. Eight units, based on the utility records. She lives there with her daughter, who's four years old."

"Four," Kelsey said. "Wonder if that explains the falling-out with her parents. Sounds like she might have been pregnant when she left home. Boyfriend still in the picture?"

"I don't know."

Ben zoomed out. Two blocks south of the building was a square of green. Ben clicked on it. A street-level picture of a park popped up on the screen.

"Sandburg Park." Ben looked at Gage.

Everyone fell silent. Kelsey sipped her beer.

"I told Gordon about my Facebook theory, but he blew me off," Ben said. "I figure, you live in California. Maybe you could ask one of your buddies to drive up and do some reconnaissance, maybe pay her a visit."

Gage didn't say anything. He stared at the map, looking pensive.

"This girl's been hounded by federal agents for years," Gage said. "She's had her phone tapped. She's probably been followed. She's been interviewed recently. I doubt sending a two-hundred-fifty-pound SEAL to her door is going to put her at ease." He turned to Kelsey. "I'm thinking we need some soft skills."

Kelsey looked at the picture on the screen. "That's

a long way to go for a conversation. What if you're
wrong?"

"What if I'm not?" Ben said.

She glanced at Gage. His face looked determined,
and she knew what he was thinking. Even if this was a
long shot, it was the best lead they had.

"Flying or driving?" she asked him.

Kelsey scanned the area around her for threats but saw
mostly pierced teens and Reebok-wearing mall walkers.
She turned down a row of cars and slipped into a space.

Gage opened one of his eyes. "Where are we?"

"Almost to San Bernardino."

He squinted at the glare and checked his watch. "It's
ten. You were supposed to wake me up at nine."

"You needed the sleep."

They'd opted to drive instead of fly, because even
if they managed to get on and off a flight without
attracting the FBI's attention, Gage had flat-out rejected
the idea of traveling without his gun.

Now he gave her a grumpy look. "Tell me why we're
at a mall."

"It's either this or a Laundromat."

He closed his eyes and groaned.

"My jeans could walk around by themselves," Kelsey
said. "And that shirt you've been wearing for five days
is extremely ripe. Doesn't it bother you?"

"No."

She pushed open the door. "Well, I've reached my
limit. Come on, I'll buy you a Cinnabon."

Gage sighed. He got out of the SUV and looked at
her sullenly as he stretched his arms over his head.

"Let's make this quick," he said. "I want us in San Francisco by five."

Kelsey led the way to the mall entrance, and an enormous weight lifted off her shoulders as she stepped through the tinted-glass doors. The cool air, the power walkers, and the Muzak coming through the speakers made it seem like a typical Monday morning in Anywhere, USA. The prospects of mass murder and bioterrorism seemed impossibly remote.

They passed a kiosk, and Kelsey inhaled the scent of fresh java. Without a word, Gage stopped and plopped down a ten-dollar bill in exchange for two extra-extra-large cups. Caffeine in hand, they made their way through the food court to a spacious atrium lined with shops.

"Look!" Kelsey picked up her pace as she spotted Old Navy. "Just what we need."

She entered the store and walked up to a manne-quin wearing a stretchy cotton top in Caribbean blue. Normally Kelsey wasn't much of a shopper, but just the prospect of doing something as mundane as trying on blouses after seven full days of off-the-charts stress made her feel giddy. She snatched a hanger from the rack and looked over at Gage, who was grabbing a couple of black T-shirts off a display table.

He turned to look at her. "You ready?"

"We just got here."

His jaw tightened, and she could see him trying for patience. He looked at the shirt in her hand and then glanced at the mannequin.

"Uh-uh."

"What?"

"No cleavage. We're trying to keep a low profile. Here." He turned around and took a dark blue T-shirt off the table behind him. He must have noticed her look of disbelief. He grabbed another one in sky blue.

"Those are *men's* shirts."

"Perfect for you. The less attention you attract, the better." He turned to a nearby shelf and grabbed a navy baseball cap. He settled it on her head, then looked her up and down critically. "Even better. You can't see your hair."

"Don't be ridiculous."

"In case you forgot, you've spent the last week on the run from people who want you dead. I'd just as soon not take a bullet because you're trying to make a fashion statement."

She sighed. Then she glanced over his shoulder. "Look, why don't you get us some breakfast." She took the heap of T-shirts from him. "I'll be finished here in ten minutes."

Looking less than convinced, he exited the store and headed for a nearby food kiosk. One thing she could always count on was Gage waking up with an appetite.

She glanced around the store, and her good mood persisted as she noticed all the sale prices. The road trip had put a huge dent in her funds. After a lightning-fast shopping spree, she joined Gage at a bench, where he was munching a pretzel.

"Mustard for breakfast?" She crinkled her nose.

"Yours is plain."

He handed her a small paper bag, and she nibbled on the snack as they strolled back toward the entrance. She glanced at him beside her in his Bears cap and jeans. Here they were, an ordinary American couple cruising the mall and eating pretzels. It was just the sort of everyday activity she'd always yearned to do with him. She felt a wave of resentment for their jobs—both of them—which had made a normal relationship impossible from the very outset.

"What?" Gage looked at her.

"Nothing." She nodded at the small pink shopping bag in his hand. "What's in there?"

"Couple things."

She peered around him and caught a glimpse of red lace tucked amid pink tissue paper. "I thought you said nothing flashy," she said.

"No one's going to see this but me."

"Pretty confident, aren't you?"

"I'm a realist."

"I think you mean optimist."

They passed a mom with a double stroller and two apple-cheeked boys in denim overalls. Kelsey felt a different type of yearning.

Did Gage ever look at children and think about his future? He came from a big family, but he'd never once mentioned plans to have one for himself. In all the time they'd spent together, he'd never talked about it. And she'd been stupid enough to let him get away with that. Sometimes when it came to Gage, it was like her brain switched into low gear. From the first time she'd met him and felt that flutter in her stomach, her brain had sent up a warning: *He's too far away. He's gone all the time. He could get wounded or, God forbid, killed. He's an adrenaline junkie and he'll never settle down.*

And what had she done with all those prudent warnings? Nothing. She'd followed her heart.

And the result? His rejection had hurt her in a way Blake's lying and cheating never had.

"Hey." Gage nudged her shoulder. "What's wrong?"

"Nothing."

"Something's bugging you."

She didn't want to share her real thoughts, so she switched to the topic that had been on her mind during her four-hour shift behind the wheel.

"You know," she said, "for years I've worked with cops and detectives and people who have devoted their careers to law enforcement. For the life of me, I can't understand how Trent could do this."

"You mean go to the dark side?"

"Knowingly help someone who wants to kill innocent people."

Gage shook his head. "My guess is money."

"That's just so . . . disgusting," she said, for lack of a better word.

"Money makes the world go 'round."

"But doesn't the FBI take notice if one of their agents suddenly gets rich? I mean, isn't that how that CIA caught that spy? He started living large and driving a Mercedes."

"Maybe he plans to sock it away somewhere. Or leave the country. Who knows."

"And for a scientist to do it . . . that's almost as bad. It makes me sick."

"Yeah, I think Spurlock's motive was a little different, though. Mark said he spent his career developing the anthrax vaccine. You ever read about the doctor they eventually charged with the letters? He was working on the vaccine, too, and the research program was in trouble. Funding was about to disappear. The theory was, he wanted to draw attention to how vulnerable we are to bioterrorism and how much the government needed to fund his program."

"Again, it boils down to money."

"But maybe that's a good thing. Money's traceable," Gage pointed out. "And a couple of corrupt bureaucrats—that doesn't keep me up at night. I'm worried about Ramli."

Gage pitched his coffee cup in a trash can. Kelsey spotted a restroom sign.

"I'm going to make a pit stop and change into these clothes." She fished a plastic bag out of her purse that contained Gage's meager supply of toiletries. "Don't forget to take your pill," she said.

She slipped into the restroom and spent a few minutes cleaning up. The euphoria she'd felt over their little shopping excursion had faded, and her shoulders were again tense with worry.

What if Marissa Ramli was a dead end? What if her brother carried out his plan?

And on a more personal note, what if Gage really did get arrested and charged with murdering a federal agent? She tried to imagine him sticking around to be put on trial by the government he'd devoted his career to defending—the same government that now seemed intent on ruining his life. She couldn't imagine it. If it came down to that, what she *could* imagine was him disappearing into the wind, and her never seeing him again.

She emerged from the bathroom and looked around. No Gage. She walked closer to the food court and scanned the people standing in line for coffee and breakfast sandwiches. She didn't see him. She glanced over her shoulder at a store that sold sports memorabilia. Her pulse picked up as she did a slow turn, looking at every storefront.

Finally, she spotted him in a hair salon and walked over to join him. He stood in the middle of the waiting area, oblivious to the curious looks he was getting from the hairstylists as he gazed up at a TV mounted on the wall.

Kelsey glanced up at the screen. A newscaster stood on the White House lawn, and Kelsey read the headline scrolling beneath her: ANTHRAX ATTACK.

CHAPTER 19

"Are you watching this?" Ben asked as soon as Kelsey picked up the phone.

"We just saw it."

"Two people dead," he said. "Both postal workers who fell ill over the weekend. The letter was addressed to the president's chief of staff, but it never made it past the sorting center. The terror threat level's been elevated and there's a run on antibiotics at D.C.-area pharmacies."

Gage unlocked the SUV and tossed their packages in back. Clearly, he intended to drive the next shift. The question was, where were they going?

"What's Mark think?" Kelsey asked, keenly interested to hear what a world-renowned profiler thought of this latest development.

"He's standing right here. You can ask him yourself." She heard the phone being handed over as Gage started the car.

"Mark? What do you make of this?"

"It's definitely bad," he answered, "especially in terms of timing. We'd hoped to have days, maybe weeks more to investigate, but this signifies that he's exited the planning stage and is now focused on execution."

Kelsey bit back a sarcastic comment. She was no profiler, but it was obvious to her that he'd entered the execution phase when he chased them into the desert with an assault rifle.

"What do you think this means in the scheme of things?" she asked. "Is this really the big attack? A letter?"

"I'd say that's doubtful. This doesn't strike me as nearly spectacular enough for him."

She glanced at Gage behind the wheel as he turned out of the mall parking lot. "That's what Gage thinks, too."

"First of all, it lacks originality. We had letter attacks more than a decade ago. Also, this is a relatively low body count, considering the weapon he has at his disposal."

"Gage and I were just discussing that."

"I was expecting a subway attack. In an enclosed space like that, the pathogens don't disperse as quickly as they would outdoors, and they're not vulnerable to the sun's ultraviolet rays. Commuters enter the contaminated space, breathe the deadly material, and then get whisked away so another batch of people can be infected. It's like a lethal assembly line."

"Does anyone know where the letter was mailed?" Kelsey asked Mark. "Headline News didn't have a lot of details."

"Salt Lake City, postmarked Wednesday," Mark said. "That's unconfirmed, but that's what Gordon got from someone he knows at Quantico. And I'm inclined to think it's right because it fits the timeline of Ramli's suspected whereabouts."

Kelsey relayed the details to Gage as he entered the on-ramp to Interstate 10 west.

"I'd bet money this is just his opening move," Gage said. "He's a demo man. You saw the video. Killing off postal workers with a tainted letter doesn't have nearly enough bang for this guy."

"Gordon's about to board a plane to Washington," Mark told her. "He's convinced it's the site of the next attack."

"What do you think?" Kelsey asked.

"I'm not sure. It could just as easily be New York, Boston, any city with a subway system or major airport would be my guess. We need intel on his whereabouts. Are you still on your way to the sister's?"

"We still are." Kelsey glanced at Gage, who was driving exactly the speed limit. The last thing they needed was to get pulled over.

"Good, because we just got a new update on that Facebook page. The message is about a Braves and Astros game at five tonight at the park."

"Is there really a game tonight?"

"Ben says yes, but it's at seven o'clock, so this is worth checking out. It's conceivable that he could have mailed that letter and traveled to San Francisco by now. He could be meeting up with his sister to get money, documents, who knows."

"Sounds like kind of a long shot," Kelsey said.

"Gordon said the same thing, but he's sending an agent up there to help with surveillance. I've got a number so you guys can coordinate."

As Kelsey rummaged for a pen, he recited a number with a San Antonio area code.

"What's his name?"

"*Her* name is Elizabeth LeBlanc."

"LeBlanc. I've never heard of her. She's out of Blake's office?"

"Shit, you're kidding me," Gage said. "They're sending LeBlanc?"

"What's wrong?" she asked. "You said you wanted more agents. She can help with surveillance."

"I think she's new," Mark told her. "But she was up there already pursuing a lead, so she's available."

"And we're assuming 'park' in the message refers to the park near Marissa's house? Sandburg Park?"

"Could be Minute Maid ballpark in Houston," Mark said. "That's where the actual game is being played tonight. But if this is a meet-up, we obviously don't want to miss it. Can you get there in time?"

"We should, barring any unforeseen disasters—which, given our recent track record, means maybe."

"Keep us posted."

She got off with Mark and looked at Gage. "Gordon's headed to D.C. He's convinced he's planning something big against a political target. He's focused on Washington."

"I bet he's also focused on getting his family out of the city."

"Can you blame him? Anyway, there actually *is* a Braves game tonight, so this could turn out to be nothing. What's your problem with this LeBlanc woman?"

"She's green as grass."

"Well, at least she's available. If we see anyone who

looks even remotely like Ramli, she can help us tail him."

"That's not happening. This woman's FBI Barbie. He'll spot her in a minute. She tried to tail me from San Diego to Piney Creek, and I lost her in no time."

"She's that bad?"

"She sticks out. That's really all they've got?"

"All they've got for us. This feels like a token effort, because Gordon's convinced he's in Washington. Which would actually be better news, because they're much more equipped to handle a threat like this."

Gage shook his head. "Let's hope he's right."

Elizabeth hurried along the sidewalk, looking for Bay Area Bread Company. She spotted it—a redbrick building with yellow awnings, just as he'd promised. Also as promised, there was a white pickup parked in the alley beside the building.

Elizabeth opened the door and slid in.

"You're late," Gage said flatly.

"Something came up." She pulled the door shut and gazed across the street at the postage-size patch of real estate known as Sandburg Park. Several boys were tossing a Frisbee. A group of old men sat at concrete tables playing chess. "What happened?"

"He's a no-show," Gage said. "Same with the sister."

"What about cars?"

"Nothing suspicious. If he's still in a white four-door, we haven't seen it. Marissa drives a yellow Mini Cooper, and we haven't seen that, either."

"Where's Kelsey?" Elizabeth asked, scanning the park benches.

"I put her on overwatch."

She gave Gage a questioning look, and he nodded across the street at a redbrick building about eight stories tall.

"That's apartments?"

"Ground floor's retail," he said. "The rest is residential. She slipped in behind some people an hour ago and made her way to the terrace on the roof."

Elizabeth eyed the rooftop. She couldn't see Kelsey, but anyone up there would have a clear line of sight to the building two blocks north, where Marissa lived with her daughter.

"Not a bad setup," Elizabeth said.

"Yeah, Gage didn't want her too close to the action."

Elizabeth shot a startled look at the cell phone in the cup holder. She hadn't realized it was on speakerphone.

"Nice outfit," Derek Vaughn said. "Thought you were coming as a jogger."

"Like I said, something came up." She glanced over her shoulder. "Where are you?"

"Park bench, southwest corner. You should recognize the Bears cap."

Elizabeth spotted him lounging on a park bench. He had a Bluetooth hooked to his ear and was once again eating. It looked like a hot dog this time.

"What came up?" Gage asked, pulling her attention back to the case.

"I was just over at Berkeley following up on a lead. This originated with Kelsey, actually. From the notepad she left in her uncle's cabin."

Elizabeth pulled out her own notepad and flipped it open. "A UC Berkeley phone number. Turns out Blake

Reid had several conversations with one of their faculty members, a Dr. Shamus, the Friday before he died."

"Microbiology?" Gage asked.

"That's what I thought, too, but his doctorate is in civil engineering. He's on vacation right now—his honeymoon, actually—so I talked to one of his colleagues in the engineering department. Aside from teaching, Shamus does consultations for major urban projects. His biggest project to date is the recent redesign of the Washington-area Metro system."

She paused to let the implications of that sink in.

"So, Gordon's theory is gaining ground. Ramli might be targeting the capital. The FBI believes he's there now, most likely setting up surveillance of the target."

Gage looked at her for a long moment. He picked up his phone.

"You catch all that?" he asked. "Let me let you go. I need to call Kelsey." He clicked off and dialed a number with his thumb. "Hey, it's me. Come on down, you need to hear this."

Adam picked up on the first ring.

"The money's late," Trent told him.

Pause. "Is this a secure line?"

"What do you think?"

"The money will be there. I've had to make some changes to the plan."

"That part of the plan isn't changeable." Trent peered through the binoculars. "You might be interested to know I've got my eye on your sister's house. You were supposed to pick up the package today."

"Someone else took care of it."

"That wasn't part of the plan, either. Bolton doesn't like surprises." Trent shifted the binoculars to the front door of the building. "I've been seeing your niece around. Cute girl. What is she, four? Five?"

No response.

"Been seeing some other people around, too. People like Gage Brewer." He waited for a reaction. "You said you took care of him in the desert."

"Brewer won't be a problem."

"He'd better not be, or it's on your head."

Again, no response.

Trent lowered his binoculars and stepped away from the window. He checked his watch. "It's nine A.M. in Hong Kong. You've got exactly three hours to make that transfer, or we're pulling the plug."

"Is that a threat?"

"It's a fact. We're done fucking around, and we have a long reach. You might be able to slip away, but they won't. Three hours."

Dial tone.

Trent stuffed his gear into the backpack and slung it over his shoulder. He crossed the empty apartment and opened the door slightly. The hallway smelled like cooked fish. Trent checked for nosy neighbors, then made a beeline for the elevator bank, where a hunched old woman stood leaning on a cane. She'd already pressed the down button, and Trent avoided her gaze as he pulled off his unseasonably warm leather gloves and stuffed them in his pocket. The elevator doors dinged open. He waited impatiently as she hobbled on. Someone in the corner reached over to hold the door for her.

"Thank you, dear."

"No problem."

Trent stepped in behind her, and the doors started to close.

Kelsey's gaze met his. For a split second, shock. Then adrenaline took over and she lunged through the closing doors. Her jacket snagged. He had her. She let out an ear-piercing shriek as she twisted free of the fabric and raced down the hallway. A muffled curse behind her as the elevator thudded shut.

Her heart skittered with relief, but it was short-lived as she glanced up and down the corridor. What floor was she on? Where were the stairs? Behind her, at the far end of the hallway, an exit sign. She bolted for it. She shoved the door open and found herself in a concrete stairwell. A door banged open below. Footsteps echoed through the chamber like gunshots as Trent sprinted up.

She took the steps two at a time and shoved through the door at the very top. The rooftop terrace. She raced to the wall and peered down at the neighboring building. Fear zinged through her now as she realized she'd underestimated the drop.

A door squeaked open. Footfalls, coming fast. Kelsey scrambled over the wall and dropped onto the adjacent building, landing hard on the concrete. She scampered to her feet and sprinted past a row of planters to the door.

Locked! She saw the keypad beneath the doorknob. She cupped her hand and peered through the glass. A workout room. Treadmills. Weight machines. Every damn one of them empty.

She glanced over her shoulder. No Trent. Did he know she was here? She scampered around the side of the building and hid from view as her breath came in shallow gasps and she tried to get her bearings. Terror gripped her as she looked around and saw nothing but rooftops and clouds.

A muffled *thud*. The rapid slap of footsteps.

She rushed to the far wall and looked over. Another building, thank God, but it was at least a ten-foot drop. She glanced around desperately. A metal utility ladder led down. She made a run for it. In the corner of her eye, a dark blur.

She lunged for the ladder and practically slid down the rungs, cutting her hands on the rails as she went. She glanced around. This building was older. No plants, no workout room up here—only a giant vent and a cinder-block structure, which she fervently hoped had an access door. She sprinted to it and dashed around the corner. Relief spurted through her as she spied the door. No keypad this time, but it was locked. She peered through the dusty window.

Footsteps.

On a burst of panic, she jerked the cap from her head and used it to protect her fist as she punched through the glass. The shattering noise sent a shot of terror through her as she stuck her arm inside and groped for a latch.

Please, please, please.

Her fingers encountered the bolt. She flipped it, jerked her arm back through the window, and yanked open the door just as a dark shape rounded the corner.

Screaming, she dove through the doorway and into the stairwell. Pain burned her scalp as he grabbed her by the ponytail. She mule-kicked backward and connected with his body.

"Fucking *bitch*!"

She raced down the steps, barely touching them as she rounded landing after landing. He was behind her. He was gaining. She took one more flight and wrenched open the door.

She was in a dim hallway lined with numbered doors. She tried the first one, then the second.

"Help!" She pounded on another locked door. "Somebody *help*!" She glanced frantically over her shoulder as the stairwell door squealed open.

Across the hall, a door opened. She barreled through it, startling the tenant who'd ventured a peek into the hallway.

She slammed the door and locked it as an old man watched her through Coke-bottle glasses. She glanced down and realized her hand was bleeding from punching the glass.

"Fire escape! Where is it?" She rushed for the nearest window and looked out. She had to be on the sixth or seventh floor.

"Is there a fire escape?" she demanded.

"What the hell is this? Who are you?"

The door rattled. Kelsey glanced at it, unnerved. She shot a glance into the kitchen and caught sight of something just beyond the window.

She rushed across the room and shoved a dropleaf table out of the way. "Go into the bedroom!" she barked, fumbling with the window lock. Her hand was slick with blood. "Call 911!"

She lifted the windowpane and squeezed through the

opening, hoping Trent wouldn't be able to do the same.
She glanced at the alley below and prayed the rusty
slats would hold her weight. She climbed down the first
vertical metal staircase. Her phone rang, startling her,
and her foot missed a rung. She crashed to her knees on
the grate. Through metal slats she saw Dumpsters and
delivery trucks way, way below. The metal squeaked
under her and she fought a wave of nausea.

Her phone buzzed again. It would be Gage, wondering where she was.

"Gage!" she shrieked, too terrified to look for him as
she struggled to focus on the endless vertical stairs.

Five more levels.

Above her, shouting.

Four more levels.

She glanced up and saw Trent's head poking out
from the window. The entire metal frame shifted and
groaned as he climbed onto the platform. She watched,
horrified by his agility, as he descended two entire levels
in a matter of seconds.

In his hand was a gun.

Gage shoved his phone in his pocket and skimmed the
sidewalk. "Where the hell'd she go?"

Agent LeBlanc shook her head. Gage spotted Derek
crossing the street and waved him over.

"She's not answering."

Derek looked up and down the block, just as Gage
had been doing for the last ten minutes.

"Think she stopped for coffee or something?" Derek
asked.

"No." Apprehension tickled the back of his neck. He eyed the rooftop again.

"Maybe we should—"

"Quiet!" Gage cut him off. "You hear that?"

"What?"

In the distance, a scream.

She grabbed the railing and scrambled down. *Three more levels.*

Her hands slipped on the rails. She was bleeding. Her heart pounded wildly as Trent closed in on her. *Two more flights.*

She glanced up.

Pop.

The bullet was like a firecracker right beside her head. She leaped onto the last level, where a hinged metal ladder lay flat atop the grate. No time to position it, so she dropped to her stomach and dangled her legs off the side.

It's too far, she thought, looking down. She shimmied to the edge, and her knuckles were white on the metal slats as her legs dangled in midair.

Pop!

She let go.

CHAPTER 20

"Kelsey!"

Gage and Derek sprinted around the corner as Elizabeth struggled to keep up. She'd heard gunshots. Those had definitely been gunshots, and they weren't far away. Gripping her weapon and praying she wouldn't have to use it, Elizabeth shoved past pedestrians and raced across the street, then stopped short as a taxi whizzed past her, horn blaring. Stunned by the close call, she stood paralyzed for a moment, then lunged for the sidewalk. She rounded the corner, but Gage and Derek had already disappeared from view.

She jerked her phone from her pocket and pressed the button to connect with 911.

"Shots fired at—" Where the hell were they? She recalled the sister's address and rattled it off. "Officer needs backup!"

"One moment, please."

"Immediate backup!" She shoved the phone into her pocket and sprinted down the narrow alley. She reached a one-way street and checked right, then left. Should she turn or keep going? She raced for the next

SCORCHED   299

intersection and checked in both directions. She spotted Derek just as he vanished around a corner. She took off after him.

Another shriek. She halted to listen. It was *behind* her.

Doubling back, she reached the street she'd just crossed and ran down it. She passed an alley and saw a flash of movement.

Another flash of movement jerked her attention up, where a man in a dark suit was clattering down a fire escape. He dropped to his stomach on the last level and leaped to the ground.

"FBI! Freeze!" she yelled.

He froze, crouched on the ground with his back to her, facing the direction where the other person— Kelsey?—had just dashed around a corner.

"Hands in the air!" Elizabeth pointed her gun at his back as she approached. He was silhouetted in the alley, against the bright flow of traffic.

She'd heard gunshots. But where was the gun now? Elizabeth darted her gaze into doorways, between Dumpsters, looking for threats.

"We're on the same team," he called, slowly rising to his feet.

"Hands where I can see them!"

"Relax, I'm with the FBI. I'm with you." His arms moved downward.

"Hands *up*!"

Beyond him, cars and trucks and cyclists whisked past, oblivious to the confrontation happening right in their midst. God, where was her backup? Her pulse raced as she moved cautiously toward him. Where was his weapon? She recalled him hurrying down the fire escape. He would have tucked it in his pants or his holster.

And then she spotted it. It was on the ground near a puddle. He must have dropped it and it skittered out of reach.

She relaxed a fraction.

"Turn around," she ordered. "Slowly."

Slowly, he turned around. Relief flashed across his face.

"Hey, I know you." His arms started to move down.

"Hands *up*!"

He smiled. Very friendly, except that his hands were in the air and her gun was pointed straight at his chest. She strained to keep her arms steady.

"You're the new agent," he said. "Elaina, is it?"

"Elizabeth."

In the distance, sirens. Panic flitted across his face, then disappeared. Another smile. "Hey, we're on the same team, Elizabeth. I'm—"

"I know who you are."

His gaze narrowed. The smile returned, but it didn't reach his eyes now.

"You were after Kelsey Quinn," she said. "You've been after her since the night of Reid's murder. She was there, wasn't she? She saw you kill him. And then you staged the scene."

The smile vanished. His face hardened. His gaze flicked right and she knew he was thinking about that weapon. A warning whispered in her head. She'd pushed him too far.

• • •

Kelsey careened around the corner and found herself in yet another alley. Terror squeezed her chest. This neighborhood was a labyrinth. She glanced around as she ran down the narrow passage, looking for an escape, a hiding place. She heard sirens, but they sounded blocks away, back near the park.

She tripped on a pothole and fell against a Dumpster. She paused to look over her shoulder. No Trent. She ducked behind the giant metal bin and bent over to suck down big gulps of air. The alley smelled of garbage and urine. A wave of dizziness washed over her as she braced her hands against her burning thighs and gasped for oxygen.

Where had he gone? And where had Gage gone? Remembering the missed call, she pulled her phone from her pocket and stared down at it, dazed.

A sharp whistle and her head snapped up.

"Kelsey!"

It was Derek at the end of the alley. He jogged toward her, pistol in hand. Kelsey pushed off of the Dumpster and stumbled toward him.

Behind her, a door banged open.

"Whoa!" Gage stopped short as he stared down the barrel of the gun.

"Shit, man." Derek lowered the weapon. "Announce yourself. I almost took your head off."

Gage looked at Kelsey and felt a punch of fear. "Fuck, you're bleeding."

She slumped against the brick wall. Her cheeks were flushed and she was gasping like she'd just run a marathon. "He's here. He was chasing me."

"Who?" Derek asked.

"Trent Lohman. With a gun."

"Kelsey, you're *bleeding*." Gage took her by the shoulders and lowered her to the ground, which she let him do with almost no resistance.

"I'm fine."

But she wasn't fine. Not by a long shot. Blood saturated her arm. He tugged her sleeve up. "Shit, Kelsey." His heart lodged in his throat as he searched for a bullet wound.

"I'm fine. *Ouch!*" She pulled away.

"I need to look at this. What happened?"

She laughed—and it sounded a bit hysterical. "I punched through a window." She tilted her head back and looked up at the sky. "I was trying to get off the roof. Trent was chasing me."

Gage stripped off his shirt to make a bandage for her wound. He exchanged a look with Derek.

Trent Lohman was a fucking dead man.

"Step over to the wall." Elizabeth tried to sound calm as she pointed her weapon at his center body mass. "Put your palms against it, feet spread."

Trent Lohman didn't move. He watched with an icy gaze as she stepped over to his gun and—not taking her eyes off him—crouched down to pick it up. She tucked it into the waistband of her pants. The sirens grew nearer, and he darted a glance over her shoulder.

"What are you doing, Elizabeth?"

She raised her weapon. "I said, hands against the wall."

"Or what? You going to shoot an unarmed man? A fellow agent?"

"I'm going to arrest you." Her mouth was so dry, she could hardly speak. Her heart was racing.

"No, Elizabeth, you're not." His voice was low now, and she could barely hear it over the approaching sirens. "You're going to turn around and walk away and pretend this never happened."

He took a step back. And another. Fear gripped her. He glanced at her gun. Fully loaded, the Glock weighed thirty-one ounces. Right now it felt like thirty-one pounds.

He looked into her eyes. She stepped closer. Seconds ticked by. She knew he saw the tremor in her arms because his lip curved in the faintest smile.

He bolted.

"Stop!"

She sprinted after him. He raced around the corner. She burst into the sunlight. Brakes screeched. Horns blared.

She heard a sickening thud.

CHAPTER 21

Kelsey loathed hospitals. She hated the smells, the sights, the crowded waiting rooms. She hated the delays. She and Gage had been here for three hours, and even though a young intern had stitched her up ages ago, they were still stuck in an exam bay.

The doors to the corridor pushed open, and Kelsey watched with curiosity as a woman came toward them with a purposeful stride. She stopped just outside the curtain.

"Dr. Quinn? I'm Elizabeth LeBlanc." She cast a tentative look at Kelsey's arm and seemed to decide not to offer a handshake. "How are you?"

"Almost finished, I hope." Kelsey glanced at the nurses' station, where her paperwork seemed to have been sucked into the Bermuda Triangle. "How are *you*?" she asked, studying the agent's face. It wasn't as pasty as it had been earlier, when she'd been watching a pair of ME's assistants zip Trent Lohman into a body bag. But still the woman looked a bit shell-shocked in her wrinkled pantsuit, her blond hair pulled back in a messy bun.

"What's the word from Gordon?" Gage asked. His steely expression said he was in no mood for brush-offs.

"I just got off the phone with him. A lot's happened. Are you sure you want to hear it?"

"We're sure," Kelsey said, surprised by the agent's candor. Everyone else they'd talked to tonight—including Gordon, whom Kelsey had called while she was having her arm sutured—had demanded all kinds of information, but provided little in return. About all they knew right now was that Trent was dead, Gordon was still in Washington, and CNN was doing all anthrax, all the time.

The media was having a field day. All reports so far indicated they were dealing with inhalation anthrax, which was scariest from a public health perspective. The news stations were hungry for visuals, though, and kept running pictures of cutaneous anthrax, which was characterized by skin legions and grotesque sores. The pictures were frightening, and it was no wonder there was a run on antibiotics in Washington, D.C.

The agent glanced at a television mounted in a nearby waiting area. "So you've seen the news?"

"Three more letters," Gage said.

"Four," she corrected. "The most recent one hasn't been announced. We've now had a total of four letters turn up in D.C., one in New York, and another that just showed up in a mail-sorting facility in Los Angeles. All were addressed to political targets, such as senators or cabinet members."

"Any fatalities?" Kelsey asked.

"Another postal worker. And a staffer who works for a New York congresswoman is in ICU. She opened the mail Friday and started experiencing respiratory problems over the weekend."

Gage shook his head.

"It's hard to find a silver lining here, but"—she took a deep breath—"the positive news is, Gordon is no longer alone in trying to address this threat. The entire Department of Homeland Security has been spurred into action. We've got elevated security levels at airports, malls, stadiums. We've got stepped-up security at train stations and subway entrances. We've even got police posted at several D.C. pharmacies to deal with the run on antibiotics."

Kelsey looked at Gage and was pretty sure she knew what he was thinking. Just days ago, he'd been within arm's reach of the man who started all this.

She turned to the agent. "Why do I get the impression you didn't really come here to tell us all this?"

"You're right." She took out her phone. "I have a photograph to show you."

She pushed a few buttons and handed the phone to Kelsey. The picture on the screen was clearly an autopsy photo, and Kelsey's stomach clenched as she recognized the face.

"That's the man from Blake's." She looked at Gage. "The man who came after me." She turned to LeBlanc. "Please tell me he's not really a cop."

"Manuel Artigas. He was a career criminal down in South Texas. Detectives investigating his hit-and-run 'accident' now think he was murdered by Trent Lohman. They have an eyewitness who provided a description of the car that struck Artigas. Traces of

SCORCHED   307

paint from the victim's clothes match paint from the bucar Trent was using that day."

"Bucar?" Gage asked.

"A Bureau car. A vehicle from the motor pool."

"You're saying this man was Trent's accomplice, and Trent murdered him, too?" Kelsey asked. She looked at the picture again. The man was Latino, which would fit with the hair evidence recovered by Dr. Froehler at autopsy.

"The new theory of the case is that Trent hired Artigas to help kill Blake after Blake stumbled across Trent's connection to this ACB terrorist cell."

"This all started with me," Kelsey said, feeling a sharp pang of guilt. "I asked him to help ID those bones, which led to the ACB cell in the Philippines."

"Which led to that training video, in which Ramli is the ringleader," LeBlanc said. "We may never know for sure how it happened, since both Blake and Trent are dead. But it appears Blake had some sort of tip-off that Trent was closely involved with this group. Maybe Trent tried to cover something up and Blake got suspicious. Or maybe he tried to stymie Blake's questions about the group. We've gone back and analyzed both of their phone records and it appears that Blake systematically called a list of people Trent had been contacting on his cell phone. Personally, my guess is that Blake got hold of the phone and copied down the numbers for investigation."

Kelsey glanced at Gage and felt a faint stirring of hope as the scenario started to take shape. Not once had the agent mentioned evidence against Gage.

"Again, we may never know just how it unfolded, but that would account for Blake's calls to Dr. Shamus at Berkeley and Robert Spurlock, aka Charles Weber, up in Utah. Blake called Spurlock repeatedly, but he never answered his phone and the call went to voice mail."

"Spurlock was dead by then," Kelsey said. "Postmortem interval indicates he was killed at least a week before Blake's trip there."

"Which might explain why he gave up on the phone and decided to pay him a visit." LeBlanc paused. "He must have had at least some inkling of the importance of all this by that point."

Kelsey looked away and closed her eyes. All this because she'd asked him to run some tests for her.

"Hey."

She looked at Gage.

"Cut it out," he said sternly.

"What?"

"The guilt. If your case hadn't tipped him off about what Trent was doing, something else would have. And we'd still have this threat on our hands, only we'd probably be in the dark about the FBI connection." He looked at LeBlanc. "Am I right?"

"Most likely, yes."

"So, the investigation shows that Trent killed Blake," Kelsey said. "What does that mean about his supposed 'alibi'? Can we get Bolton, too? He's part of the effort to frame Gage."

LeBlanc glanced over her shoulder, clearly uneasy with even the mention of his name. "That part is not as straightforward. There's been a misunderstanding about Bolton's statement to investigators—the statement in which he gave Trent an alibi."

Gage folded his arms over his chest. "I'd love to hear this."

Another glance over her shoulder, and Kelsey started to get annoyed.

"Evidently, Bolton told investigators Trent was in a meeting with him in Washington at the time of Blake's murder. That was Trent's original alibi. Now Bolton's saying they had the meeting by Skype after Trent missed his flight. Obviously, that makes for a much flimsier alibi because we can't determine the exact time of Blake's death."

"I could," Kelsey said.

"Leave it alone." Gage gave her a sharp look. "You don't want to get any deeper into this. And it doesn't matter, anyway. Bolton's off the hook."

"But that's not right," Kelsey protested. "He comes off as innocent."

"He may actually *be* innocent," LeBlanc said.

Kelsey gaped at the woman. The word *naïve* popped into her head.

"Gordon tells me forensic accountants have uncovered a money transfer into a Hong Kong bank account for Trent Lohman."

"A money motive, just like we thought," Gage said.

"We wouldn't even know about the payment, except that we've had our eye on this organization for a while," LeBlanc continued. "It poses as a legitimate business, but we've been investigating whether it funnels money to terrorists. It evidently funneled money to Trent, but we have no indications that Bolton received payments like that. We really have no solid evidence Bolton is involved in this at all, beyond making an ambiguous statement to investigators."

"What about the fingerprint evidence?" Gage asked.

"Gordon asked me to update you on that, too. Apparently that *also* was the result of a mix-up. The lab now says the print they found on the beer bottle in Blake's apartment is inconclusive."

Kelsey felt outrage bubbling up in her chest. "How is that possible? That print was the basis for an arrest warrant! And what about the hair?"

LeBlanc looked puzzled. "What hair?"

"The human hair—not Blake's—that was recovered from his body at autopsy. It probably belongs to Artigas. It definitely doesn't belong to Gage."

"I don't know what you're talking about. I've been over all the reports and I don't know anything about a hair."

"It was sent to Quantico."

The woman just looked at her, and Kelsey felt a renewed wave of outrage. Clearly, someone had manipulated the physical evidence.

"I understand your frustration." The woman glanced at Gage. "Gordon does, too. He wanted me to assure you that he's looking into how this could have happened."

Gage shook his head and looked away, obviously disgusted.

Kelsey glanced down the hallway to see Derek coming toward them. He'd changed out of his jogging gear and was now in his typical civilian attire of jeans, T-shirt, and cowboy boots.

"What'd I miss?"

He directed the question at the FBI agent, and Kelsey noticed she seemed flustered all of a sudden.

"I was just giving Lieutenant Brewer here an update on recent developments." She glanced at her watch. "But I'm dragging this out." She looked at Gage. "What I most needed to tell you is how sorry I am, on behalf of the Bureau, for your ordeal."

Gage didn't say anything.

"The warrant for your arrest has been dropped. You're free to go back to your base, your life, your vacation." She smiled weakly. "Although I realize it's almost over now."

Kelsey looked at Gage. He was off the hook. *Finally.* Which meant he was off the hook in other ways, too. He was free to go back to San Diego, as Kelsey had known he would all along.

"Well, that's it." The agent looked at Kelsey, then Derek, then Gage. "I'll just . . . get out of your way. Have a safe trip back to base, Lieutenant."

"Thank you." Gage nodded crisply.

Kelsey watched her leave.

"So." Derek slapped Gage on the back. "Good news, huh?"

Gage looked at Kelsey.

Derek smiled. "How's the arm, Kels?"

She glanced down at her bandage. "Fine. All stitched up." She looked up, but he was busy exchanging keys with Gage. Derek's pickup had been closest, so Gage had used it to rush her to the hospital.

"Your rental's parked in the visitors' lot," Derek said. "Your pickup's—"

"I know, I saw it." Derek slapped him on the back

again. "See you back at base, 1400 tomorrow. Don't be late." He turned to Kelsey and she got a back slap, too. "You take care of that arm."

He strode away, and she looked at Gage. "Gee, he seems in a hurry to get on the road."

Gage didn't say anything. He never shared much about his buddies' personal lives, but Kelsey could tell FBI Barbie was going to have her hands full tonight.

"Sit tight," Gage told her.

"Where are you going?"

"To track down that paperwork. I want to get the hell out of here."

Elizabeth stopped on the sidewalk and took a deep breath. The night was damp. Chilly. She squeezed her arms around herself and gazed out at the street, where a rainbow of lights reflected off the slick pavement. Traffic zoomed past and Elizabeth watched it, trying to recall where she'd parked.

She couldn't even recall what she was driving today. A rental. Something dark, four doors. She vaguely remembered signing papers for it at the airport this morning at the beginning of what had turned out to be the longest day of her life.

Elizabeth looked at her watch. She'd been awake for nearly twenty hours, subsisting on M&M's and a river of coffee. She had phone calls to make, reports to write, and a mountain of e-mails to answer as soon as she checked into whatever motel was going to be her home tonight.

And yet she couldn't stop thinking about that sound, that bone-chilling thud that had marked the end of a man's life. She'd recognized it the instant she heard it, and it had come back to her over and over again as she stood at the accident scene, giving her statement and talking on the phone. She'd stayed there for hours dealing with a thousand different logistics, and then more when she'd gone into the San Francisco field office to give yet *another* statement. Through all of it, she'd kept thinking about that sound and feeling grateful that Trent's wife hadn't been there to hear it. Elizabeth had never laid eyes on the woman. She had no idea if she knew what a morally deficient person she'd married. She had no idea if she had a clue about her husband's corruption. But even if she did, Elizabeth was glad she hadn't been there today to hear a sound like that.

Elizabeth wrapped her arms around herself again. Her chest constricted, and she felt the anxiety rushing back again. She closed her eyes and took a deep breath and tried to make it go away.

"Hey, there."

She turned around, not really surprised by the voice. She watched him walk toward her, tall and strong and sure of himself. Had she actually been waiting for him? Surely she was smarter than that.

He stopped and gazed down at her with those whiskey-brown eyes. He'd changed clothes somewhere, but hadn't managed to shave, and Elizabeth's nerves fluttered.

"Where you headed?" He gave her a half-smile.

"Work."

"At this hour?"

"I've got mountains of reports."

"Can't they wait till tomorrow?"

"No."

She looked away, pretty sure he could see through her.

"That's a shame." He draped an arm over her shoulder. Her muscles tensed, but she let his arm stay there, all warm and heavy. "Because I know this bar. And it looks to me like you could use a drink."

Marissa stepped into her daughter's room.

"What is it, sweetie?"

"I can't sleep."

She walked to the bedside and switched on the Sleeping Beauty lamp. Leila was having a tough time settling down tonight. There had been all the sirens outside and CNN blaring in the kitchen. Plus she'd always been able to sense when her mother was upset. Marissa sank onto the side of the bed and tucked the covers up.

"Would you like me to read you a story?"

"Yes!"

"How about *Goodnight Moon*?" A bit young for her, but it usually worked like magic.

"*Nightmare in My Closet.*"

"We did that one already."

"Please?"

Marissa fished the book out of the basket beside the bed. It was one of Leila's favorites. She loved the part where the boy shoots the monster with his cork gun and reduces him to tears. If only it were so easy.

"Okay, but this is the last time tonight."

A knock sounded at the front door and Marissa jumped to her feet.

"Who is it, Mommy?"

"I don't know. Maybe Mrs. Whitney. I'll be right back." She closed Leila's door behind her and hurried to the front door. No one had buzzed her, so it was either a neighbor or someone who'd slipped into the building. She peered through the peephole and felt a jolt of fear.

She swung open the door. "Are you crazy? What are you doing here?"

Gage pulled into the parking lot of yet another crappy motel. This one faced the highway and was tucked between a Squeaky Clean Car Wash and Madam Chen's Chinese Buffet. The two-story building offered cable TV and guaranteed traffic noise. It also offered a straight shot to the airport, so—as Kelsey had pointed out—Gage could drop her off to catch a flight before heading down the coast to report for duty.

"Hey, good news," she said. "Looks like they have a vacancy."

He glanced at the neon sign as he whipped into a space. "Stop."

"What?"

He shoved open the door. "Don't pretend you're happy about this."

She got out, too. "Actually, I'm very happy. You think I *liked* the idea of you facing charges for something you didn't do?"

Gage shot her a look as he crossed the sidewalk and jerked open the door. He took one glance at the fake plants in the lobby and knew the place was going to be a dump. A tattooed teenager sat behind the reception counter playing a hand-held video game. He put it aside and looked up at them.

"I need a room." Gage handed over a credit card.

"I'd think *you'd* be happy, too." Kelsey rummaged through her purse. "You don't have to worry about getting intercepted by a pair of MIBs the minute you set foot on base."

"Goddamn it, would you *stop*?"

The kid looked up from his computer screen. "Uh, we've got a king or a double."

"King." Gage turned to glare at Kelsey. "Put your money away."

She stuffed the money back into her wallet, looking annoyed. It was about time. She'd been relentlessly cheerful for the past hour.

Gage scrawled his name on the paperwork as the kid passed him a key card.

"You're in 206. That's up the stairs and—"

"We got it." He took the card and led Kelsey up a flight of stairs that had been carpeted circa the Reagan Administration.

"I don't know what your problem is tonight," Kelsey said, "but you barely said ten words to me at the hospital. And even less in the car."

They passed an ice machine alcove, which of course had no ice machine. Gage reached the room and shoved the card into the key slot.

"I would think you'd be happy for a change." She followed him into the musty room. "But you've been nothing but hostile."

"Hostile?" He flipped a light switch. "You think I'm being hostile?"

"Yes."

"Someone tried to put a bullet in you today." He flung his keys on the dresser. "I sat in a fucking ER and watched some twelve-year-old doctor sew up your arm. You're damn right I'm hostile."

Her eyebrows arched. "*That's* what this is about? My stitches?"

"You could have been killed!"

She looked incredulous. "Welcome to my world, Gage."

"Are you actually downplaying this?"

"Not at all. I can only imagine how stressful it must be to worry about someone for *five whole minutes*!"

He gritted his teeth and turned away from her. He didn't want to talk about this right now. He was too furious.

Behind him, a light went on in the bathroom and the door slammed shut.

Gage sank down on the bed. He rested his elbows on his knees and scowled down at the dingy carpet. He'd fucked up royally today. When he'd set up that surveillance op, all he'd been thinking about was getting Kelsey out of the way. It had never occurred to him that they might not be the only ones watching Ramli's sister.

He scrubbed his hands over his face. It was a stupid mistake, and he blamed way too much driving and way too little sleep. But those excuses weren't worth shit. He had better training than that. And his carelessness had nearly cost Kelsey her life.

Gage squeezed his eyes shut and rubbed his forehead. So many mistakes, not the least of which was bringing

her to some fleabag motel a few short hours before he
had to report for duty.

Gage pulled off his shoes and hummed them into
the corner. He took off his belt and holster. He went
to the window, where a flimsy curtain did nothing to
muffle the traffic noise. As he watched the streaming
headlights, he felt a deep well of regret for so many
things he didn't know how to change.

He listened to the pipes run. He imagined her
standing under the water, surrounded by steam. He
closed his eyes and pictured it and felt that same slow
burn that had been with him since the day he'd met her
in the West Texas desert. No matter where he went or
how long he stayed away, he couldn't distance himself
from it. He craved her like water, and the thought of
leaving her again, without even the comfort of knowing
she was back here waiting for him to come home this
time—it was damn near choking him.

When he reported for duty tomorrow, he was going
overseas. He knew that. He also knew this was no training mission. By the time he came back, she might have a
ring on her finger, and it might be from Ben, or Aaron,
or fucking Mark Wolfe, FBI profiler extraordinaire.
Gage's gut clenched with fury just thinking about it.

And yet he couldn't blame her for making a choice
like that.

What could he offer her? He couldn't give her a big
lifestyle or stability or even his presence most of the time.
The one thing he *could* offer her was a chance to uproot
her life and give up an incredible job she loved—a job
where she was respected in her field and did something
good for humanity on a regular basis—so that she could

move to California, where she'd be miserable and alone most of the time.

The water shut off. Gage stared out at the traffic and thought about all the anger and jealousy and regret he'd had festering inside him for months. And just when he thought he'd gotten past it, he realized there was no end in sight.

The door opened. He felt the slight change in temperature as steam wafted into the little room.

God, he was an idiot. How had he ever thought he'd managed to make this better? He'd made it worse. For both of them. But now Kelsey was going to be the one hurting most because—for the very first time—he understood what she'd been talking about. He understood what had twisted her up inside and made her lash out at him with that damn ultimatum.

Fear, plain and simple. Today it had hit him like a bullet in the back.

She padded up behind him and, to his surprise, wound her arms around him.

"Hey," she whispered.

He glanced down at her bandage, which she'd somehow managed to keep dry. But her skin was damp. He could smell it. The scent of her surrounded him.

She leaned her forehead against his back. "We've got seven hours together."

"Six."

She pulled him around to face her. Her wet hair was combed back from her face, and she was wearing one of his new black T-shirts.

"I don't want to spend it fighting."

"How do you want to spend it?" he asked, because it

felt like his line, but his heart wasn't really in it. He was so, so sick of this.

Instead of saying something clever, she reached up and stroked her thumb over his cheek, where his beard was coming in. She probably thought he'd been forgetting to shave, but really, he needed it for work.

Not something she wanted to hear tonight.

She gazed up at him with a look he knew well, and his pulse picked up. She slid her arms around his neck and pressed her breasts against him.

"Stop looking like you have the weight of the world on your shoulders." She took his hand and slid it slowly under the shirt. His fingers encountered warm, damp skin and a thin strip of lace. The half-smile she gave him was the sweetest, most generous thing he'd ever seen. She rose up and nuzzled him just below the ear.

"Gage?"

"Yeah?"

"Kiss me."

CHAPTER 22

His mouth crushed down on hers, and she felt a flood of triumph as his hands gripped her hips and she tasted his pent-up need. *This* was the man she wanted tonight—not sullen and cold, but hot and demanding. His warm palms slid down her body and pulled her against him.

She leaned back to look at him. It was dark in the room, with just a narrow shaft of light coming in from the bathroom. She smiled and combed her fingers through his hair as she brought his head down for another kiss. She wanted to lose herself in it—in his breath, his taste, the wonderfully familiar scent of him. She kissed him until her head began to swim and all the reservations she'd had about doing this again melted away. She wanted the here and now. She wanted his mouth and his tongue and his strong arms wrapped around her so tightly she could scarcely breathe.

She wriggled out of his hold and pulled at the hem of his T-shirt. He jerked it over his head and flung it away, then reached for hers. His heated gaze moved over her as he dropped the shirt to the floor. She went into his arms again and felt the exhilarating friction of

skin against skin as he tipped her head back for another
kiss. She loved the hard contours of his body. She slid
her hands around his lean waist and dipped them into
the back of his jeans to pull him even closer.

"Kelsey."

The word was urgent, and she responded by moving
her hips against him. He gripped her around the waist
and picked her up off the floor, and she clutched his
neck and wrapped her legs around him as he staggered
to the bed. They fell onto it with absolutely no grace
and she started to laugh, but he cut her off with a kiss
and settled his weight between her thighs. She loved the
feel of him there, and she tried to squeeze him as close
as she could. He pulled back and reached across her to
turn on the lamp.

She flinched. "What—"

"I want to see you."

His gaze moved over her and lingered on the red lace.
The look in his eyes turned molten hot. He'd always
liked her in red, even though she'd told him over and
over it wasn't right with her coloring. But he didn't seem
to care about any of that as his big hands glided over her
body. He leaned his head down and his beard tickled
her skin as he kissed her breasts. Then he shimmied
lower and trailed his tongue over her stomach, making
her squirm. She felt the slide of lace moving down her
legs, and as much as she loved that, she wanted tonight
to be about him. She grabbed his arm and pulled him
up, so he was on his knees and straddling one of her
thighs, and she unfastened his jeans.

His gaze glinted down at her. She reached for him
and was surprised when he clasped her wrist and pinned

her hand against the mattress. He took her other one and pinned it there, too, then dipped his head down to focus on her breasts again.

She writhed under him and looked at the trail of hair disappearing into his open jeans. She tried to inch lower, but his grip on her wrists tightened. Then his mouth was on hers again and his weight settled heavily between her legs, and she moaned softly. He let her hands go and pinned her there with his hips as he kissed her with that intensity she'd never felt with anyone else.

She loved this. She loved *him*. Her hands glided over his arms, his shoulders, the valley of his spine, and for once she didn't wish he was anything other than what he was. He was a warrior. He was fierce and strong, and he'd cut her so deeply she knew she'd never heal completely. She'd tried so hard to push him out of her life, along with the pain of his rejection, but it hadn't worked. They were inextricably linked—now more than ever, since he'd come searching for her and risked his life again and again to keep her safe. That's who he was—a protector. And she couldn't change that about him any more than she could change the way she was going to feel tomorrow when he went back to his job. She pushed the thought from her mind and thought instead about the now, about the warm thrill that spread through her body as he touched her.

She gripped his shoulders and felt the tension of all that suppressed power he kept locked inside his body, waiting for the right moment to explode. He had so much control, so much intensity, and whenever he directed it at her like this, she felt completely helpless to resist what he wanted. He nudged her legs apart with his thighs and she opened her eyes to gaze up at him. The expression on his face was serious, more serious than she'd ever seen it, as he positioned himself above her.

He dipped his head down and her heart seemed to stop as he kissed her gently on the lips before shifting her hips and plunging inside her. He supported his weight with his arms and she closed her eyes and held on as he moved against her. What he did to her, the way he did it, felt so right, so *perfect,* and she wanted to stretch the time out. They moved together, sweaty and straining, until there was nothing between them but a single burning need and she knew that even his impressive control was reaching its limit. She dug her nails into his shoulders and gasped his name as it finally snapped.

Kelsey stared up at the ceiling as her heart rate slowed and her thoughts floated back down to earth. When he'd gotten up from the bed she'd turned down the covers, and she lay on her back now beside him, enjoying the first sheets she'd felt against her skin in days. Outside the window, the traffic noise reminded her where they were and how soon they needed to leave.

She felt his gaze on her and turned to look at him.

"What?"

Instead of answering, he took her hand and kissed her knuckles. She looked away. Her gaze landed on the digital clock on the nightstand. *Do not cry.* She'd thought this through in the shower, and her plan for tonight did not include dissolving into an emotional puddle.

She turned to face him and propped up on an elbow. She traced her finger over his scar, making a little figure eight over the raised pink skin.

"So." She trailed her fingertip down to his navel and then back up again. "How long until . . . ?"

He cocked an eyebrow at her.

"Because I was thinking." She shifted over him and watched his attention drift down to her bare breasts. "Madam Chen's is right next door. And I could really go for some hot-and-sour soup right now. What about you?"

He looked startled. "You want soup?"

"I bet they close in fifteen minutes, so we'd have to hurry. We could take a break and then"—she bent down to kiss his chest as she watched his eyes—"I could give you something to think about when you're off . . . wherever it is you're going."

He smiled slightly. "Something to think about?"

"Maybe . . . *fantasize* is a better word." She kissed his chest again, softly, letting her tongue trail over his skin. "I'll take requests. That way you'll have something to occupy your thoughts when you're, I don't know, sitting in the Humvee, bored out of your mind."

"You're going to act out my fantasy?"

"*After* we take a break. I don't want to put you in the hospital."

He moved and suddenly she was on her back. He gazed down at her with a glint in his eyes, and she smiled.

"Who needs a break?" he asked.

"Well, I'm just guessing, but—"

He shut her up with a very thorough kiss. When he

was finished, he'd somehow managed to trap her hands against the mattress again.

She wrapped her leg around him. "Tell me," she whispered. "Tell me one of your fantasies."

"I've got way more than one."

"Then you'll have to prioritize."

"It can be anything?" His voice was low and dangerous as he searched her face.

"Anything."

He kissed her on the mouth and her skin started to tingle. "Any fantasy at all?"

"Yes," she whispered.

He leaned down and his breath was warm against her ear. "Give us another chance."

She blinked up at him. God, he was serious. "*That's* your fantasy?"

"Yep."

"I meant something sexual."

He shifted on top of her. "Trust me, it's very sexual." He kissed her breast. "And it's exactly what I want to think about when I'm in the Humvee, bored out of my mind—coming home to you."

She swallowed. She'd meant this to be playful, but he was making it way too serious.

She closed her eyes. When she opened them again, he had his head propped on his hand and he was looking at her.

"Gage—"

"I know you still love me."

Her throat tightened. She felt a flutter of panic and looked away from his eyes to the beard he'd been growing all week. He was going to Afghanistan or Pakistan or some other dangerous place, and her heart hurt just thinking about it. She reached up and touched the bristles.

"You won't say it, but I know. I knew it when you saw my scar."

She gave him a questioning look.

"Last woman to see it, you want to know her reaction?"

Jealousy clogged her throat. "No."

"She said, 'Wow, cool.'" He brushed her hair out of her eyes. "You? You looked like you might cry."

She glanced away, and now her emotions were churning. She didn't want to think about him with someone else, but it was only fair. She'd been *engaged* to someone else.

Of course, that was after he'd dumped her.

Yet another thing she didn't want to dwell on tonight. How had she lost control of this conversation? Now her stomach was tied up in knots and she was feeling defensive.

"I don't want to go down that road again, Gage."

"What *do* you want?" His voice had an edge now. "Do you even know?"

"Yes."

"What is it?"

She scooted out from under him and sat back against the pillow. She pulled the sheet up under her arms as he watched her closely.

"I want . . . what a lot of women want." Why not tell him? Maybe it would make him see how far apart they were. "I want a husband who can be my companion. I want a house. I want kids."

"You want a baby?" He looked so surprised, she had to smile.

"Generally, kids start as babies, so . . . yeah, I guess I want one. Or two."

Now she'd totally freaked him out. He glanced at the strip of condoms on the nightstand and she slapped his arm.

"I'm not talking about *now.* This *minute.* But soon. I'm in my thirties, so I've been thinking about it a lot lately."

The look on his face made her sad. He was just now seeing how impossible this was, and she'd seen it for months.

She gazed down at her lap and smoothed her fingers over her bandage. Her stitches felt sore, but she hadn't wanted to take a pain pill that might numb her senses tonight.

"You know, when I was little," she said, "we used to be a regular family. We'd eat dinners together, go camping. My mom's a teacher, so she was off in the summers. We used to go on picnics and sometimes my dad would come if he could get away from work. Christmas would roll around and he'd get out the ladder and put lights on the roof. Every Fourth of July, he'd put out the flag." She looked at Gage. "He was really proud of Joe's service. Even as a kid I could see that."

He was watching her, but she couldn't read his expression at all.

"Then one evening my mom opens the door and there's this trooper standing there. My dad was gone. That was hard enough to deal with—this big hole in our lives. And after a while . . . it was like my mom started to disappear, too. She didn't make picnics any-more, or put out the flag. She never got out the ladder."

She looked at him. "I don't want to be like my mom. I don't want to be this lonely shadow of a person, and that's how I feel all the time you're away." She paused. "I don't want to be alone anymore, Gage."

He tipped his head back and raked his hand through his hair. "I hear what you're saying, but . . ." He looked at her. "You're asking me to leave the teams, Kelsey. I can't do that. That's like asking me to cut off my arm."

"No, you *don't* hear what I'm saying." She looked him in the eye. "I understand now, Gage, and I've ac-cepted it. That's why I'm not asking."

"Dial it down, LeBlanc. You're getting too rowdy."

Elizabeth glanced at the man on the stool beside her. *Attractive man,* she corrected herself. In case she'd failed to notice, the dozens of other women sliding looks in his direction served to remind her.

"Seriously, you haven't said a word since we got here. What's the problem?"

She turned to face him and reaffirmed the fact that this was a mistake. She should be holed up in some room with her laptop, not sitting in a pub.

"This just—" She glanced around. "I haven't been in a bar like this in a while."

"What, you mean one that serves beer?" He caught the bartender's eye—no surprise, since the bartender was female and had a pulse. "Speaking of, what are you drinking?"

Elizabeth looked at the row of bottles lined up in front of the mirror.

"Beer? Rum and Coke?" he prompted. When she didn't respond, he looked at the bartender. "Give us a sec, would you?"

"A martini, please. Tanqueray. Make it a double."

He blinked at her. "Well, damn. All right, then." He turned to the bartender. "Make it two."

"You drink martinis?"

"I do tonight." He smiled. "I'm good like that. If it's wet, I drink it."

She glanced around again, still uncomfortable. She really didn't go out much—not that she planned to tell Derek that. It would just give him one more advantage tonight. For some reason, it seemed like they were keeping score.

The bartender made their drinks and delivered them with a warm smile for Derek. Elizabeth was pretty sure she'd missed a wink somewhere along the way.

He lifted his glass. "Here's to good outcomes."

Her stomach churned. "A man getting hit by a truck is a good outcome?"

"I mean Gage." He clinked glasses with her. "An innocent man not getting hauled off to jail is a good outcome."

Elizabeth looked down at her drink, no longer thirsty.

"Drink up, Liz."

She took a gulp. It went down like water and quickly turned to fire.

"So, you're headed back to Texas tomorrow?"

She nodded, certain if she tried to talk, she'd sound like a frog.

"Morning flight? Now, that's brutal."

"I've got meetings tomorrow afternoon." There. That sounded almost normal.

"You work too hard," he told her.

The gin was already starting to kick in. She plucked the toothpick from her glass. Maybe nibbling on an olive would balance out the alcohol.

"You need a vacation. Why not take a few personal days, enjoy the coast? You ever driven down Highway One?"

"No."

"Best drive in the world. Perfect view of the ocean."

A commotion arose in the back of the bar, and she glanced at the cluster of men near the dartboard. That was all she needed tonight—a bar brawl. But a quick check of their faces told her the shouting and shoving was good-natured.

She glanced back at Derek and he looked amused.

"That was your cop face."

She raised her brows at him.

"I recognize it." He smiled. "You used it on me back in Utah." He set his glass on the bar. "What, worried you might have to haul those guys in for disorderly conduct?"

"I'm not hauling anyone anywhere tonight unless they hold up a bank in front of me." She sipped her drink again. "I've filled out enough paperwork today to last me a year. Next topic. How did you know about this place?"

"Buddy of mine told me about it."

"Who, Gage?" She leaned her elbow on the bar and

rested her chin on her fist. He gave her one of those smiles, and she noticed he had nice teeth. It was the sort of thing her mother would notice.

"This might come as a shock, but Gage isn't my only buddy. Mike Dietz told me about this place."

"Oh my God." She sat up straighter.

"What?"

"That was *textbook*. Your gaze just darted up and to the left when you said that."

He gave her a curious look. "That drink's going to your head."

"It is not." She laughed. "You are *lying* about your friend Mike Whoever-He-Is. Admit it."

"What are you talking about? Mike's from Oakland. Took me here last time we were up visiting. Damn, when was that? Back last fall sometime."

She downed another sip, feeling a rush of unexplained pride for nailing him. "Nice try with the details, but you are *such* a liar. You've never set foot in this place before tonight."

A slight smile twitched at the corner of his mouth, and she slapped the bar.

"I knew it! How did you do that? On the way over here, you were like a homing pigeon. What was that? Three blocks? Four?"

"Five."

"How did you know?"

He shrugged. "Pretty good bet. Anywhere there's a hospital, there are bound to be people blowing off steam after a rough day, right? There are plenty of watering holes around here."

"And you chose this one because . . . ?"

"It looked halfway decent." He set down his glass, and she noticed it was nearly empty. "And I figured if we walked too far, you'd change your mind and leave me hanging."

She shook her head. She picked up the toothpick and plucked another olive off the end. "I can't believe you lied to me." She gave him a stern look. "Again."

"I can't believe you fell for it. Again." He eased closer. "Pay attention, Liz. It's all in the delivery. You plan to tell a lie, you have to sell it." He clinked her glass again, but it was empty now. The attentive bartender stopped by, and he signaled for another round.

Elizabeth watched him and a warm buzz settled over her. She glanced at her watch. She really needed to leave now. She'd hardly eaten today and the liquor was starting to get to her.

Fresh drinks were delivered and she took a sip, watching him over the rim of the glass. When he wasn't being infuriating he was really attractive. And nice. And she really should go. Elizabeth put down her glass and looked at him. She knew what she *should* do, but didn't want to. She was actually enjoying herself.

A wave of guilt crashed over her. How could she enjoy anything today of all days?

"Uh-oh." He pushed her glass closer to her. "Drink up. I sense a confession coming on."

"Why do you say that?"

"You've got that look." He smiled. "I've been the recipient of a few booze-induced confessions, and you definitely have one on the tip of your tongue."

She picked up the new toothpick—this one was green instead of red—and nibbled another olive.

"Spill it. I'm good at this."

"I don't have any confessions. I just—" She closed her eyes. "Let's just say it was a shitty day."

She glanced up at him. His expression was serious now and she looked down at her glass.

"I've never seen a man die before. It was—" She swallowed the lump in her throat and glanced up at him. What on earth was she saying? She was talking to a *combat veteran*. She closed her eyes and sighed.

"Hey."

She looked down at his hand, which now covered hers on the bar.

"Don't do that to yourself. He deserved what he got."

She looked away.

"Man stepped in front of a truck. That's way *better* than he deserved, if you ask me. He killed himself."

"If I'd *arrested* him successfully, he'd still be alive."

Derek shook his head, and she watched him, wanting him to talk her out of her depression over this. She couldn't get that sickening thud out of her head.

"Trent Lohman had one of the best law-enforcement jobs in the world. He was part of an elite group. He blew it."

She looked at him, and part of her knew he was right. But she still felt guilty.

Derek leaned closer. "He carried a badge and a gun. People trusted him, respected him. He deceived and manipulated people, probably right up to the end."

Elizabeth drew back.

"Am I right?"

She fiddled with the glass, turning it on the bar.

"What'd he do, try to talk you out of it? Try to cut you in on his deal?"

She cleared her throat. *He called my bluff,* she wanted to say. But she didn't say that because she didn't want it to be true. Maybe it wasn't true. Maybe she really would have arrested him if he hadn't run. She definitely would have tried. Would she have succeeded? She wasn't sure. And that was what haunted her. All that training—months and months of it—and when the stakes were high, she hadn't even been able to make a simple apprehension.

She closed her eyes. To her complete mortification, she felt tears forming. He patted her hand, and some of the tears leaked out.

"God." She laughed nervously and swiped her cheeks. "I'm sure this is exactly what you wanted to do tonight. How's that leave working out for you?"

"Yeah, it's been eventful."

"Driving to Utah," she said. "Running through alleyways. Spending hours locked in a car with Frost."

"Hey, Vernon and I are pals now. He didn't tell you?"

"Really?"

"Nah, not really. He hardly said a word to me all morning. And I have to say, I would have much rather you'd been the one to slap those cuffs on. But, all in all, my leave hasn't been bad. I've gotten to end it having drinks with a beautiful woman."

She snorted.

"What?" He pretended to be offended.

"You SEALs are tenacious."

"I'll take that as a compliment."

She smiled and took a sip. She was feeling a little better, actually. Her shoulders were starting to loosen, and she felt warm all over. She knew it was the Tanqueray. But it was also the man. He was way too cocky and an outrageous flirt, but somehow he made her feel better.

"Why are you being so nice to me?" she asked.

"Nice?"

"I mean, besides the obvious."

He leaned an elbow comfortably against the bar. "What's obvious?"

She rolled her eyes.

"You know, you're very cynical about men."

"Sorry. I don't mean to be a bitch."

"No, it's good. I should get you to talk to my little sisters. The bullshit-detector gene totally missed them. Scares the hell out of me."

She smiled. He'd just admitted he'd been bullshitting her this whole evening. At least that's what she thought he'd just admitted. Her brain felt a little fuzzy. Actually, a lot fuzzy.

She leaned down and picked up her purse from the floor and pulled some money out.

"You don't want to finish that drink?"

"I've had enough." She stood up and caught herself on the bar. He grabbed her elbow but didn't make a big deal about it as he pulled out his wallet and left money on the bar. Nice tipper. It was right up there with good teeth on her mom's top-ten list.

Go home, Elizabeth.

She made it to the door with impressive poise and stepped out into the damp night air. A view of the bay was visible between two buildings, and she noticed the lights of the bridge poking up through the fog.

The fog comes on little cat feet.

"What's that?"

She glanced up at him. Had she said that out loud? It was definitely time to go if she was reciting poetry. She glanced up and down the street.

"Where's your car?"

She looked up at him.

"Not that I'm not suggesting you drive anywhere." He put his hand on the small of her back and guided her toward the direction they'd come from.

"So you're just wondering . . . ?"

"I like to gather as much intel as possible at all times."

A little warning bell went off in her brain. *So he can close in on the target.*

"Think I'll cab it," she said.

"Where're you staying?"

Good question. "Uh—"

"I'm over at the Dragon Inn." He nodded across the street at a rundown-looking motel.

"Yeah, right."

"Seriously."

She glanced at the motel again. It was a tall and narrow brick building with a tall and narrow sign out front in red neon.

"You are not staying there."

"Sure I am."

"It says 'No Vacancy.'"

"I got their last room." He stepped closer, and his broad shoulders blocked out the streetlights. Elizabeth's heart started to pound as she gazed up at him. The breeze whipped into her jacket and pressed her blouse against her skin, but she felt the heat of him right in front of her. He reached down and tucked a lock of hair behind her ear. "Want to share it with me?"

Her throat went dry. Before her brain could form a response, he leaned down and kissed her mouth, very lightly.

She didn't move. She gazed up into those dark eyes and felt a magnetic *pull*. She imagined what that three-day beard would feel like against her bare skin, and her heart started to pound even faster. But then she imagined him getting up in the morning and leaving without a backward glance.

"Come on," he whispered, and through the haze she felt that pull again. "Say yes."

CHAPTER 23

Kelsey's eyes opened at the sound of the phone, but she'd already been awake. For the past hour, she'd been lying there with Gage's arm draped over her waist, waiting for the inevitable number to appear on the clock.

Gage sat up and switched on the lamp. "Where is that?"

"My purse."

He dragged her purse off the chair and pulled the phone out. He looked at her. "Ben." She reached across him but he answered it. "Yeah." He looked at her again. "She's right here."

Kelsey gave him a reproachful look as he handed her the phone and got out of bed.

"Hi, Ben. What's up?"

"Sorry to wake you." He sounded miffed. "Some interesting developments this morning."

She looked at the clock. It was 5:20, so that meant 7:20 at the Delphi Center. He was in early.

"I did a phone dump and a credit-card check for Trent Lohman."

"Trent Lohman's dead."

"I know. I talked to Gordon Moore. But listen to this. You want to hear what his second-to-last credit-card purchase was before his death?"

Kelsey sighed. "What?"

"An economy-class plane ticket for July fourteenth that goes from Washington-Dulles Airport, through New York–LaGuardia, and then on to Hong Kong."

She brushed her hair out of her eyes and tried to orient herself. "That's in two weeks."

"Yeah."

"Well, that makes sense, right? Did Gordon tell you about the Hong Kong bank account? He was probably going there to get his money."

"Yeah, I know, but you want to hear his final credit-card purchase?"

"What's the problem?" Gage asked, zipping his jeans. He folded his arms over his chest and propped his shoulder against the wall.

"Something about Trent Lohman," she told him. Then to Ben: "What was the purchase?"

"This transaction was yesterday morning. He bought a first-class plane ticket for the red-eye flight from San Francisco International to Washington's Reagan International Airport."

"So?"

"It was the last seat on the plane. He paid an arm and a leg for it and it has him landing in Washington this morning at 7:19 A.M."

"Yeah?" She still wasn't following.

"Kelsey, think about it. It looks like he planned to spend the next two weeks on the East Coast. Not only that, but in the very city that Mark and Gordon and everyone in Homeland Security seems to think is Ramli's target location for an anthrax attack. And not only *that,* he planned to be in three major East Coast airports during that time frame. But where is he *not* going? Where is he so eager to get away from that he buys an outrageously expensive ticket so he can hop on a red-eye?"

Kelsey was fully awake now.

"You want to know who else made last-minute plans to hop a red-eye last night?" he asked.

"Who?"

"Marissa Ramli and her daughter, Leila. They took the eleven-forty P.M. to Chicago."

"What's in Chicago?"

"Who knows? That's not the point. The point is—"

"You think everyone's looking at the wrong coast," she said. "You think his target is San Francisco."

A persistent bleating noise pulled Elizabeth from sleep. She lifted her head up and pain exploded behind her eyes. She groped for the phone as the blurry red clock numbers came into focus: 5:37.

"LeBlanc." It sounded like a rasp.

"Special Agent Elizabeth LeBlanc?"

She sat up slowly and switched on the lamp. She didn't recognize the voice. Ditto the bedspread bunched around her waist.

"Speaking."

"With the FBI?"

"This is Agent LeBlanc, yes. Who is this?"

"This is—" Static. "—Shamus. Sorry to just now be returning your—" More static. "—and now St. Croix. I hope I'm not waking you."

"Dr. Shamus?" She tried to think around the intense pounding in her head. "I've been trying to reach you." Her gaze landed on a pair of cowboy boots on the floor beside the chair.

"My apologies, but I've been away on my honeymoon. Is there something you needed? I have six messages."

Elizabeth watched, shocked, as a giant shape moved on the sofa. Memories flooded her: the pub, the drinks, an old-fashioned elevator with one of those doors that pulled shut.

Derek swung his legs off the couch. He raked his hand through his hair and looked at her.

"Are you there?" came the voice over the phone.

"I'm here." Elizabeth took a quick inventory. She was dressed, but what the hell had happened? And why did she have a deep-rooted certainty that she should feel embarrassed right now?

"Um . . . thank you for calling me back, Dr. Shamus. I was . . . Actually, I need to ask you about several of our agents. They called you recently about a project you consulted on. The D.C. Metro."

"Agents Lohman and Reece."

"Reid."

"Right. *Reid,* I guess it was. Yes, I spoke to them at length. They needed information—" Static. "—more questions?"

"I'm sorry." She rubbed her forehead. "Could you repeat that?"

Silence.

"Hello?" She stood up. "Dr. Shamus?" Elizabeth stared at the phone in her hand. The call had dropped.

She glanced across the room at the man watching her intently.

"That was Dr. Shamus," she said inanely.

"The Berkeley guy."

She looked at the phone again. She looked at Derek. "Last night . . ." Her stomach knotted. "Did we—"

"No." He gave her a sharp look and reached for his boots. As she watched him pull them on, she remembered an endless corridor with red carpet. She remembered a heady combination of lust and nerves and, again, embarrassment.

"Nothing happened at all?"

He sighed. "Not unless you count puking your guts up on the way over here."

"You're kidding," she said, but her brain was kicking into gear now, and she had a sudden memory of kneeling in a bed of ivy while a hand gripped her arm.

"Oh my God. I threw up on your shoes, didn't I?"

He didn't say anything, and she wanted to sink through the floor.

"I'm so sorry."

"Forget it. What'd the professor want?"

The phone in her hand rang, and she rushed to answer it. "Dr. Shamus?"

"Again, my apologies. Some of the places we've dropped anchor are a bit rustic. You were asking about the rail project?"

"Yes," she said. "The Bureau is investigating a potential terrorist threat."

"So they told me."

"I was wondering what part of the Metro, specifically, the agents questioned you about?"

"I'm sorry?"

"Agent Lohman in particular—was there a specific area you discussed with him? An area you thought might be more vulnerable to attack?"

"The D.C. Metro?"

"Yes."

"Agent Lohman didn't ask about D.C. We talked about Bart."

"Who?"

"BART. Bay Area Rapid Transit," Shamus said. "In San Francisco."

Rick Bolton stepped out of the J. Edgar Hoover Building and pulled a roll of antacids from his pocket as he made his way down the steps. Not even nine A.M. and already his ulcer was flaring up. He reached the intersection and crossed Pennsylvania Avenue.

This was going to be one hell of a week, and it had barely begun. He hadn't even gone home last night, he'd been so swamped with the anthrax letters. Just when he thought he might tear himself away, he'd received the news about Trent Lohman. Now he was headed into Tuesday in a rumpled suit and operating on only a few hours of sleep, stolen on the couch in his office.

His phone vibrated in his pocket and he pulled it out. Florida area code, but he didn't recognize the number. It would either be his ex-wife calling about the tuition payment that was due this week or his daughter wanting money for her summer trip to Belize. He let it go to voice mail.

Bolton's gut burned. No one—least of all his direct reports, who were supposed to help him—had a clue about the kind of stress he was under. Only a handful of people had any concept of the complexity of his job. They didn't realize how layered and far-reaching these organizations were. Fighting terrorism wasn't about eliminating one man or even one group. It was about stopping a disease before it spread unchecked into the world's healthiest democracies.

Bolton reached the National Gallery sculpture garden and slowed his pace. He noticed the National Guardsman, who looked about twenty, stationed near the entrance. He had been posted there to keep an eye on people—especially those with backpacks. The kid didn't recognize Bolton. He had no idea that he was there today as a direct result of Bolton's orders. He had no idea that Bolton was anyone noteworthy, that he'd dedicated the last twenty-five years of his life to serving his country, or that he'd racked up three ulcers, two ex-wives, and a double-bypass in the process.

Bolton took a deep breath as he crossed the garden and tried to make himself relax. He sat on a concrete bench near the fountain and pulled out his phone. He checked his watch. Not yet nine. He still had time, but he needed to keep it short and get back to his office.

"Barney."

"Hey, it's me," he said. "What's M&O Pharm looking like?"

"It's expected to hit eighty-two today," the broker informed him. "You ready to get out?"

"If it breaks one hundred, sell it off."

Silence.

LAURA GRIFFIN

"Barney?" He glanced at the fountain that was generating a lot of background noise. Listening devices were everywhere in this town.

"Yeah, that's . . . unlikely to happen. Yesterday's fourteen percent gain is huge for this company, especially with the recent decline in pharmaceuticals. They're having a good run-up because of the anthrax letters and all this Seprax shit, but it's expected to cool off as soon as the news dies down."

"Listen to me." He glanced at the guardsman. "When it hits one hundred, dump it."

Pause. "All of it?"

"Every goddamn share."

Kelsey clenched her teeth with frustration as she navigated the beginnings of rush-hour traffic. It was just after seven o'clock.

"How much farther?" she asked Gage, who was in the passenger seat for a change.

"Looks like four blocks."

She glided into the right-hand lane but had to slam on the brakes as a delivery truck halted in front of her. She pounded the horn.

"Go around," Gage instructed.

She waited for a break in traffic, then pulled around the truck and zipped into the right-hand lane.

"Do you even know where you're going?" she asked.

"Derek said it isn't hard to find."

She ran a stale yellow. They were en route to BART's security headquarters, where Elizabeth LeBlanc urgently needed two extra sets of eyes to monitor video footage and hopefully pick out Adam Ramli from the thousands of Bay Area commuters now pouring into the system.

"You're going to make yourself late," Kelsey said now. "Both of you. And this might not be happening today."

Gage didn't respond, and she shook her head as she ran another yellow. She hadn't been able to talk him out of this, and now they were speeding toward the epicenter of what might be a terrorist attack.

But might just as easily be nothing.

Gage's phone buzzed and he snapped it up. "We're almost there . . . Okay, good." He clicked off. "He's meeting me at the entrance."

"What about LeBlanc? Where's her backup? The FBI should handle this."

"Yeah, well, soon as they figure out which way is up, they can have at it. Stop here."

She swerved into a drop-off lane reserved for taxis and glanced around.

"Where am I supposed to park?" she asked, panicked. He was trying to rush off without her. He was trying to sideline her again. She'd known what he was up to the instant he'd tossed the keys at her back at the motel.

"I'm sure you'll find something." He pushed the door open. "I'll call you when we get in there and let you know where to meet us."

"Like hell you will." She grabbed his hand. "I know what you're doing, Gage."

"Kelsey." He shook his head. "There's no reason for you to jump in the middle of this."

"I can help ID him! You know I could and you're—"

"Just follow the plan, okay? Find a place to park and wait for my call." He turned to look over his shoulder as Derek emerged from the subway station.

She felt another spurt of panic. "Gage, please. Let the FBI deal with this."

"We will."

"You don't know what he's planning."

"I know I'm not going to sit around and wait for a bunch of suits to show up while some terrorist launches an attack!"

Kelsey closed her eyes. It was exactly what she was afraid of. They weren't going to wait for anyone.

He reached over and cupped his hand behind her neck. "Relax, okay? We'll get this under control. Hell, he may not even be here."

"You don't believe that."

He looked at her, and she knew she was right. He believed this was happening here. Now. He believed this was the zero hour. It was that damn sixth sense he talked about—that frog vision.

Only this time, she had it, too.

Elizabeth gazed at the wall of video monitors and tried to appear undaunted. Tried and failed. Picking one man out of the thousands of commuters flooding through gates and waiting on platforms was next to impossible. And yet she kept trying because she felt certain he was out there. Dr. Shamus had told her that Trent Lohman grilled him for nearly an hour about the design intricacies of this commuter rail system—ostensibly in order to help the FBI safeguard against a potential terrorist plot. What Shamus hadn't realized was that he was talking with one of the plotters.

"Is this really all you've got?"

She glanced up at the extremely unhappy-looking SEAL standing at her elbow. Gage Brewer held a computer printout showing the FBI's most recent picture of Adam Ramli. The man wore a beard, green military fatigues, and a deadly scowl. Gage also held a second printout showing Ramli's passport photo in which he was clean-shaven, smiling, and impossibly young looking—the all-American kid next door.

"He's not going to look like either of these," Gage said. "He'll be trying to blend in with the twentysomethings out of Silicon Valley. There are thousands pouring through here, and these security people are just staring at the screens. They'll never recognize him."

"Which is why we need more eyes," Elizabeth said. "Where's Kelsey?"

"On the way." Gage's face hardened and he looked again at the monitors.

"Check it out," Derek said, pointing at a screen. "What's that man doing?"

They all eased forward, crowding one of the security people seated at a bank of monitors.

"Just checking his backpack," the guy said. "See?" He gave them a cool look as the innocuous commuter zipped his pack shut and stepped on an escalator. "Good thing we didn't take him down."

Elizabeth ignored the sarcasm. Clearly these people were less than thrilled about this drop-in visit by an FBI agent and two oversized "associates" dressed in ball caps and jeans. She, Gage, and Derek made quite

a trio, and Elizabeth knew their disheveled appearance
was making it difficult for the shift leader in charge of
security here to take her seriously, despite the badge
she'd flashed when she'd arrived. Since the instant she'd
walked in here, he'd been highly skeptical. Elizabeth
had already called the San Francisco field office to
report the threat and request immediate backup, but no
one had shown up yet, and she had a sneaking suspicion
she wasn't being taken seriously by them, either.

"What's to say he hadn't already released the toxin?"
Derek asked. "He could have come through here hours
ago."

"Not according to our detectors," the shift leader
said. "After 9/11, we installed biohazard sensors at
every station. We've had them checked three times
since yesterday when the alert went out about the
anthrax letters. As of six A.M. this air was negative for
biohazards."

Elizabeth was encouraged by the news but dismayed
by everyone's ho-hum response. Apparently this security
team routinely dealt with crank calls and false alarms,
and no one seemed eager to shut down a rail system that
transported more than three hundred thousand people
a day based on Elizabeth's tip. But she knew this was
real. Even if the info from Ben Lawson at the Delphi
Center hadn't reinforced the theory that something was
going down today, Gage's and Derek's body language
would have convinced her. The super-cool spec ops
warriors who ate terrorists for breakfast were on red
alert.

"Whoa, got something."

Everyone turned toward the childlike voice of a

young woman seated at a computer monitor. While the other dozen or so security personnel here were monitoring real-time developments, she and several coworkers were combing through older footage from when the trains started running at four A.M.

Elizabeth leaned over her shoulder now and watched a group of people standing on a subway platform.

"What did you see?" she asked.

"Well, it was very brief, but I *thought* I saw a man slip into the tunnel."

"Rewind it."

She did. Everyone peered over her shoulder at the grainy video image. The commuters were mostly loners dressed in a range of clothes from business suits to athletic shorts. A clump of teenagers stood at one end of the platform horsing around with one another. All of them wore backpacks or had satchels slung across their bodies.

"See him?" The woman pointed at a man dressed in jeans and a hooded sweatshirt. "Watch what he does."

"Pretty big backpack," Derek observed.

"Can you recognize his face?" Elizabeth asked them.

Gage shook his head. "Not with the hood."

The man stepped toward the platform. Another step. Then—blink—he was gone.

Elizabeth's breath caught. "He disappeared."

"Let's see if he comes back," Derek said.

They waited tensely, all eyes trained on the screen.

"Where is that?" Elizabeth asked.

"Montgomery Street Station," the woman said. "In the Financial District, underneath Market Street."

Elizabeth's stomach tensed. Gage traded looks with

Derek, and she knew what they were thinking. Of the forty-four stations within this system, only fifteen were underground, so they'd been focused on those. Anyone who'd researched the best place to carry out an attack would be looking for a densely populated and enclosed space.

Elizabeth held her breath as she watched the monitor. No one emerged from the tunnel. In the dark corner of the screen, a flicker of light grew bigger as a train approached. People edged toward the yellow stripe.

"If he went in, he has to come out," Gage muttered.

And then he did. The man with the hood hopped back onto the platform just moments before the train glided to a stop.

"Freeze it," Gage ordered.

The man on the screen halted, suspended in time. His hood was cinched around his face and the backpack was gone.

"That's him," Gage said.

"What time is this?" Derek demanded.

"Uh, looks like . . . seven oh two. That's fifteen minutes ago."

Elizabeth whipped out her phone and frantically dialed for backup. She glanced at the shift leader, who no longer looked skeptical. Meanwhile, the SEALs were already out the door.

"Montgomery Street Station!" she yelled. "We need to move."

Gage leaped through the doors the instant they opened. He and Derek elbowed their way through the crowd and across the platform, where another train was hissing to a halt.

Gage stopped and waited at the wall where Ramli had disappeared. He pressed his fist against the tiles, and with every second that ticked by he imagined millions of deadly spores taking to the air.

"What's the word on that evac?" Gage asked Derek beside him. The whole way over here, he'd been on the phone with Elizabeth, who was a train behind them.

Derek shook his head.

Gage had already called Kelsey and told her to stay the hell away. She'd agreed without argument, which was why he expected her to show up at any second.

The doors whisked shut and the train groaned forward. It became a silver streak and then was gone. Gage hopped into the rail pit and was almost pulled to his knees by the suction.

"Watch out for that third rail," he said, taking out his flashlight. "It packs a thousand-volt punch." He led them into the tunnel, sweeping the flashlight beam around.

"You take that wall, I'll take this one," Derek said as they set out at a jog.

The walls, the ground, the rails—everything was covered by a thick layer of grime. The tunnel smelled wet, and Gage remembered they were near the bay. A rat scuttled into a drainage pipe. About twenty yards away, he noticed a shadow within a shadow and rushed toward it. It was some sort of access nook, with a metal ladder stretching up to the maze of pipes and ducts above.

"We got a package," Gage said. He neared the spot and shined his flashlight on it. It was the backpack they'd seen earlier, only it looked slack and empty hanging from the ladder. Gage glanced up. A few rungs above his head was something else—something that had likely been *inside* the backpack. He stared at it for a moment.

"Holy shit."

"What?" Derek asked.

"A birdcage."

"A *what*?"

"A cage with an IED inside."

"What the fuck?"

"No idea," Gage said. The setup was unlike anything he'd seen. Why build a cage around something that was going to explode?

This cage was smaller than the others he'd seen in Utah—about the size of a shoe box turned on its side—but it was made of the same wire mesh. Inside was a homemade explosive. Gage's blood ran cold as he saw the lightbulb and remembered Mark's words. *All he'd have to do is put it in a fragile container—a bottle, a jar, a lightbulb . . .* Gage shifted positions to view the other side and noted the timing device with green digital numbers: twenty-four.

"Think that's minutes or hours?" Derek asked.

The twenty-four became a twenty-three.

"Fuck." Derek looked at him.

The ground beneath their feet vibrated. A distant rumble. Gage glanced down the tunnel as the train rounded a curve and the first light winked into view.

"This nook's only big enough for one of us." He looked at Derek. "Haul ass back to the platform. Tell Elizabeth and every cop you can find they've got twenty-two minutes to clear this place out."

CHAPTER 24

Derek notified everyone he could and got back to Gage just as another train roared through. Gage squeezed himself out of the nook and stepped onto the ladder.

"Here." Derek handed him a pair of latex gloves and a paper mask that he'd swiped from a janitor's cart. "Not exactly a hazmat suit, but can't hurt."

Gage pulled on the gloves. "How's that evac going?" he asked, not looking up from his work. He had the flashlight pressed between his neck and shoulder as he used his pocketknife to slice through a strip of duct tape that attached the cage to the rungs.

"It's under way. The challenge is getting the trains to stop coming. Four different lines run through this station, so closing it is a big fucking deal. Practically means shutting down the whole system, and the security guy said their daily ridership is three hundred fifty thou. How's the time?"

"Fourteen minutes." Gage made another careful slice. He was in the zone. Cold as ice. Hands steady. Laser-sharp focus on the task at hand.

"You sure you want to move it?" Derek asked.

"Yep." One last slice, and it was free. Carefully, Gage pulled it away from the rungs. "Good news is, this explosive's a joke. We're talking extremely low-order detonation. Bad news—if it pops at all, it breaks the lightbulb where he put the anthrax."

"Shit."

"Exactly. Let's get this out of this tunnel."

Derek led the way, making sure the path was clear. The ground started vibrating and he heard a distant clatter.

"I thought they were shutting this place down," Gage said tightly.

"So did I."

In the distance, a shriek of metal. Derek hopped onto the platform and glanced around, surprised to see the area clear. But that was going to change as soon as that train stopped.

"Here." Derek held out his hands and took the device from Gage. The approaching train showed no sign of stopping and the shriek reached a deafening pitch. Gage hitched himself onto the platform. The train whisked past almost as soon as he was out of the pit.

Derek stood motionless as the train streaked by, trying not to think about how he held a weapon of mass destruction in his hands.

"You okay?" Gage looked him in the eye.

He nodded.

Gage glanced around the platform. It was eerily empty except for an owl-eyed security guard stationed at the base of the escalator. The sound of bullhorns at the top told Derek the transit police were still evacuating.

"We need an enclosed room," Derek said.

"Not a bathroom—too many vents and pipes."

"Storage closet." Derek nodded in the direction of a dull gray door on the far wall.

Gage tried the door. Locked.

Derek glanced down at the timer: Eleven minutes.

Gage jogged to another door.

"Jackpot."

It was a tiny closet packed with mops and cleaning supplies, and Gage wasted no time heaving everything out of it. Derek kneeled down and carefully placed the IED on the concrete.

Gage immediately crouched down and went to work on the wiring. "Here's what I need," he said. "A metal container. Something airtight. Think paint cans, storage drums."

"You *moved* the bomb?"

They looked up to see Elizabeth standing in the doorway. "It's not a bomb," Gage told her. "It's barely a firecracker."

She gaped at them. "Why didn't you wait for our bomb squad?"

Gage shot Derek a look. It was a plea, really. He needed her out of here so he could concentrate.

Derek stood up and steered her away from the closet. "It's not a bomb," he reiterated. "But it's very fragile. We thought we'd get it out of the path of a train moving eighty miles an hour." He reached for the knob of a neighboring closet and tried it again. He poked his head back in the storage room.

"Yo, Brewer, toss me that knife."

Gage tossed him the knife, and Derek jimmied the

lock as Elizabeth looked on. He glanced up at her. "You got a lock pick on you, now's the time to speak up. Or an airtight metal container?"

"Are you making light of this?"

"Not at all."

Elizabeth's phone buzzed and she jerked it to her ear. "LeBlanc."

Snick. Door open.

"Yes, let her through. She's with me. Okay, when?"

Derek jerked open the door and switched on a light. He surveyed the contents of the room: more mops and buckets, another janitor's cart, a shelf stocked with toilet paper.

A metal toolbox.

"We've got an FBI bomb squad en route here," Elizabeth said. "They'll be here in fifteen minutes. We should wait for them."

"No time," Derek told her, upending the toolbox and dumping everything out.

"But they're experts in ordnance disposal!"

"Oh, yeah? And where do you think they get those guys?" Derek ripped out the plastic trays. "Hundred bucks says half of them are former SEALs."

Derek squeezed past Elizabeth and took the box to Gage. "No paint cans."

"Hazmat team's also en route," Elizabeth reported. "ETA two minutes."

Gage didn't flinch. He was intent on carefully removing the timing device from inside a hole he'd created in the mesh cage. Derek looked at the clock. Eight minutes.

"Is it defused?"

Derek turned around to see Kelsey in the doorway. She was flushed and breathless and looked like she'd run the whole way here.

"Almost," Derek told her.

Gage shot him a look that said *Get her out of here.*

"What can I do?" Kelsey asked, looking determined. She'd conjured up a pair of gloves and a face mask, probably from the same janitor's cart where Derek had swiped his.

Gage didn't glance up. "You can walk up that escalator and catch a taxi to the airport."

She looked at Derek. "What can I do?"

"Nothing."

Derek checked the clock. Seven minutes. He glanced at Gage. Still ice cold. Hands steady. The only sign of stress was the bead of sweat that slid slowly down the side of his face.

Kelsey stepped into the room. "Gage, look at me."

To Derek's amazement, he did.

"You see a lot of people around here who are vaccinated against anthrax? I see three. Now, give me a goddamn job."

Gage glanced at the toolbox. He glanced at Kelsey.

"I'm about to put a lightbulb in there that's filled with anthrax spores. See what you can do with that."

Kelsey disappeared. Derek watched the clock. Another minute ticked off. Kelsey returned with an armful of toilet paper rolls and started lining the box.

Derek watched as Gage cut a final wire. The timing device went dark and everyone breathed an audible sigh of relief. One problem dealt with, another one to go. Gage slowly pulled the timer through an opening he'd cut in the wire mesh. Then he gingerly picked up the cage containing the IED and lowered it into the toolbox, which was now lined with fluffy white paper and cushy rolls. Everyone held their breath as Gage carefully closed the lid. He clicked the latches. The tiny room went silent as four pairs of eyes gazed down at the lethal red box.

And then they heard thunder.

The SWAT guys came in like storm troopers. There were two large teams equipped with face shields, weapons, full-body armor. An FBI hazmat team arrived moments later and took over custody of the red metal box.

Kelsey combed the sea of emergency workers and spotted Gage and Derek standing off to the side talking. They looked grim for two men who had just thwarted a terrorist attack. Kelsey walked up to them.

"Biohazard sensors here are still reporting clean air," she said.

Gage glanced at her, then at Derek.

"What's wrong? You're upset we didn't get him?"

"Would have been nice, don't you think?" Derek asked.

"They've got BOLOs all over the place and agents at every airport and border crossing. They'll find him."

Both of them stared at the map, not answering.

"There's something more. What is it?"

"Gage doesn't like the timer," Derek told her.

Kelsey looked at him. "What about it?"

"I'm pretty sure it was set for one hour," Gage said. "Why'd he do that?"

"Well . . ." Kelsey blew out a breath. "Probably so he could get away, right? Mark told us he's not suicidal. Based on his profile, he wanted an exit strategy."

"Yeah, but he didn't need an hour," Derek pointed out. "It only takes a minute to jump on a train, get the hell out of here."

"Plus there was no boom," Gage said. "No big moment. Nothing splashy. I don't think this is it, Kelsey."

A chill snaked down her spine. "You think there's more?"

"Don't you?"

She turned and looked at the subway map, as if that would provide answers. Both of them seemed fixated on it.

"What if . . ." Derek rubbed the back of his neck as he studied the map. "What if he wanted to maximize casualties by doing something more in that time window?"

"Okay." Kelsey stared at the map. "Like planting another device?"

"Something different," Gage said. "A real bomb this time. This guy's a demo man. I can't shake the feeling that he's got more in him than this stealth attack."

Kelsey stared at the map, thinking. An idea started to crystallize as she gazed at all the colored train routes. The lines covered Oakland, San Francisco. The routes converged into one big artery as they crossed the bay through the transit tube, which was deep underwater.

"What if he . . ." She trailed off as she looked at the map. Montgomery Street Station was at the valve where those lines entered downtown.

"What if he what?" Gage prompted.

"What if he used the timer so he could do something else before the spores released?" She looked at Gage. "Maybe something attention-getting that would force people into the subway. He'd maximize casualties *and* get his dramatic moment—kind of a two-for-one attack."

"How do you force people into the subway?" Derek asked.

"Take away their cars?" Gage suggested.

"No," Kelsey said. "Take away their bridge."

Elizabeth had just fielded what had to be the fifth phone call from Gordon when she spotted Derek striding toward her.

"Where's that bomb squad?" he asked her.

"On the mezzanine level, doing a final run-through. Why?"

"You have any pull with them?"

"I don't have any pull with anyone," she said. "What's going on?"

"We've got an idea, and I think it's worth checking into, but we need to go now."

Elizabeth looked at him for a long moment. "I'm listening."

He outlined the theory as she stood there silently, compiling a mental list of all the flaws in it.

"So, this is pure speculation," she said when he finished.

He nodded.

"I can tell you right now, there's no way the SAC—the

Senior Agent in Charge here—would send a team over there on some hunch. Do you have anything solid?"

His jaw tensed. "No."

"Then I'll talk to him, but I can't guarantee he'll even consider it."

He muttered a curse and checked his watch. "At least try him, would you?" He moved to leave, and she caught his arm.

"Wait, where are you going?"

"To catch up with Gage and Kelsey. I've burned five minutes standing here talking to you."

"You really believe in this?"

"You think I'd be wasting your time if I didn't? I'm going to drive to the bridge, see if I spot anything suspicious." He paused to look at her. "You want to come?"

She glanced around at the crowd of emergency responders. No one here even knew who she was. She wouldn't be missed until it came time to fill out the gazillion forms that were going to result from the incident.

"Time's ticking, Liz. Are you in or out?"

"I'm in."

"You know, nothing looked amiss on the way over here," Kelsey said as they approached the toll plaza to drive back over the Bay Bridge into downtown. "This really is a long shot."

Gage didn't say anything. He'd had that super-alert look on his face for the entire eastbound trip across the bay.

"The more I think about it, it's simply not possible for him to blow up this bridge," she said as traffic slowed to a crawl. "It's built to withstand earthquakes. And wasn't it reinforced after the last big one?"

"He doesn't need to blow it up," Gage said. "He just needs to create an incident. If he causes a traffic jam big enough to get news attention, commuters will opt for the subway."

They edged closer to a toll booth, and Kelsey looked enviously at the lanes for people with fast passes. They didn't have one, and even with eighteen toll booths their progress was slow.

Kelsey looked at Gage. "You sure you don't want to bag this theory and head down the coast? If you speed, you might still be able to make it in time."

Not really, but she wanted to throw it out there. She didn't want to get blamed for making him late to report for duty, even though in her mind saving the lives of potentially thousands of people should get him off the hook.

Gage still didn't say anything. He had that *look* again, the one he'd had earlier when he'd been kneeling beside the IED. Kelsey stifled a shudder. They'd come minutes away from disaster, and yet he'd been rock-steady. How he did it, she had no earthly idea.

She dug money from her purse as they neared the toll booth. Gage rolled down the window and they heard a faint chorus of horns up ahead. Kelsey glanced around. A tow truck sped through the fast lane, yellow strobes whirling.

"What's going on?" Gage asked the attendant.

"I don't know." The woman glanced over her shoulder. "Maybe a stalled car? Something's got traffic tied up on the bridge."

Gage looked at Kelsey. "That's him."

Eastbound traffic was light, and Elizabeth and Derek made it across the bay without incident. As they looped around for the return trip west, Elizabeth's phone rang.

Derek glanced at her as she took the call. Her eyes widened. "When?" she asked, and he got a very bad feeling in the pit of his stomach. "Okay, thanks." She hung up and looked at him. "Marissa Ramli just walked into the FBI's Chicago office. She says her brother plans to blow up this bridge today."

CHAPTER 25

Gage trained his gaze on the swirling yellow lights as the tow truck pulled over. Traffic had ground almost to a halt, and he wanted to leapfrog all of it and see what was going on.

"Can you see the car?" Kelsey asked, craning her neck.

"No." They were looking for Ramli's white sedan, but he could be driving anything by now.

Kelsey rolled down her window and the sound of blaring horns filled the SUV. She shimmied out and sat on the windowsill to get a better view.

Her phone rang, and she slid back into her seat to answer it. She listened a moment and looked at Gage. "The FBI just got a bomb threat about this bridge."

Gage cursed.

"From Marissa Ramli." She stuck her head out the window again. "Gage, I see it!" she yelped. "It's a yellow Mini!"

Gage spotted it about fifty yards ahead. Marissa Ramli's Mini Cooper was perpendicular to the traffic flow, blocking two entire lanes.

Gage pulled over. "Stay here," he ordered, yanking out his SIG. He slid out of the SUV, careful not to get smacked by an oncoming car, but the roadway was practically a parking lot. He ran for the Mini, darting his gaze around for any sign of Ramli. Sirens wailed behind him, drowning out the horns.

Gage reached the daisy-yellow car. No Ramli.

The tow truck driver—a 350-pound Giants fan, by the looks of his T-shirt—waddled toward the car. "Hey, where'd he go?" He spat tobacco juice on the asphalt and glanced out at the bay. "He a jumper?"

Gage ignored him as he peered in the window. His heart skipped a beat. The backseat was packed with explosives.

"I hear sirens," Elizabeth said, glancing around.

"Other side of the toll plaza," Derek said.

More sirens and she turned around. Another pair of police units bumped over the shoulder and bullied their way through the traffic to reach the fast-pass gates.

"Fucking A, there he is."

Elizabeth whipped her head around. "Where?"

"Right there. Black hoodie. See him?"

Elizabeth spied the pedestrian cutting across a patch of grass between two roads.

Derek thrust the truck in park and shoved open the door.

"What are you doing?" she demanded.

"Taking him down. What are *you* doing?"

Elizabeth got out, too. She watched the figure moving diagonally away from them. What if it wasn't him? How could they be sure?

"Adam!" she shouted.

A slight turn of the head. He broke into a run.

Elizabeth took off after him, whipping out her gun. "FBI! Freeze!"

He kept going, but Derek was gaining on him as Elizabeth pulled up the rear. Horns blared from all directions, and she felt a revolting sense of déjà vu as they darted through the cars.

Ramli cut left into a grassy area between a road and a parking lot. Derek burst forward and tackled him to the ground.

"What is it?" The driver stepped closer. "He inside?"

"Stay back," Gage said, looking for wires that might indicate a booby trap. He spotted them right away, connected to the seat. The bomb was rigged to blow if someone tried to dislodge it.

Gage rushed around to the other side and saw a timing device. *Shit.* This guy liked timers, obviously, and this one was set for six minutes.

Sirens grew closer, but even the police were stuck in the quagmire.

"Hey!"

Gage turned around as a pair of cops approached on foot. Luckily, they didn't see the gun, and Gage quickly tucked it under his shirt.

Gage raised his empty hands in a *back away* gesture. "I'm with the bomb squad!" he yelled over the noise. "This vehicle is rigged with explosives."

The cops exchanged looks. Was he a wacko or was he for real?

"Listen to your radio," Gage said. "It's all over the scanner."

One of them spoke into the receiver clipped to his shoulder, listened to something, and then gave his partner a nod.

"We've got units on the way," the man called.

"Listen up—you guys need to *clear this area*," Gage ordered. "You understand me? This thing is on a timer."

They looked dumbstruck.

"You have five minutes!"

They leaped into action, and Gage turned back to the car. The driver of Tommy's Towing must have heard what he'd said because he was waddling back toward his rig at top speed.

"Can you defuse it?"

Gage glanced at Kelsey. *Shit,* why did she have to be here right now? He took her shoulders.

"Kelsey, listen to me. You need to leave."

She nodded. "I leave when you leave."

Fuck.

"So can you defuse it?" she repeated.

"Not in five and a half minutes."

He glanced around, tuning out the traffic noise, the horns, every goddamn thing but the problem at hand.

And Kelsey. She was impossible to ignore.

"Can we evacuate and just let it blow?"

He shook his head. "This is a double-decker bridge." Gage glanced toward the traffic jam, where the cops had already set up wooden barricades and were attempting to turn traffic around. "Even if they get the upper deck cleared in time, there's all that traffic under us." He looked at the car. "I have to move it."

As the words left his mouth, the tow truck grumbled to life. Gage sprinted over to it and pounded on the door.

"Hey!" he shouted through the open window. "We need this rig!"

Tommy shook his head. "Sorry, bud."

Gage whipped out his SIG and pointed it at the man's face. "I'm commandeering this vehicle. Now, you can leave, but it's going to be on foot."

The man stared at him. Anger flickered in his eyes. But something else was there, too. Guilt? Conscience?

"Now."

The door squeaked open. "You take the wheel," he said, lumbering down. "I'll handle the winch." He spat tobacco juice. "Sometimes she sticks."

Gage jumped into the still-warm driver's seat as Tommy jerked open the Mini's passenger door and popped the car into neutral. Gage checked his watch. Four minutes. He glanced at Kelsey, who stood calmly beside the SUV, watching him with that crazy mix of fear and trust in her eyes. She wouldn't leave, just like before, at the train station. She was terrified, but she wouldn't get the hell away from him.

He put the truck in gear and lurched forward a few feet, then reversed and maneuvered in front of the Mini. This was a platform rig, and his plan was to back it up against the side of the bridge and slide the little yellow car into San Francisco Bay.

But he only had three and a half minutes. He glanced at the rearview mirror.

"Let her out!" the driver yelled.

Gage flipped the red switch. He heard a groan as the winch started to go out and the platform tilted down to touch street level. Gage jumped down and rushed back to help him secure the hook, but he seemed to have it under control, so Gage slid behind the wheel again and flipped the switch to reverse the process. The groan changed pitch. The line pulled taut. The car moved forward and Gage waited an eternity for the platform to level out. It was still moving when he threw the truck into reverse and backed right up to the wall of the bridge.

"Shit!"

He heard the alarm in the driver's voice and leaped down. Gage's stomach plummeted as he saw the problem. The platform where the car's tires rested was a good ten inches lower than the top of the wall.

Gage's pulse spiked. Ten inches was impossible. He tried to stay cool, but he was feeling the sharp bite of panic now.

All around him, sirens wailed. The asphalt beneath his feet vibrated. The wind whipped against his face as he gazed at the tires and ran through possibilities.

"A ramp." He glanced up at the driver, who looked about ready to piss his pants. Gage rushed back to the tow truck.

"Gage!"

He turned to see Kelsey hurrying toward him, dragging two police barricades behind her. *Two* ramps.

I love this woman, he thought as he rushed to take them.

"Get in the tow truck," he told her. "Pull the line in some more—the red button."

Kelsey hitched herself behind the wheel as Gage heaved one of the barricades over the hood and handed it to the tow truck driver. As the car rolled forward a few more inches, Gage positioned the wooden plank to form a ramp between the truck platform and the concrete wall. Tommy mimicked his actions.

Gage glanced through the Mini's window and checked the clock. "Twenty seconds!" He pointed at the driver. "We push on three, got it?"

Tommy nodded, and he and Gage crouched down at the front of the car, their hands braced against the bumper.

"One! Two! *Three!*" With a mighty grunt, Gage threw his weight against the car. A few red-faced seconds ticked by. He felt the instant they overcame the inertia. The Mini rolled back and up. They kept pressing, pressing, and suddenly the weight was nothing— like pushing a sled across the snow at his parents' house. The car tipped over the wall and Gage thrust his arms forward to catch himself as he pitched toward the platform.

Boom!

The invisible force picked him up and hurtled him back against the truck.

Elizabeth glanced up in time to see the fireball soaring down into the bay. She stared at it, openmouthed, then looked at Derek.

"Call Gage," she said, but he was already dialing.

Ramli muttered something and Elizabeth looked at him. He was on his knees in front of her, hands cuffed behind his back. A smug smile curled the corner of his mouth as he gazed at the bridge. He glanced back at her, and she searched his eyes, looking for some shred of . . . something. Whatever she was looking for wasn't there.

Elizabeth swallowed her contempt. She took a deep breath.

"You have the right to remain silent."

CHAPTER 26

They followed the signs to San Francisco International Airport, and Gage got a familiar sour taste in his mouth. He looked at Kelsey behind the wheel, and she had the same tight expression she'd been wearing all afternoon. Gage hated these moments. He never knew what to say because there really wasn't anything. No matter what he said, it sucked all the way around.

He looked out the window. "Thanks for returning the rental."

"No problem," she said, and her cheerful tone grated on his nerves. "I've got plenty of time until my flight."

"I bet you went a bit over the mileage limit," Derek said from the backseat. He sounded cheerful, too, but in his case it was genuine.

While Gage had been stuck for hours in an FBI debriefing room, Derek had tracked down their CO, who'd been in a transport plane, just minutes away from going wheels-up with the rest of their team. After explaining the situation, Derek managed to convince Hallenback to overlook their unauthorized absence.

Soon after that, the CO had called back and ordered him and Gage to get their asses to the East Coast and catch the next flight to Frankfurt, where he'd find a way for them to rejoin their team.

So Derek was feeling very proud of himself. Meanwhile, Gage felt like shit.

Kelsey's hand rested on her leg. Gage reached over to take it, but she pulled away.

"So, Derek, I meant to ask you." She glanced in the rearview mirror. "What'd you do with your pickup truck?"

He leaned forward. "Popped the keys in the mail to Dietz's parents. They live in Oakland." He looked at Gage. "You ever met Mike's little brother?"

"No."

"He's headed to UCSD in about six weeks. Said he'd take it down there for me."

Gage glanced at Kelsey. He shot Derek a glare.

"That is, if we're not back by then," Derek said. "Who knows, right?"

Kelsey stared straight ahead. Gage's gut clenched as she pulled up to the passenger drop-off area.

"Kelsey, thanks for the ride." Derek clamped a hand on her shoulder. "You take care now." He looked at Gage and tapped his watch. "See you inside, bro."

A blast of air and traffic noise entered the SUV as Derek hopped out.

"So." Kelsey looked at him. "Do you have your passport?"

"Yeah."

"Your real one?"

"Yeah." He searched her face, hating the look in her eyes. He'd seen it so many times before. She was determined not to cry.

"Be sure to take your pills," she said. "Do you have them?"

He didn't answer.

"Do you?"

"Come here." He reached over and pulled her to him. He cupped her face in his hands and kissed her until she kissed him back and he tasted the salt of her tears.

She pulled away. "You need to make your plane."

Gage clenched his teeth. He didn't want to leave like this. He didn't want to leave at all. But it was worse—especially for her—if he sat here and dragged it out. He grabbed his bag and opened the door.

"I'll call you."

She didn't say anything. She just looked at him, and he could tell she was struggling not to nod, or agree, or do anything that would officially start their relationship again at the eleventh hour.

"Brewer!"

Gage turned around. Derek stood in the automatic door. They were going to be late.

"Go," Kelsey said. "You're going to miss it."

Gage got out. "I'll call you."

She didn't respond, and he closed the door and turned around to face the wall of glass. A big aquarium of travelers rushing in every direction. So many people. So many goddamn anonymous people with no connection to one another.

I don't want to be alone anymore, Gage.

Fear clawed at him as he walked toward the door.

One foot in front of the other. His feet felt like lead.

He turned around. The Explorer was moving away from the curb. He lunged for the door handle. She jabbed the brakes as he yanked the door open and jumped inside.

"What'd you forget?"

He shoved the gearshift in park. He pulled her to him and kissed her—hard.

"Marry me."

She stared at him.

"It's what I should have said last night. *That's* my fantasy."

"You want—"

"I want you. Us. Marry me, Kelsey."

"But—"

"I've got siblings, cousins, a whole mess of nieces and nephews. I can give you those things you want. I can give you a family."

Horns blared behind them, and she whirled around.

"Brewer!"

He turned to see Derek waving him over. Gage ignored him and looked at Kelsey.

"I love you and I'm tired of leaving." He leaned over and kissed her one last time. "Don't argue for once. Just think about it."

Gage got out and slammed the door. He started jogging toward his friend, and his shoulders were suddenly light. Weightless. She hadn't answered. But he'd finally said the right thing.

Elizabeth hurried across the parking lot, searching for her car. With her luck, they'd probably towed it from the hospital lot since it hadn't moved from its space in two days. She glanced at her watch and sloshed coffee on her shoes.

Forty-five minutes. She probably should have picked a different hotel last night—one near the airport—but by the end of the day, she'd been dead tired, and she'd found herself crawling into a cab and asking for the Dragon Inn. At the time she hadn't been thinking about the five-block hike to her rental car, but she was thinking about it now as she rushed to make her plane. The phone in her purse chimed, and she whipped it out.

Not another delay. All she wanted was to get home.

"LeBlanc."

"This is Gordon Moore."

"Hi. How are you?" She hadn't heard from him since yesterday when they'd been in the midst of the crisis.

"I wanted to touch base with you," he said.

She smiled with satisfaction. Supervisory Special Agent Gordon Moore wanted to touch base with *her*. She spotted her rental car and strode over to it.

"I thought you'd be interested to know that Rick Bolton was arrested and charged this morning."

"Wow." She halted beside the car, hardly able to believe it. "By who?"

"The Securities and Exchange Commission."

"You're kidding."

"We're still working on a raft of other charges, but these were easier for now. He's been charged with insider trading in connection with the sale of some pharmaceutical stock. He just made a fortune on one of the companies that manufactures an antibiotic used to prevent anthrax."

"Wow, that's . . ." She didn't know what to say. "That's pretty unbelievable."

"Believe it. And don't worry, we'll get him on the rest of it, too. It's just going to take some time. But I wanted you to know."

Elizabeth stood there, trying to digest it. Rick Bolton had been arrested. Trent Lohman was dead. Adam Ramli—thanks to her—was in custody and undergoing questioning. He hadn't revealed anything about stateside associates or a sleeper cell of any kind, but whether he ever did or not, she knew there had to be more.

There were always more.

There were always threats.

That's why she, and Gordon, and Derek, and Gage had a job. She felt a swell of pride knowing she'd done hers right this time.

Elizabeth cleared her throat. "Thank you for the update, sir."

"Thank *you*. You were an integral part of this investigation. You ever need anything at the Bureau—anything at all—I want you to call me."

She was speechless.

"LeBlanc?"

"Yes, that's . . . Thank you, sir. I appreciate that."

"It's Gordon," he said, and she thought she heard amusement in his voice. "Take care of yourself."

He hung up, and she stared at the phone in her hand. *If you ever need anything at the Bureau.* It was an incredible offer. She wondered if she'd ever take him up on it.

Elizabeth unlocked her car and felt a wave of optimism. The day was looking up. She might actually make her plane. She slid behind the wheel and found herself staring at a blue Bears cap. Laughter bubbled up in her throat. She picked it up and saw the note taped beneath the brim. *Call me,* followed by a phone number.

Tears welled in her eyes. She took out her phone and started to dial. Her finger hovered over the last digit. What would she say to him? What would *he* say? Was he even in the country anymore?

She felt a pang of empathy for Kelsey Quinn. How did she live with the stress?

But it was only a phone call. Elizabeth pressed the last number and waited through three rings. She was both relieved and disappointed when she heard his recorded voice.

"Vaughn here. Leave a message."

The low-key drawl brought a smile to her face.

"Hi, it's Elizabeth. I don't know how you got into my *locked* car, but I guess it's one of those SEAL tricks."

She stared at the cap for a moment, recalling the very first time she'd seen it.

"Rumor has it you and Gage caught up with your team. I'm not sure where you're going, but—" A lump rose up in her throat. She cleared it away. "Wherever it is, be careful."

And please, please don't get hurt. The world needs more men like you.

But she left the last part unsaid because even though she'd made her first big arrest, she still had moments of total wimpiness. Such as right now. So she kept it light and hoped somehow he'd know.

"Anyway, thanks for the hat," she said. "And sorry again about your boots."

CHAPTER 27

Ten weeks later

Kelsey was slipping on her lab coat when Mia poked her head into the office.

"Oh good, you're here."

"Just got in from lunch," Kelsey said. "Why? What's up?"

"Sheriff Denton's up in the lobby raising hell. Said you were supposed to meet with him at noon to go over a report?"

"That's tomorrow."

"Well, he's hassling the new receptionist. You might want to go talk to him."

The phone on Kelsey's desk rang and Mia disappeared.

"Damn it." Kelsey huffed out a breath. She grabbed the case file and dashed out of her office, mentally rehearsing what she hadn't yet put in her report: The bones recovered from an abandoned well in Denton's county—thought to be those of a missing twenty-six-year-old Caucasian female—had been identified as belonging to a middle-aged white male. The sheriff was going to resist her conclusion, and she rehearsed her talking points as she rode the elevator up. The doors dinged open and she stepped into the lobby.

And saw Gage.

Her heart seemed to drop out of her chest. He stood there watching her. Finally he walked over, since her feet were cemented to the floor.

"Hi." He smiled down at her, and she threw her arms around him. She pressed her cheek against his shoulder and squeezed until her arms hurt.

"What are you doing here? I thought you were coming Friday!"

He pulled back. "Surprised you, huh?"

"Who let you in here?" She wiped the tears from her cheeks and grinned up at him.

"Mia. She called down to the gatehouse and gave me a green light."

Kelsey leaned up and kissed him.

"Dr. Quinn?"

She turned to the receptionist seated behind the desk. Far from looking "hassled," she looked perfectly relaxed. And perfectly delighted by the lab's latest visitor. She beamed a smile in their direction.

"It's Manny Villarreal on line two," she said.

"Could you take a message?"

"He's left three already."

"Oh. In that case, just tell him I'm in a meeting. I'll call him later this afternoon." She turned back to Gage. "I can't believe you're here early." She glanced around. "Do you want to sit outside? Fewer interruptions."

She took his hand and led him to the door, still

unable to believe he was really *here,* and that his big, warm fingers were laced through hers.

"When did your flight get in?"

"I drove."

"You *did*?"

They stepped into the cool air. A front had moved in last night, and the sky was a sparkling blue—the same color as his eyes.

"Rolled into town about noon." He looked out over the wooded landscape as she stopped at a picnic table. He sat down beside her, straddling the bench. "I don't have a key to your house, so I thought I'd swing by here."

"I thought SEALs didn't need keys." She couldn't wipe the grin off her face. He was here two days early. They had two extra nights together.

"Yeah, well, your neighbor was in her driveway giving me the fish-eye, so . . ." His voice trailed off as he combed his fingers into her hair and leaned in to kiss her properly. Her heart filled with unexpected joy. He was *here.* His mouth was warm and he tasted faintly of coffee, probably because he'd been up all night driving. She cupped his face in her hands and brushed her fingers over his stubble. He only had about a day's worth, and she felt even happier because when he shaved his beard, it usually meant he wasn't going away soon.

When the kiss ended, she was practically in his lap.

"How long till you get off?" he asked in a low voice.

"Couple hours." She kissed him.

"This place have a security cam?"

"Hundreds, I think. Why?"

The gazed shifted over her shoulder. "Because I'm thinking of taking you for a walk in those woods."

She smiled. "Uh, bad idea. There's a cadaver in those woods. Don't you see the buzzards?"

A ring tone emanated from her pocket. She pulled out her phone and set it on the table to read the screen: M. VILLARREAL.

She saw Gage looking at it.

"You're wondering who Manny is."

He looked at her. "Yeah, I am."

"I've been meaning to talk to you about him."

His jaw tightened as she took his hand.

"Manny Villarreal is the assistant director of the International Forensic Anthropology Foundation. He offered me a job."

Gage lifted his eyebrows. "I thought you liked your job here."

"I do. I love it." She squeezed his fingers. "But this job's in Los Angeles." She waited a beat, watching his eyes. "South of Los Angeles, actually. About forty-five minutes from San Diego."

He watched her intently, but she couldn't read his reaction.

"You're planning to leave the Delphi Center?"

She looked down at their joined hands. "I've been doing a lot of thinking. Seeing what you did in that subway tunnel . . ." She glanced up at him. "It was incredible. All that training you guys have, all that expertise. So few people can do the things you do. Whereas with me . . . death happens everywhere." She took a deep breath. "So if you're based in San Diego, I think we should be in San Diego. You should be with your team."

Gage looked at her for a long moment. "You'd do that for me?"

She nodded.

He wrapped his arms around her and pulled her against him. She felt the warmth of his body, the beat of his heart against her ear. This was the right thing. She knew it. It was new and unfamiliar and scary, but it was right.

He hugged her tightly. "That means a lot, Kelsey." He kissed the top of her head, then he eased back and looked down at her.

"Don't take it."

She stared up at him. "The job? Why not?"

"Because I left the teams."

She blinked at him. "You—"

"I took an honorable medical discharge." He looked down, and Kelsey felt a deep stab of pain for him. "My shoulder is shot—literally. It's been slowing me down for a year now, and it got worse after I injured it on this last tour." He looked at her. "It's time."

She didn't know what to say. She had never expected to hear those words from him. Tears welled up as she realized what a loss this was for him, for his teammates.

"Are you sad?"

"No." He looked away. Then he looked back at her. "Yeah, a little." He shrugged. "I always figured I'd stick around the base and maybe train the next guys." He ran his thumb over her knuckles. "But these last ten weeks, I've been doing a lot of thinking about you. Us."

Her heart thumped harder. She'd thought he'd dropped the big news, but he was building up to something.

"There are two metro areas within an hour from here that have SWAT teams," he said. "And there's the bomb squad in San Antonio."

"Oh my God." She laughed and covered her mouth. "What?"

"Nothing, it's just . . ." A tear slid down her cheek. "I never thought I'd be elated to hear that my fiancé wanted to be on a SWAT team."

"Yeah, well, I wouldn't make a good instructor, anyway. I'm not sadistic enough. And I work better on a team."

"You're sure about this."

"I'm sure." His voice was resolute and he squeezed her hand. "I want to move on to the next phase of my life now, Kelsey. And I want it to be with you."

He looked down at her and his genuine smile told her he was okay with this. It was a change, but it was a good one. He seemed ready for it.

He reached over and tucked a lock of hair behind her ear. "So, how soon can you get out of here? There's some other stuff I've been thinking about for ten long weeks."

She smiled. "Well, I have a full afternoon, but . . ." She checked her watch and stood up. "I could probably leave at four if I hurry. You could go to my house and rest or get something to eat."

He stood, too, and pulled her against him. "Three." He kissed her. "And bring the lab coat."

She took the key chain from her pocket and unhooked her house key. She folded it into his palm, and her heart skittered as she realized the significance of what she'd just done. She tried to imagine waking up each morning with his warm body beside hers. She tried to imagine what it would feel like to start each day *with* him instead of just thinking about him and battling worry and loneliness.

He frowned down at her. "What's wrong? I thought you'd be happy."

She took his hand. He'd come so far for her. For them. He deserved to know what was really in her heart.

"You remember that motel in San Francisco?" She looked up at him. "The one by the airport?"

He nodded.

"You asked me what I wanted, and I told you a house and kids and a man in my life. Even then I knew, I didn't want those things with anyone—I wanted them with you." She gripped his hand. "I never stopped being in love with you, Gage. Even when everything fell apart. Even through the fighting, the breakup, the other people. Even through the months away. I didn't want to, but I loved you through all of that."

"I know."

She smiled. "You knew?"

He kissed her forehead. "I always knew, Kelsey. I was just waiting for you to figure it out."

Turn the page
for a sneak peek
at the next spine-tingling Tracers novel
from Laura Griffin

SHOOT TO KILL

Available soon from Pocket Books

∫

Maddie Callahan's newest clients seemed to have everything—youth, looks, money—which was precisely why she doubted their marriage would work. But she kept her opinions to herself as she snapped what she hoped was the final shot of the day.

"That should do it for the church backdrop. So, we're all set?"

"What about the footbridge?" The bride-to-be smiled up at her fiancé. "I can post it on the blog with our engagement story."

"Whatever you want, babe."

Maddie stifled an eye roll and turned to check out the park. It wasn't overly crowded—just a few people walking dogs—but their light was fading.

"I know it's getting late." Hannah held her hands together as if in prayer and looked at Maddie. "But could we get something *real* quick?"

"We can if we hurry," Maddie said, collapsing her tripod and looping her camera strap around her neck. She waited for a break in traffic and led Hannah and Devon across Main Street to the park, where she deposited her equipment beside the lily pond. She glanced around, cataloging the details of the composition. The wooden footbridge formed a low arc over the water. Sunlight glistened off the pond's surface, creating a shimmery, storybook effect that Maddie had taken advantage of before. As one of the few natural backdrops in this congested college town, the park was a good place for wedding photos—or in this case, engagement shots. Normally, Maddie liked using it, but this appointment had run way over schedule, and she was anxious to get back to the lab. She opted to skip the tripod and keep this quick.

Maddie composed the shot as Hannah arranged her future husband behind her. In matching white oxfords, faded jeans, and cowboy boots, the couple's look today was what she thought of as Texas preppy. Hannah settled their clasped hands on the side of the bridge, putting her two-carat diamond prominently on display.

"How's this?" she asked.

"Perfect." Maddie snapped the picture. "I think I got it. Just a few more and . . . that's it. You're done."

Both pairs of shoulders relaxed. Devon looked at his watch, clearly relieved to be finished with what he probably thought was a marathon photo shoot. He had no idea what awaited him on his wedding day.

Hannah turned and smiled up at him. "Do I have lipstick on my teeth, sweets?"

He grinned down at her. "No. Do I?"

Maddie lifted her camera one last time as he reached down to brush a lock of hair from his fiancée's face.

Click.

And *that* was the money shot. Maddie knew it the

instant she took it. The ring wasn't in the picture, but she hoped they'd order a print anyway. Maybe they'd put it in a frame on their mantel, where they could glance at it occasionally and be reminded of the genuine fondness they'd had for each other before the years set in.

And, really, what more could anyone expect from a wedding picture?

Her mission accomplished, Maddie collected her equipment.

"How soon can we see something?" Hannah asked as she joined her on the grass.

"Oh, I'm guessing—" Maggie checked the time. Damn, it was already 5:30. "I should have these posted to the site by tomorrow—plenty of time to pick one for Sunday's paper."

The bride-to-be looked crestfallen. "You mean not by tonight?"

Maddie took a deep breath. She mentally counted to three. Yes, her day job paid the bills, but freelance work was the icing on her cake. And that business relied heavily on referrals.

"I'll do my best," she said brightly, even though it meant turning her whole evening upside down. And that assumed she wouldn't get called out for some emergency. "I can probably get you something by midnight. If I do, I'll email you the password for the gallery."

"Thank you! I *really* appreciate it. Everyone's dying to see how these turn out."

Maddie wasn't sure who "everyone" was, but she managed to keep a cheerful expression on her face as they exchanged good-byes. Then she hitched her tripod onto her shoulder and trekked across the park.

Her stomach growled as she headed for the garage where she'd parked. She cast a longing look at the sandwich shop on the corner. Food would have to wait. She needed to get back to the lab and send out a half dozen files before she could possibly call it a day.

She ducked into the shade of the parking garage, avoiding the stairwell in favor of the ramp. The blustery February wind had died down, and the air was thick with car exhaust. Maddie hugged the concrete wall so she wouldn't get clipped by a driver rounding the corner. She reached the third level and spotted her little white Prius tucked beside a pickup. She dug the phone from her purse and checked for messages. Her boss, her sister, her boss, her boss.

Shoes scuffed behind her. The skin at the back of her neck prickled. Maddie paused and pretended to be reading something on her phone as she listened.

Silence.

Her pulse picked up. She resumed her pace.

More footsteps.

She whirled around. No one. She clutched the phone in her hand and darted her gaze up and down the rows of cars. She searched for anyone lurking, any ominous shadows—but she was alone.

Almost.

Anxiety gnawed at her as she surveyed her surroundings. It was light out. The streets below hummed with traffic. Still, she tightened her grip on the tripod. She tucked the phone in her purse and felt for her pepper spray.

In the corner of her eye, movement. She pivoted toward it and registered two things at once: *man* and *ski mask*. Fear shot through her. Maddie swung the tripod around like a baseball bat as the man barreled into her, slamming her against the pickup. The tripod jerked from her grip and clattered to the ground. Hands clamped around her neck. Maddie punched and bucked as fingers dug into her skin. She tried to scream. No air. Gray eyes glared at her through the holes in the mask.

She smashed the heel of her hand into his face and felt bone crunch. He staggered back. Maddie jerked sideways. He lunged for her, grabbing the collar of her jacket. She twisted out of it and bolted for the stairwell.

"Help!" she shrieked, yanking open the door. She leaped down the stairs, rounded the landing, then leaped down more stairs. Her butt hit concrete, but she groped for the railing and hauled herself up. Hinges squeaked above her. Her pulse skittered. Footsteps thundered over her head.

"Someone *help!*"

But they were alone in the soundproof shaft. Another landing, a door. She shoved it open and dashed through. She searched desperately for people, but saw only rows and rows of cars. Another door. Light-headed with terror, she pushed it open and stumbled into an alley. On her right, a passageway lined with Dumpsters. On her left, a gray car parked at the mouth of the alley. Someone was inside.

Maddie rushed for the car. It lurched forward. She halted, stunned, as it charged toward her like a rhino. Behind her a door banged open. Maddie sprinted away from the door and the car. The engine roared behind her as she raced down the alley. The noise was at her heels, almost on top of her. Panic zinged through her like electric current as her arms and legs pumped. The car bore down on her. At the last possible second, she dove sideways behind a Dumpster and felt a great whoosh of air as the car shot past. The squeal of brakes echoed through the alley.

Maddie darted through the space between the back bumper and the Dumpster. She raced for the street. Despair clogged her throat as she realized the distance she'd covered. Where was the ski-mask guy? The people and traffic noise seemed impossibly far away. She raced toward the mouth of the alley as fast as her burning legs could carry her.

The man jumped from a doorway. They crashed to the ground in a heap of arms and legs and flying elbows. Her skin scraped against the pavement as she kicked free of him and scrambled to her feet. He grabbed the strap of her camera and her body jerked violently. She landed on her side as a fist pummeled her and pain exploded behind her eyes. She managed to roll to her knees as another blow hit her shoulder. She fell forward, but caught herself on her palms and kicked backward, desperate *not* to end up on the ground under him.

She struggled to her feet, but her vision blurred, and the strap was like a noose around her neck. The vinegary taste of fear filled her mouth. He heaved his weight into her, smashing her against the wall. The strap tightened again. Maddie gripped it with her hands. She tried to buck him off, but he was strong and wiry and determined to get her into a headlock. His arm clamped around her throat. She turned her head to the side and bit *hard* through the fabric of his T-shirt.

The grip loosened for a moment, and she twisted free of the strap, the arms, the fingers clawing at her. Adrenaline burst through her veins as she realized this might be her only chance.

She rolled to her feet and rocketed down the alley, toward the noise and cars and people that meant safety. *Faster, faster, faster!* Every cell in her body throbbed with the knowledge that he was behind her. Her heart hammered. Her muscles strained. *Faster!* For the first time, she thought of a gun and imagined a bullet tearing through skin and bone. She surged forward, shrieking hoarsely and racing for the mouth of the alley.

Behind her a car door slammed. Tires squealed over the asphalt. She glanced back as the gray car shot down the alley, moving away from her. Taillights glowed. Another screech of tires as the car whipped around the corner.

Maddie stopped and slumped against the side of the building. Her breath came in ragged gasps. Her lungs burned, and it felt as if her heart were being squeezed like a lemon. Something warm trickled down her face. She touched a hand to her cheek and her fingers came away red.

Tears stung her eyes as she looked down at herself. Her purse was gone. Her camera was gone. Her phone was gone. *She* wasn't gone, at least. She was here—in one shaking, terrified, Jell-O-like piece. But her knees felt so weak she didn't know if they would hold her up. She closed her eyes and tried to think.

She couldn't stay in the alley. But she couldn't go back in that garage—maybe never again. She looked out at the street, at the steady flow of cars and people.

Her gaze landed on the neon sign in the window of the sandwich shop. It glowed red in the gray of dusk, beckoning her to safety with its simple message: *Open*.

Maddie pushed away from the wall. On quivering legs, she stumbled toward the sign.

The two men were cops, she could tell at a glance. Maddie watched them from her place beside the patrol car, where she'd been sequestered for the past half hour answering questions from a rookie detective who'd probably been in diapers when she got her first speeding ticket. Maddie knew almost everyone in the San Marcos police department, but didn't it figure the first responder to her 911 call would be someone she'd never laid eyes on before—someone who didn't have the slightest interest in doing her a favor by moving things along. Added to the scraped chin, the swelling jaw, the lost purse, and the stolen Nikon, it was just another addition to the crapfest that had become her day.

And if her instincts proved right, the party wasn't over yet.

Maggie watched as the two mystery men walked up to the patrol cars parked in front of the sandwich shop. Definitely cops. But they were more than that, clearly. She pegged them for feds based on their dark suits, and that guess was confirmed when one of them flashed a badge and exchanged words with the patrol officers milling on the sidewalk. Stan Grimlich—a cop she *did* know—had just emerged from the shop with a steaming cup of coffee. He said something brief and gave a nod in Maddie's direction, sending them her way.

Damn. Maddie checked her watch. Whatever these

two wanted, it wouldn't likely be quick. She looked them over. The one leading the charge appeared to be in his midthirties, like she was. His shaved head, coupled with his solid, stocky build, would have made him look like a bouncer—had it not been for his suit and the determined scowl on his face that said *cop*.

Maddie shifted her gaze to his friend. Taller, probably six-one. Broad-shouldered, muscular, lean at the waist. He had sandy-brown hair that was cropped short on the sides and longer on top. The word *military* popped into her head. It wasn't just the haircut and the build, but the supremely confident way he carried himself. He was watching her, too, but in contrast to his partner's expression, this guy looked utterly relaxed.

"Are you *sure* you don't want to get this looked at?"

She turned her attention to the EMT handing her an ice pack. Maddie pressed the pack to the side of her face, where a bruise was forming.

"I'm good."

"Because it's entirely possible you could have a concussion."

"Thanks, but I'm fine." And a trip to the emergency room was the last thing she needed tonight. She had an aversion to hospitals.

"Well." The woman shrugged and flipped shut the lid to her first aid kit. "Suit yourself. I can't *make* you take commonsense precautions."

"Madeline Callahan?"

She turned, startled. She'd known he was coming, but she hadn't expected such a deep voice from someone so young. He stared down at her, hands resting at his hips, suit jacket pushed back to reveal a semiautomatic pistol and—as she'd suspected—an FBI shield. She returned her gaze to his smooth, clean-shaven face. If she was right about the military thing, he must have graduated from the Academy about a week ago.

"I'm Special Agent Brian Beckman with the FBI. This is Special Agent Sam Dulles." He nodded at the bald guy. "We'd like to ask you a few questions, ma'am."

Dulles leaned back against the patrol car parked perpendicular to the one where Maddie stood. Clearly, he intended to hang back and observe. Maybe this was a training exercise.

"Ma'am?"

She looked back at the young one. Beckman. He was watching her intently with those hazel eyes.

"Could you take us through what transpired here, please?"

Transpired. Typical copspeak. Maddie folded her arms over her chest and leaned against the side of the car. "It was a mugging."

His eyebrows tipped up. "Could you be more specific?"

"Someone attacked me in the parking garage. Stole my purse, along with my brand-new camera."

"Your camera?"

"I'm a photographer. I was doing a photo shoot down at the park—a couple getting married."

Both men were regarding her with frank interest now, and she had the feeling she was missing something.

Beckman eased closer, as if to hear better. "We'd like you to walk us through the entire incident, ma'am. Step by step."

Irritated by the ma'am-ing, she shot a look at Dulles.

"Since when does the FBI have jurisdiction over a mugging?"

No answer.

"Maddie?"

She turned to see Stan walking toward her, hand outstretched. Her brown leather purse dangled from his fingers.

"Oh my God! Where was it?" She beamed a smile at him and snatched up the bag.

"Nicholson found it under a truck near your car. Phone's in there, too. You just had a call come in."

"Thank you! You have no idea how much trouble this saves me." Maddie already had the phone out, and her heart lurched when she saw the text from her boss. It was just as she'd feared. She was needed at a crime scene, ASAP. He'd sent her a message coded 911, followed by a street address.

Maddie stashed the ice pack into her purse and shoved the phone into the pocket of her jeans. Now she *really* needed to leave.

"Ms. Callahan?"

She glanced up. The young agent was watching her expectantly. So was his partner.

"Listen, you see Officer Scanlon over there? The one with the notepad? I guarantee he'll be turning in a full report before he clocks out tonight. You can get the details from him."

"We need them from you," Dulles said, speaking up for the first time. He was still leaning against the side of the car, with a disapproving look.

"Is there a specific *reason* the FBI is involved here? I told you, it was a mugging."

"Looks to me like an assault, too," Beckman said evenly.

"Okay, fine. But I really need to be somewhere, like, an hour ago, so unless you can explain how this is relevant—"

"We're investigating a federal case."

"A federal case involving . . . ?" She waited as they exchanged looks.

"There was a theft across the street from here at about five thirty." Dulles nodded toward the park. "Given the timing, we think it could be connected to your incident."

Maddie glanced across the street, where a bank faced out onto the park. A bank robbery certainly would explain the feds, but why weren't there any police cars?

"Take us through what happened," Beckman said, all trace of politeness gone.

And so Maddie did.

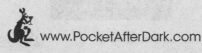

Want a thrill?

Pick up a bestselling romantic suspense novel from Pocket Books!